UNNATURAL PRAISE FOR DAN SHAMBLE, ZOMBIE P.I. . . .

"The Dan Shamble books are great fun."
—**Simon R. Green**

"Sharp and funny; this zombie detective rocks!"
—**Patricia Briggs**

"A dead detective, a wimpy vampire, and other interesting characters from the supernatural side of the street make *Death Warmed Over* an unpredictable walk on the weird side. Prepare to be entertained."
—**Charlaine Harris**

"A darkly funny, wonderfully original detective tale."
—**Kelley Armstrong**

"Master storyteller Kevin J. Anderson's *Death Warmed Over* is wickedly funny, deviously twisted and enormously satisfying. This is a big juicy bite of zombie goodness. Two decaying thumbs up!"
—**Jonathan Maberry**

"Kevin J. Anderson shambles into Urban Fantasy with his usual relentless imagination, and a unique hard-boiled detective who's refreshing, if not exactly fresh. *Death Warmed Over* is the literary equivalent of Pop Rocks, firing up an original world with supernatural zing, bold flavor, and endlessly clever surprises."
—**Vicki Pettersson**

"*Death Warmed Over* is just plain good fun. I enjoyed every minute it took me to read it."
—**Glen Cook**

Also by Kevin J. Anderson

*Death Warmed Over**

*Stakeout at the Vampire Circus**

*Unnatural Acts**

Clockwork Angels

Blood Lite anthology series (editor)

The new *Dune* novels (with Brian Herbert)

Hellhole series (with Brian Herbert)

The *Terra Incognita* trilogy

The *Saga of Seven Suns* series

Captain Nemo

The Martian War

Enemies and Allies

The Last Days of Krypton

Resurrection, Inc.

The Gamearth trilogy

Blindfold

Climbing Olympus

Hopscotch

Ill Wind (with Doug Beason)

Assemblers of Infinity (with Doug Beason)

The Trinity Paradox (with Doug Beason)

The Craig Kreident Mysteries (with Doug Beason)

Numerous *Star Wars, X-Files, Star Trek, StarCraft* novels,
movie novelizations, and collaborations

*starring Dan Shamble, Zombie P.I.

Hair Raising

Dan Shamble, Zombie P.I.

KEVIN J. ANDERSON

KENSINGTON BOOKS
www.kensingtonbooks.com

KENSINGTON BOOKS are published by

Kensington Publishing Corp.
119 West 40th Street
New York, NY 10018

Copyright © 2013 by WordFire, Inc.

All Kensington titles, imprints, and distributed lines are available at special quantity discounts for bulk purchases for sales promotion, premiums, fundraising, educational or institutional use.

Special book excerpts or customized printings can also be created to fit specific needs. For details, write or phone the office of the Kensington Special Sales Manager: Kensington Publishing Corp., 119 West 40th Street, New York, NY 10018. Attn. Special Sales Department. Phone: 1-800-221-2647.

Kensington and the K logo Reg. U.S. Pat. & TM Off.

ISBN-13: 978-0-7582-7738-1
ISBN-10: 0-7582-7738-5
First Kensington Trade Paperback Printing: May 2013

eISBN-13: 978-0-7582-7739-8
eISBN-10: 0-7582-7739-3
First Kensington Electronic Edition: May 2013

10 9 8 7 6 5 4 3 2 1

Printed in the United States of America

This novel goes out to my fellow
Superstars Writing Seminar authors

David Farland
Brandon Sanderson
Eric Flint
Rebecca Moesta

Together, we make a great team
trying to figure out
the writing and publishing business
faster than we can teach our students.

CHAPTER 1

People do bizarre things to amuse themselves, but this illegal cockatrice-fighting ring was one of the strangest pastimes I had ever seen.

Rusty, the full-time werewolf who raised the hideous creatures and threw them together in the ring for sport, had hired me to be on the lookout for "suspicious behavior." So, there I stood in an abandoned warehouse among crowds of unnaturals who were placing bets and watching chicken-dragon-viper monstrosities tear each other apart.

What could possibly be suspicious about that?

No case was too strange for Chambeaux & Deyer Investigations, so I agreed to keep my eyes open. "You'll have a great time, Mister Shamble," Rusty said in his usual growling voice. "Tonight is family night."

"It's *Chambeaux*," I corrected him, though the mispronunciation may have been the result of him talking through all those teeth in his mouth, rather than not actually knowing my name.

Rusty was a gruff, barrel-chested werewolf with a full head—and I mean *full* head—of bristling reddish fur that stuck out in all directions. He wore bib overalls and sported large tattoos on the meat of his upper arms (although his thick fur hid most of them). He raised cockatrices in run-down coops in his backyard.

Cockatrice fighting had been denounced by many animal rights groups. (Most of the activists, however, were unfamiliar with the mythological bestiary. Despite having no idea what a cockatrice was, they were sure "cockatrice fighting" must be a bad thing from the sound of it.) I wasn't one to pass judgment; when ranked among unsavory activities in the Unnatural Quarter, this one didn't even make the junior varsity team.

Rusty insisted cockatrice fighting was big business, and he had offered me an extra ticket so Sheyenne, my ghost girlfriend, could join me. I declined on her behalf. She's not much of a sports fan.

In the cavernous warehouse, the unsettling ambient noise reflected back, making the crowd sound twice as large as it really was. Spectators cheered, growled, howled, or made whatever sound was appropriate to their particular unnatural species, getting ready for the evening's show. Several furtive humans also came to place bets and watch the violence, while hoping that violence didn't get done to *them* in the dark underbelly of the Quarter.

This crowd didn't come to see and be seen. I tried to blend in with the other sports fans; nobody noticed an undead guy in a bullet-riddled sport jacket. Thanks to an excellent embalming job and good hygiene habits, I'm a well-preserved zombie, and I work hard to maintain my physical condition so that I can pass for mostly human. Mostly.

Previously, the warehouse had hosted illegal raves, and I could imagine the thunderously monotonous booming beat accompanied by migraine-inducing strobe lights. After the rave craze ended, the warehouse manager had been happy to let the space be used for the next best thing.

The center of attention was a high-walled enclosure that might have been designed as a skateboard park for lawn gnomes. The barricades were high enough that snarling, venomous cockatrices could not leap over them and attack the audience—in theory at least. Although, as Rusty explained it, a few bloodthirsty attendees took out long-shot wagers that such a disaster would indeed happen; those bettors generally kept to the back rows.

While Rusty was in back wrangling the cockatrice cages to prepare the creatures for the match, his bumbling nephew Furguson went among the crowds with his notepad and tickets, taking bets. Lycanthropy doesn't run in families, but the story I heard was that Rusty had gone on a bender and collapsed half on and half off his bed. While trying to make his uncle more comfortable, Furguson had been so clumsy that he scratched and infected *himself* on the claws. Watching the gangly young werewolf go about his business now, I was inclined to accept that as an operating theory.

The fight attendees held tickets, scraps of paper, and printed programs listing the colorful names of the cockatrice combatants—Sour Lemonade, Hissy Fit, Snarling Shirley, and so on. The enthusiasts were a motley assortment of vampires, zombies, mummies, trolls, and a big ogre with a squeaky voice who took up three times as much space as any other audience member.

I saw werewolves of both types—full-time full-furred wolfmen (affectionately, or deprecatingly, called "Hairballs" by the other type), and the once-a-month werewolves who transformed only under a full moon but looked human most of the time (called "Monthlies" by the other side). They were all werewolves to me, but there had been friction between the two breeds for years, and it was only growing worse.

It's just human, or inhuman, nature: People will find a way to make a big deal out of their differences—the smaller, the better. It reminded me of the Montagues and the Capulets (if I wanted to think highbrow), or the Hatfields and the McCoys (if I wanted to go lowbrow) . . . or the Jets and the Sharks (if I happened to feel musical).

Rusty had asked me to pay particularly close attention to two burly Monthlies, heavily tattooed "bad biker" types named Scratch and Sniff. Even in their non-lycanthropic forms, and even among the crowd of monsters, these two were intimidating. They wore thick, dirty fur overcoats that they claimed were made of Hairball pelts—no, nothing provocative there!—coated with road dust and stained with blotches that looked like clotted blood.

Untransformed, Scratch wore big, bristly Elvis sideburns and a thick head of dark brown hair in an old-fashioned DA hairstyle; apparently, he thought this made him look tough like James Dean, but it actually succeeded only in mimicking Arthur Fonzarelli in his later shark-jumping days. His friend Sniff shaved his head for a Mr. Clean look, but he made up for it once a month when his entire body exploded in thick fur. His lower face, though, was covered with a heavy beard; he had a habit of stroking it with his fingers, then sniffing them as if to remind himself of what he had eaten last. Both had complex tattoo designs on their arms, necks, and probably other places that I did not want to imagine.

Known troublemakers, Scratch and Sniff liked to bash their victims' heads just to see what might come out. They frequently caused problems at the cockatrice fights, but since they placed large bets, Rusty tolerated them.

In recent fights, however, a lot of the money had disappeared from the betting pool, as much as 20 percent. Rusty was sure that Scratch and Sniff were somehow robbing the pot, and I was supposed to catch them. Now, these two struck me as likely perpetrators of all manner of crimes, but they didn't look to be the *subtle* types who would discreetly skim 20 percent of anything. My guess, they would have taken the whole pot of money and stormed away with as much ruckus as possible.

Furguson wandered among the crowd, recording the bets on his notepad, then accepting wads of bills and stuffing them into his pockets. As he collected money, he took care to write down each wager and record the ticket number. For weeks, Rusty had pored over his nephew's notations, trying to figure out why so much money went missing. He counted and recounted the bills, added and re-added the bets placed, and he simply could not find what was happening to so much of the take.

Which is why he hired me.

Suddenly, the Rocky Balboa theme blared over the old rave speakers that the warehouse owner had confiscated when the ravers stopped paying their rent. Eager fans surrounded Furguson, placing their last wagers in a flurry, shoving money at the gangly werewolf like overcaffeinated bidders on the floor of the New York Stock Exchange.

Now, I've been a private detective in the Unnatural Quarter for years, working with my legal crusader/partner Robin Deyer. We had a decent business until I was shot in the back of the head—which might have been the end of the story, for most folks. But me? I woke up as a zombie, clawed my way out of the grave, and got right back to work. Being undead is not a disadvantage in the Quarter, and the number of cases I've solved, both before and after my murder, is fairly impressive. I pride myself on being observant and persistent, and I have a good analytical mind.

Sometimes, though, I solve cases through dumb luck, which is what happened now.

While Rusty rattled the cages and gave pep talks to his violent amalgamated monsters, the *Rocky* theme played louder, and frantic last-minute bettors waved money at Furguson. They yelled out the names of their chosen cockatrices, snatched their tickets, and the bumbling werewolf stuffed more wads of cash into his pockets, made change, grew flustered, took more money, stuffed it into other pockets.

He was so overwhelmed that bills dropped out of his pockets onto the floor, unnoticed—by Furguson, but not by the audience members. As they pressed closer to him, they snatched up whatever random bills they could find. In fact, it was so well choreographed, the whole mess seemed like part of the evening's entertainment.

Scratch and Sniff had shouldered their way to the edge of the cockatrice ring, where they'd have the best view of the bloodshed. Despite Rusty's accusations, I could see that the big biker werewolves had nothing to do with the missing money. As the saying goes, never attribute to malice what can be explained by incompetence—and I saw the gold standard of incompetence here.

I let out a long sigh. Rusty wasn't going to like what I'd found, but at least this was something easy enough to fix. His clumsy nephew would have to either be more careful or find another line of work.

The loud fanfare fell silent, and Rusty emerged from the back in his bib overalls. His reddish fur looked mussed, as if he had gotten into a wrestling match with the vile creatures. The restless crowd pressed up against the fighting ring. Rusty shouted at the top of his lungs. "For our first match, Sour Lemonade versus Hissy Fit!"

He yanked a lever that opened a pair of trapdoors, and the two creatures squawked and flapped into the pit. Each was the size of a wild turkey, covered with scales, a head like a rooster on a bad drug trip with a serrated beak and slitted reptilian eyes. The jagged feathers looked like machetes, and sharp, angular wings gave the cockatrices the appearance of very small dragons or very large bats. Each creature had a serpentine tail with a spearpoint tip. Their hooked claws were augmented by wicked-looking razor gaffs (I didn't want to know how Rusty had managed to attach them). Forked tongues flicked out of their sawtooth beaks as they faced off.

I'd never seen anything so ugly—and these were the *domesticated* variety. Purebred cockatrices are even more hideous, ugly enough to turn people to stone. (It's hard to say objectively whether or not the purebreds are in fact *uglier,* since anyone who looked upon one became a statue and was in no position to make comparative observations. Scientific studies had been done to measure the widened eyes of petrified victims, with a standard rating scale applied to the expression of abject horror etched into the stone faces, but I wasn't convinced those were entirely reliable results.) Regardless, wild turn-you-to-stone cockatrices were outlawed, and it was highly illegal to own one. These were the kinder, gentler breed—which still looked butt-ugly.

One creature had shockingly bright lemon-yellow scales—Sour Lemonade, I presumed. The other cockatrice had more traditional snot-green scales and black dragon wings. It hissed constantly, like a punctured tire.

The two creatures flapped their angular wings, bobbed their heads, and flicked their forked tongues like wrestlers bowing to the audience. The crowd egged them on, and the cockatrices flung themselves upon each other like Tasmanian devils on a hot plate. The fury of lashing claws, pecking beaks, and spitting venom was dizzying—not exactly enjoyable, but certainly energetic. I couldn't tear my eyes away.

Sour Lemonade's barbed tail lashed out and poked a hole through Hissy Fit's left wing. The other cockatrice clamped its serrated beak on the yellow creature's scaly neck. Claws lashed and kicked, and black smoking blood spurted out from the injuries. Where it splashed the side of the pit ring, the acid blood burned and bubbled.

One large droplet splattered the face of a vampire, who yelped and backed away, swatting at his smoking skin. Scratch and Sniff howled with inappropriate laughter at the vampire's pain. The spectators cheered, shouted, and cursed. The cockatrices snarled and hissed. The sound was deafening.

Just then the warehouse door burst open, and Officer Toby McGoohan entered, wearing his full cop uniform. "This is the police!" he shouted through a bullhorn. "May I have your attention—"

The ensuing pandemonium made the cockatrice fight seem as tame as a Sunday card game by comparison.

CHAPTER 2

Shouting "Fire!" in a crowded theater is a well-known recipe for disaster. Shouting "Cops!" in the middle of an illegal cockatrice fight is ten times worse.

Officer McGoohan—McGoo to his friends (well, to me at least)—reeled in surprise at the chaos his appearance caused. His mouth dropped open as he saw dozens of unnaturals, already keyed up with adrenaline and bloodlust from the cockatrice fight, thrown into a panic.

"Cops! Everybody run!" yelled a vampire with a dramatic flourish of his cape. He turned and ran face-first into a hulking ogre. In reflex, the ogre flung the vampire against the pit ring with enough force to crack the barricade. Inside, the cockatrices still thrashed and hissed at each other.

Several zombies shambled at top speed toward the back exit. The human spectators bolted, ducking their heads to hide their identities. A bandage-wrapped mummy tripped and fell. Other fleeing monsters stepped on him, trampling his fragile antique bones and sending up puffs of old dust. After the mummy got back to his feet, the clawed foot of a lizard man caught on the bandages, and the linen strips unraveled as he ran.

At the door, McGoo waved his hands and shouted, "Wait, wait! It's not a raid!" Nobody heard him, or if they did, they refused to believe.

The skittish ogre smashed into an emergency-exit door, knocking it off its hinges. The door crashed to the ground outside, and monsters fled into the dark alleys, yelling and howling.

McGoo waved his hands and urged calm. He might as well have been asking patrons in a strip club to cover their eyes. As I headed toward him, I saw that he hadn't even brought backup.

Gangly Furguson ran about in confusion, bumped into unnaturals, and caromed off them like a pinball. Scratch and Sniff looked at each other and shared a grin. As Furguson ran within reach, they grabbed the skinny werewolf and used his own momentum to fling him into the newly cracked pit wall, which knocked down the barricade. A blizzard of haphazard currency flew out of Furguson's pockets.

The cockatrices broke free and bounded out of the pit, slashing with razor gaffs at anything that came near. They were like hyperactive whirlwinds, flailing, attacking. Sour Lemonade latched its jaws onto the shoulder of a zombie who couldn't shamble out of the way quickly enough. Hissy Fit swooped down and attacked a vampire that had been burned by acid blood; the vamp flailed his hands to get the beast away from his neatly slicked-back hair.

Taking matters into his own hands, Rusty grabbed Hissy Fit by the scaly neck, yanked it away from the vampire, stuffed the cockatrice into a burlap sack, and cinched a cord around the opening. "Furguson, get the other one! We better get out of here!"

Furguson, however, flew into a rage at Scratch and Sniff for bashing him into the wall. He bared his fangs and howled, "Shithead Monthlies!" Hurling himself on Scratch, the nearer of the two, he raked his long claws down the werewolf-pelt overcoat, ripping big gashes. With his other hand, he tore four bloody furrows in the biker werewolf's cheek.

Sniff plucked Furguson away from his friend and began punching him with a pile-driver fist. Scratch touched the blood from the wounds on his cheek, and his eyes flared. Oddly, the tangle of tattoos on his neck and face began pulsing, writhing, like a psychedelic cartoon—and the deep wounds on his face sealed together. The blood coagulated into a hard scab that flaked off within seconds, the flesh knitted itself into scar tissue, and the tattoos fell quiescent again.

I had never seen a body-imprinted healing spell before. Very cool.

Amidst the pandemonium, I reached McGoo. He looked at me in surprise. "Shamble! What are you doing here?"

"Working. What about you?"

"I'm working, too. Just answering a disturbance call, Scout's honor. Your friends sure have hair triggers! Did I catch them doing something naughty?"

Rusty tore a two-by-four from the cockatrice barricade and waded in toward Scratch and Sniff. He whacked each of the biker werewolves on the back of the head, which left them reeling while he pulled his nephew from the fray. He shoved the burlap sack into Furguson's claws. "Take this and get out of here! I'll grab the other one."

With the struggling, squirming sack in hand, the gangly werewolf bolted for the nearest door. Bills were still dropping out of his pockets as the poor klutz disappeared into the night.

The two biker werewolves shook off the daze from being battered by a two-by-four. They puffed themselves up, peeled back their lips, and faced Rusty, but the big werewolf swung the board again, cracking each man full in the face. "Want a third one? Believe me, it'll only improve your looks."

I looked at McGoo. "We may need to intervene."

"I was just thinking that." He sauntered forward, displaying the arsenal of unnatural-specific weapons that he carried on his regular beat in the Quarter.

Both biker werewolves snarled at Rusty. "Damned Hairball!" After another round of hypnotically twitching tattoos, the bloody bruises on their faces healed up.

McGoo stepped up to the troublemakers and said, "Say, know any good werewolf jokes?"

After a glance at his uniform, Scratch and Sniff snarled low in the throat, then bolted into the night as well. Outside, I heard a roar of motorcycle engines.

The less panicky, or more enterprising, spectators scurried around and grabbed fallen money from the floor, before they, too, darted out of the building. Rusty managed to seize Sour Lemonade from the zombie it had chomped down on and stuffed it into another cloth bag, which he slung over his shoulder. He loped away from the warehouse, exiting through the emergency door the ogre had shattered.

McGoo and I caught our breath, exhausted just from watching the whirlwind. He shook his head as the last of the monsters evacuated into the night. "This place looks like the aftermath of a bombing raid. Mission accomplished, I suppose."

"What mission was that?" I asked.

"One of the nearby residents called in a noise complaint. She's some kind of writer, asked me to see if they could keep the noise down, said the racket was bothering her."

"That was all?"

"That was all." McGoo shrugged, looking around the evacuated warehouse. "Should be quiet enough now."

McGoo is my best human friend, my BHF. We've known each other since college, both married women named Rhonda when we were young and stupid; later, as we got smarter, we divorced the women named Rhonda and spent a lot of guy time commiserating. I established my private-eye practice in the Unnatural Quarter; McGoo, with his politically incorrect sense of humor, managed to offend the wrong people, thus derailing a mediocre career on the outside in exchange for a less-than-mediocre career here in the Quarter. A good friend and a reliable cop, he made the best of his situation.

It took McGoo quite a while to learn how to deal with me after I was undead. He wrestled with his own prejudices against various types of monsters, and, thanks to me, he could honestly say "Some of my best friends are zombies." I didn't let him use that for any moral high ground, though.

As we surveyed the aftermath, he said, "I'd better go talk to the lady, let her know everything's under control."

"Want me to come along? I could use some calmer interaction after this." I had, after all, solved the case of the missing money, but I decided to wait for the dust to settle before I presented my results to Rusty.

I found a twenty-dollar bill on the floor and dutifully picked it up.

McGoo looked at me. "That's evidence, you know."

"Evidence of what? You were called here on a disturbing-the-peace charge." As we walked out of the warehouse, I tucked the bill into the pocket of my sport jacket. "That's our next couple of beers at the Goblin Tavern."

"Well, if it's going to a good cause, I'd say you were doing your civic duty by picking up litter."

"Works for me."

Behind the warehouse, we found a set of ramshackle apartments; I saw lights on in only two of the units, though it was full dark. A weathered sign promised "Units for Rent: Low Rates!" *Low Rates* was apparently the best that could be said about the place.

McGoo led me up the exterior stairs to an upper-level apartment. When he rapped on the door, a woman yanked it open, blinking furiously as she tried to see out into the night. "Stop pounding! What's with all this noise? I've already filed one complaint—I can call the police again!"

"Ma'am, I *am* the police," McGoo said.

The woman was a frumpy vampire, short and plump, with brown hair. She looked familiar. "Then you ought to be ashamed of yourself," she said. "The noise only got worse after I called! It was a mob scene out there."

She plucked a pair of cat's-eye glasses from a chain dangling around her neck and affixed them to her face. "How can I get any writing done with such distractions? I have to finish two more chapters before sunrise."

I knew who she was. I also knew exactly what she was writing. "Sorry for the interruption, Miss Bullwer."

McGoo looked at me. "You know this woman?"

"Who's that looming out there on my porch?" The vampire lady leaned out until she could see me, then her expression lit up as if a sunrise had just occurred on her face (which is not necessarily a good thing when speaking of vampires). "Oh, Mister Chambeaux! How wonderful. Would you like to come in and have a cup of . . . whatever it is zombies drink? I have a few more questions, details for the veracity of the literature. And you can pet my cats. They'd love to have a second lap. They can't all fit on mine, you know."

"How many cats do you have?"

"Seven," she answered quickly. "At least, I think it's seven. It's difficult to tell them apart."

I'd first met Linda Bullwer when she volunteered for the Welcome Back Wagon, a public service group that catered to the newly undead. More importantly, she had been commissioned as a ghostwriter by Howard Phillips Publishing for a series of zombie detective adventures loosely based on my own exploits, written under the pen name of Penny Dreadful. The first one was due out very soon.

Miss Bullwer gave McGoo a sweet smile, her demeanor entirely changed now. "And thank you for your assistance, Officer—I'm sure you did your best, especially with Mister Chambeaux's help." She cocked her head, lowered her voice. "Are you working on a case? Something I should write about in a future volume?"

"I doubt anyone would find it interesting," I said.

"That's what you said about the tainted Jekyll necroceuticals, and about the mummy emancipation case, and the Straight Edge hate group, and the attack on hundreds of ghosts with ectoplasmic defibrillators, and the burning of the Globe Theatre stage in the cemetery, and the golem sweatshop, and . . ."

I knew she could rattle off cases for hours, because I had spent hours telling her about them. She had taken thorough notes.

"It's nothing," I reassured her. "And we don't even know if your first book is going to sell well enough that the publisher will want to do a second one."

"They've already contracted with me for five, Mister Chambeaux. The first one is just being released—have you gotten your advance copy yet?"

"I'll check the mail when I get back to the office." I have to admit, I was uncomfortable about the whole thing. Vampires shun sunlight, and I tended to avoid limelight.

McGoo regarded me with amusement. "I believe we're done here, ma'am. Enjoy the rest of your quiet night."

"Thank you, Officer. And thank you, Mister Chambeaux, for your help." She drew a deep breath. "Ah, blessed silence—at last I can write!"

Just then, an anguished howl split the air, bestial shouts barely recognizable as words. "Help! Help me! *Help!*"

McGoo was already bounding down the stairs, and I did my best to keep up with him. We tracked the cries to a dark alley adjacent to the warehouse. A gangly werewolf leaned over a figure sprawled on the ground, letting out a keening howl. Beside him, two squirming cloth sacks contained the captured cockatrices; fortunately, the ties were secure.

As we ran up, Furguson swung his face toward us, his eyes wide, his tongue lolling out of his mouth. "It's Uncle Rusty!"

I recognized the bib overalls and reddish fur. The big werewolf lay motionless, sprawled muzzle-down in the alley.

"Is he dead?" McGoo asked.

Bending over, I could see that Rusty's chest still rose and fell, but he was barely conscious. The top of his head was all bloody, and it looked *wrong*.

Furguson let out another wail.

That's when I realized that someone must have knocked Rusty out and then, using a very sharp knife, *scalped* him.

CHAPTER 3

Next morning, when I got into the office, I discovered that I was suddenly a very famous zombie PI, whether I wanted to be or not.

It had been a rough night (for the undead, what else is new?). I looked more run-down than usual, or maybe "run over" is a better way to put it. While McGoo and I had combed the crime scene for evidence, an ambulance took the unconscious Rusty to the Brothers and Sisters of Mercy Hospital, the nearest medical center that could handle unnaturals. He had been stunned by an unseen assailant using a Taser and darts filled with horse tranquilizer mixed with wolfsbane. With his werewolf healing powers, Rusty would recover from the scalping—probably faster than his frantic nephew managed to calm down—although it might be a while before he regrew a proper head of hair.

As I shambled through the office door, Sheyenne was waiting for me with a big smile on her face and a sparkle in her blue eyes. Seeing her is always a good way to start a morning. I wanted to kiss her so much that I almost forgot she was insubstantial. Romance among the undead poses more than the usual share of problems.

For all her beauty and voluptuous curves, my girlfriend is a ghost, and my days of touching her whenever I wanted to were long gone. Though we had tried a few unorthodox work-arounds, mostly I content myself with remembering the brief time we had together. Now her smile glowed with enough warmth to melt even the coldest ghostbuster. I knew that something was up.

"Special delivery box arrived at first light, Beaux"—that was her pet name for me—"direct from Howard Phillips Publishing. You already know what it is!" She opened the box and withdrew a copy of a book with a garish red cover. She can move objects when she puts her mind to it, but not living—or formerly living—things.

The title said, in blood-dripping letters (of course):

DEATH WARMED OVER

A Shamble & Die Mystery

I took the book from her with very little enthusiasm. "Shamble? Great, now I'll never get rid of that nickname."

"It's not so bad," Sheyenne said. "Time to move on."

I glanced up at her. "A *ghost* is telling me it's time to move on?"

This was the first book in the line of Penny Dreadfuls ("Now only $14.99!"). The cover art showed a sunken-eyed zombie pointing a .38 toward some unseen criminal. He wore a trench coat and a low-slung fedora that did not entirely cover the bullet hole in his forehead. Now, I *had* been shot in the head and I do wear a fedora (but a sport jacket, not a trench coat), but I thought I was much better-looking than this guy.

"That doesn't look at all like me." I opened the book to a random chapter and found a lurid sex scene ... something I definitely did not remember from my real adventures. "I suppose these are going to be distributed all over the Quarter?"

"All over the country, if you can believe what Mavis Wannovich says." Sheyenne seemed delighted. "We couldn't buy advertising like this, Beaux. A private investigator who's so dedicated that even death can't keep him from his cases, partnered with a bleeding-heart human lawyer who seeks justice for all unnaturals." She picked up another copy from the box and flipped through it. "And let's not forget the detective's gorgeous girlfriend, who came back as a ghost because her love for him was so strong."

"I thought you came back to make sure I solved your murder."

"Poetic license," she said. "Don't spoil the story."

Robin emerged from her office, her nose in a copy of the novel. She looked pretty and studious. Robin Deyer—the "Die" part of the novel's fictitious "Shamble & Die"—was a young African American woman who crusaded for the rights of monsters, tackling cases that normal lawyers wouldn't consider.

"Thrilling adventures, sure, but I see it as a good platform, too. Maybe this book will call attention to the plight of unnaturals," she said. "Did you know that zombies and vampires aren't even allowed to vote? Werewolves—at least the Monthly ones—easily pass for human, unless voting happens to occur during a full moon. There was a recent case when a full-furred werewolf was turned away from the polling center based strictly on his appearance." She tapped the cover of the novel, considering. "Great works of literature can effect social change."

"I doubt this is great literature, Robin," I said.

Sheyenne was put off by my reaction. "Don't be such a curmudgeon, Beaux! Other people *enjoy* their fifteen minutes of fame. Look at all of those reality TV shows—*Survivor: Zombie Apocalypse* and *Transylvania Extreme Makeover.*"

"That's what I'm afraid of. I'm a detective, not a celebrity." Fame and publicity could ruin my career as a private investigator. It's hard to shadow a suspect discreetly if your face is plastered all over the news.

I could see it all now. I wouldn't be able to make a move without the paparazzi shadowing me; I'd be stalked by crazy fans, get inundated with hate mail or marriage proposals. Somebody might interview me about my life story and my death story, then there'd be a scandal and an exposé—*Behind the Embalming Fluid*. I could become a paid commentator on news networks, offering opinions on particularly heinous cases. Fame put stars in some people's eyes, but I preferred just to solve cases and help one client at a time.

Still, I couldn't deny the excitement on Sheyenne's face as she ran through the possibilities, so I sighed and made the best of it. "All right, Spooky. With any luck, nobody will read the book, and the series will die quietly, end up on the remainder pile. Is there really an audience for this sort of book?"

Sheyenne chuckled. "You don't come out of your crypt very often, do you?"

"There's definitely an audience," Robin added. "Even *I* know about the big Worldwide Horror Convention coming to the Quarter. It's going to be at the Bates Hotel—they're expecting hundreds of fans, celebrity guests, media."

I had forgotten about that. "All right, I admit that I have no social life."

"We're working on that," Sheyenne said with a smile. Using her poltergeist concentration, she lifted the books out of the box and stacked them on her desk. "Fifty copies."

"What am I supposed to do with so many books?" Sheyenne probably had a scheme to give away copies as thank-you gifts to satisfied clients.

Robin picked up a pen from the desk. "These are the special limited edition. You and I both need to sign them, and they'll be sold at a charity auction to raise money for Mrs. Saldana's zombie rehab clinic."

"People are going to pay money for our autographs?" I asked.

"Good money, we hope." Robin scribbled on a sheet of scratch paper, then signed inside the first book with a flourish. "Now that I'm a board member of the Monster Legal Defense Workers, I need to show them my support in every possible way."

I grabbed a pen from a cup on Sheyenne's desk and began autographing the books as Robin finished them. Sheyenne opened the cover and held the title page out for me as I scrawled. Zombie fingers have little dexterity, but even my pre-death signature had been illegible. I thought of rock stars and famous actors swarmed by fans as they scribbled their autographs before being whisked off by chauffeurs to the next destination. People like that never had a minute's peace, and no normal life. I preferred relaxing and having a beer or two with McGoo at the Goblin Tavern.

As Sheyenne repacked the signed books in the box, I said, "I'm due for my refresher rejuvenation spell tomorrow. I'll deliver these to Mavis and Alma." The two witch sisters, former clients of ours, now worked as acquisitions editors for Howard Phillips Publishing. Sheyenne had negotiated terms with the two: In exchange for my services as consultant on their Shamble & Die series, I would receive regular magical touch-ups to keep my body in adequate shape—much better than most zombies. ("Pristine" was out of the question, so "adequate" was the best I could do.)

Early onset of decay is a serious problem for zombies. Diet doesn't matter, and exercise can do only so much to keep the muscles limber. In my line of work, I get battered more often than I want to admit. (In fact, my arm was torn off once when I fought with a gigantic monster, but the arm had been successfully reattached.) Each time Mavis Wannovich worked her magic, I felt fresh as the day I was buried, so I didn't begrudge them a little inside information for the Penny Dreadful series. A deal was a deal. As a bonus, I would return the signed books to them in person.

For now, though, I had to get ready for a new client conference. The cases don't solve themselves.

CHAPTER 4

After the mayhem last night, it was a relief to get down to business and meet with the medical examiner. And this guy wasn't just the coroner—he was a Chambeaux & Deyer client as well.

Archibald Victor (emphasis on the *bald*) was an intense man with pallid skin and a cadaverous complexion. He was a diminutive, even goblinesque, human of the mad-scientist variety, with eyes as large and round as ping-pong balls and thin skittering fingers that might have made him a good pianist, though he devoted his dexterity to dissection instead.

He was completely hairless, yet for some reason—I was embarrassed to ask him why—Dr. Victor wore a dark toupee on top of his scalp, meticulously combed and moussed. It lay on his head like roadkill, obvious to the point of incomprehensibility.

Robin and I sat at the conference table. "How can we help you, Dr. Victor?" she asked, ready to take notes on her yellow legal pad.

The coroner set two pickle jars on the table in front of

Robin and me. One jar contained floating blobby tissue, a discolored organ that I could not identify; biology had never been my best subject in school. The larger jar held a rippled grayish mass that was obviously a human brain. He looked intently at us, narrowing his too-large eyes, keeping one hand on the jars, as if to protect them. "Before I engage your services, I must know that I can count on your absolute discretion. This is a private matter, ahem, and I wish it kept private."

"That's why I call myself a *private* investigator, Dr. Victor."

"And I'm bound by attorney-client privilege," Robin said. "You can speak freely."

"Good, good." He fluttered his fingers. "I'm not ashamed of my hobby—lots of people do it. Nothing abnormal about eccentric behavior."

The little coroner had my attention now. I owed him a favor anyway: During the autopsy of Snazz the gremlin, this man had proved that even though I'd been found at the scene of the murder, I was not responsible for killing the furry pawnbroker.

"We'll keep this professional, Dr. Victor." Robin clicked her pen. "How may we help you?"

He seemed embarrassed. "My wife says I'm obsessed, but in an endearing sort of way. You see, ahem, bodybuilding is a passion of mine."

I looked at his scrawny, pallid form—he was the last person I'd expect to find in a gym. And here I thought Archibald was going to say he liked to dress up in women's clothing. I wondered what strange hobby he was talking about.

McGoo had told me of a case where a psychotic dentist became obsessed with collecting human teeth; he'd only been caught because the insurance company complained that too many patients were filing claims for full sets of dentures after coming in for a routine teeth cleaning. When an insurance claims adjuster investigated, he was incapacitated with nitrous oxide and woke up giggling in the dentist's chair with bloody gums and

no teeth. The dentist had tried to flee, but was caught at the air-
port because all the fillings in the jars of stolen teeth had set off
the metal detector. . . .

Archibald Victor tapped his spidery fingers on the conference table. "How to explain this to someone who won't understand? You know how some people like to put together models
of sailing ships?"

With a wistful smile, I said, "I built a few of those plastic
molded kits. You snap them together or use model cement." I
let out a sigh. Ah, to be a kid again! "We used to float them in
the duck pond and blow them up with firecrackers."

Archibald blinked his large eyes, touched his toupee as if to
make sure it was still there, then said, "Ahem, I was talking
about something more involved than that. Truly dedicated
hobbyists build the ships piece by piece, sand and paint every
wooden part, tie the rigging rope with tweezers, cut and string
the sails. A meticulous craftsman can take up to a year to build
a single model."

The hairless coroner grew even more animated. "Now, think
of a hobbyist who builds a ship *in a bottle,* using tweezers for
every step—it requires the patience of a Zen master. And when
he's done, ah, the sense of pride and accomplishment . . ." He
drew a deep breath, let it out slowly. "The challenge of what *I*
do for fun is ten times harder."

I raised my eyebrows. "Bodybuilding?"

"Yes, ahem, I've become quite adept with 'build your own
person' kits. You assemble a human being from the skeleton up,
organ by organ, stitch by stitch."

Robin set her pencil down, concerned. "I thought that was
illegal. Weren't there raids on a few mad scientist laboratories?"

"Not exactly *illegal*—it's still a gray area of the law," the
coroner said. "I'm familiar with the cases you mentioned, but
those were extraordinary circumstances, and the mad scientists
in question are not members in good standing of the guild.

They should have known not to use non-voluntary body parts and organs. They give us all a bad name."

"Non-voluntary body parts?" I asked. "Who'd give *voluntary* body parts?"

"Oh, there are sources," Archibald said. "Usually mail-order catalogs or websites."

In a short break between answering the incessant phone calls—the press release about *Death Warmed Over* had done its work—Sheyenne entered the conference room carrying coffee for me and the coroner, green tea for Robin. Sheyenne looked at the pickle jars on the table, glanced at the preserved brain, then focused on the lumpy organ.

"Oh, a spleen," she said. "But an odd-looking one. Is it damaged?"

Archibald brightened. "Why, yes! That's exactly what I mean—it's defective. I did not get what I ordered. And though I've complained to the company, I received no satisfaction."

"You ordered a spleen from a catalog?" Sheyenne asked.

"Online. The warehouse is local, but I prefer to remain anonymous, get my components in unmarked packages delivered right to my home. It's Tony Cralo's Spare Parts Emporium, budget prices for collectors, researchers, hospitals. It's quite a booming market, ahem."

"You learn something new every day," I said.

"At least every other day," Robin added.

"I'm building two models right now at home, getting ready for a big body-building competition coming up. I received an honorable mention last year. But when the wrong piece shows up, it throws everything out of whack." He tapped the jar lid. "This spleen is in such bad condition, even your assistant spotted it at first glance."

"I did take two years of med school," Sheyenne said.

Archibald looked at Robin. "So, I want to enlist your services, ahem. Can you get my money back and stop the company from hurting other people? Look at this!" When he lifted the larger container, the formaldehyde sloshed from side to side, and the disembodied brain bobbed as if it were nodding. "This is shit for brains! Not mint condition by any means. Look at the medulla oblongata! And can you see the damage there to the cerebellum?" He made a sound of disgust. "Looks like somebody removed the brain with a meat cleaver and a set of bacon tongs."

Sheyenne nodded. "He's right. The damage is quite apparent."

Robin said, "We'll look into the matter, Dr. Victor. We handle consumer complaints as well, and we have several options. We can threaten to bring bad publicity for the Cralo Spare Parts Emporium, maybe arrange a boycott among mad scientists."

"Oh, no, no, no!" Archibald wrung his hands. "This has to be discreet. I'd be laughed at in my job, and I couldn't take the shame. I want people to think of me as a perfectly normal person, ahem." He bowed his head, and the ridiculous toupee nearly fell off. "If you come to my home, I'll show you my kits. You'd understand better."

"I could drop by, if I'm out in that area," I said.

Robin tapped her pen on the yellow legal pad. "We'll contact the company first, visit the manager, put them on notice. They need to improve their quality control, or they could lose a large part of their customer base. Don't worry, Dr. Victor—there's usually some quick way to avoid a misunderstanding. We file a lawsuit only as a last resort."

I added, "I'll see that you get a replacement brain and spleen, Dr. Victor. Maybe even convince them to throw in a free set of lungs while we're at it."

"Oh, that would be nice."

"We can't work miracles," Robin cautioned, "but we'll do what we can."

The phone rang again, and Sheyenne flitted out to answer it. She rushed back into the conference room through the wall, ignoring the door, and from her expression I could tell that the call wasn't just another book reviewer hoping for a free copy of *Death Warmed Over.*

"Officer McGoohan's looking for the medical examiner. There's been a murder—and even *he* thinks it's unusual."

CHAPTER 5

Although death isn't necessarily permanent since the Big Uneasy, it still isn't pretty. And if this murder scene was gruesome enough to disturb even McGoo, I knew it wasn't going to be a picnic.

I gave the coroner a ride in Robin's rusty Ford Maverick, affectionately known as the Pro Bono Mobile. I invited Robin to join us, but she's squeamish about seeing murdered bodies in situ. For someone who takes pride in being called a bleeding heart, she has no stomach for real blood.

But I didn't press the issue—I'd put her through enough already. Even after all these months, I still felt guilty that she'd been the one called down to the morgue to identify my body after I was shot in an alley. You'd think that having a bullet through your brain would be the worst part, but Robin and Sheyenne felt the hurt of my dying much more acutely than I did.

Personally, I don't remember any pain whatsoever, it was so fast, although it was damned uncomfortable to wake up underground in a dark and stuffy coffin, then have to work my way out. It took forever! I couldn't breathe (not that I needed to), and by the time I poked my head back out of the fresh sod, I thought that newly turned earth had never smelled so sweet. . . .

With Archibald Victor seat-belted in, I drove us over to the Motel Six Feet Under, known for its slogan "Dirt Cheap for a Dirt Nap: We'll leave the lights off for you." The coroner worried far too much about being seen arriving with me. "How are we going to explain to Officer McGoohan that I was at your place of business? You promised you'd be discreet. You can't tell him that I hired you!"

"Don't worry about it," I said. "There are a million reasons why a coroner could be at Chambeaux and Deyer Investigations."

Archibald wove his pale fingers together, then extricated them, then tangled them up in a different way. "But what are we going to *say?* What will you tell him?"

"The correct answer," I said as I pulled into the parking lot of the Motel Six Feet Under. "That it's none of his damn business."

Two police units were in the lot, lightbars flashing; a crowd had begun to form. An ambulance was already there, but the two EMTs lounged against the side, smoking cigarettes. They obviously had nothing to do, always a bad sign.

As Dr. Victor and I got out of the car, an approaching coroner's wagon rocked and swayed as it took the curves too fast, roaring down the block toward the motel, scattering curious pedestrians. The wagon carried the coroner's assistants, three ghouls who enjoyed their job far too much.

"We'd better hurry inside and have a look at the crime scene," Archibald said. "My boys tend to get so excited by a particularly gruesome setup that they scramble evidence." The body wagon pulled up with a screech of brakes, slewed sideways, and took up two spots.

The Motel Six Feet Under was a typical seedy place where

rooms could be rented by the hour, week, or phase of the moon. This motel had a special relationship with the police department, due to the sheer frequency of crimes committed there. Four spots were reserved in the parking lot for handicapped parking, one for a police unit, and one for the coroner's wagon.

With the commotion clustered around the bright red door of Room #3, we assumed that was the place to go. Archibald and I stepped into the room and immediately smelled blood, large quantities of it, as if someone had purchased a double family pack of the red stuff from a price warehouse club. The coroner's concerns about being seen with me vanished with the whiff of murder and violence. McGoo wasn't concerned about somebody's private life when he had a more-than-disemboweled vampire corpse to occupy his attention.

Archibald had left his pickle jars of organs in Robin's car and now carried his standard medical bag and tool kit. He entered the crime scene and spoke sharply, maybe to distract McGoo. "What's the situation, Officer?"

"Dead vampire found on the bed." McGoo looked relieved to see me—not for the help I could provide, but just to have a friendly face around.

"Don't see many dead vampires," Archibald said.

McGoo gestured, and we saw the corpse of a fish-belly-white vampire male manacled to the bed with a set of silver handcuffs. He'd been cut open, his insides scooped out like a Halloween pumpkin.

"His heart's gone, along with everything else," McGoo said. "I guess they wanted to be sure they took all the right organs."

Archibald bent over the body. "The technical term is that he was *disorganized*."

The incision went from the navel to the neck. The vampire was flaccid, like a deflated balloon, because nothing remained inside—no heart, no lungs, no stomach or digestive tract, no liver, no kidneys, not even a spleen (defective or otherwise). The top of his skull had been hacked off, and his brain was gone, as if removed with a large ice-cream scoop.

"Not the way you normally see a vampire killed," I said.

"Not the most efficient way, certainly," the coroner muttered. "Since vampires heal rapidly, this must have been a lot of work. But they held him in place with the silver handcuffs, so they could take their time removing every organ. And there are limits to what even a vampire can survive."

I gave my well-considered assessment. "Eww."

"Somebody sure as hell had a grudge, Doc," McGoo said. "Do I really need a complete autopsy so you can state the cause of death?"

"I can make my preliminary assessment on the spot," Archibald said.

I had heard of people harvesting a kidney from an unsuspecting victim picked up at a singles bar. I also knew that some unscrupulous vampires would intoxicate a mark, drain a couple pints of fresh blood, then let them wake up in a room without even orange juice and cookies to help them recover.

This, though, was something entirely different.

The three ghoul assistants from the coroner's wagon shouldered their way through the door, bright-eyed and jabbering. "Nice room!"

"I wonder if they have free breakfast," said another.

The third looked at the vampire corpse on the bed. "Looks like lunch is ready."

Archibald scolded them. "Boys, be professional!"

"We're ready to take the body," said one of the ghouls. "We even hosed out the back of the wagon."

All three hurried to the bed, frowning down at the inconvenient silver handcuffs that held the body in place. "Nothing's ever easy. Should we go get a saw?"

The motel manager had been hovering outside the door,

wringing his hands, trying to cope with the disaster. He, the policemen, and the coroner were all on a first-name basis. "If you cut up my headboard, you're going to pay for the damages!"

"We wouldn't cut the nice headboard. We were going to go straight through the wrists."

McGoo got out his own handcuff keys. "Standard issue. These should work." The cuffs popped open, and the dead vampire's limp wrists flopped to the bed.

"You are going to need new sheets, though," Archibald said to the manager. "And a mattress."

"No, that'll wash out. I've got a really good detergent that I buy in bulk. And the mattress has a liner—do you think I'm nuts?"

"The sheet is evidence. We keep it," McGoo said. "You know the drill by now. We try not to disrupt your business much."

"That's all right." The manager looked around, appraising the crime scene. "Murder rooms go for a premium. I can charge an extra ten bucks a night now."

"Everybody's happy, then—except for this guy," McGoo said.

The three ghouls wrapped up the eviscerated vampire in the bloodstained sheets (saving the expense of a fresh body bag) and carried the body out of the room. They knocked a lamp off the nightstand, and the manager rushed forward, yelling for them to be careful.

Seeing a vampire victim harvested of organs was certainly novel. I glanced at Archibald, remembered why he had come to Chambeaux & Deyer in the first place. I needed to have a look at that spare parts emporium as soon as possible.

CHAPTER 6

A gruesome murder scene doesn't usually whet my appetite, but it was lunchtime when I left the Motel Six Feet Under, and I decided it would be best to visit Cralo's body-parts warehouse with a full stomach and plenty of caution. After seeing the state of the vampire's corpse, it occurred to me that Tony Cralo might be involved in something far more sinister than shipping substandard organs to collectors like Archibald Victor.

Also on the day's to-do list, wrapping up a case: I had to tell Rusty what I'd learned about his missing gambling money during the cockatrice fights. Sheyenne let me know that he had already been released from the hospital and was recovering at home; werewolves are tough creatures, and Rusty, a gang leader of the Hairballs, was tougher than most. Given the assault he had suffered last night, I doubted a few missing dollars were his highest priority.

I stopped at the Ghoul's Diner for a cup of miserably bad coffee and some semblance of lunch. The sign in the window said SORRY, WE'RE OPEN. I also noticed a flyer taped to the glass door that said *Welcome Worldwide Horror Convention! Yes, We Serve Humans!*

The diner bustled and burbled with the lunch trade, and I settled for a solo stool at the counter, not wanting to hog one of the booths, which would have drawn the wrath of Esther, the harpy waitress. (Just being a *customer* was usually enough to annoy Esther.)

I cast a cursory glance at the menu and the chalkboard special without much interest—it would all taste the same to me. Albert Gould, the owner, had posted a sign on the coffeemaker, THESE GROUNDS ARE CURSED!

I pulled out a piece of scrap paper and began jotting random thoughts while I waited for somebody to take my order. In the back, Albert—a well-ripened ghoul—cooked, sweated, and oozed tendrils of runny slime into the customers' orders.

I heard the chatter of one-sided conversation as a delivery-truck driver brought in the day's load of canned goods straight from the rendering plant. The driver was a zombie in fairly good condition; he wore a green uniform and green trucker's cap. When he dropped a load of cardboard boxes on the counter, rats and cockroaches scurried out of the way. Albert turned with amazing swiftness for such a sluggish guy, using his forearm in a quick matter-of-fact gesture to sweep the bugs and rodents into a large stewpot. He stirred, then covered it with a big metal lid.

Esther came behind the counter and glared at me. Before I could say a word to her, the harpy waitress grabbed a ceramic mug and dropped it in front of me with a clatter. She splashed it half-full with the foul-smelling coffee, while also pouring a puddle across the flecked countertop.

Black and oily-green feathers stuck out from her arms like machete blades. Her hands terminated in obsidian talons, which she could use to hook several coffee mugs at a time, or snag the collars of customers who tried to depart without leaving a sufficient tip. Esther had a pointed, angular face with sharp teeth and an even sharper temper. When she skewered you with her bird-of-prey eyes, you wondered why you had come to the diner in the first place. Even so, her pale blue waitress uniform and white apron hid voluptuous and intriguing feminine curves. Unwittingly, she made you think about sex, and then made you shudder because you thought of it.

In a voice that sounded like a screech, she said, "I bet you think you're special."

In the kitchen, Albert perked up. *"Special!"* he slurred, and plopped a plate on the counter. "Last one."

"Just mix up some other slop," Esther called back, then she sneered at me. "Mister Famous Private Eye probably wants something that smells French."

I felt a cold dread in my stomach. "What makes you think I'm famous?"

Esther squawked again. "I saw the piece in the paper. Albert's going to want an autographed black-and-white photograph to hang on the wall." She flounced to the chalkboard listing the lunch specials and used one of her curved talons to scrape off the words with a flesh-cringing shriek of nails on slate.

I sipped my coffee while Esther bothered other customers. Maybe this wasn't such a good place to gather my thoughts after all. Investigating a suspicious body-parts emporium was sounding more and more like fun compared to lunch.

The zombie delivery-truck driver turned his cap around and came out of the back, pouring a mug of coffee for himself, demonstrating long familiarity with the diner. Esther glared daggers at him, but he paid no attention to her. Instead, he spotted me, saw the empty stool to my left, and came over. "Dan? Dan Chambeaux?"

I looked up from my piece of scrap paper that was still absent of insightful case notes. He was a blond-haired, gray-skinned blue-collar zombie. "Don't you remember me, Dan? It's *Steve*. We were dirt brothers. You helped me out of a tight spot—literally." When he grinned, I saw his teeth were still in relatively good condition.

Then I did remember. "Steve! Steve . . . Halsted, right?"

"Sure thing!" He clapped me on the back. "You look different out of your funeral suit, buddy. If I hadn't seen your picture on that book cover, I would never have recognized you."

Steve Halsted and I had risen from the grave on the same night. I'd emerged, dirt-encrusted and disoriented, not long before the guy in a nearby plot also crawled out. Reanimation is a tough time for everybody, and we had told each other our respective stories, exchanged contact information, and promised to stick together.

Over the months since, I had lost touch with him, though. I knew Steve left behind an ex-wife (no love lost there) and a young son, but we really didn't have much in common, so we drifted apart. I had my cases and a succession of personal emergencies, and I assumed Steve got on with his own unlife.

He said, "I was going to call you—I still have your card." I never could figure out why anyone had buried me with business cards in my pocket.

I ran my eyes over his uniform. "I see you got a job working as a delivery driver." It's always best to state the obvious.

"How did you know that?" he said, then laughed and brushed at his uniform. "Oh, I forgot, you're the detective. Yeah, that's me, delivering goods all around the Quarter. But it's about the only pleasant thing that's happened to me since coming back. I meant to give you a call to see if you or your lawyer friend could offer some advice. It's a sticky situation—and a stinky one—but I never got up the nerve to find you until I saw the piece in the newspaper talking about how you and your partner always stick up for unnaturals and never turn down a case."

"I haven't seen the article myself, but I'm pretty sure it was referring to the fictional adventures of a fictional zombie PI."

Steve chuckled. "Oh, you don't fool me, buddy!"

Albert staggered out of the back with a bowl of something that looked like a mix between magma and vomit. He opened his left hand to spill out a sprinkle of still-squirming cockroaches as garnish on top of the unappealing substance.

"New special," he said in his low, slurred voice.

Steve glanced down, took a deep sniff. "That looks good, Albert. I'll have one of those, too."

The ghoul proprietor shuffled back into the kitchen.

Talking about Steve's case seemed more appetizing than the food. "So what's the problem? Tell me about it, and I'll let you know if we can help."

Steve had a sad look as he got up and refilled both his coffee cup and mine without spilling a drop. "It's my ex, Rova. I just got this job, and I'm barely scraping by, but now she's filed a motion to garnish my wages, claiming past-due child support. I didn't even know I was supposed to keep paying, now that I'm dead. I thought that's what the life insurance money was for."

"I've never heard of postmortem wage garnishing," I said. "That's cold!" Robin might indeed have something to say about that. "I have to warn you, it'll be an uphill battle. Courts don't look kindly on deadbeat dads."

"I want to be sure that Jordan's taken care of," Steve said. "I'm not trying to get out of my responsibilities, but I don't trust Rova to use the money for our son's benefit. My insurance was supposed to cover all of his expenses, even put him through college, but Rova says that money's gone now, and she wants more from me. Worse, she's denying me visitation rights. I can't even see my own son."

I took a bite of the stewlike concoction and crunched down on something squirming and juicy.

"How does it taste?" Steve asked.

"We'd better just talk about your case."

Esther came by just as Albert served up another bowl of the new special; she swooped it from under the heat lamps and dropped it with a clatter in front of Steve. "We don't do separate checks." She tore off a ticket for both meals and set it next to my place. "Gratuity already added for parties of one or more."

I focused on Steve. "What's the problem with a zombie having visitation rights with his kid? That you might give the boy nightmares?"

"Hmm, he did scream the first time I tried to see him."

Steve seemed nearly as well-preserved as I was. "That's surprising. You don't look *that* scary." I meant it as a compliment, although not all monsters would have taken it as one.

"Oh, he didn't scream because I'm a zombie—it's because I'm *me*. I made a policy of not bad-mouthing my ex, for Jordan's sake, but Rova doesn't have the same attitude. She's poisoned my own son against me."

"And you say she spent all the insurance money?"

"Fifty thousand dollars! I thought it would be enough, but Rova took the money for herself, invested it in some beauty parlor she opened in the Quarter, said it was a surefire deal, the next best thing to printing your own money."

"She might have been a tad optimistic," I said.

Steve ate his stew, preoccupied. "I just want to make sure my kid is taken care of, you know? Could you look into it for me, buddy? See if I have any legal options?"

I glanced at my still-empty sheet of paper that should have been covered with brilliant deductions by now. "I've got appointments this afternoon, but why don't you stop by our offices later? I'll introduce you to Robin Deyer, my lawyer partner. Do you need the address?"

He pulled out the rumpled Chambeaux & Deyer Investigations card I had given him on the night we both came out of the grave. It looked as if he never took it out of his pocket, even when he laundered his uniform. He grabbed the check. "Let me get this, buddy. It's good to have a friend who understands your problems."

"We're dirt brothers, Steve. What are friends for?"

CHAPTER 7

Rusty the werewolf had been surly before, and I doubted that being scalped had improved his disposition, but I had an obligation to my client. I'd solved his case, whether or not he liked the answer. Out of consideration, though, I told Sheyenne not to send him the final bill until after he had recuperated.

Rusty lived in a dilapidated row house in a run-down part of town, not because he couldn't afford the rent elsewhere, but because the homeowners' association rules were less strict here. His front windows were boarded up since plywood was cheaper than glass, and he didn't like the view toward the street anyway. A chain-link fence surrounded his yard. A prominent warning sign on the fence said, BEWARE OF ALL MY DAMN PETS! I had been here twice before, and I knew Rusty could be more fearsome than his guard animals.

In the neighbors' front yard sat a rickety hearse on cinder blocks. Someone was burning trash in a rusty oil barrel. Dogs barked and howled incessantly because they had nothing else to do. Spiky dead weeds seemed to be the preferred form of landscaping.

When Rusty held weekend kegger parties for his rough-and-tumble Hairball gang members, he invited the neighbors, but they were afraid to come. His neighbors had their own dark secrets: coven rituals, lodge meetings, serial-killer boot camps, and quilting circles. Children didn't generally come around here selling Girl Scout cookies or Boy Scout popcorn.

I rapped on the screen door, and someone jerked it open with such force that the hinges didn't have time to squeak. Awkward-looking Furguson stood there bristling, his yellow eyes wide. He held a double-barreled shotgun that wavered from side to side. I raised my hands, not so much terrified of the gun as I was of Furguson's clumsiness. I didn't want to spend hours using tweezers to pick buckshot out of my dead skin because of a klutzy Hairball.

"Whoa, Furguson! Put that thing down, or at least point the barrel at someone who deserves to be shot!"

He seemed mortally embarrassed. "Sorry, Mister Chambeaux. Can't be too careful after what happened to my uncle." He let me into the house.

"That's who I came to see." I felt sorry for the kid, not sure how Rusty would punish his nephew, but I had been hired to solve a mystery, not to determine the consequences of the answers. "How's he doing?"

"Recovering, and just as stubborn as ever. He drank a gallon of vinegar tonic, said it was good for his constitution." Furguson was perspiring; sweaty werewolf fur smells like a wet cat under a low-powered hair dryer.

I didn't want to wake up a recovering werewolf who was in pain. "Is he resting quietly?"

"Resting?" Furguson let out a chuffing laugh. "What do *you* think?"

"So, out by the coops, then?"

"He spends more time with the animals than with me, I think. He says they're cuter."

I went through the small kitchen and out the back door into the fenced-in backyard. A broken fishing boat sat on a trailer, covering part of what would have been the lawn if anything had grown there. The rest of the yard was crowded with six coops covered with chicken wire and tar paper. Rusty incubated the prize cockatrice eggs, raised the chicks, and nurtured the creatures into adulthood. Then he tried to get them to kill one another.

The big werewolf stood out in the yard now, wearing his overalls, carrying a bucket of slimy entrails, which he ladled into the feed bins. "Here chick chick chick!" He slopped more intestines into the next bin. Rustling and hissing creatures swarmed forward, scales glinting in the light, beaks clacking. They squabbled as they gorged themselves. I saw a flash of lemon-yellow scales, bronze-green ones, and bright scarlet.

When Rusty turned around, even I was startled at his appearance. His scalp was a raw scab, like a skin wig turned inside out and painted with dried blood. Thanks to his lycanthropic healing abilities, the top of his head had scabbed over, though I doubted the fur would ever grow back the way it had been.

"Rusty, it's good to see you on your feet."

"Someone didn't ever want me on my feet again." He touched his head and winced. Parts of the wound that covered his cranium continued to ooze yellowish pus that crusted over. "If you're here to sell me shampoo, I won't need much of it anymore."

I laughed, because it was the polite thing to do.

Rusty growled. "Humor's a coping mechanism to keep me going until I find and kill the bastard who did this."

"Shouldn't you let the police handle it?" I asked. "Officer McGoohan was there at the scene. He won't ignore something like this."

"Hah! The same cop that tried to break up our cockatrice fight?"

"About that . . . there was a misunderstanding. McGoo just came to ask you to keep the noise down because one of the neighbors complained."

"*Now* you tell me. I knew I shouldn't have used those old rave speakers. It was the *Rocky* theme, wasn't it?"

"Among other things."

"We won't be doing the fights again for a while—I've got other priorities. Cockatrice fighting gets trumped by a blood vendetta any day. Did you find out anything about my missing money last night?"

"Afraid so," I said. "I solved the case."

Rusty growled. "Then why are you afraid?"

"Because you're not going to like the answer."

"I *already* don't like it—I've been losing money! Was it Scratch and Sniff, like I thought?"

"It was . . . an accident." I hesitated, and Rusty drew his own conclusions. He growled in disgust now instead of anger.

"You mean it was my nephew? He's one big walking accident."

I sighed and explained how, although Furguson had carefully recorded all the bets, he'd been sloppy stuffing the bills into his pockets.

"Damn that boy! When he tries to answer the call of the wild, all he gets is a busy signal! This is serious business. It's not as if I can take him over my knee and spank him anymore." He shook his scabby head. "My sister's son. I promised her I'd watch out for the kid, although why she'd trust her only son to a full-time werewolf makes no sense at all." He heaved a big sigh. "That kid is so clumsy, we don't dare let him use anything but these little round-ended scissors. I can't even let him trim his own facial fur."

Grumbling, he continued to ladle entrails into the cockatrice feeding troughs. Scaly, fork-tongued chicks wobbled about, flapping their not-yet-developed dragon wings and pecking at one another. Another cage held several nests built out of bent nails, which cradled leathery-shelled eggs. In three of the nests, fat warty toads sat on the eggs; in two others, vipers coiled around the clutches.

A lemon-yellow cockatrice fought with a crimson one, and they tumbled around inside the cramped cage in an orange blur, spilling offal all over the place. While they fought for the last scraps, the other cockatrices in the cage ate the ignored meal, so that when the two squabblers finished beating each other up, nothing remained.

Rusty went from cage to cage, inspecting. "I've been doing a lot of crossbreeding. Cockatrices are magnificent beasts, beautiful colors, even make nice family pets if they're raised right. I hear they're good with kids."

Two of the coops were entirely enclosed with tar paper, which blocked the view of the monsters within, but I could hear them rustling and hissing like a manifestation of intestinal distress. I figured that Rusty put some of his prized cockatrices in dark solitary confinement so they'd be hungry and angry for the next fight.

"So, I leave you to decide how to discuss the matter with your nephew," I said. "I hope you've found our services satisfactory. Sheyenne will send you a customer comment card in your final bill."

The cockatrice racket was deafening, but Rusty wasn't bothered by it. He continued to brood, flexing and unflexing his clawed hands. Finally, he threw the empty entrail bucket across the yard in a gesture of uncontrolled anger. It banged against the tar-paper side of the solitary-confinement coop, eliciting a round of bone-chilling snarls and cackles. I silently reaffirmed my desire to *not* see what the coops contained.

Rusty's eyes were fiery. "Oh, we're not done, Mister Shamble. I want to engage your services for a much more important matter, but I can't think what it is, off the top of my head." He tapped his raw scalpless skull, winced, then chuffed at his own joke and shook his head. "No, I don't see that using humor makes it any better." He extended his clawed hand. "I need a private detective. I want you to find out who did this to me and come up with proof."

"I'll take the case, but only if you tell me everything, especially the parts you didn't tell the doctors or the police."

"I didn't see the bastard. It was a dark alley, full night, and I was busy trying to hold my cockatrice in the bag. Those things don't like to be confined. Since I thought the fights were being raided, I was in a hurry to get out of there. Before I knew it, I got hit with two darts of full-strength animal tranquilizer laced with wolfsbane, and a Taser for good measure. Knocked me flat. Then some butcher took a knife and hacked off the top of my head."

I forced myself to look closer, telling myself it couldn't be any worse than the gutted vamp in the Motel Six Feet Under. Actually, it looked as if a neat, straight line had sliced away the scalp, causing no damage to the skull.

"I know damn well it was the Monthlies. I should have whacked Scratch and Sniff a few more times with that two-by-four. Shoulda used the end with the nails, too! But I'm a nice guy, Mister Shamble—a pacifist at heart. Look what it got me."

There was definitely bad blood between the two types of werewolves, a long-standing feud that went beyond mere rowdiness at a cockatrice fight. I guessed there would be a lot more to this case.

"You don't know for certain it was them," I cautioned.

"I know damn well for certain! I just can't prove it."

"So you're asking me to get the Monthlies," I said.

"Oh, yes—and blood will flow!"

CHAPTER 8

When you get invited to visit a mad scientist's lab—even if it's just a personal home workshop—you might think twice. But Archibald Victor wanted me to see his innocent do-it-yourself people kits.

I think he wanted to reassure me that his hobby was no more bizarre than collecting stamps or baseball cards. I'm not a judgmental guy in the first place. As a private investigator, I've represented monster brothels, a witch transformed into a sow, a bank robber ghost, an arsonist who claimed to be William Shakespeare, and a werewolf contesting her prenuptial agreement. Who was I to look askance at somebody who liked to stitch body parts together?

Still, at Chambeaux & Deyer, we try to give our clients the personal touch. I was happy to make a house call.

The coroner and his wife lived in a nice double-wide in a trailer park that had been converted from a bankrupt drive-in theater. At neighborhood get-togethers, the trailer-park management showed grainy old monster movies on the big patched screen. The tenants viewed them as comedies.

I was surprised that the Quarter's coroner could afford only a modest residence, considering the work he had to do (including all the repeat customers). But Dr. Victor and his wife were newlyweds, starting a life for themselves, and they didn't live beyond their means. I wondered how much he spent on his unusual hobby; I assumed mint-condition organs didn't come cheap.

When I rapped on the door of the mad scientist's house trailer I certainly wasn't expecting the woman who answered. I've never seen so much hair on a woman other than a werewolf. She was covered with it: long, curly locks that fell down to the middle of her back, long eyebrows that drooped to her cheeks, and a lavish beard that extended from her lower eyelids down to her ample bosom.

"You must be Mister Chambeaux! Archibald told me you'd be stopping by." She extended her hand, and her grip was warm and soft, indicating that she did not scrimp on lotions. The manicured nails were painted rose-petal pink; long and silky hair covered her forearm and the back of her hand. Everything about her had a freshly shampooed strawberry scent.

"Pleased to meet you, Mrs. Victor," I said.

"Please, call me Harriet. Come inside. My husband's in his lab." She closed the trailer door behind me and kept talking. "Yoo-hoo, Archibald! That detective is here."

"I'll be right there, love," he called back. "Just as soon as I finish installing this bronchial tube."

"Sorry the place is a mess," Harriet said. "Archibald takes over every table and countertop with his model-building hobbies and chemistry experiments. Someday, he's going to make us rich with a great discovery. He always tried to impress me when we were dating—I think he still is. He's such a sweetheart." She bustled about. "Could I get you a snack? Some crackers and cheese? I'm just getting ready for work."

"No, thank you, ma'am. I'm fine."

As I stood in the trailer's small living room, she put on a delicate necklace and bracelet, which were all but swallowed up in bodily hair. She primped her facial curls in front of a mirror. "Harriet isn't actually my real name," she said conversationally. "Just a stage name from when I worked for Oscar Kowalski's vampire circus. I was the most popular bearded lady they ever had."

"So you're not an unnatural, then?" I asked.

"No, it's just a hormone condition. I maintained a sunny disposition and made a good living, but I never liked being treated as a freak. Dear Archibald took me away from all that."

As if she had summoned him, the coroner emerged from the trailer's back room, shucking a pair of black rubber gloves and adjusting his prominent toupee to make himself presentable.

"I'm off to work, sweetie." Harriet picked up her purse and gave her husband a peck on the cheek.

He worshipfully stroked her full beard. "I love running my fingers through your hair."

Harriet giggled. "Now, don't get carried away—we have company. I'll leave you boys to your business."

After she left the trailer, Archibald stared after her like a lovesick puppy. "Don't know what I did to deserve her . . . or what she sees in me."

I had no idea how to answer that, so I didn't even try. "Let's have a look at your kits, Dr. Victor. I have another appointment later this evening." Actually it was my usual get-together with McGoo at the Goblin Tavern, but I wanted to keep this meeting on a business footing.

"Follow me to the back room. I'm just finishing a particularly challenging assembly."

Archibald's hobby area took up half of the trailer. A small bed was tucked off in the corner, and I couldn't imagine how Archibald and Harriet both fit on it, unless they snuggled tightly—which, as newlyweds, they probably did. Jars, tubes, and bottles of every conceivable type covered the countertop around the single bathroom sink, but the vanity was divided in two, as if by an imaginary line. One half was crowded with shampoos, crème rinses, mousses, hair sprays, and arcane beauty treatments—Harriet's side, I presumed. The other part contained beakers, flasks, test tubes, Bunsen burners, separation coils, differentiation cylinders, boxes of powders, jars of liquids.

"Concocting a new energy-drink recipe, Dr. Victor?" I asked, remembering his penchant for such things.

"No, no—an innovative new hair tonic. Top secret—it's going to make us rich, *rich!* I could rule the world!" He started to cackle, then caught himself. Embarrassed, he pulled me away from the vanity and sink. "Actually, I prefer the quiet life, never understood the appeal of ruling the world. That's not why I brought you here."

On a pair of sturdy fold-out utility tables rested two of his build-your-own-person projects in different stages of completion. One was a very tall human, nearly complete: The arms, legs, and torso were stitched together out of parts that originated from different sources; the varying shades of skin color gave the patchwork form a sort of calico appearance. The body cavity was propped open with Popsicle sticks and dowels.

I looked closer. "Why is one leg shorter than the other?"

He frowned. "Slight imperfections are to be expected. These bodies are individually handmade. It increases the collectible value."

"But won't he have trouble walking once you reanimate him?"

"Oh, these aren't for reanimation—just art objects. I'll enter them in the upcoming body-building competition, and I have a standing show over at the Night Gallery. This one still needs an acceptable spleen, as I showed you earlier. And, of course, a mint-condition brain." He tapped the kit's head, which had been sawed open, the top of the cranium set aside. The skull cavity reminded me of an empty garage waiting for a car to be parked there.

The second table held a skeleton on which some major muscle groups had been sutured with thick black threads. A set of lungs, looking like deflated balloons, had been tucked inside the rib cage, only recently attached. From the long canine fangs in the bony jaw, I assumed the head was a werewolf skull. Two eyeballs, one brown and one blue, had been installed, but the rest of the body needed a lot of work.

Archibald cracked his knuckles. "This hobby gives me an appreciation for the body's intricacies. As a coroner, I spend my days taking bodies apart, so it's gratifying to put them back together again in my spare time. Only the most skilled hobbyists start with the bare bones. And this"—Archibald tapped the long, yellowed fangs—"this is a genuine werewolf skull, very rare. Most werewolves revert to human form upon death, but this poor fellow died of a Gypsy curse—hardening of the arteries, I think—which messed up the reverse transformation. This one component cost me a fortune!"

I looked around the workshop. "If the hobby is so expensive, how do you afford it all?"

"I do consulting work to raise a little spare cash. So far, it's mostly mummies who bring their canopic jars and ask me to re-install their organs because they feel empty inside. Once a week, I donate time to the Fresh Corpses Zombie Rehab Clinic."

I thought about the crime scene at the Motel Six Feet Under. "Do you think the murdered vampire had anything to do with hobbyists like yourself?"

The coroner gasped. "I'd be appalled to think so!"

"Why else would anyone plunder the organs?"

"You may be aware that there's quite a demand for vampire organs on the black market—they just keep going and going, no matter how detached they are from the main body." Actually, I wasn't aware of that, but it made a twisted sort of sense. "Discriminating customers pay a lot for still-functional pieces."

I walked around the hobby table, seeing all the preserved pieces just waiting to be installed in the body-building kits. "How can you be sure all these body parts are obtained legally? My partner can't make a consumer protection case on your behalf if you're buying from a shady supplier."

He shook his head so vigorously that the toupee slid askew. "Body-snatching laws have been significantly tightened since the Big Uneasy. Many zombies came back to find themselves missing vital parts. Plenty of complaints filed."

I was glad that hadn't happened to me. "I see how it would be a problem."

"That's why I buy only from reputable dealers. I'm the coroner—I wouldn't want to expose the department to a scandal! I assume Tony Cralo's Spare Parts Emporium is fully licensed."

"I'll definitely look into Mister Cralo's operation—with complete discretion," I said.

Suddenly, a cauldron-like gurgling came from the shower stall in the half bath, sounding like a drowning victim in the first stages of reanimation. Alarmed, Archibald rushed to the bathroom. "Not that drain again!" The shower drain bubbled, burbled, and splurted effluent as it backed up with a stench worse than a sewer dweller's belch. Archibald snagged a long-handled rake propped against the shower and began fishing around with the tines, uprooting long, tangled masses of hair that had refused to go down the drain. The little coroner looked like a farmer moving hay with a pitchfork.

He set the tangled wad on the floor outside the shower, then emptied a gallon jug of drain cleaner down the shower drain. Fumes began to sizzle and smoke, and the coroner flicked on the bathroom exhaust fan.

"My dear wife is beautiful, and I love her hair, but she always forgets to use the hair trap or clear the shower stall after she's finished."

"At least you don't have that problem," I quipped, before I remembered how sensitive he was about his baldness.

He blushed and tried to block my view of his chemistry experiments on the countertop. "Just wait until I find a hair tonic recipe that works."

"Good luck with that." I glanced at my watch. "Thanks for showing me your work, Dr. Victor. I'll be back in touch after I visit the Spare Parts Emporium. I'll make sure you get a replacement brain and spleen."

"And see if they'll throw in an extra set of lungs, as you promised."

"I'll do my best." I left the trailer very much looking forward to having a beer with McGoo.

CHAPTER 9

The Goblin Tavern is the Quarter's favorite watering hole, a well-known hangout for monsters of all types (and a few humans, too).

That evening, I was on my usual bar stool with a tall, cold draft in front of me and my best human friend McGoo on the adjacent stool. Francine, the regular salty-humored bartender, was back on the job after an embarrassing disagreement with the new management. Yes, all was right with the world.

"How was your day, McGoo?" I slurped the foam head off my beer.

"About the same as yesterday, Shamble."

"Lousy, you mean?"

"That's about it."

As the bartender walked by, I said, "Francine, how was your day?"

"Same as McGoo's."

"Sorry to hear it," I answered.

She shrugged. "At least I'm still alive, which makes my day better than yours."

"You've got a point."

"So, a zombie shambles into a bar," McGoo said, before I could tell him I wasn't interested in another joke. "And on his shoulder, he's got a huge red parrot with long tail feathers and a big black beak."

"Those are called macaws," I said.

McGoo gave me an impatient gesture. "He's got this big red *macaw* on his shoulder. The bartender takes one look and says, 'Holy cow, where did you get that thing?' "

Francine butted in, "And the *macaw* says, 'Out at the cemetery—there's hundreds of them!' " She let out a cackle. "Yeah, I've heard that one before." She poured gin and crushed ice into a shaker, just a drop of vermouth, and dispensed an extra-dry martini for a dapper-looking Aztec mummy who sat in the corner of the bar, reading a codex.

Francine lit a cigarette and took a puff, leaving bright pink lipstick on the filter. She was a hard-bitten woman in her late fifties who colored her hair an unnatural shade of woodchuck brown. She didn't take any disrespect from her customers, gave advice from her own personal experiences when appropriate, and cared for the Goblin Tavern patrons better than any previous bartender had—certainly better than Ilgar, the former owner.

After she'd been laid off in favor of a more unnatural employee, her regular customers protested, and Robin filed an antidiscrimination suit. Francine got her job back, after agreeing to wear a funereal black miniskirt and cobwebby fishnet stockings (honestly, not something most customers wanted to see); she accepted the terms only on the condition that she be allowed to smoke on duty. Henpecked and desperate to have the beloved bartender back, the new owner Stu admonished Francine that cigarettes were bad for her health; more importantly, he warned her to stay away from the flammable customers whenever she had a lit cigarette in hand. (She kept her distance from mummies in particular.)

Stu was a portly, good-natured human who always greeted his customers, joked with them, and pretended to be their best friend. He had cobbled together the financing to buy out the Goblin Tavern after the collapse of the Smile Syndicate. He was in over his head, but he soldiered on, sure that business would get better. McGoo and I did our part to support the local tavern by drinking there as often as possible.

Stu emerged from the back office, jaunty and cheerful. "Thought you'd need a little help behind the bar, Francine." He grinned at all of us, bobbing his head. "The tour bus is due to arrive, and it'll be full of early convention-goers. Have to make a good impression. Maybe they'll blog and post about it."

It took me a moment to remember what Robin had said. "You mean the Worldwide Horror Convention?"

"Yes, sir, Mister Chambeaux. This should be one of our busiest weekends ever—and, boy, could we use the customers. The Goblin Tavern placed a big ad in their program book, shared a page with the Full Moon Brothel. They're having a convention special, too."

"Madame Neffi wouldn't miss a chance to advertise for customers," I said.

"She wants to be plugged into the convention traffic. We've got flyers stuffed into every registration packet as well."

McGoo wasn't convinced. "Aren't the convention-goers mostly human?"

"Sure, but I'm guessing they're an adventurous lot. I made up a special sampler platter."

"Hey, Stu," McGoo said. "What's cuter than a zombie baby?"

"I don't know. . . ."

"A zombie baby with a bunny's head in its mouth."

Francine went to console a middle-aged vampire who was drowning his sorrows in a glass of AB negative. I half listened as he poured out his sob story: He'd been a successful cat burglar until he broke into the wrong house and startled the vampire who lived there; the vamp bit him on the neck and turned him. Then, once the burglar became a vampire himself, he could no longer enter a home uninvited, which immediately ended his career as a thief. Now the guy didn't know what to do with himself.

With a roar of engine noise and a puffing squeal of air brakes, a large motor coach pulled up in front of the Tavern and disgorged twenty humans with cameras and book bags, all of them wearing clip-on badges that identified them as pre-registered attendees of the Worldwide Horror Convention; three wore ribbons that said *Professional Guest*.

Many of the fans were dressed in elaborate monster costumes, some of which looked better than the real thing—two immaculate Bela Lugosis, a werewolf with a prosthetic muzzle and fake fur glued on her face, and two undead who seemed to think that pale foundation, liberally applied eye shadow, smears of misplaced rouge, a bit of shoe polish, and a fake scar were all they needed to turn themselves into zombies.

Stu greeted the tour group at the door, wearing a big grin. Planning for the bus's arrival, he had pushed together six tables and pulled around chairs. The rearrangement cramped the room for the dartboard and the shiny new billiards table Stu had just installed (insisting on fiberglass pool cues, so there would be no risk to vampire customers from the long, pointed wooden sticks).

Francine left the depressed cat burglar and went to take orders from the convention group. Because they were tourists and not likely to become repeat customers, Francine gave adequate but not necessarily scintillating service. For their own part, the tourists—knowing they were not going to be repeat customers—would feel no need to tip well, regardless of the service.

Usually, when a tour group left the Tavern, Francine would complain about the crazy concoctions they ordered. She blamed Stu for creating the special twelve-page "Monster Martinis" menu, and she had to keep looking up the recipes.

Hearing a rumble of motorcycle engines outside, I looked through the window to see two large choppers pull up. The burly bikers Scratch and Sniff dismounted and came inside, looming large in their matted werewolf-pelt coats. At their waists dangled meat cleavers with rusty blades and sharp edges that gleamed silver. (Apparently, the two called their trusty cleavers Little Choppers, as opposed to the big choppers they rode.) The werewolves in human form surveyed the customers, obviously not impressed. Over at the empty billiards table, they shucked off their stained fur coats and draped them on stools, which gave them a chance to show off their myriad tattoos.

"Yo, Francine!" Scratch bellowed. "Bring us the usual!"

"Yeah," said Sniff. "One of everything!"

Francine looked up from the table of tourists. "I'll be there when I'm finished taking this order."

"We already gave you our order." Scratch primped his slicked-back hair.

The intimidated tourists stared at the big men. Francine lifted her chin and turned to the two bikers. "I said, wait your turn. These people are tourists. Show them a little Unnatural Quarter hospitality."

Holding fiberglass pool cues like cudgels, the pair strode over to the table of conventioneers. Sniff sniffed at the costumes, but the fake full-furred werewolf particularly drew his ire. "Little lady, what do you want to dress like that for? It's embarrassing."

"Aww, Sniff, she looks better than most Hairball chicks. Besides, she can wash that off when she wants to. Real Hairballs are stuck with what they look like."

Francine planted herself in front of the two burly men. "I

don't want any trouble here, and you're not going to give me any. Don't you know better than to piss off a bartender? Someday when you least expect it, I'll put a depilatory cream into your drink."

"Easy, Francine. We're not causing any trouble," Sniff said. "Just welcoming these people to the Quarter. Got no problems with regular humans."

Stu scuttled back to the bar, doing his best to defuse a situation that Francine had already defused. "What'll it be, boys? First order's on the house."

"Stu, don't encourage them," McGoo said. He'd been ready to intervene in case things got ugly, but I never doubted that Francine could handle it.

With exaggerated fake smiles, the two Monthly werewolves sauntered back to the billiards table and racked up a game. They ordered light beers in large mugs. I offered to take the drinks over to them, and Stu looked relieved that he didn't have to face Scratch and Sniff. Some zombies tend to lurch, but I walked over, careful not to slosh any of the beer.

The billiard balls had been painted like bloodshot eyeballs, another homey touch Stu had instituted at the Goblin Tavern. Holding pool cues and studying the balls across the table, both Monthly werewolves looked up at me.

Sniff sniffed. "Weren't you at the cockatrice fight?"

"I didn't think you'd noticed."

Scratch aimed with great care, sliding the pool stick back and forth on his posed fingers, and missed the ball entirely, whacking the felt surface of the table. His partner let out a sneering laugh. He fumbled the next shot, too, knocking the cue ball off the table. Now I understood where he had gotten the nickname of *Scratch*.

Scanning their myriad tattoos, I thought it would be a good icebreaker. "When you two got scratched up at the fight, I saw those tattoos come alive."

"Good healing spells, huh?" Sniff rubbed his beard, sniffed his fingers.

"They're not just tattoos." Scratch flexed his biceps to show off the pattern. "They're *voodoo* tattoos. I don't think they work on zombies, though."

I looked closer. "What does that mean, 'One-Percenter'?"

"Means we're one percent human," said Sniff. "I wouldn't tell you which one percent, though." They both laughed.

Always on the case, I fished for information. "Did you hear Rusty the werewolf got scalped after the fight?"

"Probably improved his looks." Sniff hooted and chuckled again.

I lowered my voice. "You guys, uh, didn't happen to have anything to do with that?"

"Scalping old Rusty?" Scratch pulled out the meat cleaver at his side. "If I was gonna do something, Little Chopper here would take his head clean off, not just his scalp."

Looking at the two, I believed them, though I doubted Rusty would.

No longer interested in me, they went back to their game. Sniff knocked an eyeball into the left corner pocket. "We should tell Miranda Jekyll to put a pool table at her werewolf sanctuary."

Scratch fumbled again and knocked a ball off the table. "When we're up there during the full moon, you wanna play *billiards?* That's our chance to run wild, roam the wilderness, feel the hot blood pounding."

"No, I mean during the daytime, before the moon rises," said Sniff.

"Oh, right. Sure, that's a good idea."

I left them to their game.

Chapter 10

Next morning, when my dirt brother Steve Halsted came to our offices, he looked forlorn and nervous, pulling off his green trucker cap and kneading it in his hands. I smiled with as much reassuring cheer as I could manage and introduced him to Robin and Sheyenne.

Steve shook Robin's hand and attempted to do the same with Sheyenne, though his hand passed directly through her ghostly form. "Sorry," he said. "Old habits die hard."

I had already told them the bare bones of Steve's situation, including a few specifics about Rova Halsted, his ex-wife. Robin liked to do everything by the book, having (sometimes unreasonable) faith that the right side would always win. I, on the other hand, was less sure of automatic happy endings. I preferred leverage.

I took Sheyenne aside to whisper in her ear, "Any interest in digging up a little dirt on the ex-wife?"

"Well, you're hard to resist when you blow in my ear. . . ." She gave me a sultry smile. "It would be my pleasure."

Robin led Steve into the conference room, and he seemed uncomfortable to be talking to an attorney, but was reassured to have me in the room. "Dan pulled me out of the grave when I was having a hard time—and now I'm having a hard time again." He drew a breath, shuffled nervously. "He said you might be able to help?"

As we sat down to discuss the case, Robin said, "If you haven't paid your original court-imposed child support, it'll be difficult to generate sympathy from the judge." She tapped her pencil on the legal pad. "Although it's highly unusual for an ex-wife to go after a dead husband."

"Ex-husband," Steve said. "Dead *and* divorced. I guess that makes me a double-ex-husband." He leaned forward, resting his elbows on the table. "It's not that I don't want to take care of my son. I'm a responsible parent. Jordan was the only reason I took out that life insurance policy in the first place."

Robin scribbled notes on her legal pad. "But your wife Rova received the money?"

"Ex-wife. But she's not dead, so it's only one ex. I told Rova that if anything ever happened to me, I wanted that money to go for Jordan's expenses: nice clothes, a good college."

"Was she the beneficiary?" Robin let out a barely audible sigh, but I caught it. "The status of life insurance proceeds has been muddled for years in the courts, with several lawsuits pending—zombies demanding the money for themselves, rather than their beneficiaries, and then insurance companies counter-suing to get their money back because the policyholders, while dead, are still ambulatory and are still capable of earning a living. Of course, the problem gets worse—in both cases—because the beneficiaries have usually spent all the money on funeral expenses, and new cars, long before the matter gets to court."

Once Robin got started talking about the nuances of cases, she built momentum. I loved to see her enthusiasm, but I tried to get her back on track. "Robin, so what about Steve's money for Jordan?"

She cleared her throat, embarrassed. "Sorry, Mister Halsted. In many cases, the divorce settlement voids any documents that name an ex-spouse as a beneficiary. How detailed was the paperwork delineating funds for your son's benefit?"

Steve shifted in his seat, awkward. "We just filled out the forms in one of those do-it-yourself books. Is there a standard blank for that? I wasn't really expecting to die when I did."

Now Robin's frown deepened. "You left the money to her, but there was no binding agreement that the money was to be put into a sheltered account in Jordan's name?"

"Oh, nothing formal like that. I thought I could trust her."

Robin hung her head and groaned. "Sometimes clients are their own worst enemies. In my experience, most divorced parents would rather eat glass than cooperate with each other."

"After I died, Rova took the fifty thousand dollars and went in with a partner to open a beauty salon. Now all that money's locked up in shampoos, crème rinses, and pedicure chairs. How can I make sure that it gets used for Jordan's benefit?"

Sheyenne floated into the room. "Their salon is called the Parlour (BNF)—whatever that means. Rova Halsted filed papers and all the necessary permits, founded the business with someone named Harriet Victor."

I perked up. "Harriet Victor? That's the coroner's wife—I just met her." Now that I thought about it, I wasn't surprised that the lavishly tressed bearded lady would be interested in, and have a great deal of practice with, styling hair.

"Yeah, that's the place," Steve said. "Never been in it. When I need a haircut, I go to a barber, not someone who calls herself a *stylist*." He shook his head. "I don't like to speak ill about Rova . . ."

Robin said, "I encourage you, Mister Halsted. Please speak ill about her *to us*. It could be relevant."

"To tell you the truth, she's . . . not very good at doing hair."

"That's for sure," Sheyenne said. "Rova Halsted has her stylist's license, but couldn't find a job outside the Quarter—too many complaints, even got fired from one of those haircut factories. So now she works on unnaturals."

Did I mention that Sheyenne is amazing at what she does?

"I guess monsters aren't so picky," Steve said.

"Tell that to the old-school vampires," Sheyenne said. "Some of them are as vain as high school girls on prom night."

"Rova used to cut my hair. That's why I usually wear this hat." He set his green cap on the conference table, hung his head, and admitted, "Rova's actually a dangerous hairdresser."

"How can anyone be a *dangerous* hairdresser?" Robin asked, jotting down the information in hopes it might be relevant. "Has she hurt people with scissors? Burned anyone with hair dye or curling irons?"

"No, I mean she's dangerous to people who *see* her customers. Her haircuts are so bad they've caused accidents, distracting drivers as they pass." He glanced at his watch. "I have to get to work soon. Deliveries to make, and I don't dare lose this job—especially not if I have to pay child support." Steve fished out his trucker's wallet, which was chained to his belt loop. "Here are some snapshots. Me and Jordan, good times. Rova won't let me have any other pictures. These are just the ones I was buried with."

The wallet photos were well-thumbed: a grinning boy in a Little League outfit, another one of him and his dad with fishing poles and proudly dangling very small trout they had caught. He flicked through the photos, showing another one with the boy in a rather alarming buzz cut that looked as if it had been trimmed with a lawn mower instead of hair clippers.

"Rova cuts his hair, too," Steve said.

"I gathered that," I said.

Sheyenne said, "Such a cute kid."

Steve couldn't take his eyes from the snapshots. I could tell he was about to start crying, and my heart went out to him.

Robin rose from her chair. "Let me look up some precedents. I can make the case that you've already paid fifty thousand dollars' worth of child support with the insurance, but your wife squandered it. Before we agree to pay her more, it's only fitting we have the court set up parameters, establish how exactly Rova is allowed to use the funds on your son's behalf." Seeing the determined look on her face, I began to feel that this might turn out all right after all.

"I want my boy taken care of," Steve insisted. "That's all I need to know."

"We should be able to negotiate visitation rights, if you'd like."

Steve lit up. "I'd love that, but Rova says I'm not allowed to see him anymore because I'm dead. The visitation ruling doesn't apply anymore."

"She can't have it both ways," Robin said. "If you're too dead to see your boy, then you're too dead to pay child support."

"Rova always used to confuse me with her contradictions." He forced a chuckle. "Whenever I pointed out to her that two completely opposite things couldn't be true at the same time, she just got angry."

"Lawyers are good at straightening out contradictions, Mister Halsted." Robin shook his hand again. "I'll be on this. Do you have contact information for her attorney?"

Steve shuddered. "You're not going to like him. He isn't a very likeable person."

Robin wasn't bothered. "We're professional colleagues. We don't have to like each other."

"His name is Donald Tuthery, and he works for the Addams Family Practice."

Robin started to write down the name and froze. "Oh. Well, I'll see what I can do. Sheyenne will set up a meeting with all parties as soon as possible, maybe even tomorrow." She flashed him a smile that I could tell was entirely false, but it convinced Steve. He thanked her and went off to work.

CHAPTER 11

Today was filled with reminders of the past.

Miranda Jekyll wasn't exactly an old friend, but she was a former client and a satisfied one at that. Robin had successfully broken the strictures of her prenuptial agreement with Harvey Jekyll, and we had seen to it that her evil husband was convicted of numerous horrendous crimes (which satisfied Miranda even more). The scandal had rocked Jekyll Lifestyle Products and Necroceuticals, while still leaving a fortune and a half for her.

When Miranda came for a visit, she didn't just "stop by"; rather, she *arrived*. Her hair was dyed a striking and potent cinnamon color, styled, swirled, massaged, and moussed into a precise sculpture that would have surpassed Rova Halsted's wildest dreams as a stylist. Miranda wore lacquered nails, layers of expensive necklaces, too much makeup, and too much pheromone-laced perfume, and the whole package was wrapped up in a tight red dress.

"Why, sweethearts!"—she pronounced it *sweet-hots*—"So grand to see you again! I just had to say hello, now that I'm visiting the Quarter . . . temporarily. As temporarily as I can possibly manage. You remember Hirsute, my deliciously masculine companion?"

The large hunk of male that accompanied her looked as if he had gotten carried away ripping bodices and ripped himself right off the cover painting of a romance novel. Flowing dark hair, shirt artfully torn to display his sculpted chest, square jaw, very large hands—and he didn't talk much. Though they looked human, Miranda and Hirsute had a feral glimmer in their eyes that signaled to a discriminating observer that they were both Monthly werewolves.

"Good to see you again, Mrs. Jekyll," I said.

"Oh, please, sweetheart, it's *Ms.* Jekyll, and I only keep Harvey's last name because of all the money involved. Besides, I'm sure it annoys the little worm no end. How is he doing by the way, after being executed and all?"

"Getting by," I said. "He just moved out of the Quarter into a small house in the suburbs." I didn't want to reveal that Robin and I had been instrumental in the matter, by filing lawsuits against locals who were trying to keep unnaturals out of their nice normal neighborhood. Even I still had a hard time believing that we had helped the loathsome man.

"I hope Harvey stays far away." She glided into the offices, holding Hirsute's muscular arm as if it were an anchor to steady herself. "Ah, I've missed the Unnatural Quarter! The seediness of this place reminds me just how wonderful it is to be somewhere else. Most of my time is spent out at the sanctuary up in Montana—that's my true calling in life. Hirsute makes it so pleasant there."

Miranda ran her long fingernails across his bare chest. He growled seductively, deep in his throat. As if to compete, Sheyenne brushed up close to me, giving me an unfortunately unfelt ectoplasmic snuggle.

"What brings you here, Ms. Jekyll?" Robin asked.

"I'm back to do my regular check-in at the factory, make sure my minions aren't ruining things." She brightened, her eyes twinkling. "*And* I've been invited as a celebrity guest speaker at the Worldwide Horror Convention tomorrow. They begged and begged until I finally had to agree. They're paying for our room at the Bates Hotel, even told us we could dine in the con suite, whatever that means, but it's a suite, so it must be fancy." She batted her eyes—the artificial eyelashes looked like a folded daddy longlegs. "But I see I'm not the only celebrity in town. You, Mister Chambeaux, are quite the famous detective."

We had received plenty of publicity in the wake of the JLPN scandal and our recent cases against Senator Balfour's Unnatural Acts Act, the Smile Syndicate, and solving the murder of the gremlin pawnbroker Snazz. But I feared Miranda was talking about something else.

"I saw the advertisement for your novel, sweetheart. If it's about the true adventures of a zombie detective, I wonder if *I* might be in there? A small cameo part perhaps? Every book like that needs a femme fatale."

"I wouldn't know, Ms. Jekyll. I haven't read the novel myself." After a brief pause, I saw an opportunity and took it—you never know where information might lead. "Since you're here, maybe you'd like to help out in another case? Recently a werewolf was attacked in the Quarter, stunned unconscious and then scalped."

"Scalped? Oh, my! But it wasn't even a full moon."

"The victim was one of the full-time werewolves," I said.

"Oh." Her alarm turned to distaste. "I have little to do with the Hairballs, if I can help it."

I pressed on. "The victim hired me to look into who attacked him. Not many leads so far, though he's suspicious of two troublemaker Monthly werewolves, Scratch and Sniff. They mentioned they've been to your sanctuary?"

"There was a time when 'troublemaker werewolves' was a

redundant statement," Miranda said with a sniff. "I know those two. Rowdy, unruly boys, but they can't help it. They're just hot-blooded. At least they're *real* werewolves, the ones that transform under a full moon, not those other types."

"I don't understand," Robin said. "You don't consider the full-timers to be real werewolves?"

"Sweetheart, a werewolf *transforms*. Human during the day, majestic beast under the light of the full moon. If you're covered with hair all the time, there's no transformation, is there? Hairballs are just like trained talking dogs."

Hirsute surprised us by speaking up. "They look like Wile E. Coyote."

"I've noticed friction between the two types of werewolves," I said. "Does it go beyond rivalry? Maybe to the point of gang warfare? A blood feud? If you could tell us anything about the long-standing grievances, that might help us solve the case."

Miranda waved her colored nails in the air. "Sweethearts, do I *look* like I get involved in politics? Of course not. It's none of my concern. Hirsute, escort me back out onto the street. I want to walk up and down the boulevard and show you off."

"I would be most honored to do so." He took Miranda's hand and nibbled on her knuckles, much to her delight.

"I'll see you at the convention, Mister Chambeaux. Perhaps you can dine with us as my guest in the con suite?"

"I doubt I'll be going to the Worldwide Horror Convention," I said, wondering what I would do there.

But Miranda just laughed as she walked out the door. "Of course you will, Mister Chambeaux. Of course you will."

CHAPTER 12

The Unnatural Quarter is a dark, convoluted place that has bad parts of town and worse parts of town. Even after my years here, there were still plenty of backstreets and byways with which I was unfamiliar, eccentric shops to peruse, restaurants to try, nightclubs to visit, alleys to avoid entirely.

Cralo's Spare Parts Emporium had not even been on my list, and now I visited the place with a certain amount of trepidation as well as—I admit it—curiosity. Good thing Sheyenne accompanied me, not so much as a bodyguard, but as a companion. There are worse things than being haunted by a beautiful blond ghost.

The Emporium—which I now realized was just a fancy name for "warehouse"—seemed like a typical chop shop, providing used, currently unused, and unusual body parts to the entire Quarter. For ambience, the warehouse was near an abandoned skeletal railroad bridge. The location was definitely toward the latter end of the bad-to-worse part of town.

Seeing the place, Sheyenne said, "I'm not surprised Dr. Victor prefers to do his shopping online."

The corrugated Quonset hut looked like a dead caterpillar in the middle of a gravel parking lot that was dotted with oil-stained brown puddles. A billboard rode on top of the curved roof, lit by a row of bent spotlights: *Tony Cralo's Spare Parts Emporium—Walk-Ins Welcome*. Another sign leaned against the open front door: YES, WE SELL DIRECT TO THE PUBLIC! SHOWROOM NOW OPEN!

"It says all parts are one hundred percent organic," Sheyenne said. "That can't be all bad."

"I can think of ways it would be all bad."

We moved forward. A few cars and pickup trucks were parked haphazardly outside the Emporium. We saw two men wrestling with a lumpy rolled-up Persian rug, which they carried through a back door marked *Deliveries*.

Several furtive customers emerged from the front door carrying wrapped packages. An older human couple, both bespectacled, wandered inside; like a gentleman, the man held the door for his wife. They looked like a pair going antiquing on a weekend.

"I'm surprised to see so many customers," I said. "Who would have guessed there's such a demand for the spare-parts trade?"

"Body building must be a more popular hobby than we thought, Beaux. Probably mad scientists window-shopping."

I figured there must be other legitimate uses—medical research, morticians needing to fill out or fix up a client, maybe even high-end gourmet flesh-processing plants for discriminating cannibalistic customers.

The foot traffic made our job easier; we didn't have to call attention to ourselves. Sheyenne and I blended in, and entered just behind the elderly couple.

Inside, the Emporium was an amazing place, well lit, with row upon row of fully stocked shelves. A color-coded map on the wall segregated the warehouse by species (Cralo catered to humans as well as most known unnaturals).

"It's like an IKEA for body parts," I said.

"You should take me to IKEA," Sheyenne said. "We could furnish your apartment."

I picked up a small wire basket for impulse buys, so we could maintain our cover as we walked up and down the aisles. There were severed hands and claws of all types, replacement lungs and hearts. A showcase area had framed samples of flayed skin and fur "For All Uses," without specifying any of the aforementioned uses.

Aisles were labeled: *Skeletal Replacement, Soft Tissue Sundries, Kidneys (Two-for-One Special)*; one whole alcove was devoted to eyeballs. A rack of hardware store drawers contained teeth, separated and labeled. Fingers and toes were in the bargain bins.

Sheyenne flitted ahead, fascinated. "Reminds me of my med school classes. I wish I'd known about this place when I was in school." She stopped in front of rolls labeled *Bulk Muscle, Guaranteed Steroid-Free.*

There were bins of bones sorted by size, as well as a grinder and a bread-making machine. A Home Fashion section advertised decorative tumors, intestines dyed various colors (sold by the foot). Feet were also sold by the foot.

Jars and cans held cranial fluid under several brand labels; spray bottles had multipurpose mucus. Self-service plasma dispensers stood next to a large aquarium in which floated glands, ducts, and small organs, kept moist and fresh. It reminded me of forlorn lobsters in a tank at a seafood restaurant.

Thinking of the eviscerated vampire corpse in the Motel Six Feet Under, I wondered if the Vampire Parts section had any new arrivals. "We should tell McGoo about this place."

"You think he wants to take up body building?" Sheyenne asked.

"I think he might be curious as to where all these body parts come from."

A floor salesman was explaining to an older necromancer, "Our specimens are of the highest quality. Flash-frozen or vacuum-sealed in bags to preserve freshness."

"But where do they all come from?" the necromancer asked, his eyes sparkling with wonder. "It's been years since I've seen a selection like this."

"Some come from murder victims, some from executed murderers, unclaimed bodies in the morgue, maybe an indigent or two. A few fell off the truck." The salesman chuckled. "Some were *run over* by a truck. We buy in quantity so we can keep the prices down. The titles are free and clear on everything we sell."

With a sober nod, the necromancer tapped his chin. "I'd hate to have someone come shambling by asking for their pieces back."

"That's never happened, I assure you, sir!" the salesman said, bustling off with the necromancer. "We have a complete customer satisfaction policy."

"We'll see about that," I muttered. When Archibald Victor had tried to lodge a complaint, he couldn't reach their customer service department. No one had answered the phone or responded to his written complaints.

As was typical for a large store, when I tried to find a salesperson to help us, they were entirely invisible. Finally, at the back of the warehouse Sheyenne found an office marked *Floor Manager, Xandy Huff,* and she guided me there.

The door was partly closed, and before I could knock, I heard shouts from the office. "We shouldn't have kept you on after the first time, Francis—you're fired! Give me your badge!"

"B-but Mister Huff—I need this job!" It was a nasal phlegmy voice, not entirely human. "How am I going to eat?"

"Eating's what got you into trouble in the first place—this isn't a restaurant! How can I justify this to Mister Cralo?"

"Please don't tell him!" The voice quavered, palpably frightened. "Just give me my paycheck, and I'll leave."

"Mister Cralo decides whether you even get your last paycheck. We'd be within our rights to deduct the lost materials from your wages. Come back tomorrow after I've discussed it with him. For now, I want you out of here!"

The door flung open, and a sick-looking, greasy-skinned ghoul tottered out, panicked and uncoordinated. He had lank, lumpy hair; his face was emaciated. His crooked and broken teeth looked like random glass chips. Sniffling and sniveling, he careened into me, then walked directly through Sheyenne's incorporeal form. "Excuse me. Sorry!"

He reeled away, and Sheyenne remarked on the oily smear the ghoul's residue had left on my sport jacket. "I suppose it needed cleaning anyway."

I pushed into the floor manager's office, taking advantage of the man's emotional state. Better to spring my problem while Huff was in a huff, when his guard might be down. "Excuse me, Mister Floor Manager . . ."

The man behind the desk had a bald pate surrounded by a fringe of dark hair, and his jowly face was punctuated by a thick black mustache. He did not look like the sort to give encouraging talks to his employees, even when he wasn't having a bad day.

"Damn ghouls, eating on the job." He stuffed an employee badge (presumably from the freshly fired ghoul) into an envelope and slid it into a metal rack of time cards on the wall behind him. "What do you want?" He ran his gaze up and down my form. "You need a job? We just had an opening. You look like you're used to handling dead things."

"I'm here for a customer."

"A customer?" Xandy Huff changed his entire demeanor; he even managed a half smile. "How can I help you? Please call me Xandy—short for Alexander, but not quite Andy."

"I'm Dan Chambeaux, private investigator, and this is my associate Sheyenne. One of our clients, a Dr. Archibald Victor, asked me to help him pursue a complaint and investigate your operations. He showed us evidence of substandard parts, damaged goods, and mislabeled items that he's ordered from your catalog."

Xandy looked uncomfortable. "I don't see how that could happen. Why didn't he contact us directly instead of hiring a detective?"

"He's called numerous times and sent several letters."

"Oh. Our complaint line has been disconnected to better serve our customers, and all complaint letters are carefully looked into, on a regular basis."

"How regular?" Sheyenne asked.

"At least every six months."

"That explains a lot," I said. "Before pursuing legal action, our client wants to invoke your complete customer satisfaction guarantee."

"Certainly!" The man seemed very solicitous. "We believe in customer satisfaction."

I took out a folded piece of paper from my jacket pocket. "This is a list of items and order numbers, primarily a brain and a spleen, both of which were damaged. Dr. Victor would like to receive appropriate replacement organs or get his money back."

"We also think he's entitled to an extra set of lungs, to make up for the inconvenience," Sheyenne added.

Annoyed, Xandy Huff took the list and skimmed it. "The spleen is no problem, got plenty of those, if you have his receipt and his original purchase order. But the brain, that's difficult. There's always a shortage of brains around here. You'll have to talk to Mister Cralo himself."

"What about one hundred percent customer satisfaction?" Sheyenne asked.

"You'll be satisfied. Mister Cralo prefers to deal with complainers face-to-face. He makes them an offer they can't refuse. So far, we've had no repeat complaints." Huff glowered at us both, as if he thought we would be intimidated, but I'm not a zombie who gives up easily.

"And where can I find Mister Cralo?" I asked. "I'll go speak with him right now."

Xandy seemed alarmed. "Really? Do you have any idea—?"

"No idea whatsoever, but I do need to get this resolved."

Sheyenne added, "Dr. Victor is our client, and at Chambeaux and Deyer we also have a customer satisfaction guarantee."

"Suit yourselves. It's your funeral."

"Already had one," I said.

"Me, too," Sheyenne said.

Xandy gave me an address. "Mister Cralo spends most of his time at the Zombie Bathhouse. You can find him there."

"Zombie . . . Bathhouse?" Sheyenne's ghostly form shuddered. "I'm afraid you're on your own for this part, Beaux."

CHAPTER 13

By the time we left the Spare Parts Emporium, a weather front had come in. A fog bank smothered the sky with miserable gray, accompanied by a cold drizzle that refilled the pothole puddles in the parking lot.

A panel truck drove off so full of body parts wrapped in white butcher paper that the back doors had to be secured with a bungee cord. The panel truck roared away, hitting every one of the potholes, splashing rooster tails of brown water into the air. Just before it left the Emporium parking lot, the bungee cord snapped, and body parts fell all over the ground. Yelling at each other, the driver and his companion got out and rushed around reloading the truck, and then hurried off again.

In the ramshackle tenements a few blocks away, a swamp creature was hanging laundry on a line to soak up the mist, freshening up lacy underwear that was not designed for any sort of body I wanted to imagine. I heard a banshee doing a gut-wrenching—and heart-stopping—rendition of "Singin' in the Rain"; windows shattered, and neighbors shouted at her to stop the racket.

Sheyenne gave me an air-kiss and flitted off to the office. "I'll let you find the Zombie Bathhouse. Need me to bring your bathing suit?"

"I'll be fine, Spooky." I couldn't convince her that it wouldn't be so bad. I couldn't convince myself of that either.

Not far from the Spare Parts Emporium, the skeletal wreck of an abandoned railroad bridge loomed out of the fog like an economy-sized gallows big enough to offer group discounts. Shadowy figures lurked under the bridge in a squalid shantytown. Homeless unnaturals gathered there, bound together by fiscal situation rather than their unnatural species.

As I shuffled out of the gravel parking lot, feeling the damp cold mist on my damp cold skin, a gruff voice called. "Shamble, is that you? Dan Shamble!"

"It's *Chambeaux*." I looked over at the shanties and cardboard boxes under the bridge.

Ominous figures stood around a trash fire in an oil barrel, but the voice came from a large, sagging cardboard box. A hairy werewolf crawled out of the box and stretched, putting a hand to his back as if his body ached. He motioned me over. "Don't you remember me? It's Larry." He scratched a patch of matted fur. "I used to be more intimidating."

I came over, surprised. Larry was a werewolf hit man who had served as Harvey Jekyll's personal bodyguard; now he made his home in a cardboard box from the kind of discount coffin you could buy off the shelf at one of those price warehouse clubs. He had a tattered old blanket and a pillowcase stuffed with wadded newspapers. The scruffy-looking werewolf hadn't washed or trimmed his fur in some time.

"Larry, what are you doing here?" I shook his hand, then shook my head. "What happened to you?"

"Lost my job. Jekyll let me go after he moved into his cozy house in the suburbs with their neighborhood watch and block parties—said he didn't need a bodyguard anymore." He flexed his claws. "It was a crappy job anyway. And he was a terrible boss."

"I'm not surprised. Jekyll was a terrible human being, and then he became a terrible zombie."

"I have my pride," Larry continued. "I actually quit—he didn't fire me. *I quit.* Never wanted to work for him in the first place. It was demeaning."

Seeing that he now lived in a cardboard box under an abandoned railroad bridge in the drizzle, I had to wonder what his definition of *demeaning* was.

"You couldn't find other work?" I asked. "There must be plenty of jobs for bodyguards or hit men. This *is* the Unnatural Quarter."

"You'd think so." Larry tried to growl, but it sounded like the phlegmy aftereffects of pneumonia. "But I'm a pariah because I worked for Harvey Jekyll."

"Well, Larry, you dig your own grave, you have to rise from it."

He brushed a paw down his chest, as if to show that he didn't care. "I'll scrape by, Shamble. I don't need much." He stretched, then gestured me to follow him. "Come here—I want you to meet a friend of mine." He moved toward one of the burning barrels.

Cold water dripped from the framework of the bridge above, and bats circled in playful mating dances. The area under the bridge itself was a trash dump piled with old cans, boxes, broken glass. Some of the debris was arranged in neat piles, even assembled in what might have been called artistic sculptures; gravity rearranged the rest.

A troll came up to us. He was a few inches shorter than me and had leprous scales, pointy ears, and a face with all the wrong angles. He wore a padded fleece coat salvaged from the garbage.

Larry introduced us. "Dan Shamble, this is my friend Tommy Underbridge. He helps the less-fortunate unnaturals here."

The troll reached out a big-knuckled claw to shake my hand. "Good to meet you, sir. Care to join us for dinner? I'm making a large community pot." A cauldron was suspended over the low flames of the barrel's garbage fire. Something bubbled, and the aroma wasn't entirely awful.

"Goat stew," said the troll. "Stringy, but delicious."

"Where do you find goats out here?"

"They come out here to eat the garbage, try to cross the bridge, and get stranded. That's when we trip 'em and trap 'em."

An ogre who wrapped himself in a stained Scooby-Doo blanket raised his big shaggy head. "Damn goats, trying to steal our garbage. Serves them right." The ogre picked a rusty can from a pile, tossed it in his large-jawed mouth, and began crunching happily.

"Goats are getting scarce around here," Larry said. "But there's always the rats—plenty of those."

To be polite, I asked, "And what's your story, Tommy? How did you become a homeless troll?"

Tommy cackled. "Homeless? This is my home, exactly where I want to be. Beautiful view, lots of friends, and a bridge to live under! What more could a troll want?" He raised his hands. "This is our community center."

Larry picked up an empty can, with which he scooped up a serving of goat stew. "Want some, Shamble?"

"No, thanks. I ate at the Ghoul's Diner yesterday. My stomach's still a little queasy."

"I understand." With a gesture of his head, Larry indicated the Spare Parts Emporium. "Don't bother shopping there. Prices are too high. If you need organs or body parts, come see me. I can set you up, cash only."

"I wasn't trying to buy anything. Just investigating a case, a customer service complaint." I narrowed my eyes, thinking of the dis*organ*ized vampire in the Motel Six Feet Under. "And where would *you* get body parts?"

"Donations," Larry said.

Tommy had been cheerful, but now his mood changed. "You shouldn't get into that racket, Larry. It's beneath you."

"Beneath me? I'm living in a dump, and I've got a cardboard box for a bedroom."

"And you should be happy with what you have," Tommy said. "Lots of monsters going missing these days, Mister Chambeaux—and I doubt they're all moving out to the suburbs like Harvey Jekyll did."

I said, "I was about to go meet with Tony Cralo in person. I'll mention it to him."

"Cralo? Whoa!" Larry said. The homeless monsters suddenly looked uneasy. "While you were in the Emporium, did you buy yourself a set of jumbo-sized balls? Nobody goes to see Cralo."

"I have to follow where the leads take me," I said. "The cases don't solve themselves."

"So, uh"—Larry fidgeted as he slurped his goat stew, while Tommy the troll ladled up several cans and passed them to homeless monsters—"if you have any work I could help with—on a consulting basis—just let me know. I'll be here in my box. You need the address?"

"I can find it," I said, then paused. "Come to think of it, I do have a case that involves werewolves. Rusty, the leader of the Hairballs, got assaulted and scalped the other night."

"Heard about that," Larry said. "But you probably didn't hear that it's happened before. Nobody cares when bad things happen to homeless monsters." He led me to two mangy-looking werewolves who hadn't had a bath or a grooming in quite some time.

Both homeless werewolves wore dirty stocking caps that had been knitted from colorful yarn, back at the dawn of time. The fuzzy beanies were pulled down all the way to their pointed ears. "Dan Chambeaux, this is Arnie and Ernesto, two of my werewolf pals. Guys, he's investigating what happened to Rusty." Larry nodded at the two. "Go ahead, show him. He needs to know."

Embarrassed, Ernesto and Arnie glanced at each other, then pulled off the stocking caps. Both of them had been scalped. The crowns of their heads were scabbed, rubbery-looking, angrily healed.

"They got it two nights apart, a week ago."

This made the case more complicated. So Rusty wasn't just a single revenge target. "You think it's a case of scumbags attacking the homeless? That's called trolling."

"Don't you bad-mouth trolls," said Tommy.

Larry shook his head. "It's a gang disturbance between Hairballs and Monthlies. That's where I'd put my money, if I had any money. Trouble's been brewing for a long time."

"What started it?" I asked.

"Bad blood, a personal insult, but Rusty's so embarrassed he won't even talk about it. Something to do with the Voodoo Tattoo parlor. Scratch and Sniff were behind it, Rusty never forgave them, and Hairballs and Monthlies have been at each other's throats ever since." He puffed up his chest. "I'm a proud member of the Hairballs myself, been over to Rusty's house for a couple of his kegger parties."

"Couldn't they help you out of your situation?" I asked.

Larry looked away and scratched the fur on his muzzle. "I'm not that desperate yet. I'd be ashamed for them to see me like this. But sooner or later . . ." He squared his shoulders, flexed his claws again. "If gang rivalries heat up, they'll need all the muscle they can get—and I've got muscles."

I pondered all the details I'd learned from this single visit, and for good measure—or maybe good karma—I slipped Larry a twenty-dollar bill. (I think it was the one I had found on the floor of the cockatrice-fight warehouse.) A good investment, I decided.

CHAPTER 14

Out of the fog and into the steam.

The two words *Zombie Bathhouse* said it all—and deterred most customers. The bathhouse was a brown brick building that covered half a block, and most of the floor space was subterranean. Sturdy arches framed doorways that looked like the mouths into a sewer. A skilled tombstone artisan had incised the address and the name of the place into the stone.

I hesitated at the doorway, then steeled myself and entered the bathhouse. As I went down the slick stone steps, a stench wafted up, overpowering, although some might have considered it inviting. The thick, humid air was pregnant with brimstone smells and mineral salts. I hoped Archibald Victor appreciated that I was willing to shamble the extra mile for his case. It was a lot of work just to file a complaint properly.

I didn't know whether this place fell on the fair-trade or rough-trade side of the equation. Some customers come into a massage parlor really and truly for a relaxing muscle massage, and I had no idea how many undead came to the Zombie Bathhouse to get a *bath*. Nevertheless, Tony Cralo was here. He had an intimidating reputation, but I would talk with him, man to . . . whatever, and hope I got the "happy ending" I expected.

The main area held a large swimming pool in which bobbed dozens of naked zombies in various stages of decomposition. Steam wafted up from the water. Separate whirlpool baths offered special treatments from freezing ice plunges to ultra-hot mineral soaks. One tub was a veritable cauldron, and the bubbling water foamed and swirled; only one zombie dared to venture into that tub, which looked far too much like a stewpot to me. There was even a wading pool for kiddie zombies.

An undead attendant stopped me at a turnstile gate. "Fifteen bucks for a soak." He looked as if he'd been a librarian in his previous life.

"I'm looking for a man named Tony Cralo," I said. "I was sent here."

The zombie cashier's eyes widened. "In that case, my sympathies, and I wish you the best of luck. But it'll still be fifteen bucks for a soak." He ran his gaze up and down my patched-up sport jacket. "No street clothes allowed."

"Do you have bathing suits for rent?" I asked.

"We have towels and winding sheets."

"Give me a set, then. And a locker key."

I pushed through the turnstile, and the clerk handed me a stack of fabric. "This establishment assumes no responsibility," he said. "Especially for body parts that fall off."

"I don't plan to soak that long."

"Most people don't." The cashier went back to reading his paperback book.

I took the towel and winding sheets into the changing room, claimed a locker, and disrobed. I regularly worked out at the All-Day/All-Nite Fitness Center, so I was accustomed to seeing various naked monsters horsing around in the showers. I remembered one roughhousing group of vampires cracking other patrons with gym towels, all fun and games until they inflicted permanent damage on the crumbling bones and bandages of an old mummy who had been trying to get himself back in shape.

After they disrobed, zombie customers shuffled out into the pool room. Some wrapped towels around their waists, others didn't bother. With their sagging butts and leprous blotched skin, some with ribs and scabs showing, no one spent much time looking at the customers anyway.

I was in good repair, and the series of bullet wounds across my torso had been packed and stitched up by the best sawbones and taxidermist in the Quarter, but scars and stitches don't fade from zombie skin. Maybe I would ask Mavis Wannovich if she could do anything when I saw her for my restorative appointment that afternoon.

Zombies shuffled around the pools, dropping towels and flip-flops, climbing into the relaxing waters. A bathhouse attendant walked around with a skimmer net, scooping out slime and chunks of debris that floated to the top of the pool. Some of the more limber zombies frolicked about, splashing or dunking one another. One zombie's eyeballs had fallen out of the sockets, and his friends snatched them away in an impromptu game of Marco Polo. Most of the zombies, though, just soaked away their aches and pains.

I went to the attendant as he fished out hunks of detached skin and dumped them into a reclamation bucket. "Could you tell me where to find Mister Cralo?"

He sized me up. "Private pool number two. Don't tell him I sent you."

I found private pool #2, a separate Jacuzzi. Two linebacker-sized zombies in business suits blocked my way. They were the only ones in the entire bathhouse wearing street clothes. Their suits bulged in places that shouldn't have bulged.

"Excuse me, I'm here to see Mister Cralo."

One of the goons looked over his shoulder. "You holding court, boss?"

"I'm relaxed enough," a voice drifted from the steaming whirlpool. "Who is it?"

"Dan Chambeaux, private investigator," I said.

Cralo heard me and called past his two bodyguards. "A private dick? This is a nude bathhouse, not much private dick around here." He chuckled. The bodyguards chuckled. So I chuckled, just to be part of the gang. Then Cralo said, "Check him, then send him over."

"You'll have to remove your towel, sir," said one of the bodyguards. I let the towel fall, and the two men eyed me without being impressed. "He's unarmed, boss."

They let me through, and I stood before the Jacuzzi of Tony Cralo, an imposing monstrosity of a man. He lounged back against the rim as the hot water roiled around him. "Dan Chambeaux. Climb on in and have a soak. Ease your troubles."

I'd been invited by a powerful man who seemed to intimidate everyone, so I had to agree, even though I would rather have stayed on the sidelines. But the cases don't solve themselves.

Cralo was an enormously fat zombie. His bloated skin was just on the ripe side of putrefaction, his eyes sunken into their sockets and surrounded by folds of puffy skin. He squirmed in discomfort and emitted a loud basso fart that sounded like a howitzer going off. A huge bubble broke the surface of the water, and I swear the fumes were visible like greenish-brown pipe cleaners bent into odd shapes.

"Damned outgassing," Cralo said. "Never had good digestion before I died, and now . . . with a body my size, it's only natural." He let out another much smaller fart, then sighed. "Come on in, what are you waiting for?"

I paused for as many seconds as I dared, to let the fumes clear, then lowered myself into the whirlpool next to him.

"Feels good, doesn't it? That's special hot sulfur water piped in here. Good for the skin, good for the health." He rested the back of his head on the edge of the tub.

"Yes, it does feel good, Mister Cralo," I said.

"I don't know if these aches and pains are caused by me being overweight, or being dead." He heaved another sigh. "What can I help you with? Who's trying to charge me with something now? I'll post bail and get my lawyers right on it."

"I'm not the police, Mister Cralo. Just looking into a matter for one of your Emporium customers. He's an avid body builder, and several of his orders have been defective. He can't get anyone to respond to his complaints. In particular, he needs a replacement brain and a spleen. He'd appreciate a set of lungs, too, if you can spare them."

Cralo leaned forward in the pool like a sea monster approaching for the kill. "Xandy Huff couldn't take care of you?"

"He's the one who sent me over here, said you took care of all complaints personally."

"Damned minions, can't think for themselves . . . but I guess that's not what I pay them for." He chuckled. "If that's the worst problem I have all day, then I'm going to have a good day. My Emporium does a brisk business supplying mad scientists, resurrectionists, hospitals, medical research companies, even that new zombie rehab clinic. We do good work for the community as a whole, but we try to pay attention to our smaller clients as well. One Hundred Percent Customer Satisfaction, Mister Chambeaux—that's my policy. I'll see to it your client gets a replacement brain, spleen, and whatever else he needs. Stop by and see Huff tomorrow. Tell him I said so."

I was taken aback, after all the ominous warnings and disbelief I had encountered. "That's it? You're just going to say yes?"

Cralo leaned back, closed his eyes, and concentrated on the warm brimstone water. "Nobody's ever had the nerve to lodge and follow up on a complaint before. I'll give you props for that." He was obviously finished with me.

"Thank you, sir. It's been a pleasure."

Another large, fragrant bubble shot to the surface of the whirlpool, and I climbed out of the tub as quickly as I could, retrieving my towel from the business-suited bodyguards. I went back to the locker room to clean up and get dressed.

After this, I definitely needed my restoration spell from the Wannovich sisters.

CHAPTER 15

Life had been rough for me since my death. A career as a private investigator in the Unnatural Quarter is fraught with hazards, and Robin had suggested—though not seriously—that I find a safer profession. A zombie accountant, perhaps.

I had been beaten up by demon goons, gunned down in the street, framed for the murder of a gremlin, even had my arm torn off by an ugly monster. But this is what I do, and it's not likely to get simpler. I'm not the sort of guy who could settle for a cushy desk job.

To mitigate the wear and tear on my body, I set up regular appointments at Bruno and Heinrich's Embalming Parlor to top off my fluids, touch up my makeup, and do all the cosmetic things necessary to make me presentable to the public. Unlike other well-preserved zombies, though, I had an edge—my side agreement with Mavis and Alma Wannovich. I offered the witch sisters inside details about my cases for their new Dan Shamble books, and they gave me a monthly restorative spell. Quid pro quo.

I arrived at their apartment carrying the box of autographed

Death Warmed Over special editions for the charity auction to benefit the Fresh Corpses clinic. I wiped my shoes on a quaint welcome mat that said *Abandon Hope, Ye Who Enter Here* and rang the bell.

Mavis opened the door, wearing her stars-and-moons witch's hat, which covered an explosion of tangled black hair that looked like a smoke spell gone wrong. "Mister Chambeaux, welcome! Delighted you could make it. We're going to have a busy week—all of us." She was plump and bubbly; her black dress barely surrounded her girth.

I didn't know what she meant. "It's always a busy week." I carried the heavy box of books inside and set it on a counter. Each copy of the special edition had a small inset marble tombstone with the copy number engraved in the stone.

Mavis opened the box. "Wonderful! We'll get these over to the Worldwide Horror Convention. MLDW is running the charity auction, and these autographed first editions are sure to be hot items."

The Wannovich sisters had a small, homey place with cross-stitched samplers on the walls featuring verses from the Necronomicon, funereal lilies in a vase on the table. Odd-smelling potpourri bubbled from miniature cauldrons over black candles. A wide variety of curious roots and herbs grew in planter boxes and vases throughout the residence. A small shrine-offering sideboard stood against one wall, cluttered with unusual trinkets, amulets, vacation photographs, and even a shrunken poodle head.

Mavis's sister Alma, who had been irreversibly transformed into a sow by an attraction spell gone wrong, also worked at the Howard Phillips Publishing Company. Though the witches had offices in the main building, they took reading days and worked part time out of their home—hence the dozens of manuscripts piled on the floor.

Alma rooted through the slush pile, shoving her pig snout

into the papers and nudging them around. She snuffled at the prose as if she hoped to find either truffles or some literary gem. The sow looked up at me, snorted a greeting, blinked her beady close-set eyes, and turned back to the manuscripts.

"Come on, Alma—you have to help me with Mister Chambeaux's treatment. And then we'd better clean up for our company. The ladies will be here soon."

Alma knocked over a thousand-page manuscript held together by several rubber bands. *My Immortal Loves, Volume 1,* by Fred Nosferatu. A more scholarly text, judging by the number of footnotes at the bottom of its manuscript pages, was *Scandal in the Church,* by Q. Modo.

Mavis tidied up the sitting room. She had already put a plate of cheese and crackers on the coffee table. "We're having a ladies' social gathering in about an hour, Mister Chambeaux— just some other witches for tea. It's the Pointy Hat Society."

"I won't take up too much of your time, then," I said. Alma used her snout to shove the manuscripts into a haphazard pile behind the sofa, while Mavis flipped through a well-worn spell book; particular pages were marked with sticky notes.

The restorative spell itself would not take long, although it drained Mavis by the time she was finished. "If this were easy, everyone would do it," she had once told me. "But we're very happy to help *you.*"

Some restorative spells required nasty-smelling unguents applied to all of the body's orifices. Fortunately, my regular tune-up required none of that, just a few recited incantations in what sounded like pig Latin (and Alma joined in).

Mavis sketched designs in the air with an incense stick that roiled with lavender smoke, and I immediately sensed an improvement that turned the rigor into vigor. It felt much better than the brimstone mineral soak in the Zombie Bathhouse.

I stretched, flexed my arms and legs. "I appreciate it very much."

"And we appreciate *you*, Mister Chambeaux. We owe you a great deal, and not just for the cases you solved. We got our jobs because of you and Ms. Deyer, and now Howard Phillips Publishing is on the verge of its greatest success. We want you at your very best to help us with the promotion." Mavis went around the room, propping up cardboard posters that showed the garish red cover of *Death Warmed Over*. "We'd love it if you could do just a teensy amount of publicity for the book release. My instinct says this series will catch on like a funeral pyre."

"What . . . sort of publicity?"

Mavis continued, as if she were in a sales meeting. "We are thrilled with the response we've received so far, and the pre-order numbers are great. Have you seen the stellar reviews? And a cover quote from Charlaine Harris herself! Can you believe that? 'An unpredictable walk on the weird side. Prepare to be entertained.' *Charlaine Harris!*" Mavis could barely control herself.

"I'm glad Ms. Harris liked it," I said. "What sort of publicity were you expecting me to do? I'm not good at interviews."

"Oh, just an appearance—a book signing for a very specialized audience. Say . . . tomorrow? We want you to be our guest at the Worldwide Horror Convention. Howard Phillips Publishing has a large table in the dealers' room. We've taken out an ad for the novel in the program book and included a free preview copy in the registration bags." She moved around the room, setting out stacks of *Death Warmed Over* postcards and bookmarks, and engraved pencils shaped like wooden stakes. "Just one day at the con and one signing at our table, to meet your fans?"

"How could I have any fans? The book just came out."

"Some people are fast readers," Mavis said, "and the buzz has been phenomenal." Alma snorted in enthusiastic agreement. The witch pulled out a Special Guest badge adorned with a VIP ribbon, like the ones I had seen on the tour group at the Goblin Tavern. "We already picked up your badge."

I flexed my arms again, feeling the renewed vigor and flexibility there. After the rejuvenation spell, my whole body felt tingly and energetic, and I owed a debt of gratitude to these two witches. "Tomorrow is short notice, but I can make an appearance for a few hours. I've never been to a Worldwide Horror Convention before." I had to admit, I was interested in what Miranda Jekyll intended to talk about, since she was also a special guest.

The doorbell rang, and Mavis hurried to answer it. "Oh, the ladies are starting to arrive! I'm glad you're still here, Mister Chambeaux. Many of them want to meet you."

I looked at my watch. "You said they wouldn't be here for an hour yet."

"Some insist on showing up early."

Four other witches came in, all wearing identical pointy hats. They chattered, giggled, and complimented one another on hairstyles and scarves. With far too much pride, Mavis hurried the women over to introduce me. "These ladies are our friends, Mister Chambeaux. We're not exactly a coven, just a social group." While we were talking, several more witches arrived. It didn't take a detective to figure out that Mavis had told them to come early, just so she could show me off.

Alma waddled around the apartment, letting the guests place jackets and scarves onto her back, after which she tottered toward the spare room and shook them off onto the bed.

"We started out as a support group for Alma," Mavis continued. "They're still working to find a cure for her spell, but we love and accept Alma just the way she is."

The ladies had brought cupcakes and finger sandwiches. One particularly tall witch slipped a large silver flask out of her coat and passed it around. Mavis put a cauldron on the stove to boil.

The ladies treated me like a very special guest, asking how it felt to be famous, tittering over how dangerous and exciting my job must be. Many of them already had copies of *Death Warmed Over,* which they asked me to sign. Finally when the Pointy Hat Society turned their conversation to ladies' club topics that I didn't understand—primarily gossip about members who had not yet arrived for the meeting—I excused myself.

"Sorry, ladies. I have work to do. The cases don't solve themselves." I pocketed my convention guest badge and promised I would be there as agreed. All the women said goodbye in an eerie harmony.

Mavis quipped, "He's a zombie detective. He can't rest in peace until he brings criminals to justice." Then she jotted that down, thinking it might be useful as a tagline.

CHAPTER 16

Walking back to our offices in the afternoon, I soaked up the ambience, or the miasma, of the Quarter. One of the Kreepsakes chain gift shops was shuttered, its inventory of ridiculous monster souvenirs liquidated. A large UQ Tours motor coach rolled by, packed with tourists who snapped photos from behind the safety of monster-proof windows. I could hear the muffled sound of the tour guide's voice as he described noteworthy parts of town.

I did enjoy this place and felt it was my home. Years ago, I never would have imagined my career, and afterlife, would lead me here, but I felt a certain responsibility for the people, particularly the ones who came to me and Robin for help.

It was amazing, in a way, that so many monsters of various sorts—as well as a fair number of humans—managed to get along, live and let live (or maybe *exist* is a better term for it). There are ethnic neighborhoods generally divided by the type of unnaturals, and there are feuds, romances, lazy nights, nail-biting days, the aromas of exotic cooking (or spells), everyone finding their niche. Thankfully not everyone got along, or I would have been out of a job, but the Quarter wasn't much different from any other city, except for all the supernatural creatures.

A black-furred, full-time werewolf in a white apron cranked open the awning of his little tienda, setting out fruit baskets and marking up the prices on the spoiled fruit. Next to him, a vampire tended his newsstand in the shade, wearing gloves, oversized sunglasses, and slathers of sunscreen. A black gargoyle stopped to buy a package of peppermint gum.

The tour bus ground to a halt, and the human tourists crowded to one side, taking pictures of the gargoyle and the vampire, who looked up in annoyance. It made me think of Harriet Victor and her life as the bearded lady in a circus freak show. Given the publicity from the Dan Shamble books, I worried that UQ Tours would change the bus route so the gawkers could swing by the Chambeaux & Deyer offices.

I came upon McGoo entering the Transfusion coffee shop for his usual cinnamon latte. "Hey, Shamble. Heading back to the office?"

"In my own ponderous way."

"I'm headed that direction. Think we should pick up a coffee for Robin?"

"She'd like that." We ducked into the coffee shop, and McGoo even paid, which was one of the strangest things that had happened all day.

"So, what does a vegan zombie eat?"

"I don't know. I'm a rib-eye man myself."

He stretched out his answer. "Graaaaaiiiiiins!"

I let out a long groan, always an impressive sound, to further my image. Before he could tell another joke, I distracted McGoo by talking about work. "I've got a lead you might want to check out for that murdered vampire—Cralo's Spare Parts Emporium has a staggering variety of organs and body pieces. I don't know exactly where they get their inventory, but if you dig into their records, you might find a few organs—maybe even some vampire organs—that don't have the proper receipts and donation forms."

He sipped his coffee. "Thanks, Shamble. I'll look into that."

Emerging from Transfusion, we spotted the lanky Furguson sniffing around a fire hydrant. The owner of a used-clothing shop, a female Monthly werewolf, came out of the shop and chased him off. "Get away from that hydrant! Nothing for you there!" She made a disgusted sound. "Stupid Hairball."

Growling, Furguson slinked away. "Stupid Monthly."

Seeing him alone, I wondered if his uncle had chastised him, maybe even kicked him out of the house for losing so much money at the cockatrice fights. No doubt Rusty would have preferred to learn that the Monthlies were responsible, since he had already expended so much personal energy on the feud.

Hearing the coughing rumble of loud motorcycle engines, I looked up. "Here comes trouble," McGoo said.

"You're stereotyping again."

"I'm observant. Got no problem with bikers in general—just those two in particular."

I knew that motorcyclists could be some of the most tight-knit and sociable people you'd ever meet; they didn't judge, they lent a helping hand. There was even talk of a great rally through the Quarter, the Ghost Rider Classic.

But Scratch and Sniff were the bad apples of the bunch. They arrived on their chrome custom-built choppers, fur coats flapping behind them, rusty meat cleavers dangling at their sides. The two rode without helmets or sunglasses, catching flies in their teeth; they looked human and exuded feral energy. Gripping ape-hanger handlebars, they looked from side to side as the choppers cruised past. They let out wolf whistles at the clothing shop owner who stood at her doorway; she gave them a flirtatious wave. Turning toward the black-furred Hairball tienda owner, though, Scratch and Sniff hawked up wads of phlegm and spat like a double-barreled shotgun. The black-furred werewolf ducked out of the way in time, but the phlegm splattered the baskets of fruit.

"Sorry about that, man," Scratch yelled. "Didn't mean to hit the fruit."

Sniff chuckled and hooted. "Yeah, we just had hairballs caught in our throats."

Scowling, McGoo stepped into the street, wearing his cop uniform like armor. "Spitting in public is a hundred-dollar citation, boys. We don't want any trouble—hope you didn't bring any."

"Just going for a nice afternoon ride, Officer," Sniff said.

"We wouldn't dream of—"

Then a snarling cannonball of fur barreled toward the two bikers, all gangly arms and legs, flashing teeth. Furguson. He sprang at Scratch, the nearer of the two, but tripped at the last minute and fell on the pavement in front of the chopper. He tumbled into the front wheel, which knocked the chopper over so that Scratch collided with Sniff, and both motorcycles crashed.

Furguson sprang up in an instant, baring his teeth. "That's for what you did to my uncle Rusty!" He threw himself on Scratch and raked his claws down the biker's head and chest, ripping open a long, ugly wound.

McGoo and I rushed toward the fray, but the brawl exploded in a minute. The Hairball tienda owner bounded from his shop and dove on Sniff, who was trying to help his partner. Furguson moved in a flurry, slashing, jabbing—not a very good fighter, but certainly a frenetic one. Scratch and Sniff were bleeding profusely, but looked more annoyed than mortally wounded. The used-clothing shop owner ran to fight alongside her fellow Monthly werewolves, armed with nothing more than a coat hanger.

I pulled out my .38 and fired two shots in the air, which startled everyone long enough for McGoo to snag Furguson by his shirt collar and yank him away.

Scratch and Sniff struggled to grab their meat cleavers. The black-furred werewolf stood with muscles bulging, growling deep in his throat as he faced off with the clothes-shop owner, who menaced him with her clothes hanger.

McGoo had had enough. He reached for his belt, which held numerous defenses against both humans and unnaturals, and brandished a large canister. "Back off, all of you, or you'll get a face full of pepper spray. You think you're red-eyed were-wolves *now* . . ."

Scratch coughed blood, pushed himself into a sitting position. He seemed more concerned about his mussed hair than the gashes. "That was assault—you all saw it!"

Furguson snarled. "They started it! They attacked my uncle Rusty!"

"Haven't proved that yet, Furguson," I said.

I watched in fascination as the kaleidoscope of tattoos on Scratch and Sniff crawled like multicolored worms, squirming, stitching skin together until the deep gouges vanished.

Sniff brushed himself off. "Gotta love those voodoo tattoos."

"Not a mark." Scratch laughed at the embarrassed Furguson, then turned toward McGoo. "We want to file charges, Officer. That's deadly assault. He tried to kill us!"

"There's not a mark on you—as you said yourself." McGoo smiled. "But I'll be happy to take you downtown and let you file a complaint. I've been meaning to have you both answer some questions anyway about this feud with the full-time werewolves—and your involvement in the very real assault on Rusty."

Scratch backed away. "We had nothing to do with that." He

adjusted his hair so that it looked like the back end of a duck again. "Just like we had nothing to do with those other things you've charged us with in the past."

"Only this time, we really mean it," Sniff said.

Scratch righted his chopper. "We don't need to file paperwork, and this matter isn't going to any court. We'll handle it our own way." The two bikers swung aboard their choppers again. "This isn't over," they said and roared down the street.

Furguson looked infuriated and ashamed. His fur was still bristling.

"That's not the way to make it up to your uncle," I said.

"It was a start," he mumbled, then shook his head. "And I couldn't even do that right."

CHAPTER 17

Coming back from the dead isn't as bright and cheery as most people might think. More often than not, there are tragic consequences.

For my very first case in the Quarter, I'd been hired by a family to track down their missing uncle, who had risen from the grave and shambled off. When I did find the man, he was in such a decomposed state that the family was repulsed and never saw him again. It broke the poor guy's heart.

Next morning, when our walk-in client appeared (though it was more of a lurch-and-stagger-in client), I knew in my gut that this was going to be one of those situations.

Adriana Cruz was messed up, both physically and mentally. She had been quite vivacious—good figure, good looks, great personality, on the cheerleading squad her freshman year before moving on to pre-law and volunteering at a community legal center. Adriana had a bright future and ambitious plans, a whole life ahead of her.

Unfortunately, she also loved to send text messages to her

friends while she was driving, and she wasn't as adept at multi-tasking as she thought she was.

"I watched the funniest kitten-and-crocodile video you ever saw, and I was just texting a message back to my friend," Adriana said. "I hit *L O* and was about to type the last *L* when I became car number five in an eight-car pileup. Or maybe I was car number six—my memory's a little fuzzy on the details."

Adriana's good looks and good figure hadn't come through the automotive trash compactor in the best condition, to put it mildly. She held up her scarred hands, her fingers splayed at all the wrong angles. Her head was cocked to one side. Although Adriana must have arrived at the funeral parlor with "closed coffin suggested" stamped on her forehead, her mortician had gone the extra mile. Unfortunately, she'd needed a lot more than a mile.

"I'm sorry for your loss," Robin said. "How can we help you?"

"Nobody plans on being mangled," she said. "We all imagine that we'll die in front of a cozy fire at age ninety. No such luck for me."

Sheyenne joined us, her expression deeply sympathetic. "Some days, I'm thankful I came back as a ghost. Given the choice . . ."

I imagined Adriana might want us to file some sort of wrongful death suit against the other drivers in the pileup, or the cell phone manufacturer, or even her friend who had sent the funny cat-and-crocodile video clip.

It turned out to be much stranger than that.

Sheyenne led the way, politely opening the door as Adriana lurched into the conference room and slumped her battered and mismatched body down into the chair. The disfigured zombie kept talking as she adjusted her position. "I'm a responsible young woman. Twenty-eight. Most people my age don't worry about death planning, but since I was in pre-law, I know what can happen if you have a sloppy will, so I left instructions for the disposal of my remains. My parents thought I was being morbid, and I told them they were being irresponsible. We, uh, didn't always see eye to eye. But I made my last wishes known. It was completely clear."

Sounding like a voice-over in a movie trailer, I said, "But something went wrong?"

"Something definitely went wrong—I mean, in addition to being killed in an eight-car pileup." Adriana fidgeted as if trying to find a comfortable position. "I requested cremation, especially after the Big Uneasy. I didn't want to come back no matter what. It's just a matter of personal preference."

"But your parents didn't follow your wishes," Robin said, pulling out a yellow legal pad and taking notes. "Sentimental reasons?"

"Complete, utter, malicious incompetence."

I began to grasp how ugly this was going to be, if Adriana wanted to sue her family for not following her final wishes.

Adriana looked from me to Robin, saw the expressions on our faces, and she said, "Oh, it's not my parents! They sent my body to Joe's Crematorium—but, as you can see, I wasn't exactly cremated."

"They'd probably take you as a walk-in," Sheyenne suggested. "Tell them what happened. I doubt they'd even charge you for the cremation."

Adriana raised herself up, horrified. "Oh, I couldn't do that now! This is . . . this is what I am."

Still trying to get all the facts, I asked, "So, you woke up before you were delivered into the furnace? That can be awkward." Reanimation rates vary widely. Some, such as Harvey Jekyll, came back to life almost immediately; in my case, it took several days.

Again, Adriana shook her head, and it wobbled from side to side like one of those bobblehead dolls that McGoo finds so amusing. "No, I woke up in a body truck at the crematorium.

It was stacked high with cadavers, but I was the only one moving and moaning. It was hard for me to get up and walk because I just had a quick patch-up job. The mortician didn't bother to use any finesse, considering the condition I was in."

I had my mind focused on the mystery, though. "You were in a truck full of bodies being delivered to the crematorium?"

Adriana shook her head. "I was confused and disoriented, as you might guess. I rolled over and fell off the back of the truck—when the driver pulled out of the parking lot and drove away from Joe's Crematorium."

"Wait a minute, why would anybody take a truckload of bodies *away* from the crematorium?" Robin asked.

"That is the question, isn't it?" Adriana said, folding her hands on the table and getting down to the real business. I could see that she would have made a good attorney, if she'd survived law school. "I'd like to engage your services to investigate Joe's Crematorium, to make sure this doesn't happen to other zombies. Find out what's really going on."

Robin tapped her pencil on the pad. "And get your parents a full refund."

Now Adriana seemed even more agitated. "The worst part is, my family didn't even know! They received an urn that supposedly contained my ashes. They thought everything was fine."

"That's fraud, not incompetence," Robin said, her righteous anger rising, as I knew it would. "We'll find out whose ashes they really have, and we'll hold Joe's Crematorium responsible."

Adriana looked as if she wanted to cry, but found an inner strength. "I want to find out how this could have gone so wrong."

Sheyenne flitted out and returned quickly with a card for Miss Lujean Eccles's taxidermy and body-repair boutique. "You might want to give this woman a call. She's done wonders for Dan, several times."

Adriana shook her head again. "I've already tried a cosmetician, a place called the Parlour (BNF). I spent hours and a lot of money on skin wraps, lotions, various types of makeup. They even redid my hair, and it looks horrible. In my spare time, I might want to sue them as well." She looked over at Robin. "I'll keep your card."

Considering the intertwined cases, I decided it was time to look into the Parlour (BNF) before more harm was done.

CHAPTER 18

Since Harriet Victor was the co-owner, I made my visit to the Parlour (BNF) under the pretext of passing along an update on her husband's case, but I really wanted to see firsthand how Rova Halsted had spent the life insurance money. And I intended to investigate whether she was as bad a stylist as she was rumored to be.

Although Robin had contacted the opposing attorney and set up a meeting with all of us for early the next morning, Rova Halsted didn't know who I was . . . not yet. I had plausible deniability. Since her ex and I were post-death friends, she had never seen me hanging out with him. After we all met to discuss the case, however, the rules would change. This was the best time for me to gather information, when her guard might be down.

At the door of the Parlour (BNF)*, the asterisk directed me to an explanation: *(Beauty, not Funeral). There, one mystery solved.

I stepped into the Parlour, jingling the cheery bell mounted above the door. Inside, I saw several empty hair-cutting stations, a pedicure chair with a large tub for oversized feet, a manicure table complete with a display of nail polish that boasted a selection of blacks ranging from Simple Flat Black to Pitch to Oilslick. Smells assaulted my nostrils: detanglers and conditioners, bleaches and colors, perm chemicals, reptilian scale wax, freshening crèmes, fixatives, mousses, pomades, and deodorants.

The lavishly bearded Harriet Victor was tending a female demon whose entire body—and I mean *entire* body—was covered with pubic hair (which smelled accordingly). Harriet was giving her a full-body perm on an aesthetician's table.

A pale-skinned undead woman, who had been stitched together from various pieces, had her hair done up in a pyramidal beehive. She sat under a hair dryer, preening in front of a handheld mirror. "I love the long white streaks. I'm going to be a bride!"

At the cash register, a female full-time werewolf was paying, and the human woman ringing up the sale handed her a receipt. "Here's a coupon for your next visit."

The werewolf flinched, as if the coupon were cursed. "No, thanks. I won't be needing that." When she turned around, I saw that her face fur was trimmed and chopped so badly that it looked to be the work of a drunken, nearsighted Edward Scissorhands. The werewolf touched her face, groaned deep in her throat, and hurried out of the Parlour (BNF).

The human woman—Rova Halsted, I assumed—closed the cash register. She could have been pretty if she hadn't practiced her questionable skills on herself. Her hair was a randomly colored mop, like a collection of sample swatches from a hair-color line. She looked up at me. "How can I help you?"

Before I had to make up a story, Harriet called out. Her lips curved upward in a broad smile that fluffed out her curly beard like catfish whiskers. "Mister Chambeaux! Are you looking for Archibald? He's at work."

I thought quickly. "He told me to be discreet, so I thought I'd ask you to pass along a message."

She clicked her tongue against her teeth. "Oh, Archibald and his silly secrets! He thinks everything is such a grand mystery. Does anybody really care? I love him all the same."

Even so, I chose my words carefully. As a general rule, I didn't want a mad scientist upset with me. "Regarding the matter of the . . . the *business* trouble he was having, I spoke to the owner, and I've been promised adequate replacement parts. I'll deliver them in person tomorrow."

Harriet nudged the pubic-hair demon to roll over onto her back, then continued massaging deodorant oils into the creature's shoulders and arms. The wafting stench of body odor was overpowering, even to my deadened nostrils. A forest of tangled wiry hair extended from her solar plexus all the way down to her knees. "Oooh, that feels good, don't stop," the demon said, and Harriet continued her massage.

Rova went to attend her undead bride customer, swinging aside the hair dryer so she could squeeze more bleaching chemical in a zigzag streak from the temples to the top of the beehive hairdo. "Permanent means *permanent*—our guarantee."

Harriet talked to me as she continued working the demon's short hairs. "You look a little pallid, Mister Chambeaux. We could offer you a tanning session for half price, a friends-and-family discount. You need to get out in the sun more."

"It's not lack of sun exposure—embalming fluid takes the color away," I said. "Do your tanning beds get much use?"

"Unfortunately, no. I . . . misjudged the market."

Sheyenne had uncovered all the business details for me already. Harriet had originally opened a tanning salon, since not all monsters hid in the shadows or avoided direct sunlight. Even so, it was a niche market and an undead tanning salon wasn't the best idea anyone had ever had—vampires couldn't use the service, werewolves didn't care, and no matter how much sun a zombie got, undead skin would retain its deathly pallor. After leaving the circus, Harriet sank her life savings into the business and nearly went bankrupt.

Then she met Rova Halsted, who was desperate for work as a beautician, unable to keep a job in the outside world. As a result of Steve's death, she had a large life insurance check, which she used to expand the tanning salon into a full-fledged parlor (beauty, not funeral).

Now Harriet spritzed freshening spray and feminine deodorant over the pubic-hair demon. She even tied a bright red ribbon in one of the wiry locks of hair that protruded from the woman's head. "I like making people beautiful, in their own particular way," she said to me in a wistful-sounding voice. "After all those years in the freak show, I had enough of people not accepting me for who I was, so I came to appreciate everyone for who they are."

After Rova replaced the hair dryer over the bride's head, she went back to look at the appointment book. "I have one more client for the day, Harriet. A full preening, but after that I have to pick Jordan up from day care by six o'clock."

"You have a son?" I asked. Disingenuous is my middle name.

She was surprised by my interest. "Yes, he's eight." She eyed me up and down as if I had tried to hit on her. "I am single, but not looking—certainly not for a zombie."

Harriet gave a scolding cluck of her tongue. "That was rude, Rova. Mister Chambeaux is a professional."

The woman gave me a brusque apology. "Sorry—you can't help that you're dead." She closed the appointment book. "I was just dreading my next appointment."

"Apology accepted. It wasn't my place to ask." I'd learned all I expected to, so I decided to take my leave. As I opened the door of the Parlour (BNF), however, I nearly ran into the next customer.

She bristled with razor-edged black-and-green pinion feathers over an unfortunately curvaceous body; she had a face that immediately set you on edge and a hard smile that would scare away the hungriest carrion bird. Esther the harpy waitress stopped me in my tracks.

"Dan Chambeaux!" she said in her piercing voice. "Stop right there—I want to have words with you."

Chapter 19

It's unnerving to be buttonholed by a harpy, especially an angry harpy. (Or is that redundant?)

Esther ruffled her plumage so she seemed to be more in the valkyrie category. She poked my chest with one of her talons and nudged me back into the Parlour (BNF). Now, I'm not cut out to be a larger-than-life hero, regardless of how my character might be portrayed in the Dan Shamble Penny Dreadfuls, but I saw no way to duck under her sharp feathers and escape.

Finished with the bride, Rova Halsted looked up with a decidedly forced smile. "Hello, Esther. Ready for your preening?"

"Of course I am! Why else would I come here?" Esther's sharp, raucous tone reminded me of brawling crows. "I don't have time for the usual chitchat—this famous detective and I have something to discuss. Do your work while we have a private conversation, but no listening in!"

Rova was unfazed. "Not to worry. I never listen when my customers jabber."

I asked, "What's this all about, Esther?" As far as I could remember, I had left her a tip the last time I ate at the Ghoul's Diner. She'd been known to walk the streets of the Quarter, hunting down recalcitrant customers and demanding her due.

"I'm hiring you for a case. Actually, I need that lawyer partner of yours to file a lawsuit, but she never comes into the diner, so how am I supposed to talk with her?"

I was relieved that this was a business matter instead of some personal grudge against me. "Well, you could come to our offices, like most clients do."

"What? Is she too good for us? Something wrong with the food?"

"Robin usually brings a bag lunch."

The bride examined herself in the mirror, studied her newly painted nails, touched the white-streaked hairdo. Esther rounded on her. "Stop hogging the chair. It's my appointment now. Don't you have someplace to be?"

"Yes, I do," the bride said with a sniff, then added in a syrupy voice, "*I'm* going to meet my husband-to-be for a romantic lunch together while we talk about our wedding." As she flounced out of the Parlour (BNF), she added over her shoulder, "*You* obviously need to get laid—very badly."

"How dare you!" Esther shrieked, flashing talons and fluttering her machete-like feathers. "I've been very badly laid plenty of times!"

Indignant, Esther dropped into the vacated chair while Rova tied an apron around her neck and gathered up brushes and pots of chemicals. The harpy continued her stream of bitter complaints, though I was the only one listening, and I had no interest whatsoever.

"I have a boyfriend," Esther continued, sounding defensive. "A rich and powerful one, too—my own sugar daddy! He rides in a limousine and takes me to the fanciest places. Better than any man who would've settled for that bitch."

Esther was flaunting plenty of bling that she didn't wear around the Ghoul's Diner—gold bracelets, jeweled rings on her talons, even a designer scarf around the wattles of her neck. Rova began the long process of combing the harpy's plumage, filing and sharpening her long talons, oiling the fine scales on her forehead.

"And does your . . . boyfriend have anything to do with the matter you wish to discuss?" I was looking for an excuse to leave as soon as possible.

"Of course not! Why the hell would I want to sue him? He'd stop giving me nice things if I sued him."

"So what is the lawsuit about, then?" I asked.

Esther made a disgusted noise that sounded as if she'd gotten a piece of gravel stuck in her gizzard. "I see I'm going to have to treat you like a schoolchild and start at the beginning."

"I recommend that," I said.

She made that disgusted sound again. "Zombies are known for brains, but obviously not the ones inside their skulls."

Always cheerful, Harriet Victor finished with the pubic-hair demon, who admired the red ribbon as she left the Parlour, smelling fresh as a spring morning. Rova, not much of a conversationalist herself, continued to work on the pinfeathers and then the larger feathers on the harpy's arms.

Esther jerked from side to side, trying to concentrate on me. "Somebody left me a tip—a tip that I don't like." Considering her personality, she should have been happy with any tips at all, but I wasn't stupid enough to say that out loud. "It's cursed, and that wizard left it to me on purpose. He's never been happy with my service."

Again, I refrained from pointing out that no one was happy with Esther's service.

As Rova dodged out of the way, the harpy squirmed and pulled out a small black coin purse. "Instead of leaving cash, this moron gave me a medallion." She yanked and tugged until she withdrew a gold medallion on a chain. Two simple words had been stamped on its face: *For Luck.*

I still didn't see what was wrong. "It's a luck charm."

"I can *see* it's a luck charm—but I didn't realize until later that it's a *bad*-luck charm! I thought he was trying to make up for being such an asshole customer, but ever since he gave this to me, I've had a run of constant bad luck, and that wizard is to blame. I've dropped countless plates and cups. My orders are screwed up. Large parties come into the diner two minutes before closing time. Customers take the wrong copies of their credit-card receipts. It's awful!"

I listened with an expression of rapt interest because that was important to Esther, but I had seen her drop dishes and cups, screw up orders, and rail at the customers long before being given any cursed jewelry items.

"Worse, he keeps coming in, acting as if nothing ever happened! He wants to see how miserable I am. I'm never accepting a tip from him again!"

Still looking for a way to slip out the door, I asked, "How exactly can Chambeaux and Deyer help you?"

"Don't be an idiot. I want to sue his ass, then I want to sue the rest of his body. Make sure you add all that pain-and-suffering crap, too."

"I'll look into the matter and give it all the attention it deserves," I said. "If you're sure it's a bad-luck charm, why don't you just get rid of it? Throw the medallion away and stop worrying about it?"

"I tried that, you moron! I threw it into a Dumpster, into a trash can, dropped it down a sewer drain—it always reappears! It's magically connected to me. As I said, the damned thing is cursed. Weren't you listening?"

"I wasn't clear on the specifics," I said.

She swiveled her head and snapped at Rova. "And you need

to hurry up! The limo will be around to pick me up in half an hour, and I've got to look my best! Can't have the fat slob thinking I'm unattractive."

Though I remembered the misery that Rova Halsted was inflicting on my friend Steve, I felt sorry for her at the moment. Just a little bit. But I got over it. "We wouldn't want that," I said.

"Thank you!" the harpy said, exasperated. "At least *he* understands! And if a *man* can understand, then even an idiot stylist can!"

Rova gave her a cold smile. "Would you like your wings clipped?" She had already gotten out a large pair of hedge-trimming shears and seemed anxious to use them.

"Not today, no time. And you, Chambeaux—don't just stand there. Get on my case!" Esther thrust the medallion toward me. "Take this. You'll need it for your investigations."

I backed away as politely as I could, in case it truly was a bad-luck charm. "Not necessary. I have everything I need. Let me do some investigating."

"You better give my case the highest priority, or you can serve *yourself* the next time you're in the diner."

That might have been preferable, but instead of provoking Esther, I said, "I give every case the highest priority."

While she looked momentarily satisfied, I hurried out of the Parlour (BNF) into the gathering dark.

CHAPTER 20

Each client is important to us at Chambeaux & Deyer Investigations, but after that less-than-pleasant experience, diving into an abrasive harpy's problems was not the first thing I wanted to do. A gang war among werewolves seemed more important than Esther's well-deserved string of bad luck.

Twice now, I had seen the arcane tattoos come alive on Scratch and Sniff, and Larry the werewolf had mentioned that Voodoo Tattoo was partly responsible for the blood feud between Monthlies and Hairballs. I decided to stop by and see what I could find out.

Voodoo Tattoo was a little boutique business tucked away in one of the Quarter's innumerable dark alleys. More than just a place for body art, it also doubled as a collectible doll shop. The façade was run-down chic, and a pulsating neon sign flickered the words *Voodoo Tattoo* on and off. Signs in the windows listed the specialties: *Tattoos: Temporary or Permanent (depending on species)*, *Special Discount on Do-Overs*, *We Offer Piercings of All Types*, and in smaller letters, *Silver Available upon Request,* with an even smaller disclaimer beneath that *Customer Assumes All Risk, No Refunds for Fatalities.*

The place was dim, lit by deep red floodlights. I could smell a thick, sour stench of seaweed-and-ganja incense mixed with cloves. Catalogs of tattoo designs sat open on a countertop, next to a heavy reprint volume of the Necronomicon. Shelves along the walls held dolls that represented specific people, although crudely fashioned (denoting either artistic license or a lack of representational skills). Tags dangling from the dolls' toes listed very high prices. According to an index card thumbtacked to a shelf, the proprietor took special commissions: *Get One For Your Enemies—Better Yet, Get Two!*

The Voodoo Tattooist, Antoine Stickler, was a tall, coffee-skinned Jamaican vampire with a mass of dreadlocks that Medusa might have envied. A muscle shirt showed off his biceps, which sported yin and yang symbols and peace signs. He was bent over a client sprawled on the single padded bed, and when I entered the shop, Antoine turned his dark eyes to me and flashed a smile that showed off his fangs. "Be with you in a minute." He sized me up. "Can put some bright color on that gray skin of yours."

His voice had a clear spice of Jamaican accent but with careful attention to detail so that he pronounced the words without an excessive Caribbean blur. As a vampire, he might have been working on erasing his accent for half a century or more. He bent back to his customer, humming—I swear, I'm not kidding—"Don't Worry, Be Happy."

The client was a small bookwormy vampire who had his shirt off and lay facedown on the tattooing bed. The Jamaican was finishing up a bold tattoo, covering the right shoulder blade with spiky capital letters: *BITE ME!* Definitely not what I'd expect to see on this little bookworm, but who could tell a person's double life? Even so-called "respectable" people sometimes sneaked off to rough bars to follow their baser desires—the definition of which was certainly broad in the Quarter. As Antoine continued to poke and swirl with his pulsating tattoo gun, the vampire squirmed and whined. "Ouch, ouch, ouch!"

"It'll be okay. Got some skin cream to take care of that—special ingredients." When he had finished the letters in *BITE ME*, Antoine rubbed a dark red gooey gel over the tattoo area, which hardened quickly like a large scab. "Okay, now go home, crawl into your coffin, and sleep it off. When you're ready to go party tonight, your tat'll be perfect."

The vampire sat up. "And how long will this one last?" With great care, he pulled on a formal white business shirt, buttoned it, and artfully tied his necktie. After he shrugged into a conservative gray suit, he looked like a banker, lawyer, undertaker. I suspected his coworkers would be shocked if they discovered the tattoo.

"It'll last a week, that's all," Antoine said. "Then you come back and get a new one."

"I might change it next time. Let me think about it." The vampire businessman glanced at me, looked away as if embarrassed, and scuttled out of the tattoo parlor.

"Aren't tattoos supposed to be permanent?" I asked. "Yours fade in a week?"

"It's vampires—they regenerate too much." Antoine passed a hand over his arm in a clean-slate motion. "Skin heals, ink goes away, and I have a clean dead slab all over again. Good for repeat customers." He touched his own biceps, rubbed his fingers around the yin-yang and the peace symbol. "I do myself every five days. I wish I'd gotten inked up right when I was still alive."

Antoine Stickler was a mellow guy, relaxed and patient. He seemed ready to watch the world go by, equally satisfied whether the shop was busy or empty. After introducing myself, I asked him about the self-healing tattoos I'd seen on the two biker werewolves.

"Ah, Scratch and Sniff." Antoine chuckled. "Rowdy boys, practical jokesters, but there's nothing funny about those tats. My best work, I think." He went to the illustration catalogs on the countertop, but instead picked up the Necronomicon. It was one of the deluxe illustrated and annotated editions released by Howard Phillips Publishing.

"Me, I like to expand my palette. I've done too damn many dragons and broken hearts, skulls with daggers, bulldogs, Celtic knots . . ." He made a face. "But when I saw the illustrations in the Necronomicon, I decided to diversify my menu. Scratch and Sniff wanted the new tats right away."

"So werewolf tattoos don't fade like vampire tats do?" I asked.

"No. Werewolves have tough skin, keeps the ink. Once they pay for a tat, no way does their hide let it go. Those boys are covered with healing spells, but they also have gang tattoos—proud Monthlies! Course, as soon as Monthlies started getting loyalty ink, then the Hairballs had to have theirs. I was so busy for a month, werewolves were coming one after another after another. Had to set special hours—Monthlies in the morning, Hairballs in the afternoon. Didn't want any trouble.

"I spent a lot of time listening to them chatter—I'm a *good* listener, and there's a lot of time for conversation when I do big, complicated designs. Heard grumbling and growling on both sides. What an earful! Messed up my attitude, day after day, but it's over now. Everybody on each side has loyalty ink, and I can get back to regular customers."

"So what was the problem?" I asked. "I heard that your tattoos started the feud somehow?"

Antoine tossed his long dreadlocks, like bullwhips. "Scratch and Sniff, they're jokesters, like I said. Really funny, too—

unless you don't have a sense of humor. So, when Rusty came in to get his gang ink, they paid me for a special. I swear I misunderstood what they said . . . but I think they wanted me to." He snorted. "Making fun of my accent!"

"And how did that exacerbate the bad-blood situation between the Monthlies and the Hairballs?" I had always wanted to use the word *exacerbate* in a sentence.

The big Jamaican vampire seemed embarrassed. "I should have known they weren't poking fun—they were just being mean. After all, Rusty is the Hairball leader, big badass, rough and tough, and he came in here for an extra-special tat to make him *important*. But Scratch and Sniff, they convinced me I didn't understand him right, that Rusty really wanted a tat to make him *impotent*. So that's what I gave him. And werewolf tats—well, they're as permanent as permanent can be."

Antoine scratched his dreads. "Rusty wanted to rip my head off and stuff my mouth full of garlic right then and there, but he knew that would start a full-on war between werewolves and vampires. And it wasn't my fault! He knew Scratch and Sniff were behind it, so he chose that fight instead. Rusty tries to keep the impotence tat a big secret, but secrets of that sort . . . well, they're too funny to keep secret for long."

No wonder Rusty hadn't been willing to give me details. "So that's why the Monthlies and the Hairballs don't like each other."

Antoine whistled. "No, sir—not at all. Monthlies and Hairballs already couldn't stand each other! I think it's because they're so much the same." He hung his head. "Then I went and made it worse. And that Rusty, he holds a grudge!"

"You know he was attacked?" I asked. "Someone slashed his scalp clean off."

"Yeah, I heard about it. Nasty business. And three or four other Hairballs got attacked, too, every one scalped. Must be some gang thing. Doesn't make any sense. The world sure has changed since the Big Uneasy, and it needs to keep changing. Why can't we all just get along, vampires and werewolves, Monthlies and Hairballs, spiders and flies? No need for all this violence and hate."

"Some of it's just inhuman nature," I said, as if that explained things.

"But there's no *need* for it! We clawed our way to the top of the food chain, and we should act like it. There's alternatives, specially processed tofu human-flesh substitutes, voluntarily donated blood. I get my supply from the Talbot and Knowles Blood Bars, humanely obtained, one hundred percent organic, and free-range. Keeps me healthy." He gave me a playful comradely punch in the shoulder. "And look at you—obviously a zombie who takes care of himself. You don't put garbage in your body, do you? Who provides your embalming fluid? Is it sustainable, locally manufactured?"

"I hate to say it, but I do occasionally eat at the Ghoul's Diner."

Antoine winced and shook his head, making his dreads dance. "Aww, don't do that to yourself! You're already dead, why make it worse? You know how much cholesterol and preservatives are in that food?"

"Wouldn't preservatives just help me?" I wondered aloud.

Antoine tsked and flipped open one of the catalog binders. "Why don't you take your shirt off and let's look at some tats for you."

"No thanks. I was just here asking questions." I wasn't sure how Sheyenne would feel about me getting a tattoo. Maybe we could find some creative way to spruce up the repaired bullet holes in my torso. Make them into daisies?

Before I left, Antoine called to me. "How about a doll instead? I could make you a doll. Good likeness, too."

"I don't know what I'd do with it."

"You don't do *with* these dolls." Antoine grinned. "You do *to* these dolls. Come on, it'll be fun. Must be someone in your life who needs one of my special dolls?"

"Plenty of people, but I'd need to make a list," I said. "Thanks for your help."

CHAPTER 21

By the time I got back to the office late that night, Sheyenne had compiled research on various bad-luck charms, based on my description and a crude sketch I had made of the talisman Esther had received.

"I put more stock in your descriptive abilities than your artistic ones, Beaux," she said.

"There goes my hope for a second career as a face painter," I said.

"I found a selection of common charms. Which one looks most like what Esther had?" She handed me a stack of printouts from home-shopping channel websites and various special pendant promotions. As I sorted through the images, she said, "Each has a standard fine-print disclaimer that regulatory agencies have not independently verified the bad-luck charm claims, that such talismans are not intended to diagnose or cause any particular disease, that they have not been proven effective under all circumstances, blah, blah, blah."

Robin came out of her office. "The disclaimers are necessary. They give lawyers something to do."

I held up a sheet that matched the pendant exactly. "This one."

"Ooh, a high-end special edition," Sheyenne said. "Somebody really wanted to make sure it worked."

"Esther must have given the wizard enough incentive." Robin took the paper and read it slowly, nodding. "Though there's little doubt a vindictive wizard did indeed give our client a bad-luck charm, I'm concerned about the viability of the case. Even if we can prove the hazardous nature of the talisman, the wizard might respond to any lawsuit by saying he gave the tip 'with cause.' "

"Better not put Esther on the stand if it ever goes to trial," I said, and Robin shuddered at the suggestion. Sheyenne took the papers and the now-identified bad-luck charm and went back to her desk to continue her research, blowing me an air-kiss as she departed.

Meanwhile, after accepting Steve Halsted's case, Robin had set up an initial meeting with Don Tuthery, the attorney representing his ex-wife. It would take place first thing in the morning; Steve had asked for an early appointment because he had to do his daytime deliveries throughout the Quarter—and I had promised to make an appearance at the Worldwide Horror Convention for a few hours.

Digging into case law, Robin had found several vaguely relevant precedents, and she was sure Tuthery had done the same. But she seemed worried, which I found unsettling. She lowered her voice, as if she didn't want to hear her own doubts. "He's a pit bull, Dan—exactly the man you want representing you in a divorce or custody dispute. Unfortunately he's not on our side."

"We have an even bigger advantage," I said with a reassuring nod. "We've got Robin Deyer working for us."

She gave me that warm smile and went back to her research for the 8 A.M. meeting.

* * *

Steve arrived in his dark green overalls and trucker's cap, looking uneasy. To show that he understood the importance of this meeting, he had draped a polka-dotted necktie over his chest. I complimented him on it.

"I get nervous every time I see Rova," he said. "So much history there, so much bad blood. And her lawyer makes it worse with all his pushing and prodding."

"We'll push and prod right back, Mister Halsted," Robin said. "I promise. Dan, would you sit in with us for moral support?"

"Lucky for you, today is my day reserved for moral support." I wasn't due at the convention for another couple of hours.

Don Tuthery arrived at 8 A.M. to the minute, a tall serious human in a charcoal business suit and gold wire-rimmed glasses; his steel-gray hair was impeccably trimmed and combed, thereby proving beyond a reasonable doubt that Rova didn't cut his hair at the Parlour (BNF). His briefcase looked as if it might contain nuclear launch codes. I couldn't describe his teeth because he never showed them, never smiled, and barely moved his lips when he spoke.

Next to him, Rova Halsted wore a conservative black skirt and blazer, as if ready to attend her ex-husband's funeral all over again, rather than a "friendly discussion." Her mop of mismatched hair-color swatches added a bit of carnival to the funereal atmosphere. When she recognized me from my Parlour visit the previous day, her expression soured into a suspicious scowl.

Steve looked away and mumbled, "Hello, Rova."

When she started to respond, Don Tuthery raised a finger, stopping her like a schoolteacher rapping knuckles with a ruler. "Not one word, Ms. Halsted." He faced Robin, Steve, and me. "I will speak for my client in this interaction."

"If you're speaking for her, then could you at least say hi

back?" I said. His rudeness set me on edge from the very beginning.

Tuthery frowned at me. "And who is this . . . gentleman? I object to having a second zombie attend these proceedings."

"This isn't a deposition, and you're not in court before a judge, Mister Tuthery. But feel free to object all you like, if it makes you happy," Robin said. "Mister Chambeaux is my business partner, and Mister Halsted requested his presence. No need to be concerned—humans still outnumber the zombies here, three to two."

"I'm not concerned," Tuthery said. "I'm never concerned. Normally, however, I would prefer a meeting such as this to take place on neutral ground, preferably hallowed ground, but that's difficult to find in the Quarter."

Tuthery set his briefcase on the conference room table, opened it to show that it contained not nuclear launch codes, but stacks of manila folders, legal briefs, and lovely photos of doting mother Rova and cute-as-a-button Jordan, whom I recognized from the snapshots in Steve's wallet.

Tuthery took control of the meeting, even though it was on our turf. "We can resolve this today." He pulled out papers, glanced at Robin, completely ignored Steve and me.

"I'm glad your client is willing to reconsider her allegations, Mister Tuthery," Robin said.

Steve and Rova kept looking at each other and then away, both of them uncomfortable and angry, but also . . . hopeful?

"I respect you as a professional colleague, Ms. Deyer, but have you looked at the complaint? Mister Halsted simply has no case. I expect you to withdraw your claims and objections so we waste no further time on the matter."

My already-sluggish heart sank. Oh. So that was how it was going to be.

Robin's eyes flared at his dismissive and antagonistic tone. "I was about to say the same to you. The law couldn't be more clear: A person's obligations to provide spousal and child support terminate upon death. Mister Halsted is clearly dead."

"On the contrary," Tuthery said. "The Halsteds' divorce settlement decrees that so long as Mister Halsted is gainfully employed and earning an income, he is required to provide for the care of his son."

"I want to do what's right for Jordan," Steve blurted, "but I already did that! The insurance settlement—"

Robin held up her hand to keep Steve quiet. "My client raises an important point. Mister Halsted did arrange for the care of his son from the life insurance payout, an amount totaling fifty thousand dollars, which was to remain in trust for Jordan. We can file a motion demanding Ms. Halsted's financial records and vigorously investigate any mismanagement of that trust fund. Ms. Halsted did set up the required trust fund, correct? We expect to find every penny there and available for the child's care."

Rova blanched at this. She flicked a wide-eyed glance from Steve to Mr. Tuthery and back.

"Ms. Halsted, not the child, was the designated beneficiary on the policy, and she was entitled to use the money as she saw fit," Tuthery stated.

"Not according to my client."

Steve rose partly to his feet, with difficulty. "That money was for Jordan, Rova! You know it."

Though Tuthery looked annoyed, he pressed on. "Ms. Halsted invested that money, and Jordan will benefit significantly once he comes of age."

Rova burst out, "Once the Parlour makes a million dollars, I'll be able to send Jordan to Harvard, or Stanford, or both in the same year!"

"What happens if the Parlour flops?" I asked. "You could lose everything."

Rova sniffed at me. "Not a chance. It's a beauty salon, and

the Quarter needs a lot of beauty. This is a surefire bet, as guaranteed as opening a restaurant!"

Tuthery shushed his client.

"Which brings us to visitation rights," Robin said. "My client would like to see his son regularly."

"Out of the question," Tuthery said. "We shall not allow you to inflict psychological damage on an eight-year-old boy."

"You'll give him nightmares!" Rova wailed.

"But he was happy to see me the two times I showed up," Steve said.

"And that's another matter we will bring to court," Tuthery said. "Undead stalking, particularly of a minor, is a very serious matter."

"What? He's my son!"

Robin was shocked. "You have no legal grounds for that."

Glaring at Steve, Rova burst out, "You were never around to see him when you were alive! *Now* you want to make up for it?"

Steve spoke with surprising calm. "Yes, Rova—yes, I do." She just stared at him.

"I'm afraid visitation rights are entirely off the table," Tuthery said.

"*I'm* afraid that's the crux of the matter. Bottom line, Mister Tuthery: If your client wants continued child support, my client gets visitation. You will have my motion for discovery of your client's financial records by tomorrow." Robin began packing up her documents. Rova was white as . . . well, as a ghost.

"We're finished here," Tuthery replied, also packing up. He made sure we saw the beautiful, loving photos of mother and son before he put them away. "I warn you, if this goes to court, it'll be an ugly case. Think of the boy's welfare. Children shouldn't play with dead things."

Steve said, bewildered, "I just want to do what's right for my son."

Rova didn't say another word as she left with her attorney.

When we were alone in the conference room, Steve looked miserable. He tore off his polka-dot tie. "If you tell me not to worry, then I won't worry." He shook his head and adjusted his cap. "But I'm worried."

"We haven't even started to fight for you, Mister Halsted," Robin said. "Don't worry until I tell you to."

CHAPTER 22

The idea to host the Worldwide Horror Convention in the Unnatural Quarter was a stroke of genius. It must have been a particularly rambunctious meeting of the con committee when they decided to include the Bates Hotel in their convention bid. Both the convention planners and the hotel staff saw the unique relevance and attraction, even suggested making the Quarter the permanent home of the Worldwide Horror Convention, which traditionally moved from city to city.

The Chamber of Commerce hung welcoming banners on lampposts up and down the streets; the City Council proclaimed a special Monster-Loving Humans Day, and several thousand fans, writers, industry professionals, and celebrities descended upon the Bates Hotel.

According to the ribbon on my guest badge, I was in the celebrity category.

I arrived in my traditional fedora and sport jacket with crudely repaired bullet holes. I had added more mortician's putty to the bullet hole in my forehead, but I could never do as good a job as Bruno and Heinrich. I hoped the Wannovich sisters didn't expect me to wear some kind of costume.

When I entered the hotel lobby, I was surrounded by a milling mixture of normal-looking humans, humans dressed in a variety of monster costumes, real monsters wearing normal street clothes, and reporters and TV crews covering the event. It took me a few minutes just to drink it all in.

Con attendees stood at tables, filling out registration forms and getting in line to pay for their badges. The queue for the Pre-Registered badges was long and disorganized; and the crowd was growing restless, particularly when it became apparent that the line for those *not* pre-registered was moving faster.

A wizard sat behind the Pre-Reg table. Apparently, he had used a crystal ball to arrange the badges and registration packets in the order he *predicted* the guests would arrive, instead of alphabetical order. Unfortunately, his spell was flawed.

Over at the Professionals registration table, a slimy tentacle-faced creature was holding his badge and arguing with the poor human volunteer in a burbling otherworldly voice. "My name is misspelled! Yov Shuggoleth has two *G*s!" He slapped the badge down, waiting for it to be reprinted. He moaned, "I'll bet it's misspelled in the program book, too."

Fortunately, Mavis and Alma had already given me my badge, so I went to the welcome table and asked for my attendee packet. The young woman handed me a plastic bag with the convention logo printed on the front. Inside, I found a flyer, one side advertising specials for the Goblin Tavern, the other side soliciting business for the Full Moon Brothel. Both had coupons. I also found a giveaway copy of *Death Warmed Over*. Howard Phillips Publishing was really getting behind this book.

I saw Miranda Jekyll holding court, walking in a regal procession through the lobby crowds, flanked by reporters and TV camera crews. Hirsute accompanied her like a burly body-guard. "I tell you, sweethearts, it's so wonderful to be wel-comed back to the Quarter. Since my husband's very timely demise, I have tried to rehabilitate the image of Jekyll Lifestyle Products and Necroceuticals."

At the back of the lobby, a man in an extravagant gargoyle costume, complete with a pneumatically twitching barbed tail and folding green fabric wings, tried to enter an elevator with a *real* scaly demon who had even larger wings. The two of them jostled back and forth, struggling to fit inside, but neither could fold their wings tightly enough. A large ogre stood waiting for the elevator, his fat lips turned downward; finally he shuffled off to take the stairs.

Hearing screams, I went instantly on the alert when a man dressed like Van Helsing with a wooden stake and mallet ran at full speed after a slender vampire woman in a flowing white gown. But they were both laughing, and I realized they were just costumed fans in a live-action role-playing game.

A particularly frayed-looking mummy reclined on a palan-quin, carried by two fan volunteers from the convention. They stood at the Handicapped Services desk, requesting a special ac-cess placard. On the mezzanine level up from the lobby, signs advertised a blood drive at the convention: *Sponsored by Talbot & Knowles Blood Bars. Leave a Pint of Yourself Behind in the Quarter! What Flows Here, Stays Here!* Volunteers lay back on gurneys with red-filled tubes leading out of their arms while white-uniformed medical attendants took care of them. Conve-niently close to the blood-drive area was a Talbot & Knowles Blood Bar refreshment stand.

Yes, this was going to be an interesting day.

I didn't know where to go or what to do first. A sign pointed me to the dealers' room, where Howard Phillips Pub-lishing had set up their table. Maybe I could do my autograph-ing, politely say hello to a few fans, then having fulfilled my duty for the day, I could get back to work on real cases. Robin and I already had plans to investigate Joe's Crematorium that afternoon.

Somebody called out, "Look! There's that Dan Shamble guy!"

I saw a fan raise a large camera; two other fans stopped and scrambled for their phones. Then I realized that not three feet away stood another man in a fedora, with obvious pallid makeup and dark eye shadow applied to his face. The fedora was slouched low, and a fake putty bullet hole stood out in the center of his forehead. He even had black stitches covering bullet holes in his sport jacket. He didn't look a thing like me, but he grinned in my direction. "Whoa, yours looks really realistic."

"I work hard at it," I said.

The fans clamored for the two of us to pose together for a photo. I stood patiently; we were blocking traffic, but the photographers didn't seem to care. "I, uh, I need to get to a panel," I said, and flipped open the program book.

Several tracks of programming were listed, some for professional writers, some for fans. I saw "Funniest Vampire Misconceptions," "Alternatives to Brains—New Diet for the Undead," "Most Embarrassing Zombie Moments," and "Got Wood?— Stake Design and Use." I was particularly delighted to see "Real Life in Ancient Egypt—Peeling the Bandages Off." It was one of Ramen Ho-Tep's presentations, and I knew he'd find a fascinated audience here. Then I spotted "The Hairy Truth—What Every Horror Writer Needs to Know about Werewolves."

Hmm, maybe I could get some work done while I was here.

CHAPTER 23

The self-proclaimed "World Renowned Werewolf Expert" Professor Walter Zevon was giving an hour-long presentation. Normally, academics wouldn't bother to attend frenetic conventions such as this, but since many universities refused to give tenure to non-human lecturers, unnatural scholars had been striving for respect in their various fields. Professor Zevon's lecture was in Voorhees Ballroom B, a hall with about fifty seats, two-thirds of which were filled with fans, writers, and a smattering of monsters.

I slipped in late, opening the door and distracting the crowd. I mumbled an apology and closed the door as quietly as I could. I shuffled forward and took a seat in one of the back rows next to a Wiccan who was knitting a long, pink scarf.

Professor Zevon stood at the podium, a rather frail-looking elderly gentleman, a full-time werewolf with a lavish head of gray fur, a long snout, and most of his teeth. He adjusted round spectacles and looked down at his notes, intent. His shoulders were hunched. A pair of younger furry werewolves sat in the front row; two of his academic students, I guessed.

"We provide this lecture as a service to all readers and writers, in order to promote accuracy in horror fiction. We strive to increase understanding and tolerance of lycanthropes throughout the world." Zevon's tongue lolled out, and he licked his muzzle. "We also want to save you the embarrassment of making real howlers of mistakes."

A few people politely chuckled, but not many.

"First, some definitions," the professor continued. "There's been confusion about werewolves in general. As you look around you, some of us, such as I and my students here"—he gestured to the two Hairballs in the front row—"are obvious werewolves. We wear our fur proudly and permanently. We don't hide who we are. We don't blame our condition on some Gypsy curse. We are the true werewolves, not the ones who are human most of the time and only do an occasional transformation. Those once-a-month, full-moon-only, quote-unquote werewolves are like temp workers, mere hobbyists rather than true professionals."

There was muttering in the audience, and two large figures rose out of their seats. "You'd better take that back, Professor."

Scratch and Sniff. I was surprised they had purchased badges to sit in on a lecture at the convention. They'd probably come for the sole purpose of heckling Professor Zevon.

"Boys, boys, don't pick on the poor, senile fool." I was surprised to see that Miranda Jekyll occupied a seat in the center of the room, flanked by an entourage of reporters taking notes. She didn't deign to rise to her feet. "Professor, sweetheart, I'm afraid you're toiling under the delusions of academia. Your research is flawed."

At the podium, the elderly werewolf bristled. "How so?"

"If you would study the very *basics* of werewolf lore, you'll note that *transformation* is an indispensable part of the equation. Werewolves look like humans, except during the full moon, when they transform and unleash the bestial part of their nature."

Miranda flashed a broad grin, showing her bright white teeth. "Some might call it the *best* part." She stroked her red finger-nails along the bulging arm of Hirsute, who sat next to her. "Since a Hairball never changes, you're not *technically* a were-wolf. You're just a"—she twitched her hand as if searching for the word, but I knew Miranda had thought of her snappy comeback even before sitting down—"a large hairy dog that's been taught how to talk and dress up."

The Hairball students in the front row growled, baring their long canines and rising to their feet. One said, "Just because you can't keep your hackles up for more than a day or two at a time doesn't make you a werewolf."

Scratch and Sniff were ready to leap over the rows and charge the stage, but convention security (two golems wearing headsets connected to walkie-talkies) stepped forward. "Calm down. No trouble here. If you don't like the topic, go to an-other panel."

Professor Zevon regarded Miranda Jekyll as his main oppo-nent. "And where, might I ask, did you get your degree in ly-canthropy, madam?"

"I don't need a degree to know what's true, sweetheart."

The professor dismissed her and pushed a button on the po-dium to activate an overhead projector, showing the first slide in his presentation. "If there are no further interruptions, I would like to discuss personality types in relation to fur color."

"This is a bunch of bullshit!" Scratch said. "Let's go to the dealers' room and pick up some bootleg anime." The two big tattooed Monthlies made as much disturbance as possible as they worked their way out of their row, elbowing each other, laughing loudly before they slammed out of the room, banging the doors.

I wanted to ask about the friction between the two types of werewolves, since we'd just seen a demonstration of it, but the professor continued his lecture, going into excruciating detail about daily life as a werewolf, his preferred diet, methods of fur care, even the consistency of his bowel movements. It was far too much information, and not at all the kind I needed.

In the front row I noticed Linda Bullwer, the vampire ghost-writer, with her cat's-eye glasses in place, scribbling notes, probably for the next Dan Shamble book she would write. I hoped she would leave out the part about the bowel movements.

I decided to hold my questions until the end of the lecture, when the golems held up a sign announcing a five-minute warning, then cut off the discussion. The next panel, "A Beginner's Guide to Sewers and Catacombs," required a lot of setup. I didn't have a chance to ask anything.

Miranda Jekyll drew much of the audience with her as she flounced out of the ballroom. Too many fans crowded around the professor for me to get close, so I would have to see him later. I decided it was time to do my duty and take my stint at the Howard Phillips table, sign a couple of books, and then go back to work on my cases.

The convention dealers' room was like an Arabian bazaar of the bizarre. Used books, rare first editions, homemade jewelry, magical items, gaudy items, and gaudy magical items. A zombie was hunched over in a massage chair, moaning as the masseuse whispered soothing words into his ear and rubbed his shoulders. The Unnatural Acts adult novelty shop was doing a brisk business at their booth with chains, leather straps, whips, corsets, feathers, spikes, and truly mystifying harnesses that came with an instruction sheet sealed inside a plain brown envelope.

Another kiosk sold personal ectoplasmic defibrillators from Harvey Jekyll's spin-off company. One of the dangerous contraptions was on display, but not hooked up to any power source. An index card noted that it was "For Display Purposes Only."

The same vendor had a panoply of wooden stakes and mallets, squirt guns filled with holy water as well as refill jugs, hexes, charms, silver bullets, garlic, and wolfsbane. The garlic and wolfsbane were sealed in zipper-lock plastic bags, but several allergic vampires still sneezed, their eyes red and watery, and they complained about the stench.

I found Mavis Wannovich behind a table next to tall retractable posters for Howard Phillips Publishing and stacks of catalogs touting their new releases; *Death Warmed Over* was featured prominently on the catalog cover. A pyramid of the books stood in front of two empty chairs, next to a poster: *Meet the Real Dan Shamble! Signing Books Here Today!*

Alma rooted among the cardboard boxes behind the table, tipping them over to spill new product onto the floor, which Mavis then placed on the table. Before I could get there, Linda Bullwer scuttled through the dealers' room crowd, came around the table, and took one of the vacant seats behind the pile of books. Mavis called out, "Oh, look, everyone! Here's Penny Dreadful, the author of the Shamble and Die series!"

The vampire writer nudged her cat's-eye glasses higher on her nose, took out a pen, and sat smiling, waiting for the queue to form.

When I shuffled up, Mavis heaved a sigh of relief. "Oh, Mister Chambeaux, you're finally here. We've had so many questions. You're going to get a long line."

"If you say so."

I came around to meet the beaming gaze of Linda Bullwer, who reached out to shake my hand. "This is such an honor, Mister Chambeaux. I hope our book does well."

Mavis handed me a regular pen as well as a fountain pen and a cup of fresh blood from the Talbot & Knowles Blood Bar. "In case somebody wants you to sign with this."

To my surprise, people actually began to gather in front of the table, each one carrying a copy of *Death Warmed Over*.

Alma used her bulk, waddling up and down the line to nudge the fans into some semblance of order.

The first fan was a young man with two copies of the book. "Could you please sign this, Mister Shamble?"

"It's Chambeaux," I said.

"Great! I've got one for a friend, too. I already read it. I loved it! Especially the part where you died!"

"No spoilers!" someone yelled from the back of the line.

"He *starts out* dead," the fan sneered back.

I autographed the novels, then passed them over to Linda Bullwer, who began to write a lovely inscription. The fan glanced at her. "And who are you? Why are you writing in my book?"

"She wrote it," I said.

"Oh." The fan frowned. "Well, okay then, I suppose."

The fourth person in line asked me to sign in blood, and I used the fountain pen and the cup from Talbot & Knowles. Once he started that trend, *everybody* wanted their book signed in blood. They asked me questions about my cases. They asked how many more Dan Shamble books I was going to write, and I deferred to Linda Bullwer, again pointing out, "This is the real Penny Dreadful. She's the author."

"I'm already working on the next volume." She smiled graciously. "The material is so rich. Provided sales go as well as we hope, we could have a long-term series."

One woman came up to me, leaned over the table, and extended a meaty forearm. "Bite me! Please, bite me! I want a souvenir of the con."

I was flustered. "No, but thank you."

"It doesn't say anywhere on the sign that you won't bite fans."

"I'm making it a new policy," I said.

One fan had a stack of twelve copies, and he insisted on signature and date only. Another one pestered me for writing advice, and I referred her to Linda Bullwer, but the fan didn't seem to understand that I hadn't actually written the novel. Two more gave me "great ideas for cases" in future books in the series.

"And Miranda Jekyll is here, too!" said a very enthusiastic older man. "Do you think she'll sign my copy, the part where she's mentioned in the book?" Knowing Miranda, I was sure she would, and told the man so.

At first I assumed that the fans were only getting in line because they'd received the book for free in their registration packets, but many of them had purchased multiple copies, and quite a few had read the whole novel already.

I had planned to be there for only an hour, but the line continued. And continued. I was truly embarrassed by all the attention.

Fortunately, or unfortunately, the line degenerated into near panic when alarms went off. At first I assumed that some overly enthusiastic gamer had pulled a fire alarm—until I heard sirens outside.

Finally one of the con security golems came in, his clay face sculpted into an expression of dismay. "It's Professor Zevon! The ambulance is taking him to the hospital right now."

"What happened?" I asked.

"Somebody assaulted him out in the parking lot. He's been scalped!"

CHAPTER 24

The ambulance rushed the freshly, and unfortunately, topless Professor Zevon to the Brothers and Sisters of Mercy Hospital. In the parking lot of the Bates Hotel, crime-scene techs stretched out yellow tape, pushing back the crowd of both real and fan unnaturals who observed the goings-on with interest. Some figured that this must be part of the convention fun; several were already reviewing the "incredibly realistic staged event."

McGoo paced around a chalk outline that marked where the professor had sprawled. The crime-scene tech had been quite meticulous, adding details of fingers, even wrinkles of clothes; for the top of Professor Zevon's formerly furred head, the tech had used dotted lines to render where the scalp had been.

McGoo shook his head. "This is crazy, Shamble. Why would anybody do this? He was just an old professor—how could he have any enemies?"

I told him about the disturbance at the werewolf lecture and what Antoine Stickler had told me about the feud between the Monthlies and the Hairballs. Rusty did seem an obvious target, but I couldn't understand why gang members would target an old lecturer (or, for that matter, the homeless werewolves who had also been scalped). In explaining violent irrational behavior, though, *Just Because* is often a good enough reason.

McGoo wore a queasy expression. "I'm putting Scratch and Sniff on my list of suspects, just for the hell of it."

I couldn't argue with the conclusion, but these assaults were nastier than the work of mere thugs. Personally, I thought scalping a victim also showed more imagination than one would expect from Scratch and Sniff, but a good investigator follows the clues wherever they take him.

I left the Worldwide Horror Convention, having done my duty, although I doubted my afternoon with Robin at Joe's Crematorium would be any more enjoyable.

Sheyenne briefed me on what she had learned about the proprietor, Joe Muggins.

"You're so good at uncovering background information, Spooky, I think you deserve a PI license of your own," I said.

"I do deserve one, but you can be the front man of the agency. Besides, you're the one with the fedora." She pulled up the information she had gathered. "Joe Muggins is a vampire, and his criminal rap sheet, even his juvenile record, is still available from his prior life."

"Anything interesting?"

"He's been arrested for arson several times. He liked to play with matches, build blazes, even set his sister's bedspread on fire."

"Sounds like he settled on a career that matches his skill set and interests," I said. "Not everybody's cut out to be a crematorium manager."

Armed with the pink copy of Adriana Cruz's cremation receipt, Robin and I headed off. Something smelled wrong about Joe's Crematorium.

After the Big Uneasy, cremation had become a big business.

While some people hoped to come back as zombies, vampires, or other types of undead, many had a horror of joining the walking dead, so they rewrote their living wills to insist on cremation. Joe's Crematorium had capitalized on the craze, offering specials, running ads at bus stops and on public benches.

Robin and I pulled up in her Pro Bono Mobile in front of a large cinder-block building. Tall stacks curled rich black smoke into the air. A bright fabric banner was stretched across the drab walls: *We Do Viking Funerals!* A big signboard on the door advertised *This Month Only: Two-for-One Special.* Trucks had pulled up to the rear, and I saw giant piles of cordwood stacked there, as if someone were preparing for winter.

We got out, and I looked around curiously, sniffing the smoke in the air. To my surprise, I heard loud motorcycles starting up at the back of the building, and two choppers roared off with wrapped packages precariously balanced on their large saddlebags. Scratch and Sniff gunned the engines and accelerated out of the parking lot.

Robin looked after the two. "What were they doing here?"

"I'll ask next time I see them," I said. "I need to have a chat with those boys anyway."

We entered through the crematorium's homey-looking front door, which was surrounded by flower boxes and nicely trimmed hedges. The receptionist was on the phone and waved us over to a small couch. I picked up a brochure from a tabletop stand. *Consider Cremation . . . For Your Family's Peace of Mind. And Your Own.* Easy-listening music played over the intercom.

The receptionist put her hand over the mouthpiece and yelled through an open door to the back. "Hey Joe! Walk-in customers." She looked human, but her voice had a familiar *edge* that told me she was a Monthly werewolf.

A short, business-suited vampire came out—and I immediately recognized him as "Bite Me" from the Voodoo Tattoo parlor. He recognized me too, looked away in embarrassment, and reassembled his greeting-the-bereaved demeanor. "I'm so sorry to hear about your death, sir. We can take care of your every need."

"My needs have already been met," I said. "I'm here on be-half of one of our clients."

Robin opened her briefcase. "A former customer of your crematorium—a very dissatisfied customer."

Joe Muggins fidgeted. "My, my! We almost never get com-plaints from our customers. There should be very little left of them to complain."

"That's exactly the problem, Mister Muggins. There's a *lot* left of this client. Adriana Cruz is still walking around, and not very happy about it." Robin handed over the pink slip and the receipt.

"My, my!" he said again. "If you send her back, we'd be happy to cremate her at no extra charge."

"That isn't what my client wishes," Robin said in a stern voice. "And we want to make certain this does not happen again in the future."

Taking the pink slip, Joe went to the computer, moving the receptionist aside as he tapped away and called up Adriana's cremation certificate. "Ah, here it is. Yes, she was cremated five weeks ago, a no-frills ceremony, no add-ons. Her ashes were delivered to her family. They chose a streamlined budget-model urn, but still very nice."

"The family received somebody's ashes," I said, "but they weren't Ms. Cruz's."

Joe shook his head, flustered. "I don't see how this could be. We always tell prospective customers to take care of their bod-ies, and if they don't, *we'll* take care of them."

Robin's expression grew harder. "I assure you, Mister Mug-gins, our client is walking around as a zombie. Something went terribly wrong with your procedures. *Whose* ashes were deliv-ered to the Cruz family? How did our client's cadaver not get put into the furnace, even though your records show she was? What sort of quality-control measures do you have in place?"

He swallowed hard. "Check with the Better Business Bureau and the Chamber of Commerce. I've got an A plus rating with the BBB, and I've been a member of the Chamber since I opened my business. I assure you, there have been no other complaints. I run a clean business, and from now on I'll make sure I light the fires myself."

"I'm sure you'd enjoy lighting the fires, Mister Muggins," I said in a dangerous voice. "We've looked at your prior record. And maybe we should look into your . . . extracurricular activities, too?" I knew that a mousy guy like that wouldn't get a *Bite Me* tattoo just to show his pet cats.

Now he seemed mortified. "There's no need to get personal, Mister Chambeaux." Then, in a very small voice, he added, "Please?"

I shrugged. "No need . . . at the moment." I had no intention of exposing his private life—any more than I worried about Archibald Victor's eccentric hobby. Unless it had some bearing on the case.

Robin continued, "We obviously have clear and substantial grounds for a lawsuit. If there've been other instances, we could file a class-action suit. And we couldn't help but notice the wood you have stacked in the back. I assume your furnaces use gas jets to ramp up and maintain the required two thousand degrees? What exactly is the cordwood for?"

Now the vampire was quite panicked. "The . . . wood? It's a premium service we offer—in addition to the Viking funerals. Some clients prefer the choice of hickory or mesquite smoked. The neighbors say it smells nice." He fidgeted, straightened his tie, handed back Adriana Cruz's pink slip. "There's no need for any unpleasantness. How can I make restitution? I've offered to cremate your client for free. We could even throw a big going-away party, champagne for everyone . . . maybe toss in a free cruise for her parents afterward? I'll certainly investigate the matter internally to ensure that the mistake is never made again."

"To begin with, you could refund the entire cost of the cremation," Robin suggested. "Plus an additional consideration for pain and suffering."

The little vampire swallowed hard, then nodded. He knew he was defeated. "Of course . . . in fact, I insist—so long as your client signs a release and an appropriate nondisclosure agreement. Bad publicity could harm our business. There are other crematoriums in town, you know." He handed us a brochure as well as discount coupons and told me to give him a call if I ever reconsidered my own cremation.

I had a growing suspicion that more was going on here than a simple administrative glitch and one accidentally uncremated body. According to her story, Adriana had woken up in a truck filled with corpses, and the truck had been driving *away* from the crematorium.

No, I wasn't done investigating yet.

CHAPTER 25

After leaving Joe's Crematorium, Robin drove back to the office, but I decided to walk. It had already been a long day and I wanted to stretch my legs, reduce the stiffness; this would take the place of half an hour on the treadmill at the All-Day/All-Nite Fitness Center, although it would have been better if Sheyenne had been with me, two postmortem lovers on an afternoon stroll through the dark side of town.

Besides, I needed to stop by the Spare Parts Emporium to pick up the replacement brain and spleen Tony Cralo had promised, maybe even a bonus set of lungs, and then I could wrap up Archibald Victor's case. Customer satisfaction all around.

When I arrived, I saw that another weather front of cold gray drizzle had socked in the body-parts warehouse, and brown water refilled the pothole puddles in the gravel parking lot. Like a giant's erector set, the abandoned railroad bridge loomed out of the mist, beneath which I could see huddled figures, trash fires, and the large cardboard boxes of the residential complex for homeless unnaturals.

When I entered the Spare Parts Emporium, I had to dodge a

man with a hand truck piled so high with boxes that he couldn't even see over the top. Customers milled about. Passing mummies, zombies, even a gargoyle with a handwritten shopping list, I made my way toward the floor manager's office.

This time, naturally, since I didn't *need* any assistance, two customer service reps rushed to me and asked, "May I help you, sir?" One looked human, but I guessed he was a Monthly werewolf; the other was a stocky female zombie.

"No, thanks. I know right where I'm going," I said, but then paused. "Say, you don't happen to sell werewolf scalps, do you?"

The two looked at each other. "Why would anyone want werewolf scalps?"

I stopped myself from replying with "Why would anybody want *anything* in here?" deciding that would be rude. Instead, I said, "Just curious. It's a specialty item."

The female zombie suggested, "If you fill out a form at customer service, we might be able to special-order it for you. How many do you need?"

"No, thanks. I was only asking for a friend."

The two looked at each other again, raised their eyebrows, and nodded knowingly. The werewolf wiggled his bushy eyebrows and said, "Yes . . . 'for a friend.' "

Then I had another thought. "Last time I was here, there was a ghoul who helped me . . . an attractive young lad, black teeth, sunken cheeks, deathly pallor?" I knew he'd been fired, but disgruntled former employees give the very best background dirt.

"Oh, you mean Francis." Distaste was plain on the female zombie's face. "He actually *helped* you?"

"He did what he could."

"He doesn't work here any longer."

"Just thought I'd ask." I headed to the back of the warehouse.

When I reached the floor manager's office, Xandy Huff was on the telephone. Behind him, on the metal rack of envelopes and time cards, the slip that had belonged to Francis the ghoul was gone. I heard Huff acknowledge "receipt of the order," then he hung up and looked at me.

Before he could say anything, I quipped, "I see my friend Francis picked up his severance check."

Huff's face fell into an annoyed grimace. "That ghoul? We won't be seeing him again." I watched the slow-moving gears in his mind clank together until he remembered me. "Wait a minute, you're that zombie detective guy. Francis didn't have anything to do with you." He grew suddenly wary. "Or did he file some kind of complaint?"

"Did he have something to complain about?"

"Absolutely not." Frazzled, Huff wiped beads of perspiration from his forehead. "I have a full-time job as it is. And now the police want to triple my work. Years' worth of records and receipts! I don't see why they're on a witch hunt—if they're hunting for witches, they can just look them up in the business directory."

I didn't mention that I was personally responsible for all this extra work, having pointed McGoo toward the Emporium as a possible link.

"Mister Cralo usually hires attorneys to fight every step of the way, but this time he's taking a different approach." Huff heaved a long sigh and hung his head. "He told me to provide records of everything—*everything!* Hold nothing back, he said—copies of every record, every body part, every transaction, for as long as we've been in business. I had to hire an army of temp goblins in our accounting department, and four golems just to haul boxes of records."

"Think of it as doing your civic duty, Mister Huff." I knew perfectly well what Cralo was doing—trying to hide a needle of truth in a haystack of paperwork.

Huff gave me a long-suffering look. "Are you here to gripe about something else? I thought I took care of your complaint already."

"You sent me to see Mister Cralo personally."

"Yes, that usually takes care of any complaints. We never see the customer again."

"Well, I did as you suggested, I went to see your boss in the Zombie Bathhouse, and I resolved the issue. He told me to come back today and pick up a new brain and spleen, plus extras."

Huff's eyes went wide and he lowered his voice in disbelief. "You actually went to see Mister Cralo? Nobody does that!"

"He invited me into his Jacuzzi and everything." I shuddered to remember sitting in the fetid whirlpool with the fat, outgassing crime lord.

Huff swallowed hard. "You're a brave man, Mister Chambeaux." He shuffled papers on his desk.

"You should read the novel," I said. Good thing he hadn't seen me in my less-brave moments. "In addition to the replacement brain, Mister Cralo said you'd give my client a new spleen, a set of lungs, and a discount on any future orders. Then the case will require no further action on our part. My client has an important body-building competition coming up, and he needs those organs."

Huff was flustered. "I'm sure you're right. I just have to double-check that with Mister Cralo."

"One hundred percent customer satisfaction," I reminded him.

"Yes, of course. And you went through the appropriate procedures." He shook his head. "But we don't have the replacement brain ready for you yet. I can get you the spleen and lungs—ship them directly to the customer. Come back tomorrow."

"Is this how you get return customers?" I asked. "Just have them keep coming back because their order isn't ready?"

"Believe me, Mister Chambeaux, I don't want to see you any more often than necessary." He double-checked records on his computer screen, shook his head. "I really don't have a brain."

"So . . . you're saying it's a no-brainer?" He didn't laugh at my joke, but it wasn't much of a joke anyway.

The phone rang again, and he made an impatient gesture. "Please, come back tomorrow. Right now, the body parts you need are not in stock, but we'll get them. I've got about a ton and a half of paperwork to prepare."

I thought Archibald would be happy enough with that. He could get started with the spleen and lungs at least.

On my way out, I strolled up and down a few of the aisles, where my two eager customer service reps were shelving boxes in the Ghoul section. The sales reps stacked crates of various ghoul body parts, each with a bright red label that said *Fresh Today!*

I wondered if Francis had been not so much fired, but rather disassembled and recycled.

CHAPTER 26

When my Best Human Friend showed up at our office with a bright grin, I knew I should have been suspicious. As my second clue that something was up, McGoo started the conversation with, "I've got to call in a favor, Shamble—a big one."

I should have asked exactly what he wanted before agreeing, but what are friends for? My automatic response was, "Sure, McGoo. Anything you need."

With an embarrassed grin, he called into the hall. "Bring everything in, boys!" That was another bad sign.

Two uniformed cops and a sturdy golem wheeled in hand trucks piled with bankers' boxes. It looked as if they had come from a clearance sale at the Ark of the Covenant warehouse.

Sheyenne hovered beside me, giving me a questioning look. "What did you get us into, Beaux?"

Robin emerged from her office to see what the commotion was about. Regarding all the boxes, she said, "I haven't seen so much paper since I got my copy of the Unnatural Acts Act."

McGoo explained with a shrug. "I followed up on your hunch, Shamble, and requested records from the Spare Parts

Emporium. I asked for everything they had. I didn't expect all this stuff! It's supposed to make us think the fat zombie's operation is aboveboard, that he has nothing to hide."

Sheyenne drifted over from her desk. "Anybody can fake records. We can't exactly double-check with the donors to make sure they surrendered their body parts voluntarily." Her normally beautiful smile became hard and determined. "But I'm good at digging."

"Their next of kin should have the counter-copies of the receipts," I said.

Robin looked at the mountains of documents and raised her chin. "I've seen this technique before. Sometimes the party being investigated will bury you under an avalanche of paperwork in hopes that you won't be able to sift out the one or two compelling pieces of evidence you need. Were you specific in your warrant, Officer McGoohan?"

He looked embarrassed. "I just asked for their records. This is what they gave me."

The golem thumped down his hand truck, and the uniformed policemen began unstacking the boxes in the middle of our reception area.

"What do you expect us to do with them?" I asked. "This goes far beyond a consumer complaint case." But if Tony Cralo had anything to do with the disorganized vampire corpse in the Motel Six Feet Under, we were dealing with a murder. And though Sheyenne always insisted that we concentrate on paying clients first, we might also look into the fate of Francis, the ghoul who'd been fired for eating on the job. The Spare Parts Emporium could be like a walk-in-sized closet full of skeletons.

"As I said, I need your help. Somebody's got to look through all these records to find discrepancies. Say, like a *detective*. The precinct doesn't have the manpower to go through it all, and you know *I* can't do it—I can't even balance my checkbook."

"You still have a checkbook?" I asked. "Nobody carries a checkbook anymore."

"I only use it in the express checkout line at the grocery store," McGoo said. He let out a long sigh at the sheer number of boxes. "I wasn't figuring *you* could do much, Shamble—but these two lovely detail-oriented ladies . . ." He gave a flirtatious smile that failed miserably.

Robin looked over at me. "Dan, did you pick up the replacement brain for our client?"

"No, I got the runaround. The floor manager told me to come back tomorrow, but he promised to send over a new spleen and lungs."

"I'll believe that when it actually happens." Robin sniffed. "We would be happy to look into this, Officer. We might identify another entire set of wronged customers so we can expand our case, if necessary. I smell class-action suit."

"I smell *something*," I added.

"If you can do that, Robin, then I'll owe you a coffee," McGoo said.

"You'll owe me a coffee plantation," she said. "But I'll accept the coffee for the moment. Keep me caffeinated so I can bury myself in the case."

One of the uniformed cops pulled a cardboard lid off a box. "Should be everything you need. They sent everything." He rustled among the papers. "These are receipts for junk-food purchases for vending machines in the employee break room."

The other cop held up a folder. "Monthly formaldehyde bills. And full donation receipts for charity write-offs, regular deliveries to the Fresh Corpses Zombie Rehab Clinic."

"We're going to need the whole conference room table," Robin said. "Sheyenne, do we have any intake appointments for the next day or two?"

"None scheduled."

"Good." Robin nodded at the boxes of records, and determination was carved on her face. "Let's sprawl."

"Day or two?" McGoo said. "This looks like months of work."

Robin said, "I'm a fast reader."

He looked relieved and brightened further. "What about the scalps? Does Cralo deal in werewolf scalps?"

"Not that he would say—I already checked," I answered.

McGoo shook his head, but a strange quirk of a smile hovered on the corners of his lips. "I keep looking into the murdered vampire, and I come up empty." His grin grew larger as he looked expectantly at us. "That was a joke! Get it, *coming up empty*—like that vampire?"

"So . . . about the case?" I asked. "Any leads?"

McGoo heaved a sigh. "You dead people have no sense of humor. We've identified the victim. Name was Ben Willard, worked part-time as a hemoglobin barista at one of the Talbot and Knowles Blood Bars. More importantly, he was active in the rough-trade clubbing scene, liked to dress up, act tough. He'd pick up anyone who was still ambulatory, whether warm- or cold-blooded, then he'd go have a good time."

"The Motel Six Feet Under is a real destination spot for that," I said. "The manager was offering 'change your own bedsheets' discounts."

"Vamps think they're invincible," McGoo said. "And whoever Ben Willard picked up that night proved too much for him."

His helpers wheeled the empty hand trucks down the hall to the stairs where they clattered, bump-bump-bump, down to street level. McGoo followed them out, calling back, "Let me know as soon as you find anything. I have to get back to my beat, but these guys will bring up the rest of the load."

I looked at the stack of boxes in our reception area. "The rest?"

"It's a big Emporium, Shamble. They wanted to be thorough."

Since I wouldn't be much help studying receipts or balances on bank statements, or calculating whether the volume of formaldehyde purchased was reasonable for the business Cralo conducted, I made myself useful by lugging the heavy boxes into the conference room.

Robin directed me like a stage manager and sighed in disgust as she tried to prioritize the cartons. "These boxes aren't even labeled! How am I going to organize all this?"

"Through talent, sheer persistence, and determination," I said.

Robin sniffed. "That goes without saying. But I still wish they were alphabetized."

Over the next couple of hours, we worked together to sort the relevant records (body-part inventories, donation forms, and receipts) from the silly records (water, sewer, and utility bills; parking-lot pothole repairs—not too many of those); and fan letters (mostly from a group of schoolchildren who had toured the Emporium on a field trip).

As expected, many organs were sold to mad scientists and body-building enthusiasts like Archibald Victor, as well as hospital transplant wards. Many scratch-and-dent or slightly damaged floor samples had been sent over to the Fresh Corpses Zombie Rehab Clinic for a (rather large) tax write-off.

I had an idea. "Maybe I should stop by the clinic, see if Mrs. Saldana can give me any background on the Emporium." When it came to tracking down the origins of those spare body parts, I was the best person to do the arm-and-leg work.

Sheyenne interrupted, "I think *we* should go there, Beaux. You and Robin went to the grand opening reception, but I've never seen the place. Do you think Mrs. Saldana will be working today?"

"She splits her time between the clinic and the Hope and

Salvation Mission. I'd be happy to have you along, Spooky, if Robin can spare you." In fact, spending a little more time with Sheyenne would go a long way toward brightening the dreary case.

Robin was intensely focused on the folders and boxes. To me, it looked as if a document explosion had occurred in our conference room, but she had some sort of visual organization method that I didn't want to disturb. "It's all right," she said in that preoccupied voice of hers. "I'll do better by myself, if I can just stare at this and absorb it all. I can put the pieces together."

Robin had often told me how she kept up with her studies in law school days by getting into hyperfocus, immersing herself in details, and becoming One with the legal precedents. Now she was doing a similar thing, absorbing the storm of data provided by the Spare Parts Emporium and making connections that Tony Cralo never expected anyone to find. "Getting dirty in the facts," she called it.

"All right," I said. "We'll go see what we can dig up at the zombie rehab clinic."

Sheyenne slipped her incorporeal arm through mine, just for effect, and we headed out.

CHAPTER 27

Not all zombies are as well-preserved as I am. Many take their time coming out of the ground, and by then the maggots and worms have made them less than presentable. Sometimes the initial embalming job is bad, or a mortician doesn't care enough to put the pieces back together properly when it's for a closed-coffin service. Other zombies are just plain slobs who don't take care of themselves, let their bodies fester, eat a poor diet of junk food—sometimes including brains, sometimes not. It's a rotten situation all around.

Though the worst shamblers are too far gone to want any sort of help, others just need a leg up. The charity-run Fresh Corpses Zombie Rehab Clinic was now administered by the Monster Legal Defense Workers. As a member of MLDW's advisory board, Robin had done a substantial amount of pro bono legal work for the charity, and after the recent scandals with the Smile Syndicate, they were on solid humanitarian ground again.

I entered the front doors of the clinic with Sheyenne drifting by my side. The clinic was a clean, modern facility with several wings, including a private lockdown ward for recovering brain addicts. Fresh Corpses also had a day-spa section, a dental replacement room, a necro-ophthalmologist who offered a wide selection of glass eyes, and a vault filled with replacement parts, many of them—I now knew—donated by Tony Cralo.

At the front desk, a horrifically scarred and mismatched zombie girl gave us a crooked grin. Sheyenne and I both brightened. "Wendy!" I said. "I didn't know you were working here."

"Doing my part for those less fortunate," she said in a slurred voice because her teeth, palate, and tongue had not been properly reassembled. "Other zombies have it worse than I do."

"You're looking well," I said. "Good to see you out in public."

Wendy looked away and batted her eyelashes. She was shy and self-conscious about her appearance. Unlucky in love, she had thrown herself in front of a train. But suicide victims have a higher reanimation percentage than normal deaths, and her mangled pieces had come back to life. Fortunately, the taxidermist and sawbones Miss Lujean Eccles had stitched the Patchwork Princess together as best she could. Her work had gotten better with practice.

"Is Miss Eccles here today, too?" Sheyenne asked.

"She's in the Upholstery and Repair ward. Let me take you there." Wendy lurched up from her chair and tottered off. Sheyenne and I followed.

After I'd been shot down in the street—an inconvenience, even for a zombie—Miss Eccles had patched the bullet wounds in my torso, while Wendy used her seamstress abilities to repair the holes in my sport jacket. Wendy was clearly thrilled that I still chose to wear it. "You don't have to keep that jacket, you know, Mister Chambeaux. It's such a bad stitch-up job."

"Not a chance," I said, brushing the front with my free hand. "I love it."

Sheyenne drifted on the other side of us. "That jacket has character. We won't let him get rid of it." Wendy blushed.

We saw the matronly Miss Eccles inside a room with two patients. One zombie sat by himself on a table, pulling a leather glove over shredded bony fingers, testing the fit.

At the adjacent table, Miss Eccles was stitching a triangular swatch of flesh-colored leatherette onto a rotting cheek. She hummed as she tightened the tiny stitches and affixed the replacement part where it covered the zombie's exposed molars. "Now, you have to take care of this patch," she said. "Someday, you might want to upgrade to real leather."

"Can't afford it," the zombie mumbled.

She clucked at him. "Plenty of available options for afterlife insurance and postmortem-care plans. Conscientious people plan ahead."

"Didn't expect to come back as a zombie." He stretched his mouth, flexed the new skin patch, rubbed his jaw like a dental patient checking the extent of Novocain.

Miss Eccles shook her head and said in a chiding voice, " 'Didn't expect to.' I bet an insurance agent hears those words more often than anything else."

Wendy led us into the room. "Look who's here, ma'am."

Miss Eccles looked up as we entered, and her expression lit up. "Why, Mister Chambeaux! Did you get damaged again?" She eyed me up and down for unexpected leaks or tears. "You'll have to put your name on a waiting list if you need repairs."

"I wouldn't take up a spot in the free clinic," I said. "Just had my monthly restorative spell, so I feel fine."

"I'm taking care of Dan," Sheyenne said. "You use your services for these people in need. Thanks for paying back to the community."

Miss Eccles snipped off the thread next to the zombie's face, gave him a motherly peck on the cheek, and sent the repaired undead patient on his way. "The zombies appreciate it. Most of them just need a second, third, or fourth chance."

Before attending to the second patient, she patted the Patchwork Princess on her misshapen shoulder. "I don't know what I'd do without Wendy. She's been taking self-esteem classes. Isn't she positively glowing?"

"And not in a bad way," I said. "I really can see the difference."

Sheyenne lowered her voice. "We should encourage Adriana Cruz to see Miss Eccles. I think she'd benefit from it."

Wendy said in her slurred voice, "Working here makes me realize how lucky I am."

Miss Eccles adjusted the leather glove on the second zombie, tweaking the knuckles, aligning the edge on the rotted wrist. "How does that feel? Can you flex your fingers?" The zombie did so. "The shade doesn't quite match the rest of your arm, but it's difficult to get an identical putrefaction color."

"This'll do fine," the patient said. "Stylish."

As she finished attaching the leather glove to the zombie's forearm, Miss Eccles glanced at me. "So if you don't need repairs, Mister Chambeaux, did you just come to visit the clinic?"

"It's part of a case, ma'am. We're investigating one of your suppliers, Tony Cralo. We understand that a lot of your . . . raw material comes from his Emporium."

Miss Eccles was surprised. "Mister Cralo is one of our most generous donors! As a zombie himself, he suffers from aches and pains, so he understands the plight of many of our patrons. Admittedly, he provides a lot of substandard pieces and writes them off at full value for tax purposes. We get his seconds, the slightly irregular parts or the ones near expiration dates." She clucked her tongue again.

"Sounds like a factory outlet store," Sheyenne said.

With a sigh, Miss Eccles shrugged. "We take what we can get. But if you need to look at paperwork, you should speak with Mrs. Saldana—she does the administrative work for the clinic. I just do patch-ups."

Mrs. Hope Saldana was a kindly old woman who had devoted her life to helping out downtrodden monsters. She had opened the first mission in the Unnatural Quarter, feeding, clothing, and caring for indigent monsters.

Wendy led us to the clinic's admin office, but Mrs. Saldana was pulling on her coat, ready to leave. "I wish you'd come sooner, dears! I'm heading over to the mission. Jerry's been handling the work all day, but he gets overwhelmed easily."

I didn't know where she got the energy. "Before you go, could you answer just a few quick questions about your dealings with Tony Cralo?"

"Dan meant to say 'please' at the end of his sentence," Sheyenne said.

Mrs. Saldana grabbed her purse. "This clinic wouldn't last long if we had to purchase all the materials that the Spare Parts Emporium donates to us." She turned to a pair of tall file cabinets behind her desk. "We have all the paperwork right there, receipts and forms with his contributions. We're never able to decipher them. Nothing seems to match, but we accept what is freely given and do our good works with it."

"Could we have copies of those records, Mrs. Saldana?" Sheyenne asked.

I wasn't so sure. "You think Robin wants *more* paperwork?"

"I can compare these forms with the papers Cralo gave to the police. If there are any discrepancies, I'll spot them."

And I knew she would.

Mrs. Saldana opened the drawers and began pulling out manila folders. "You're welcome to look at them, Mister Chambeaux. As far as I'm concerned, after all the help you've given me, you don't need a warrant. I trust you. Besides, Ms. Deyer is a member of the MLDW board, so she is allowed access to any of the clinic's paperwork." The old woman lowered her voice as a concerned look crossed her face. (She was very good at concerned looks.) "Mister Cralo isn't in any trouble, is he?"

"We won't know until Sheyenne has a look at these records," I said. "He may be marketing a few body parts that the original owners were still using at the time."

It took a second for that to sink in, then Mrs. Saldana's eyes went wide. "Oh, my! Well, we keep careful records of all patients we treat here at the clinic. If you need any of the donated body parts returned . . ." She shook her head, frowning. "A lot of poor zombies are going to be so disappointed."

CHAPTER 28

By the time Sheyenne and I returned from the clinic, Robin had done a spectacular job of papering every horizontal space in the Chambeaux & Deyer offices (and used pushpins to take advantage of many vertical spaces). Piles of documents had been distributed across the conference room table, the seats of the chairs, Sheyenne's desk, my desk, even the top of the microwave and coffeemaker in the kitchenette.

"Now we're making some progress," Robin said.

All visible evidence to the contrary, she has a highly organized mind. By now she'd concocted a master plan for arranging the Emporium records and laid them out according to a certain pattern. I thought of one of those optical illusions: If you tilted it just so and held your gaze in the right way, some sort of new pattern suddenly popped up in an "Aha!" moment. (Unfortunately, I was never good at those puzzles, and I couldn't see any sort of pattern now.)

"What did you find out at the clinic?" she asked.

"Wendy says hi," I said, "and Miss Eccles and Mrs. Saldana."

Sheyenne carried the folders of receipts from the Fresh

Corpses files. "And we brought more documents—donation forms we can compare with the paperwork Cralo already provided."

"Excellent!" Robin said, and she genuinely sounded excited. Go figure. She was upbeat as she bustled back and forth, carrying folders, looking through receipts and entries. She was in the zone, and we could almost hear her thoughts humming.

That was when Miranda Jekyll and Hirsute arrived, generating all the usual amount of commotion as they pushed into the offices. The two Monthly werewolves were alone, but Miranda was always followed by a large entourage of sycophants and adoring fans, in her own mind at least.

She wore a shimmering emerald dress, diamond stud earrings with stones so large and heavy they stretched out her earlobes, and enough gold necklaces to create a layer effect. Intense lipstick, intense nail polish, intense expression. She paused after walking through the door, as if waiting for applause. Heavily muscled and lavishly haired, Hirsute stood by her side like a hunk of 100 percent pure hunkness.

Miranda noticed the papers all around. "Sweethearts, you must get a better office manager."

Sheyenne took offense. "It's a work in progress, but completely under control."

"I'm working on a complex case," Robin said. "It requires a lot of my attention."

Miranda deftly dodged piles of paperwork, careful to not soil her Jimmy Choos with copy toner. "At the moment, sweethearts, *I* require your full attention. I understand you're working for the Monster Legal Defense Workers, Ms. Deyer? I need to engage your legal services."

Robin brightened. "Yes, I'm a member of the board. Very important work, standing up for the rights of underprivileged unnaturals."

"It's *charity* work, Ms. Jekyll," Sheyenne pointed out. "In your case, the normal fee structure would remain in place."

"Of course, sweetheart." Miranda sighed. "I wouldn't want word to get around that I'm a charity case."

"How can we help you, Ms. Jekyll?" I prodded, afraid she might accidentally disorganize one of Robin's careful paperwork stacks.

"It's about my werewolf sanctuary up in Montana. I originally intended it to be a place where Hirsute and I could roam and unleash our animal passions." She stroked long fingernails along the curves of his biceps, like an all-wheel-drive vehicle negotiating steep mountainous terrain. "But I hated to be so selfish. I felt obligated to open up the property, make all that wilderness acreage a refuge for my Monthly brothers and sisters during the full moon, a place where they can be free and loved, and feel safe to be who they really are. But I want to be legally protected."

Robin said, "You'd have to set up a nonprofit organization and transfer the property into the corporation's name. I'll complete and file the forms, then we can set up another meeting to review the details, go over the tax implications with you."

Miranda gave a blasé wave of her hand. "Whatever you think is best, sweetheart, but it's important. I still feel soured and unsettled by that nasty werewolf business at the Worldwide Horror Convention."

Robin gave a concerned nod. "What happened to Professor Zevon this morning was awful. I hear he's recovering in the hospital, though. He'll be all right."

Miranda grimaced, as if she had swallowed a mouse and it had gone down wrong. "Oh, I'd almost forgotten about *him.* I was talking about the snotty attitude and outright disrespect the Hairballs show the rest of us *true* werewolves."

This was as unwise as discussing politics at a family reunion, but I couldn't stop myself from reminding her, "Let's not forget that Scratch and Sniff did cause trouble on their own."

"Of course they did, sweetheart. They're *troublemakers*. It's what they *do*. But those two are anomalies—rather garish ones, if you look at their tattoos. Implying that all Monthlies are ill-tempered troublemakers is like implying that all motorcyclists are ill-behaved and destructive. Scratch and Sniff may embody the cliché, but it doesn't make it true."

Hirsute squared his shoulders. "They were unruly up in Montana last full moon, too, Miranda. We might not extend them a return invitation. I'd rather have the wilderness with you, my dear, without distractions." He lifted his square jaw and cocked his head in a well-practiced display of his profile. "When we walk among the trees under the full moon . . . and the light bathes us, and we feel the change—I love to be right there, so I can help tear your clothes off, nibble you with my fangs, taste you. Then we lope off into the underbrush. . . ."

Sheyenne rolled her eyes and flitted away. "Whoa, a little TMI there."

Miranda giggled in uncharacteristic embarrassment.

But Hirsute wasn't finished; his voice grew huskier. "I'll know that you're in heat, and I'll chase you into the meadows, where we'll make wild love. Together we will hunt prey, stalking anything that moves. And after we've killed it and torn the flesh with our fangs and claws, we'll drink the hot blood and feel energy again. We will make love a second time—and continue until the sun rises! Then we will rest for the next night of the full moon."

"Whew!" Robin fanned herself, glancing awkwardly at me.

Miranda looked as if she were about to melt, and I was afraid she'd turn into a puddle right there and ruin Robin's neat stacks of papers. She let out a long sigh. "Ah, those are my favorite days of the month." She nuzzled against Hirsute's rock-hard body. Her face was flushed, her pupils dilated, and she breathed heavily. "The full moon will be here soon, but maybe we'd better not wait to get in some practice."

She gave a quick dismissive wave to Robin. "You know what to do about the legal matters, Ms. Deyer. Call me whenever the paperwork is ready. I think . . . I think we'd better go now." She glanced at Hirsute. *"Hurry."*

As they left the office, Hirsute tossed his mane of hair, glanced back, and for some reason gave me a triumphant wink. He playfully grabbed Miranda's ass as they rushed into the hallway.

Robin put her hands on her hips and looked down at the piles of paperwork. "Now I've lost my train of thought."

CHAPTER 29

Walking the dark streets of the Unnatural Quarter was a habit of mine. Some might have diagnosed it as restless-corpse syndrome; I'm even a card-carrying member of AARZ—the American Association of Restless Zombies. In actuality, I just like to think while I walk. Sure, it might look like I'm wandering aimlessly—as many zombies do—but I'm really *working*. The cases don't solve themselves.

I walked past nightclubs, bars, gambling joints, all-night restaurants, blues clubs. I stopped before a small run-down theater, the kind that used to play second-run porno films before home video ruined the market; now the refurbished theater catered to a wider clientele. The red plastic letters on the marquee said ONE NIGHT ONLY: GOLEM MUD WRESTLING!

Directly in front of the theater, two familiar choppers were chained to a fire hydrant in a blatant Screw You gesture at parking enforcement. Raucous shouts came from inside the theater, and I knew I had to go inside (and not just to see the golem mud wrestling).

I bought a ticket from a frog creature (small body, large

head: some sort of D-level demon or nondescript sewer-dweller). He put a red vinyl wristband around my arm and said in a voice that sounded like an extended belch, "You can go in and out if you want."

"I don't think I'll need the privilege."

"The night's young."

Once inside, I was bombarded by raucous cheering, loud laughter, and thick smoke—cigar smoke, burning weeds, brimstone, even a whiff of what came out of the smokestacks at Joe's Crematorium. Vampire cocktail waitresses in slinky dresses patrolled the tables carrying trays of drinks. The bartender was a fat, gray fellow with four tentacled arms, which he put to good use concocting multiple drinks at once.

A few dozen people crowded around a center stage like a boxing ring, except this one held a plastic inflatable swimming pool adorned with cartoon dolphins. The plastic pool was filled with a sloppy brown slurry that looked more like diluted manure than good clean dirt. It bubbled like a hot, cloying mud bath.

Two clay female figures faced off in the pool; they had breasts and curves sculpted in all the right places, but the figures were streamlined like giant-sized Barbie dolls; etched lines around their breasts and waists implied bikinis, but they were so scanty that even the outlines didn't make much difference. Lumpy wads of gray clay hair hung down around the golems' flat generic faces; their expressions were threatening grimaces.

The referee called out the start of the match, and the golem mud wrestlers crashed together with a wet, painful-sounding slap. The women grappled, pushing and straining until they finally drove each other into the manure-like mud. Rolling around, they splashed brown slop in all directions, spraying the disgusted audience.

The golems slammed each other back and forth with wild abandon, punching, grabbing, slapping, kicking. One golem shoved the other's head into the mud, and when she came up sputtering, her head was misshapen from the pressure. Furious, she reached up and grabbed the clay hair of her opponent, tearing off lumpy wads, which she tossed into the mud. They gouged divots out of each other's skin; one punched her opponent's left breast, caving it in. When the wrestlers finally disentangled themselves, the damaged golem took a moment to squish and reform her body, glaring at her opponent the entire time. Both dripped with brown slop.

Scratch and Sniff were crowded close to the ringside, cheering and cursing, egging on the two golems, just as they had done during the cockatrice fight. The clay opponents looked identical, as if stamped from the same mold, so I had no idea how or why the audience could cheer for one or the other.

When the crowd recoiled as mud flew, I worked my way closer to the ring. Scratch and Sniff didn't seem bothered by the muck that spattered their faces and werewolf-pelt coats.

"Hi, guys," I said. "Mind if I join you?"

The biker werewolves scowled at me and wrinkled their noses. Werewolves, even monthly ones, are sensitive to smells, but I doubted my undead scent was any less pleasant than the manure-tainted mud.

"It's that zombie guy." Scratch rubbed a palm over his slicked-back hair, as if the brown mud were a new kind of mousse.

His partner contemplatively stroked his beard, then sniffed his fingers. "Either he's trying to be a player, or he's following us."

"Maybe we just travel in the same circles," I said. "In fact, I saw you both riding away from Joe's Crematorium today. Business there?"

"Visiting a sick friend," Scratch said with a sneer. "Why do we have to tell you anything?"

Before I could answer, a raucous cheer went up. One golem slammed the other down in the mud, picked up her adversary's right leg, and bent it like a pretzel until it was tangled around the back of her neck. The other golem struggled and flopped, trying to straighten out her limbs.

"I also saw you at the Worldwide Horror Convention. You two sure have diverse interests. Renaissance men?"

"We wanted to heckle that crackpot professor with his stupid ideas," Sniff said. "Guess he got what he deserved."

I hardened my voice, no longer trying to be cheerful. "Scalping an old man is no way to respond to an intellectual disagreement."

Hearing the accusation, Scratch growled deep in his throat, even though he still looked human. "Wait a minute—Sniff and I had nothing to do with that."

I shrugged. "Do the math. You were there, and you were also at the cockatrice fight when Rusty got scalped. Quite a coincidence, don't you think? Somebody sneaked up behind him, shot him with tranquilizers, and then ran away."

Sniff cocked his head. "Mister Zombie Guy, do we look like the type to tranq someone *before* we cut his scalp off?"

Come to think of it, they didn't. Instead, I indicated their coats. "Didn't you skin a werewolf alive for the pelt?"

The two looked at each other, self-consciously brushed at the stained fur jackets and the long-dried red clumps. "Nah, it's just synthetic fur," Scratch said. "But it looks cool. And it's part of our . . . thing."

"The dried blood is real, though." Sniff rubbed one of the clumps, then smelled his fingers. "Anti-fur protesters dumped it on us because the coats looked so real."

I supposed that was a relief. "Don't worry, I won't ruin the secret."

The mud wrestling had grown even more furious. One golem grabbed the other's fingers and wrenched them off, holding up the severed clay digits like trophies. The ref whistled a shrill, piercing note, but the wrestling golems were too intent on their battle, pummeling, cursing each other. The ref whistled and whistled again. The crowd cheered. The bartender continued to pour drinks, shaking martinis in two of his tentacles, while pulling beer with two others.

Finally Security charged the ring with a fire hose and blasted a stream of high-pressure water. The mud-wrestling golems kept fighting until they dissolved into grayish glop that filled the mud bath.

The announcer came out to ringside. "Ladies and gentlemen, we call that match a draw, but don't worry, we'll scoop up the mud and make some more golems. We still have the animation spells!"

Scratch and Sniff obviously intended to stay for the next match. "So, what sort of work do you two do for a living?" I asked them when the tumult had died down. I tried to sound cheery and conversational, best buddies.

"We work in collections," Sniff said.

Scratch was not so forthcoming. "What's it to ya, anyway?"

"Oh, just curious, since I've been hearing a lot about you two. In fact, I was at the Voodoo Tattoo parlor—heard about the practical joke you played on Rusty."

They both laughed. "Now, that's more our style! Yes, sir, big tough Rusty sure is one *impotent* guy!" Sniff lowered his head, brushed some of the mud that had splattered his beard, sniffed it, then wiped his fingers on his pants.

"We're sick and tired of being accused of everything by the Hairballs," Scratch grumbled. "Full moon is in a couple of days, and then it'll be time—claw to claw, wolf mano–a–wolf mano. We'll settle this."

"Or maybe just keep the feud going," Sniff added, and the two chuckled again.

A pair of newly formed female golems came out to the ring, fists raised, to loud cheers from the audience. This time, one had been sculpted with even bigger breasts, and the second sported a decidedly larger backside. A well-muscled hunch-back came out and dumped a tub of fresh, noisome brown mud into the plastic swimming pool.

Scratch and Sniff no longer paid me any attention, but I had a lot to ponder anyway. Unable to concentrate in the middle of a golem mud-wrestling match, I slipped back out into the streets. If I changed my mind and wanted to go back later and see another match, I still had the wristband.

Chapter 30

Next morning, I went to see Professor Zevon in the hospital. The old silverback was recovering well, thanks to his lycanthropic healing abilities, but he'd been rather frail to start with, and he had an academically low pain threshold. While Rusty had gone home within hours of being scalped, the physicians were holding the professor for further observation since they were concerned about his cholesterol levels and blood pressure.

At the Brothers and Sisters of Mercy Hospital, an old panel truck was parked in front of the emergency room. The side of the truck bore the logo and bright letters of Cralo's Spare Parts Emporium: *Nobody Beats Our Deals on Transplants.* I wondered if the truck was there for a pickup or a delivery.

Inside the hospital, I approached the information desk. The receptionist took one look at me and immediately tried to direct me to the morgue, but I assured her that I had already been there. A security guard and triage nurse pushing a gurney with a body bag came up and politely invited me to lie down, but I brushed them aside. "I have business to attend to." At the reception desk, I asked where I could find Professor Zevon.

When I finally got to the right room, the gray-furred were-wolf was lying flat on the bed, his spectacles on the nightstand, the top of his head wrapped in gauze. Two of his Hairball students kept him company; a young furry woman was reciting from a thick book—she was pretty by werewolf standards, I supposed.

As I entered the room, I nodded toward the novel. "Reading *Twilight* to the professor?"

"He likes to keep up with the classics," said the student.

Zevon tried to focus on me without his spectacles. "Excuse me, do I know you?"

"I'm Dan Chambeaux, private investigator. I attended your lecture at the Worldwide Horror Convention, sir, and I've been hired by another werewolf who was also scalped. I'm sure your cases are related. Mind if I ask you some questions?"

With a clawed hand, the student folded over a corner on the page where she'd stopped reading. "We should have protected the professor."

"It was a convention full of monsters and rowdy fans. I never dreamed we wouldn't be safe." Zevon leaned forward in the bed, snuffling in the air. "There's a bit of a taint about you, Mister Chambeaux."

"I'm undead, sir, but I'm still on the job."

"Zombies can be persistent indeed." He shook his head, then winced at the pain. "I'm afraid I can't help. I was shot in the back by a tranquilizer dart out in the parking lot. I didn't see a thing."

The male student growled. "If you attended the professor's lecture, then you saw those two Monthly bullies harassing him, and that awful woman, Miranda Jekyll! *They* scalped the professor, just to shame him."

Professor Zevon touched the bandages on his head. "I agree with the thesis. Those . . . those *part-timers* publicly threatened me, and I was assaulted very soon afterward!"

The blood pressure and pulse rate on the monitor apparatus began to bleep in a shrill, annoying tone that had the opposite effect of calming the patient.

"Please don't stress, Professor," said the young werewolf student in a soothing voice. She quickly reopened the book. "Here, let me read some more. Bella's problems will cheer you up."

The professor lay back on the bed, breathing heavily.

Though I doubted I'd convince them, I said, "I've talked to both Scratch and Sniff. They enjoy mayhem, but I'm not convinced they're the culprits."

The professor turned his muzzle away. "I don't want to hear it. Who else would do such a thing?"

"I'll let you know as soon as I find out." I handed over the sentimental get-well card and stuffed teddy bear I'd bought at the hospital gift shop. The professor thought the teddy bear was adorable.

As I left the room and walked down the hall, another full-furred werewolf emerged from the elevator. Rusty flaunted his raw and lumpy scalp, which still looked like a large balding scab. His gangly nephew accompanied him, jaunty and happy. Furguson must have gotten back into his uncle's good graces; maybe his brash outdoor attack on Scratch and Sniff had earned him some street cred in the Hairball gang.

Rusty was holding a bouquet of limp lilies. "We came to make sure the professor's doing all right."

"And vow to get revenge!" Furguson added.

"Just make sure you get the right target," I said. I looked at Rusty's fur, trying to make out the tattoo designs, one of which was the mark of impotence, but I could discern only vague outlines.

Rusty narrowed his yellow eyes. "We'll give you a couple more days to solve the case, Mister Shamble—but once the full moon hits, Hairballs are taking matters into our own claws. We've got enough proof, as far as I'm concerned."

Scratch and Sniff had said something similar at the golem mud-wrestling match. I said, "You might have more of a battle than you expect. The Monthlies plan to fight back."

Rusty chuffed. "We're counting on it! Time to set things right. At least four other Hairballs were scalped. Our lost brother Larry filled us in."

Furguson growled. "Larry, grrrrr—I wish *he* got scalped for helping Harvey Jekyll!"

Rusty placed a clawed hand on his nephew's shoulder and squeezed like a vise. "Now isn't the time for old grudges. We have to stick together to wipe out the Monthlies once and for all."

I frowned. "Isn't that an old grudge, too?"

"Not the same thing." Rusty shook his semi-shaggy head. "Maybe the professor and his students want to join us in the fight—solidarity!—though those sissies are more likely to lecture the Monthlies than rip out a few hunks of fur."

"I'll keep investigating," I said. "Don't jump to conclusions."

"Come up with the *right* conclusion, and we won't have to do any jumping."

Furguson twitched his gangly legs. "I like to jump!" They went past me down the hall toward the professor's room, and I pushed the button for the elevator.

Shrieking alarms blared, loud enough to wake the dead and then send them back into their crypts for a little peace.

"Code Arterial Red," shouted a voice on the intercom. "Surgery Two!"

CHAPTER 31

Code Arterial Red was a special alarm that indicated Violent Activity with Monsters.

Hospitals had never needed to address those types of emergencies before the Big Uneasy, but with all the new crises caused by and happening to unnaturals, hospitals had to assign more colors to their alarm-category rainbow.

As hospital security responded to the blaring summons, Furguson panicked, flailing his long arms and howling along with the noise. Rusty elbowed him in the gut. "Nothing to do with us. Come on, let's deliver the flowers." Furguson yipped in embarrassment, and the two made their way to the professor's room.

The experimental cardiac surgery ward happened to be on the same floor as the werewolf recovery ward. Human security guards ran toward the surgery center, colliding with nurses and staff who fled screaming from it. Several were covered in blood; one who had been severely mauled collapsed on the floor. Two nurses and a doctor loaded her onto a gurney and ran with her toward the ER, as if it were part of a relay race.

A burly human security guard careened out of the surgery doors and slammed against the wall. His throat was torn open; his head lolled at a broken angle. The electronic doors to the experimental cardiac surgery center glided automatically shut again.

I drew my .38—normally not allowed during visiting hours in the hospital, but I did have a permit. From inside the surgery room, I heard a snarling, more screams, smashing glass, a clatter of equipment and instruments.

I'm just a detective, not a hero, not a commando, not even a cop. But I was there in the hospital, and I was armed, and there was a lot of screaming going on. I had to do something.

The elevator bell chimed, and a flustered-looking McGoo burst out, weapon drawn. He blinked at me in surprise. "Shamble, what are you doing here?"

"Visiting a sick friend."

McGoo glanced at the dead security guard and shook his head. "How'd you like to be my backup?"

"Sounds better than waiting for more cops to arrive." We ran down the hall, weapons drawn.

"I thought this was going to be a routine hospital call," McGoo muttered in disbelief. "Got complaints about a vampire photographer acting erratically, so I brought him in. Turns out he was suffering from silver contamination due to photography chemicals in his darkroom."

"Photography chemicals? Doesn't everyone use digital cameras now?"

"He's old-school. Maybe next time he'll wear gloves."

The Code Arterial Red alarms still clamored like a monkeys-with-pans rock concert, but the screams had died to low gurgles as we crept to the door of the surgery. A male nurse whose back was slashed open started to crawl out of the room on hands and knees, but collapsed on the floor, thus frustrating the electronic doors; they tried to close on his waist, then opened, then tried to close again.

McGoo extended his firearms, one in each hand: both the revolver loaded with silver bullets and his regular service piece. We flattened into a doorway.

From inside the surgery, someone or something flung body parts into the hall, like a child having a tantrum because she didn't like her toys.

Through the blood-splattered observation window in the operating theater, I could see overturned monitors and a respirator, and the surgical table leaning tilted against one wall. Other equipment lay smashed and disassembled, as well as a surgeon (also smashed and disassembled) and several nurses—it was hard to tell the exact number, since the pieces were in such disarray.

Inside the room, the alleged patient was on a rampage. An obese woman in a blood-drenched hospital gown that hung in tatters, she had low-hanging breasts and hips the size of a small Volkswagen; her hair was a mess, her wild eyes blazing orange. Her teeth had sprouted into tusk-like fangs so long that she could barely open and close her mouth. She yowled and screamed, and slashed the air with fingers that ended in long claws.

The most noticeable oddity was that her chest hung wide open, her sternum sawed in half, the ribs pried apart and propped open with a spreader. A purplish-black heart dangled from her chest cavity, roughly attached by black sutures.

"I've heard of people wearing their hearts on their sleeves," I said, "but that's ridiculous."

"It's not a human heart, Shamble," McGoo pointed out.

The monster-patient fell upon a pack of replacement blood that dangled from an IV cart. She struggled to poke her long curved fangs into it, but couldn't find the right angle; in frustration, she tore the plastic with her claws and poured the blood into her mouth. Most of it missed and splattered her cheeks.

A prissy-looking middle-aged man scuttled down the hall,

184 / *Kevin J. Anderson*

shaking his head. He wore a suit and hospital ID badge. "What a mess! This is going to be difficult to explain, but I don't believe we can be held legally responsible. Thank heavens the patient signed all the release forms."

McGoo and I looked at each other, then pulled the administrator aside. McGoo said, "If we're going in to fight that thing, you better tell us what's going on."

"It was an experimental transplant procedure on a terminal case." The prissy man shrugged. "The chief surgeon didn't believe there was much chance of success, but we thought, what the heck?" His nervous smile didn't endear him to either of us. "Insurance wouldn't cover it, but the patient paid with her own life savings."

I looked at the carnage strewn around us. "What procedure are you talking about—exactly?"

"Oh, simple heart transplant—or it should have been simple. We obtained a reasonably fresh vampire heart. Compared with regular human heart transplants, this should have been a piece of cake, since it's almost impossible to make vampire hearts *stop* beating. So why not try it for a transplant?"

I indicated the slaughter in the operating theater. "*That* seems to be a good reason not to do it."

"Tissue rejection, apparently," the administrator said with a shrug. "Surgery isn't an exact science. It is called medical *practice,* you know. Did I mention she paid for this procedure out-of-pocket? No one is liable or on the hook."

"The families of all these victims might disagree," McGoo said.

"The hospital provides generous afterlife insurance. They'll be fine."

Looking at the mangled victims, I doubted they'd be "fine."

The monstrous transplant patient threw herself into the wall, uprooted more monitors, and crashed them to the floor.

She was slavering, ravenous, inhuman. The exposed heart hung out of her open chest.

"I have silver bullets," McGoo said. "You think those will work?"

"Only if you hit the heart exactly," I said.

"Right now it's a moving target, flopping around from side to side."

"I don't like your chances, McGoo. She's wild for anything hot-blooded, and if you got killed, then who'd be my best human friend? I'll go first. I doubt embalming fluid is on the menu." He and I both knew that as an undead person, I would be little more than an unappetizing piece of walking furniture as far as a vampire patient was concerned.

The transplant patient moaned, touched fingertips to her long curved fangs as if her mouth were sore. She seemed disoriented but ravenous.

"That thing needs to be put out of her misery," McGoo said. "Let's go. I'm right behind you."

The administrator lifted his chin. "Do what you must to resolve this unfortunate situation. It's all right. As I said, she signed the proper release forms."

I was about to suggest that the administrator go in and take care of his own problem, but decided that would be unproductive.

The automatic doors opened again as I stepped over the nurse's bloody body and into the room. Shuffling forward, I was careful not to slip on the red-smeared floor. McGoo followed me, revolver drawn.

The vampire patient whirled, glared at us, and made incomprehensible sounds. As she opened and closed her mouth, the downward-curving tusks bit into the folds of her chin, leaving divots.

"Easy, girl," I said, holding out my hand. "I'm here to make it better." Flailing her clawed hands, she swayed in agony, and the dangling heart bounced around, barely attached by black sutures. McGoo tried to track the renegade organ with his silver-bullet revolver, looking for a shot. She sniffed, smelling fresh blood, turned her fiery eyes toward him.

I intervened, waving a hand to get her attention. "Gentle. It'll be all right," I continued in a soothing voice. I hated to lie to a fiendish monster, but this thing had already murdered several people and had to be stopped. "I'm sorry this happened to you." She gave a hesitant yowl.

"I wish somebody would shut off that yammering alarm," McGoo said. "It isn't making that thing any less agitated."

"Give me some room, McGoo."

The transplant patient snarled and burbled, made a moaning sound, then slid to the floor, resting on her generous buttocks.

"It'll be over soon, I promise." I inched closer. "Simple enough. Just a quick little tug."

"Watch yourself, Shamble. Just grab it—"

"I've got this."

While McGoo hung back, the creature looked at me, showing something like gratitude in her orange eyes. She leaned forward, clutching the sides of her head with clawed hands, and squeezed her eyes shut, as if she didn't want to see what I was going to do.

Taking the opportunity, I grabbed the pulsing, purplishblack vampire heart and tore it free. Even after I ripped it from the sutures, the rubbery heart kept beating and convulsing in my hand. I flung it aside to a clear area on the floor.

McGoo aimed his revolver, shooting again and again, but the heart flopped about like a fish on a dock. The silver bullets ricocheted, and he had to fire three times before hitting it. We didn't dare leave the monstrous organ alive, or the hospital administrator might decide to do more experiments.

The woman let out another pitiful moan of pain, sorrow,

and confusion as she died—for real, this time. "I'm so sorry, ma'am." She collapsed into me, like a deflating inner tube.

McGoo and I emerged from the surgical theater to the administrator's delighted smile. By now, several backup officers had arrived, and they proceeded to secure and process the scene. My hands, sport jacket, and slacks were sloppy with blood. I was a mess, but in far better shape than the mangled corpses around us.

"Thank you, gentlemen," the hospital administrator said, sounding chipper. "So much for that transplant idea, though . . . back to the drawing board. Did you leave the organ intact so we can ask for a refund, if we track down where it came from?"

"Sorry," I said. "Accidentally damaged."

Eyes wide, McGoo said to the administrator, "You don't even know where the organ came from? How can you not have records?"

The man shrugged. "With such a rare transplant commodity, the chief surgeon wouldn't have been too picky. And he's dead, so we can't ask him." He shook his head. "This is going to be an administrative nightmare. You can't even begin to imagine!" He grumbled as he walked away. "You gentlemen have the easy part. *I* get to fill out all the paperwork."

CHAPTER 32

When Sheyenne saw me enter the office caked with dried blood, she swept forward in alarm. "Beaux! What happened? Are you all right?"

Forgetting for a moment that she was a ghost, she embraced me . . . and her arms passed right through. I gave her an air-hug back.

"I was in surgery," I said, then explained my encounter. "My guess is it was part of the vampire murdered in the Motel Six Feet Under. I wouldn't be surprised if the evidence pointed back to Tony Cralo."

"We've been finding evidence of our own, though ours is less dramatic," Robin said and turned to look around the offices. Receipts and documents were still sorted into different piles, and the project had even co-opted part of my desk, spreading like the out-of-control experiment of a mad accountant rather than a mad scientist.

Thankfully, I didn't plan to stick around the office for long. "Come up with anything useful?" I asked.

"Not much yet. But we'll get there."

I couldn't forget about the gang violence brewing among the werewolves, especially with Rusty convinced the Monthlies were behind the scalpings. If we could prove that Cralo or one of his goons was behind the scalpings, however, then the furry feud didn't have to get bloody. The fat zombie crime lord would be a bigger fish to drown. It would have been nice to wrap up the investigation, but the cases don't solve themselves, and they certainly don't solve themselves in order.

I tugged at my stained sleeve. "After I get cleaned up, I'm going to ask Adriana Cruz's parents about dealing with Joe's Crematorium. If they're willing to give me a sample of Adriana's alleged ashes, I'll call in a favor from Dr. Victor and have him run an analysis."

The Cruz house was in a quiet neighborhood outside the Quarter, a tri-level *Brady Bunch* model. I made myself as presentable as possible, pulled the fedora low enough to cover the bullet hole in my forehead, popped a breath mint in my mouth, and rang the doorbell.

A meek-looking middle-aged woman opened the door. Even before she spoke, I thought of a dark-haired Edith Bunker. "Hello, how can I help you?"

I introduced myself, and the woman called over her shoulder. "Sal, there's a zombie at the door. Says he's here about Adriana."

Mr. Cruz hollered from the living room in a long-suffering voice. "What's she gotten into now?" He sat in a recliner rocker with the leg rest extended. On TV, the joyful buzzers of a game show proclaimed the contestant's answer to be incorrect.

"I'm a private investigator, Mister and Mrs. Cruz. Your daughter hired us to investigate fraud committed by Joe's Crematorium."

Mrs. Cruz opened the door and invited me into the foyer. "We were quite surprised to see our daughter again, after her death and all. Do come in." Mr. Cruz muted the television but kept watching the game show with closed captions.

"After she went to college, Adriana didn't have much to do with us," Mr. Cruz said. "I've had the same job in the factory all my working career, about to retire in six years. Maria's a proud housewife, never wanted to be anything else, never changed her job title to 'domestic engineer' or crap like that."

"But Adriana was her own woman, wanted to be professional. She excelled in everything," said Mrs. Cruz, with a small sigh. "I think she was embarrassed by us, and even though we might not be go-getters like her, we were still proud of her. I wish we'd been closer . . . and when she died in that horrible car accident, we didn't know what to do. But Adriana had taken care of everything ahead of time. Such a responsible girl. All we had to do was follow the steps."

"She had a separate sheet printed up with bullet points," Mr. Cruz said. "Couldn't have asked for more. Our girl was always organized. Took her to the crematorium, just like she asked."

"It was quite a shock to us when she came back."

"Returning from the dead is unsettling for everyone concerned. I've been through it myself." Thinking they needed some reassurance, I added, "Being a zombie isn't all bad, though. Look at me—I'm well-preserved, I have a decent job. I'm a contributing member of society. Adriana can still make something of herself, once she gets used to her situation."

"She always said she wanted to volunteer for important activities, change the world," Mrs. Cruz said, putting a finger on her lips. "Do you know if the Peace Corps accepts zombie volunteers?"

"I couldn't say, ma'am."

Mr. Cruz worked the lever on the side of the recliner and dropped the footrest. He heaved himself out of the chair with sounds of obvious back pain, and then pointed toward the mantelpiece. "Have you figured out how to explain that? We got her ashes, right there, specially delivered from Joe's Crematorium. So if Adriana is still around, then who—or what—is in that urn? We couldn't bear to throw it away."

"That's why I stopped by today. Would you be willing to let me run some tests on the remains? If those ashes belong to someone else, they should go to the proper owner. You'll also be receiving a full refund from Joe's."

"Take the whole urn," grumbled Mr. Cruz. "It's pretty damned clear that isn't Adriana."

Mrs. Cruz hurried into the kitchen and came back with a brown paper grocery bag. She wrapped newspapers around the urn, set it in the bottom of the bag, and handed the bag to me. "Here you are, dear."

The bald coroner with the obvious toupee was happy to see me at the crime lab. He glanced meaningfully at the brown paper bag and whispered, "Harriet told me you'd stopped by the Parlour (BNF), but you shouldn't have brought the replacement brain here. That's a private matter."

"Your brain wasn't ready when I stopped by Cralo's," I said. "But they promised it's coming, don't worry. Did you get the new lungs and spleen? They should have been delivered to your home."

His expression became annoyed. "They arrived, and the lungs are fine, but the box with the spleen was crushed. The organ's totally useless."

I sighed. "I was going to have to go back there anyway."

"I have tomorrow off. You can bring the brain and spleen directly to my lab in the trailer park." He was filled with anticipation. "Now, what can I do for you?"

I reached into the grocery bag and pulled out Adriana's urn. "I need a quick favor, an analysis for a client."

The coroner frowned at the ashes. "It's a little too late for me to perform an autopsy once the body's been cremated."

"With all your resources I was hoping you could run some tests. These were supposed to be the ashes of a beloved daughter, but since she walked into our offices as a zombie, obviously she wasn't cremated. Could you at least tell me if these are human remains?" I kept thinking of the stacked cordwood behind the crematorium and what it might be for. "Neither the family nor the crematee is satisfied."

"I'd imagine not." Archibald Victor took the urn, popped the top, and bent close, sniffing as if he meant to inhale it for a particularly odd kind of high. "Doesn't smell like roasted human flesh." He licked his fingertip, dipped it in the ash and tasted it, like a cop at a drug bust checking for cocaine. "Doesn't taste right, either." He spat it out. "Too tangy. I can run some tests and get you a quick answer."

He took the urn to an experimental table that held bubbling flasks and a test-tube centrifuge. A heavy machine spinning larger flasks reminded me of a paint mixer in a hardware store. "The department just purchased this piece of equipment, a Necro-Centrifuge specially designed to separate human ash from wood ash."

"And what would you need that for?" I asked.

"Vampire murders. If someone stakes an old vampire, everything turns to dust in a flash. In some investigations, we need to separate the stake's ash from the vampire's. The easiest way is with this handy little gadget."

The little mad scientist dumped powder from the urn into one of the paint-can-sized containers, then connected a spiral tube to an empty canister. He sealed the tops and set the machine rattling and spinning. It made as much noise as a dryer with an uneven load of soaked bath towels.

We tried to have a conversation while we waited, although the loud machine made it difficult. Archibald said, "About that murdered vampire, Ben Willard—I finished studying his entire skin, found a couple of stains that weren't apparent at first. Ink stains."

"Did he have a pen in his pocket?" It could have gotten smashed while he was being murdered.

"It was tattoo ink," said the coroner. "Tattoos don't last long on vampire skin—they leak out and wear away as the pinpricks heal. The victim must have been sweating heavily, which diluted the ink. I suppose even a vampire perspires when he's having his organs removed one by one."

"Any way to tell what the original tattoo looked like?"

"Not a chance," Archibald said. "It was just a smeary blob of ink staining the sheets. No way to know."

"I might have a way," I said. I already knew where the vamp had gotten his tattoo. "I'll call you if I learn anything."

Archibald self-consciously adjusted his toupee and shut down the Necro-Centrifuge. When he opened the canisters, all the ash had traveled through the spiral tubing to fill the second canister, leaving nothing behind. He handed the full can to me. "Well, there's your answer, Mister Chambeaux. It's quite obvious."

Obvious wasn't the word that came to my mind. "Could you make it a little . . . more obvious?"

"The Necro-Centrifuge separated the wood ash into this canister. It's *entirely* wood ash, Mister Chambeaux. No human remains here at all. Definitely a crematorium scam."

"Thank you, Dr. Victor. That's what I needed to know. I owe you one."

"Just bring me my brain—and spleen—and I'll be a happy man," Archibald said. "I'm close to a major breakthrough in my hair-tonic experiments, but the body-building competition is coming up, too, and I need to have my entry ready. So much to do, so much to do."

CHAPTER 33

The following morning I met Steve Halsted at the Ghoul's Diner for a bad cup of coffee, a bad breakfast, and an update on his case (not necessarily bad). Esther the harpy was cranky, tired, and testy, as if auditioning for a PMS commercial—in other words, same as she always was. She clatter-spilled a cup of coffee for me and for Steve.

Esther butted in on our conversation. "I've already had a long shift, Chambeaux, and I'm ready to get off." Her feathers were ruffled. "Did you nail the bastard who gave me the bad-luck charm yet?"

I decided not to tell her that her case was far from our highest priority. "We've done some research. My partner believes she can prove intent on the wizard's part—that he knowingly gave the bad luck to you—although she isn't convinced that we can prove damages. The courts haven't ruled definitively on whether bad luck is transferable."

"It's sure as hell been bad luck for me!" she shrieked. "How else do you explain my mixed-up orders, all the broken dishes, all the customers being angry with me?"

Sitting in a booth, a Monthly werewolf raised his coffee cup and tried to get Esther's attention, but she lashed out at him. "You wait your turn! Can't you see I'm busy with something a lot more important than your damn cup?" She turned back to me. "Stupid customers, always demanding things. Like that giant plant we used to have in the back, 'Feed me, feed me!' Nag, nag, nag."

I interrupted her rant. "What can you tell me about the wizard who gave it to you? Do you have a name, an address? I'd like to talk with him, see if I can convince him to lift the curse."

"His name is Glenn, with two *N*s. He's a wizard. What more do you need to know? *You're* the private detective—go track him down. If I have to do all the work, what am I paying you for?"

In the kitchen, Albert the ghoul stirred his pot, which probably hadn't been washed since the mystery stew from my previous visit, and ladled out two servings of a congealed oatmeal substance. When he placed the bowls under the heat lamp, the mounded contours looked disturbingly like brains.

Esther thumped the bowls down in front of me and Steve. "I've got to get back to my tables, so I can't stand around talking all day. Let me know as soon as you find anything." She fluttered her sharp feathers. "And pay your bill as soon as you can—I'm clocking out in a few minutes. My boyfriend's picking me up in his limo."

Even though we hadn't yet taken a bite of the food, Steve and I both fished in our wallets for the appropriate amount of cash, adding a 20 percent tip because we knew what was good for us.

When we finally got around to talking about his case, Steve seemed dejected. "So, no progress? Has Ms. Deyer found a precedent that can help me?"

"She's got an interesting idea," I said. Even while auditing the records of the Spare Parts Emporium, Robin had come up with an approach that might help resolve my friend's problem. I slurped my coffee and played with my oatmeal. "Let me try to explain. When you listed your ex-wife as beneficiary for the insurance policy, I know you intended the money to go to your underage son. Even if Rova was aware of your wishes, since it wasn't explicitly written in the will or in the insurance policy, there's no way to prove your intent. Legally, Rova could do whatever she liked with the money. Now, however, you yourself can make your postmortem instructions perfectly clear. You'll sign an affidavit that clarifies your intentions for the money."

"And then Rova has to use the money for Jordan's benefit?" he asked. "It's that easy?"

I dared to take a bite of oatmeal. "You know it's not going to be that easy."

Steve twisted his green trucker cap around. "I didn't think so."

"Even if we can clear up the disposition of the money, there isn't actually any money left. Your ex-wife invested it all in the Parlour (BNF). Robin will request an audit of the beauty salon to see if there's any way to reclaim the liquid assets, but I wouldn't hold out hope. My guess is that the Parlour isn't making much money."

"I know, I've seen Rova's haircuts," Steve said miserably. "But if all that money is gone, how am I going to take care of my son? If the Parlour goes out of business, then Rova won't be able to support him either."

I wished I had something better to tell him. Don Tuthery was going to fight tooth and nail to wring every penny out of Steve, but Robin would fight with just as many teeth and just as many nails to protect her client. Neither outcome would help the young boy, however.

Before I could answer, Esther let out a raucous shriek and rushed toward the front door. A thin, bearded wizard with a sky-blue robe and pointed hat sauntered into the diner. He held a crooked staff and looked as if he had just come from a Gandalf impersonators' convention. He froze as the harpy hurtled toward him.

"You've got a *lot* of nerve—how dare you come back here!" She whipped out the bad-luck charm on its chain and dangled it in front of his face. "You take this back—lift the curse *now,* or I'll never serve you coffee again!"

The wizard spun about and fled into the street, his robes flapping, his pointy hat flying off his head (fortunately he had tied it with a string under his bearded chin, so it simply bounced on his shoulders as he ran). Everyone in the diner watched the show.

Esther remained in the doorway, her feathers bristling, bird-bright eyes flicking back and forth in search of prey. Finally, needing to damage *something,* she shredded the flyer for the Worldwide Horror Convention. The diner patrons hunched down in their booths, intent on their breakfasts and avoiding her gaze. The werewolf customer, who still had an empty cup of coffee, set his mug down and drank from his water glass instead.

When Esther stormed over, I said, "That was Glenn the wizard, I take it?"

"Yes, that was him! Why did you just sit here? Why didn't you go demand satisfaction for your client?"

"You chased him away before I had the chance."

She flared up. "Now you're blaming me?"

"It might have been a good opportunity to get his name and phone number."

"Go after him!" She jabbed one of her feathered arms toward the door, but by now the wizard had fled up the street and disappeared around a corner. "Run!"

"We're called the *walking* dead, not the sprinting dead."

"I don't like the tone of your voice, Chambeaux."

198 / Kevin J. Anderson

A long black limousine pulled up outside the diner, and Esther's mood changed like a ricocheting pinball. "Oh, he's here!" She flung off her apron, ran to the time clock, and punched out. "I'm done with my shift, Albert. Handle the orders yourself."

There were no other waitresses, and I didn't think the lethargic ghoul was in any condition to take care of himself, much less a diner full of customers.

The limo driver was a small hunchbacked lab assistant who had been downsized from a research lab and now worked as a hired driver. He wore a specially fitted tux and a black cap, but he was so short he sank down in the seat and had to reach up to grab the steering wheel. He could barely see over the dashboard.

The back door of the limo opened to reveal a very large man inside, with rolls of discolored flesh, bloated cheeks, and sunken eyes. He squirmed, as if he couldn't find a comfortable position.

As Esther flounced to the diner door, she looked momentarily cheerful. I said in amazement, "*Tony Cralo* is your boyfriend?"

"Something wrong with that?"

"No . . . just surprised, that's all," I said.

"He's fat and disgusting, he outgasses constantly, and he treats me like shit. He's just after a piece of tail feathers. But he's rich, so I'm willing to overlook his flaws."

"I remember true love," Steve said with a sigh. "It doesn't last."

Esther turned to him. "I know that, and I intend to milk this relationship for everything I can in the meantime."

She left the diner and bounded into the backseat of the limo. Tony Cralo opened his pudgy zombie arms to embrace her. She was chirpy and cheerful for a few moments, then started to rail at him for being late as the limo door closed. The hunchbacked driver pulled away.

With Esther gone, everyone in the diner heaved a sigh of relief and began to enjoy their meals. Steve had hardly touched his. He swung off the stool. "Gotta go. A delivery to make, a shipment of eggs to some Hairball werewolf—specially fertilized under the full moon or something. For his cockatrice coops."

"Rusty?" I asked. "Mind if I ride along? He's a client of mine."

"Sure, buddy. Always happy to have someone riding shotgun."

I left my oatmeal mostly untouched as well. We went out to Steve's truck.

CHAPTER 34

As I rode in the passenger seat of Steve's delivery truck, he made conversation about how he drove a big eighteen-wheeler when he was still alive. "Used to make long hauls from Cincinnati to Livingston, Montana, and all points in between. I enjoyed the big rig—spacious and powerful. It's like sitting in a house while the rest of the world rolls by." When he grinned at me, I noticed his teeth were still in good condition. "All that driving gives you time to think, listen to music, listen to an audiobook, or just watch the scenery, although the interstate freeways aren't usually scenic routes. They're Mileage Disposal Units, designed for getting rid of miles between one place and another. Drop off a load, pick up a new one, then head back."

He drove around the outskirts of the Quarter, taking backstreet routes even I had never seen before. As a delivery truck driver, he had to know the town inside and out. On his route, many of the special deliveries went to unmarked doors and dark alleys, dungeon entertainment centers, and any number of oddball shops. Steve just looked at the clipboard and address, and he did his job.

"When you're driving across Nebraska with the cruise control on, you spend your time thinking, and it's family you think about," Steve continued. "While I was still married to Rova, I'd worry about how I needed to be a better husband, spend more time at home, create a good family environment. I always put a photo of Rova and Jordan right there on the dashboard. I remember one time, in a horrific blizzard in the middle of North Dakota, the winds were howling and I couldn't see a thing. The only way I got through that was by staring and staring at that photo while I drove." Steve kept one hand on the steering wheel while punctuating his story with the other.

"If the blizzard was so bad, shouldn't you have been looking at the road?"

"Nah." He gave a dismissive wave. "Out there, the interstate's perfectly straight."

We arrived at Rusty's house with the shipment of eggs. His neighbor across the street was having a forlorn-looking garage sale, but there weren't many customers. I spotted some children's clothing, a used chemistry set, a stuffed moose head (no home should be without one), embalming supplies and equipment, and a complete set of hazmat suits in a range of sizes to fit the entire family.

A dozen cars were haphazardly parked in front of Rusty's house, three motorcycles, even a go-kart. Full-furred werewolves milled about in the front yard, going in and out through the front door. Loud music pounded from inside the house. A beer keg sat in a large tub filled with ice; the werewolves filled red plastic cups with beer from the tap.

"Need help carrying the eggs in?" I asked Steve. "I'll be your wingman."

We each took a crate of eggs from the back of the truck and carried it toward the door. The Hairballs didn't pay much attention to us.

"Got a delivery for someone named Rusty!" Steve announced.

At the kitchen table, two werewolves strained and growled in an arm-wrestling match. In a big pot on the stove, bratwursts were boiling in beer. Steve and I set the eggs on the counter. I didn't see Rusty, but I heard cheers and wolf whistles from the living room. Steve took his delivery receipt and clipboard and followed me down the hall.

The coffee table had been pushed aside, and folding chairs were set up in a circle. In the middle of the room, a werewolf bitch swayed and danced, dressed in little more than a filmy negligee. I recognized Cinnamon, one of the ladies from the Full Moon Brothel. Werewolf men hunched on the edges of the folding chairs, howling, barking, their eyes riveted as Cinnamon did a slow striptease. Furguson sat among them, intent on the stripper, but squirming on the chair, as if he hadn't taken his werewolf Ritalin that day.

Near him, I saw scalped-but-recovering Rusty sitting in his own lounge chair. He wore a red bandanna wrapped around his damaged head and didn't seem interested in Cinnamon's performance. (More evidence of the impotence tattoo.)

Furguson's foot bumped a cup and spilled beer on the carpet, much to his embarrassment. Rusty groaned. "Furguson, watch what you're doing! Now I have to get Larry to clean that up! *Larry*—janitorial duties! Now!"

Larry, the former werewolf bodyguard, slinked into the room, carrying a bucket and some napkins. "Sure thing, Rusty. I'll clean it right up." He had a trash sack and had obviously been emptying wastebaskets. "Thanks for letting me come to the kegger. It's been a long time. I hope you'll invite me again and not hold my past against me."

"Depends on how useful you are," Rusty said.

Cinnamon kept dancing. When she saw me, she gave me a wink and a long, lascivious curl of her tongue around her muz-

zle. I had helped the brothel on another case, but she was working, and I didn't want to distract her. Steve was fascinated by
the dance.

Noticing us, Rusty levered himself out of the chair and came
over. "Mister Shamble, got any proof yet? Or do we proceed
with the war as planned?" He sounded as if he preferred the latter alternative.

"Not just yet." I gestured back toward Cinnamon. "Don't
let me interrupt you watching the striptease."

Rusty grumbled. "No interest whatsoever. Doesn't do me
any damn good."

"Sorry about that. I heard about the tattoo."

When Larry finished dabbing up the spilled beer with a wad
of napkins, Rusty lashed out at him. "Don't forget to take out
the kitchen trash—and the toilets could use scrubbing. See if
anybody's barfed in them yet."

When Larry bristled at the lowly task, I remembered how
fearsome he had once been—a werewolf hit man who could
have torn me limb from limb. Now he seemed like a whipped
cur. Seeing his reluctance, Rusty snorted, "If you can kiss Harvey Jekyll's ass, you can clean some damn toilets."

Larry controlled himself and went off to do his work.

Rusty led us into the hall, where it was less crowded, since
everyone else wanted to watch Cinnamon. He flexed his heavily furred left bicep and nudged the hairs aside so I could see
the intricate webwork of his tattoo. The impressive design
showed a fanged dragon curled around a fortress tower with
flames all around, lightning bolts striking.

"It does look important," I said.

"Not funny, Mister Shamble. I should have killed Antoine
Stickler and burned down the Voodoo Tattoo parlor."

I thought of Antoine's special dolls that catered to specific
customers and/or their enemies. If they had all gone up in
smoke . . . "That could have had some bad consequences."

"I knew where to place the blame," Rusty said. "Stupid Jamaican vampire . . . He's just too mellow for his own good, said he was sorry. To make up for it, he did gang tattoos for every single Hairball, no charge. Soon as the Monthlies knew we were getting gang tats, then they had to get their own, but at least Stickler charged the Monthlies for theirs. Seems he's the only one who came out ahead through all this."

Werewolves came in and out of the backyard smoking cigarettes. On the porch, someone had fired up a charcoal grill, and another werewolf took the pot of bratwursts outside to begin cooking them for lunch.

Steve waved his clipboard. "Need a signature here, sir, then we'll be on our way. I delivered the eggs you wanted."

"And they're all fertilized?" Rusty asked. "Laid by chickens under the light of a full moon?"

Steve shrugged. "That's what the manifest says. Not like I was there for the actual egg drop. I'm just the truck driver."

"You vouch for this guy, Mister Shamble?" Rusty asked me.

I also shrugged. "I don't know a thing about the eggs, but I can tell you Steve is a decent, hardworking man. He wouldn't be trying to cheat you."

"Good enough for me." Before he could sign the clipboard, though, an outcry came from the back, a squawking and shrieking racket from the cockatrice coops, then another loud commotion, followed by shouts.

Rusty was already moving toward the back door. "You stay away from them dark coops if you know what's good for you!" He bolted into the yard, letting the screen door slam behind him. Most of the werewolves headed out of the living room to see what was happening in back. Even with the diminished audience, Cinnamon continued her dance, flailing her colorful scarves, using her claws to shred them and then throwing the strands in the air.

Through the kitchen window, Steve and I watched the burly

werewolves throw a blanket around a man-sized object—something so heavy it required three of them to lift. The werewolf by the grill turned the bratwursts, not at all disturbed.

Rusty came back into the house, so angry his fur bristled, and I suggested it might be best if we left quickly, but Steve was diligent. "I still need my signature—the boss insists."

I stopped Rusty before he could go into full warpath mode. "What happened? Anything I can help with?"

"We take care of our own—and we got some violence to prepare. This is our full rumble planning meeting."

"I thought it was a kegger."

"We do our best planning when we get good and drunk." Behind Rusty, through the kitchen window, I watched werewolves carry the heavy man-sized object over to the garage. "Better get out of here, Mister Shamble. Nothing you need to see."

Rusty signed Steve's clipboard, and we headed out the front door, leaving the Hairballs to their strategy session against the Monthlies.

Before we drove off, Steve stopped to peruse the items in the garage sale. A tear came to his eye when he found a baseball mitt and a softball, which he bought for five dollars. "Someday, I'm going to give these to Jordan."

CHAPTER 35

The following day I stopped by the Parlour (BNF), even though I had no appointment; I didn't intend to have services rendered anyway. Since Rova Halsted knew who I was now, I doubted I'd receive a friendly reception.

I looked presentable, for the most part. Sheyenne had gotten my jacket dry-cleaned, and most of the bloodstains from the hospital were gone. The dry cleaner wanted to repair the bullet holes, or at least replace the black thread with less-visible tan stitches, but Sheyenne insisted that I liked the jacket exactly the way it was. (And she was right.)

I was the only customer in the Parlour. Harriet sat in one of the beautician's chairs covered with a smock, her tresses spread out like a lion's mane. Foil strips had been wrapped around some of her locks. Her hair was wet and dark, smeared with something that was either conditioner or the remnants of an oil slick. A kitchen timer ticked at her side. Rova bent over her, using small scissors to trim the hair on the backs of Harriet's hands.

Seeing me, the bearded lady lifted one hand to wave. Rova glanced up and turned frosty. "What are you doing here?"

Harriet frowned. "Rova, please stop being rude! Remember what I told you about customer service."

"He's not a customer. He's working with my ex."

"Among other things," I said. "I'm also working with Harriet's husband on an unrelated matter."

"We don't take sides here," Harriet said. "Archibald doesn't need a friendly manner on the job because his customers are already dead, but *ours* are alive, or at least ambulatory. If we want to grow this business, we need to treat everyone well." Harriet lifted her other hand, nudging Rova to get back to work. She looked at me, batting eyelashes the size of palm fronds. "We had a slow morning, Mister Chambeaux, so that's why I'm in the chair. Rova wanted to practice her art, since customers have complained."

"They don't know what they want," Rova said.

"The customer is always right," Harriet chided again, then spoke to me. "I'm demonstrating faith in my business partner. She'll give me a facial—a facial *trim*—and try out new techniques on my hair. Besides, this way we can do the perming and shampooing and conditioning without clogging my drains at home. Archibald gets testy when I mess up his workshop, even though it's technically part of our bedroom and bath."

"The Emporium promised I would have the . . . materials he requested by the end of the day," I said. "I'll deliver them personally."

"Good! He's busy planning for the body-building competition, but he is obsessed with that new hair-restoration formula. He thinks I care that he's bald! Sweet, precious man. At least he doesn't have to worry about hair all the time. Ah, sometimes that would make life so much easier. But Archibald thinks his new tonic will make us all rich, and there's no talking sense into him. He's a man in a workshop, one project after another after another . . . never finishes one thing before he moves on to something else."

Rova used a ceramic flat iron on a large swatch of Harriet's hair, flattening all semblance of curls. The locks did not look so much styled as *crushed*.

I decided it was time to be up front. "I actually hoped I could have a word with Ms. Halsted."

After seeing how much Steve cared for his son and what an all-around good man he was, I hoped—with foolish optimism, I know—that I could crack the ice. Regardless of how hard Robin fought for her client, I did not expect Don Tuthery to back down. Lawyers in divorce and child-custody cases were not known for easing tensions or finding resolutions that satisfied all parties. With Steve and Rova at such an impasse, by the time the mess was finished, Jordan might be in college, scarred from growing up under such bitter circumstances. It didn't matter who won.

Rova's nostrils flared, and not from the fumes of the hair chemicals. "You'd better leave, Mister Chambeaux. My lawyer gave me strict instructions that I'm not to have any direct contact with Steve's attorney."

"I'm not the attorney. I'm a private detective and a friend of Steve's."

"How are you a friend of Steve's? He didn't know any private detectives."

"We came out of the grave on the same night. That sort of thing creates a special bond. He didn't ask me to talk with you. I'm here on my own initiative, to ask if we can find some way out of this without racking up more legal bills and making everyone more miserable."

"More miserable? My ex is a zombie, and he wants to play with my child! How sick is that?"

"He's just a father trying to make up for the time he should have spent with his son. Besides, he hasn't decomposed very much. Look at me—I'm a zombie, too. I'm well-preserved, I interact well with others."

Rova sounded disgusted. "It's not *normal!*"

"Do you think Jordan would rather have no father at all?"

"This is just Steve's way of trying to get back together. He never could accept the fact that I left him."

I shook my head. "I'm fairly sure getting back together is the last thing on his mind."

Rova sniffed. "I have no intention of letting my ex-husband see Jordan. He owes me child support. The divorce decree was perfectly clear in that."

The thing that seemed perfectly clear was that Rova didn't want to work out an equitable arrangement. Even if Steve did pay child support, she would still fight visitation rights. The problem wasn't about Steve being a zombie; it was her intention to hurt him by keeping him away from his son.

Talking with me made Rova more and more upset while she snipped off hunk after hunk of Harriet's hair, first trimming the back of her hand, then working her way up the arm. She grabbed a handful of thick locks covered with foil sheets and was about to cut them off when Harriet grabbed her hand.

"I don't need that much of a trim, Rova dear. You're letting your emotions get the best of you. I realize that not everyone's marriage can be as perfect as mine and Archibald's, but you must let the calm flow through you. The *haircut* is what matters. Feel the Zen of styling."

Rova breathed heavily, set the scissors down, and calmed herself.

"You'd better go, Mister Chambeaux," Harriet said in a stern maternal voice. "Rova needs to meditate and focus her energy before I let her work on my hair again."

"That is a good idea—on so many levels," I said.

Disappointed that I had accomplished nothing with my unofficial visit, I left the Parlour (BNF) and decided to focus on other cases. I wanted to make at least one client happy—even if it was only Esther the harpy.

CHAPTER 36

Without much trouble, I tracked down the identity and address of the Gandalf look-alike named Glenn. He ran a little shop next to a bakery, with a signboard that offered Wizard Services, rather vaguely defined as *Palm reading, sports predictions, life coaching, general tutoring, and other services as requested.*

When I entered his shop, Glenn sat at a small table playing solitaire and losing. His pointed hat sat on a shelf behind him, and his gray hair was matted into an odd shape. His long beard was thrown over his left shoulder, out of the way, so he could shuffle and deal his cards without restraint. I noticed he had several playing cards tucked up the sleeve, but he still managed to lose the game.

Assuming I was a potential customer, Glenn greeted me with great enthusiasm. He rose to his feet, grabbed his wide-brimmed hat, and placed it back on his head as part of his costume. "Welcome, friend! It's a magical world outside, but even more magical in here. Any problem you have can be solved through arcane means. I specialize in trinkets."

"Matter of fact, I'm here to inquire about a trinket." I fished out one of my Chambeaux & Deyer business cards. "I'm here on a case."

"Oh, a professional investigator?" His voice was thin and nasal, and rose a note at the end of each sentence in sudden wonderment, as if he preferred to use question marks rather than periods. His expression fell. "So, not a paying customer, then?"

"Just professional courtesy. But I do referrals."

"In that case, Mister Chambeaux..." Glenn the wizard produced one of his own business cards with a flourish, as if by magic (though I saw him pluck it from his sleeve). An ace of spades also fell onto the table.

After the wizard put a pot of tea on a hot plate, he sat on the other side of the table and listened to me in earnest. "You must have many exciting cases. Is this about a murder, a bank robbery? Perhaps a kidnapping or blackmail!"

"Not all of my cases are exciting." I thought of suggesting he pick up a copy of *Death Warmed Over,* but that would give him a distorted picture of my life as a zombie PI. Besides, it was bad form to try selling the book to someone my client wanted to sue for everything he was worth. I added, "We're both customers at the Ghoul's Diner."

The wizard perked up. "Oh, right—I've seen you there." His expression became troubled again. "Is the health department trying to shut down the place finally? Did a customer die from poisoning?"

"My client is actually Esther, the waitress...."

He recoiled in horror. "Oh, I'm terribly sorry for you! Esther Pester, we call her—worst waitress in the world and the most unpleasant creature in the Unnatural Quarter. I don't understand why Albert doesn't get better help." The wizard raised his eyebrows. "Is Pester in some kind of trouble...I hope?"

"Actually, Glenn, you're the one who's in trouble. Esther hired us because you left her a bad-luck charm as a tip, and now her life is miserable because of it."

Glenn smiled. "Her life is miserable? How could she tell the difference?"

I tried to talk to him, man-to-man. "Look, Glenn, I don't have to tell you she can be one vindictive harpy. Once Esther gets her tail feathers in a knot, she doesn't let things go. Our research proves that the charm is indeed a bad-luck charm."

"So I left her a tip," Glenn said with a shrug. "Sure, it was a bad-luck charm, one of my most popular models. I've been working with the tattoo artist over at Voodoo Tattoo. We plan to sell his special dolls and my bad-luck charms together as a set—for when you really want to give your enemies a double whammy."

I kept my voice cold and hard. "Knowingly leaving my client a dangerous object can be considered intentional infliction of emotional distress. She'll sue you for damages, claim pain and suffering."

"And what about *my* pain and suffering for having to endure her service at the diner?" Glenn asked. "What about her customers? Have *you* ever been satisfied with her service? Could you swear to that in court?"

"Uh, no."

"Maybe I'll call you as a character witness."

"Let's not go there. If you lift the curse, maybe I could convince her to drop the suit."

Glenn looked stubborn and angry. "If Esther Pester testifies in court, don't you think any judge or jury would want to curse her themselves?"

"She isn't required to testify, Glenn." In fact, I was certain that Robin wouldn't let such an awful plaintiff speak a word in the jury's earshot.

Glenn's shoulders slumped. "All right, so I was annoyed.

She messed up my order. She spilled coffee on my blue robes so I had to get them cleaned. She charged me for a dessert that she never served . . . and her voice just plain gives me a headache. Maybe I gave her a bad-luck charm, but the curse only works on people who *accept* the gift. She's as much at fault for being so greedy. She can't throw the charm away, it'll just reappear."

"She's already tried that. Isn't there some way you can cancel the curse?"

"No, the curse is nonrefundable, with the warranty attached to the recipient. But there is one thing. . . ." The wizard looked as if he intended to charge me for the solution—and I might have been willing to pay the price, just to be rid of Esther as a client—but Glenn relented and said, "Her bad luck will go away if she just gives it to another person. But I wouldn't expect a selfish soul like Esther to understand the concept of generosity."

"That's it? She can just hand it to someone?"

"They have to *accept* it."

The teakettle began to whistle on the hot plate, but I didn't plan to stay for a cup. Besides, I'm more of a coffee drinker. "Thank you, Glenn. If this all works out, I won't need to see you again."

"Don't forget about the professional referrals," he said, then shuffled his cards, ready to play another game of solitaire.

"I'll have my administrator put you on our contacts list."

As I headed out the door, Glenn called after me. "You know she deserves it, Mister Chambeaux. Esther Pester is your client, and you have to do what you have to do, but is it absolutely necessary to tell her the solution . . . right away?"

I didn't have plans to see Esther in the immediate future. "I suppose I could hold off for a while."

CHAPTER 37

Showing tremendous faith (or foolish optimism) in Robin and Sheyenne's abilities to sort swiftly through tons of loose papers, McGoo arrived that afternoon, grinning. "Found any discrepancies in the Cralo paperwork yet?"

I thought he was being a tad unrealistic. "McGoo, you brought them a dump truck filled with receipts and files!"

Now he looked sheepish. "I'm just anxious for answers. That vampire transplant heart might be only the tip of the iceberg. Vampire organs harvested from a body, werewolf scalps taken. Could be a really big case."

"Were you able to prove that the transplant heart came from Ben Willard?"

"No," McGoo said. "As obsessed as that administrator was with his paperwork, he didn't keep very good records. Apparently, that vampire heart fell off a truck."

"One of Tony Cralo's trucks?" I asked.

Sheyenne flitted in from the conference room, carrying several folders. "Of course we found something—and it's as fishy as a swamp creature's underwear."

Robin was more professional in her metaphors as she followed Sheyenne. "The paperwork does give us the big picture, and a lot of the pieces just don't fit together properly. The Emporium's admin department did such a good job of doctoring the details that this can't be explained as accidental bookkeeping errors." She looked exhausted but relieved, and didn't even seem to resent McGoo for putting her through so much work. "After collating the names of the donors, the dates of donations, and the body parts obtained, we had to break down the Emporium's inventory code system in order to determine who gave what and when."

Sheyenne held up a stack of folders in her spectral hands. "I visited the Emporium myself and did some personal shopping. I flitted up and down the aisles and kept track of the SKUs, then I backtracked them and extracted the specifics from these records."

"That sounds great!" McGoo grinned. "Now, can we do it one more time in English?"

Sheyenne opened the folders and spread out the papers to show us highlighted code numbers and her own sheet of translations. Robin pointed to names on the donation forms, then the code numbers from the warehouse shelves. "The discrepancies raise obvious questions. For instance, according to these records, the same person donated more than two arms or legs. And although it's not impossible in the Quarter for someone to have more than two eyes, this particular person gave up *six*, and then stopped by the following week to donate not one liver, but two."

"As a former med student," Sheyenne said, "that man is a specimen I would have liked to see in the lab."

"Definitely fishy," McGoo said. "I'd say that's enough for a warrant to do further digging."

Robin said, "I can provide a summary of the current state of body-snatching laws." She picked up several sheets of paper. "I doubt these donors exist at all—they're probably dummy names. Their body-parts inventory database manager was too lazy to create as many fake donors as they needed."

Sheyenne smiled at McGoo. "So, that means we can submit an invoice to the police department for payment as consultants, right?"

Awkwardly changing the subject, McGoo said, "Hey, here's one I just heard—what has a cat's head, a dog's tail, and brains all over its face?" He looked around, hoping someone might venture a guess, but we all refused. "A zombie in a pet store!"

After a punch line like that, I knew I had to leave. "I'm going to the Spare Parts Emporium now. I've got business of my own there."

McGoo sounded surprised. "What kind of business?"

"I need to pick up a new brain."

He scowled. "Come on, the joke wasn't *that* bad."

"It's not for me, it's for a friend."

"Sure it is." McGoo gave a sage nod. "They always are."

On the way to Cralo's Emporium, I passed the Voodoo Tattoo parlor. Antoine Stickler was alone in the shop, sitting at a worktable and playing with arms, legs, and heads—not life-sized ones, just small doll pieces. He was sewing clothes that might have belonged on Ken dolls, but his figures had thick tufts of hair covering their exposed skin and fingernails painted black. Another set of dolls, already finished, looked like humans; two were covered with carefully reproduced tattoos. One had a goatee, one had a thick DA hairstyle. As soon as I recognized the Scratch and Sniff action figures, I figured the others must represent Monthly werewolves as well.

Antoine looked up. "Change your mind about getting yourself a tattoo? I can liven up the pallor."

"My girlfriend and I are still deciding." Sheyenne could always get a design inked onto the lifelike inflatable doll she sometimes inhabited for me. And for her, I'd even get a Cupid tattoo (fortunately, she hadn't asked me to do that).

Antoine grinned. "So right, you've got to keep that girl of yours happy. I can always do couples tattoos. *His and Hers Forever,* either with permanent ink or temporary tats, whichever you prefer. A lot of guys come in here asking for *Forever,* but then they slip me fifty bucks to make it washable."

"The couples tattoo thing would be a problem, since my girlfriend's a ghost."

"Hmm. Let me think on it a bit," Antoine said as he continued to work on his effigy dolls. "If I figure that out, it could be a new market in the Quarter."

"Are you making an entire doll series of Monthlies and Hairballs?" I said. "A collector's set?"

"Commissioned work." Antoine tossed his dreadlocks and bent back to his project. "The Monthlies wanted voodoo dolls of every Hairball, and as soon as the Hairballs found out about it, they got angry and offered to buy 'em back, at twice the price. At the same time, they commissioned voodoo dolls of every Monthly."

"Sounds like a booming business. And you're getting work from both sides."

"Yeah, but all this negativity bothers me. I agreed to make the dolls only on the condition that they stay *here* for safekeeping. I'll put them on display as samples of my work. A voodoo portfolio." He looked up at me. "But those two gangs don't know I put *these* around all the dolls." Antoine picked up a handful of brownish-purple pods. "Balm of Gilead buds. 'Hoodoo aspirin,' white folk call it. Soothes the pain of arguments and quarrels, brings peace to the home."

"Does it work?"

"Can't hurt."

Maybe Esther the harpy would be interested in using some of that on Glenn's bad-luck charm. "I was at Rusty's house yesterday," I said. "He said that you gave all the Hairballs their gang tattoos for free."

"Least I could do after the *important-impotent* mix-up. I also did gang tats for the Monthlies—not the kind with magic healing, though, like Scratch and Sniff have. Too difficult— cost-prohibitive, you know. At least I got 'em all marked, just in case."

"Just in case what?"

Antoine blinked up at me. "In case the balm of Gilead doesn't work."

I said, "They're dead set on having this gang rumble during the full moon as a vendetta, even though nobody proved it was Monthlies doing the scalpings."

Antoine seemed maddeningly calm. "It'll work out."

I got down to the real reason I had stopped by. "A vampire was murdered a couple of days ago. He was handcuffed to a bed and all of his organs removed. I think he was a customer of yours."

"I get quite a few vamps—repeat customers." A troubled look crossed his face. "Not many get murdered, though."

"This one was named Ben Willard. He went out clubbing a lot."

"Oh, Mister Willard! Came in every week to get fresh tats. Always planned a big Friday night. Bad mojo, though . . . he liked it rough. Not surprised to hear he was killed."

"You saw this coming?"

"Vamps have an old saying: 'You go out in the sunlight, you're going to get burned.' A lot of vamps, especially the newly turned ones, have more testosterone than they have bloodlust. They get disappointed in sex because normal human partners are far too wimpy. So they want me to make them look edgy and tough to help them pick up some big bad creature that's just as horny as they are." Antoine went to his book, flipped to the entry for the next Friday, and drew a line through Ben

Willard's standing appointment. "You change your mind about a tat of your own, I got an opening now."

"I'll think about it," I repeated.

Antoine finished his dolls, tucking a balm of Gilead bud into the folds of their clothes, adding a dab of paint to the faces. The likenesses were really quite remarkable. He smiled at his handiwork. "Turn that frown upside down, Mister Chambeaux," he chided. "Don't worry, be happy."

CHAPTER 38

Back at the Spare Parts Emporium, I made my way to Xandy Huff's office in the rear of the cavernous warehouse; I was determined to get the right parts for Dr. Victor this time.

If need be, I could spoil the floor manager's day by telling him we'd found interesting discrepancies in the mountains of Cralo paperwork. I was sure Mr. Huff had put in a great deal of effort gathering and copying all that information, boxing it up in such a reverently disorganized fashion, never expecting anyone to make sense out of the storm of numbers and forms.

When I came in, Huff was at his desk eating a foul-smelling liverwurst sandwich. I've been inside dank crypts, waded through sewers beneath the Quarter, smelled the stench of many a rotting corpse, even sat in a Jacuzzi with an outgassing fat zombie. But the smell or taste of liverwurst turns my stomach.

Huff wiped his mouth with a napkin, set the sandwich aside. "I knew you'd come. I suppose you're getting impatient for your brain."

"My client certainly is. And when my clients are impatient, I'm impatient."

Huff opened the bottom drawer of his desk and removed a large box, gift-wrapped in black paper and tied with a silver ribbon. "Mister Cralo told me to give you this with his highest regards. It's a fresh brain, Grade A, just came in this morning. I'm sure your client will be satisfied." He nodded toward the box. "Do you want to inspect it? We can have Customer Service rewrap it for you, if you like."

"I wouldn't know the difference between a good brain and a bad one," I said.

"I thought zombies were connoisseurs."

"Not me. I'm just a regular guy. Cheeseburgers and fries. Never acquired a taste for brains. But the spleen you sent over yesterday was damaged in shipping. I'll need another one of those as well."

The manager sighed, controlled an angry outburst by doing some sort of silent meditation, or just cursing under his breath, and he wrote out a slip for a complimentary spleen, which he signed. "So, that completes our business together? I don't need to see you again?"

"Not unless I come back to do some shopping," I said.

Huff looked relieved. "I'll let Mister Cralo know you're satisfied." I realized that, as floor manager, he might suffer extreme repercussions himself if customers lodged too many complaints.

Carrying the gift-wrapped brain in a box, I went to the front counter, exchanged the coupon for a new spleen, and walked out of the Emporium with my prizes in hand. I kept a close eye on the rest of the inventory, particularly noticing unmarked boxes on the high shelves.

As I walked out into the sloppy parking lot, I wondered who had donated this particular brain and why he or she had decided it was no longer a useful organ. Now that Sheyenne and Robin had uncovered so much suspicious paperwork, I found myself questioning the provenance of *all* these items for sale, down to the amputated little-piggy toes and vermiform appendices in the bargain bins.

But Archibald Victor didn't want me to make his case public, and since McGoo worked with the coroner, I was honor bound to keep my client's complaint off the books. A mad scientist shouldn't need to be ashamed about his laboratory activities, but Archibald had not yet come out of the closet. . . .

I made my way over to the trailer park with spleen and brain in hand. I found the Victors' address and rapped on the door. Since it was only midafternoon, Harriet should still be at the Parlour (BNF), preparing unnaturals for a night on the town (or, more likely, fixing dissatisfied clients who had been afflicted with Rova's haircuts).

The pallid coroner yanked open the door. He looked flustered in his lab coat; goggles hung at his throat, and black neoprene gloves limited his dexterity as he fumbled to adjust his toupee. "Yes, what is it?" Then he recognized me. "Mister Chambeaux! Of course, you said you were coming."

"I have a delivery for you, Dr. Victor." I held out the giftwrapped box and the packaged spleen. "From Tony Cralo himself, along with his full apology. His floor manager assured me this is their best brain, and he wanted you to be satisfied."

Archibald was so excited he hopped on both feet as he let me inside the small trailer. Harriet had set out two bubbling pots of potpourri in the tiny kitchen, but the rest of the trailer reeked of odd chemical mixtures. In his home lab/workshop, Archibald had a setup of bubbling chemicals, liquid-filled flasks, electrical arcs that shocked downward from metal probes.

At the far end of the trailer, on a model-building table, I saw the hulking form of one of the bodies he was assembling piece by piece. Spools of suture thread, safety pins, and duct tape were strewn haphazardly around the model, but the coroner didn't seem to be working on it at all. He was far more interested in his chemistry experiments on the bathroom countertop. I remembered Harriet talking about how he obsessed on his numerous hobbies, like any man with a workbench.

Archibald yanked off his thick black gloves and unwrapped the spleen first, letting out a sigh of satisfaction. "Finally! This organ will do just fine."

As he started to undo the silver ribbon on the gift-wrapped brain, I wandered farther into the room to look at his bubbling experiments. "What are you working on, Dr. Victor? Is it the super hair-tonic project?"

With a look of horror, he whirled. "Please don't touch anything! In fact, I'd rather you not look at all. This is a very important bit of research, and it could be worth millions."

"I don't know anything about chemistry," I said, "or about hair tonics."

"Harriet shouldn't have mentioned my little project to you at all." Out of politeness, I turned from the mysterious and colorful liquids. "I was just about to achieve a breakthrough, but I'll have to set that aside for the body-building competition. There are a lot of entries in the male model category."

He removed the top of the gift box and lifted out a transparent container filled with clear preservation fluid and a many-contoured, fresh-looking brain that reminded me of an inexpertly swirled pile of spray whipped cream.

"So, we can wrap up the case, Dr. Victor?" I asked. "I want to extricate your name from any dealings with the Spare Parts Emporium. I happen to know there's an ongoing investigation, and you don't want to be involved in that."

He looked at me, and his toupee started to slip. "I'm not surprised. Many other clients have been affected by the Emporium's poor quality control." He held the brain jar up to the light, and his already-round eyes widened further in anger. I thought he was going to dash the jar on the floor. "Unbelievable! After all my complaints, they give me *this* as a replacement?" He set the brain down and scurried to a small rolltop desk, which he flung open, ransacked through the papers, and came out with his receipt. "Look here. My order form *plainly* indicates I require a *human* brain!" He jabbed his fingers at the jar. "Look at that one!"

I looked, but I didn't see what he saw.

In exasperation, Archibald said, "That's not a human brain, Mister Chambeaux! It's not even compatible with the spinal column! And how am I supposed to attach that medulla oblongata?" He looked at me, furious.

"I'll take your word for it," I said.

"It's a *troll* brain!" Indignant, Archibald thrust the brain jar back in the box, slammed the lid back on top, and shoved it into my hands. "This is absurd. Tell Mister Cralo that I am *not* satisfied, and I expect to receive the merchandise I purchased!" He shook his head. "I doubt it'll arrive in time now. Maybe I should just keep working with my chemistry set." He made a loud raspberry sound that reminded me of Tony Cralo's outgassing. "Troll brains! Who in the world needs a troll brain?"

"Trolls, I suppose," I said. I felt a sudden twinge of dread, suspecting that I might, after all, have some idea where they had gotten that brain.

Leaving him with the spleen, I took the box with me and left.

CHAPTER 39

I headed back to the Spare Parts Emporium, fuming and tired of being given the runaround. What was I supposed to do with yet another defective brain?

I suspected there was more going on here than the inept shelving of bodily organs. The plot had thickened, like gravy made with too much cornstarch. I vowed to find out where this inconvenient troll brain had come from, and I knew where to start asking.

It was a long walk on my dead feet back to the Spare Parts Emporium, but it was a beautiful gloomy afternoon in the Quarter. Gray skies grew dimmer as the sun set and dusk gathered on the streets. I walked past a Talbot & Knowles Blood Bar—a place filled with polished glass, flecked countertops, and checkerboard linoleum, with a vampire working behind the counter dressed as a soda jerk from an old fifties diner. I walked past an Ucky Dogs corner hot dog stand, which was attended by a lonely reptilian vendor; the dogs looked like something even a ghoul would refuse to eat.

From his stand on the corner, a soothsayer called to anyone

passing by. "I'll tell the future for five dollars!" He had a stainless-steel mixing bowl in front of him, in which he stirred various entrails, lifting them up so that they dripped and steamed. His lack of customers might have given some sense about the accuracy of his predictions, or maybe five dollars per fore-telling was higher than the going rate in the Quarter. He fon-dled the lobes of a liver and cried, "Beware! The end of the world is coming!"

I stopped. "What's the time frame on that?"

The soothsayer held up blood- and slime-covered hands, grinning at me. "No, it's just a general statement. Nothing im-minent."

"I won't worry about it, then." I tipped my fedora to him and walked on.

The soothsayer raised his voice and called out again, "The end of the world is coming! Limited-time offer to spend your five dollars and get a foretelling!" If the world was indeed com-ing to an end, I could think of better ways to spend five bucks.

For the Hairballs and Monthlies, though, Armageddon might indeed be imminent, since tomorrow the full moon would shine and the werewolf gangs would go to war—unless I could prove someone else was responsible for the scalpings.

Clasping the arm of Hirsute, Miranda Jekyll strolled along the boulevard, dressed to kill as always (or at least dressed to hunt). The two looked as if they were on their way to the opera. (The Phantom was holding a stage revival, casting himself in the starring role; he claimed it was for added veracity, but crit-ics had panned the show, since the *real* Phantom couldn't sing.) Next to Miranda, Hirsute was protective and confident, with the constant habit of tossing his thick head of hair as if to demonstrate that his locks were more desirable than any full-time werewolf's. I wondered if *he* had an alibi for the scalp-ings. . . .

Miranda and Hirsute paused to look in the window of a jewelry store, admiring the diamond earrings, necklaces, and cursed amulets. She snuggled close to her ultra-manly companion.

A battered Chevette drove up, coughing and puttering as if competing with Robin's Pro Bono Mobile for Worst Muffler Ever. When the Chevette slowed and the passenger window rolled down, I recognized Furguson riding shotgun as another full-furred werewolf drove, hunched over a tiny-diameter ghetto steering wheel made of welded chain links. Miranda and Hirsute turned to scowl at the noisy muffler.

Furguson yelled out the window, "Hey, Monthlies! Try some of our new cologne!"

He threw a liquid-filled balloon, which struck Miranda full in the chest. When it burst, brownish-gray goop splattered her. Miranda shrieked as the stain began to fume and smoke.

The Hairballs howled with laughter, and Furguson threw three more balloons in quick succession (but he was so clumsy he missed with two of them). The third balloon grazed Hirsute's chest, striking him only because he had such massive shoulders. The noxious substance covered both of them.

With a roar of rage, Hirsute bounded after the Chevette. Furguson yelped and banged on the car door, and the driver floored the accelerator. The Chevette strained to pick up speed, puttering along. Hirsute loped after it, ready to tear the back bumper off, but the car accelerated just enough to stay out of reach of his grasping hands.

I hurried over to Miranda, who pawed at the liquid staining her dress. The smell was overpowering, and I could guess what it was: Furguson had filled the balloons with cockatrice excrement. Miranda peeled off her stylish accessory scarf and dabbed at the slime. "How *dare* they? I can never forgive this!"

Hirsute bounded back to rescue her. "Are you all right, Miranda?" He looked as if he wanted to rip her dress off, just to prevent the stain from the monster feces from touching her skin, but he controlled himself.

"I'm stained and smelly. And very, very angry." She looked at me. "Mister Chambeaux, you are a witness. This is an outright assault!"

"I vow revenge upon them!" Hirsute said.

"I can identify the perpetrator if you want to file charges," I said.

Furguson's actions were just plain irrational and dangerous, actively trying to incite more violence against the Monthlies. He had already attacked Scratch and Sniff on their choppers. He was a loose cannon, or at least a loose BB gun. Was he *provoking* this rumble, just to get back in Rusty's good graces? Could he have stunned and scalped his own uncle—and the other Hairball victims—in order to rile up the gang? That didn't make sense . . . but then, Furguson didn't make a lot of sense.

When she turned to me, Miranda's face showed such fury that I could imagine what had turned Harvey Jekyll into such an evil man. "I appreciate the suggestion, sweetheart, but Hirsute and I will pursue a more immediate alternative." She actually gnashed her teeth. "We intended to stay out of this dispute—gang rivalry has nothing to do with us. But after this . . ." In disgust she touched the cockatrice poop stains on her dress. "We are joining the full moon rumble tomorrow night."

CHAPTER 40

These days, I seemed to be spending more time at Cralo's Spare Parts Emporium than at my own cluttered desk. After I splashed through parking-lot puddles the size of lunar craters—there was no avoiding them—and entered the giant warehouse, I made my way, yet again, to the floor manager's office.

Xandy Huff's office door was closed, though. He must have known I'd received the wrong brain, so he ducked out early to avoid a vengeful zombie. Probably a good idea. Maybe he thought I'd just eat it and destroy the evidence.

Not wanting to keep the unacceptable brain longer than necessary, I marched toward the Customer Service and Returns window, where a thin ghoul sat on a stool; he looked surprised that I would bother him. Apparently few customers dared to request returns from Tony Cralo, but I wasn't intimidated by their complex bureaucracy. I'd had enough of this place.

I clunked the gift-wrapped box on the countertop. "I've returned a brain twice now for replacement, and I was promised satisfaction. My client ordered a human brain, and this is a troll brain. It took two tries to get the lungs right, three tries to get the spleen, and this is our fourth attempt to get a proper brain."

The ghoul blinked heavy-lidded eyes at me. "Do you have a receipt?"

"This was an exchange. Your floor manager, Mister Huff, gave this to me."

"Anyone could say that," said the customer service ghoul. "How do I know you didn't buy this from some other body shop?"

"It's your gift wrapping. Look at the box."

"It's similar to our gift wrapping." He still sounded skeptical. "You say someone gave this to you as an exchange?"

"Mister Huff did, as authorized by Tony Cralo himself."

The ghoul fumbled with the lid, opened the box, and withdrew the container. "This is a troll brain. Different item number."

As with so many businesses, the least-motivated and least-intelligent individuals were assigned to work the customer service desk. "I *know* it's a troll brain, I already told you that. I need a *human* brain."

"Troll brains go for a higher price. You can have this one, no extra charge." The customer service ghoul reached up to grasp the dangling string of a window shade, intending to close the window.

"I don't want a troll brain. I need to return this one and get the item my client ordered."

"Ten percent restocking fee. And you need to file a formal return request."

"Already did that," I said.

"Then you have to report to the floor manager."

"Already did that, too."

"Then I'm afraid you'll have to speak to Mister Cralo in person. He's in charge of our one hundred percent customer satisfaction guarantee."

"Already did *that*," I said, raising my voice.

Still trying to think of some other way to deflect me, the flustered customer service ghoul finally took the brain jar and said, "Thank you for your feedback. I'll be sure the matter gets looked into promptly. We'll send a replacement brain to the original address. Please allow up to six weeks for delivery."

Before I could argue or even demand a return receipt, the ghoul pulled down the shade and closed the customer service window. He set out a sign with a flat plastic clock, saying WILL RETURN AT—Both of the clock hands had been snapped off.

I was ready to call in full police intervention and a company shutdown just to straighten out a simple order mix-up. On previous cases, I had faced a werewolf hit man, demon thugs, a vast genocide conspiracy against unnaturals, a Congressional act from a corrupt senator, a monster that had torn my arm off— not to mention the fact that I'd been murdered myself, as had my girlfriend. And I came through those cases all right. I was not about to be defeated by a maddening customer-satisfaction guarantee. This was a vendetta for me.

I lurched out of the Emporium and, with more determination than ever, set off toward the railroad bridge swathed in cool mist. The homeless monsters sat on the front porches of their cardboard boxes. The mangy ogre slouched on a pile of cinder blocks that had cracked under his weight; his knees were drawn up to his chest, and he stared forlornly at his hands. An exceptionally thin mummy and a tentacled demon roasted a scrawny goat carcass over a fire in a rusty barrel.

Inside the large coffin box he had claimed as his home, I found Larry lying on a deflated air mattress, his bare paws sticking out of the opening. He sat up, recognized me, and scrambled out. "Chambeaux! What are you doing here?"

"Following up on a lead," I said.

"Something to do with Rusty? Did you notice he's letting me hang out with him again? I'm going to go to the rumble tomorrow night, too! And if I do enough damage, he'll initiate me into the gang. I can even go to Voodoo Tattoo for my own Hairball tat. Things are looking up, Chambeaux."

"I'm checking on Tommy Underbridge," I said. "Have you seen him lately?"

Larry puffed his furry cheeks and blew out a long breath. "Nobody's seen that troll in two days. I think something bad happened to him." The werewolf brushed loose fur from his shirt. He appeared to be shedding. "Some of the others here think he just found a better bridge to live under, but Tommy loved it here, and he loved all of us." He gestured toward the fog-enshrouded superstructure. "What could be better than this?"

"I'm also afraid something bad might have happened to him."

"Think he was scalped, too?"

"Worse. I think he involuntarily donated his brain to commerce. But I can't prove it yet."

"It's those damned Monthlies," Larry growled. "They knew Tommy was helping us, and they must have gotten even with him. Oh, the fur is gonna fly tomorrow!"

"You know where the rumble is going to take place? I didn't get an invitation."

Larry's eyes narrowed. "They aren't handing out guest passes. It's a private matter—werewolf to werewolf."

"Rusty hired me to investigate it. I think I'd be welcome."

Larry looked calculating for a moment, then chuffed a laugh. "You know that old Smile Syndicate warehouse, the one flattened by an explosion a while back?"

"I'm familiar with it." I had been personally involved in the explosion itself, although Larry didn't need to know that.

"Warehouse district is the right place for a rumble, don't you think? Wide-open spaces, just the right part of town." He bobbed his muzzle up and down. "So better stay clear of there when the full moon rises tomorrow. Things are going to get ugly in the Quarter."

"It's always ugly in the Quarter," I said.

CHAPTER 41

The following morning Sheyenne brought me coffee at my desk and lingered. I enjoyed both her coffee and her lingering a great deal. "I miss you, Beaux. I'm starting to think you're married to your job."

"Not married to it, but it does seem to be a committed relationship." I looked up at her beautiful, semitransparent form and let out a long sigh. "I'm always glad you're here, Spooky. When these cases wrap up, I promise we'll find something exciting to do. First I have to get a breather."

"I don't have to breathe anymore," she reminded me. "And neither do you."

"Good point."

Just then, Esther stopped by to brighten our day. The harpy's plumage was ruffled, her eyes fiery—as usual—and she was dressed in her Ghoul's Diner uniform.

"I'm tired of waiting for results, especially when you're charging by the hour." When she saw the Emporium papers, folders, and notes strewn about my office she seemed mollified. "All this for *my* case? I didn't think it was that complicated."

"It's for another case, Esther," I said, which only annoyed her further.

"You're supposed to give priority to my problems. I thought we had an understanding."

I decided to lie. "I'm glad you're here—there's been a major break in your case. Robin, could you help me consult with a client, please?" I needed to get Esther away from the papers before she noticed we were digging into Tony Cralo's activities. (And also because I didn't want her to flap her wings in a tantrum and rearrange every scrap of paper that Robin had so painstakingly organized.)

Robin was much better at faking a professional smile than I was. Fortunately, it's easy for my undead face to remain expressionless when the situation calls for it. I explained—exaggerating the difficulty of my work—that I had tracked down Glenn the wizard and had a chat with him (I remembered just in time to use the word *confront* instead of *chat*).

"He admitted to giving you a bad-luck charm, and he's very sorry that he lost his patience with you. Even wizards have bad days. His pet canary died that morning, and I'm afraid he took out his grief on you."

I shook my head sadly. It was a good performance, worthy of fictionalizing in the next Shamble & Die mystery.

"I don't give a crap about his canary," she said. "If he brought it to the diner, we'd serve it up. Speaking of which, I have to get to work—and if I'm late punching in, I expect *you* to reimburse me for my lost wages."

Robin looked at the wall clock. Breakfast at the diner had been going at full steam for hours. "When were you supposed to start?"

"Ninety minutes ago, maybe more. So hurry up."

I said, "I'm surprised you keep your waitressing job. Isn't Tony Cralo taking care of you well enough?" The Ghoul's Diner, and all of Esther's customers, would be better off without her.

She snorted. "Sure, the fat zombie gives me baubles and shiny things, pampers me, takes me out to nice restaurants—but that's not enough. I'm thinking of my future. What if the relationship doesn't last?"

Sheyenne didn't like Esther (none of us did, but Robin and I covered it better). She said in an acid-sweet tone, "You must be worried he'll dump you for some other chick."

The harpy ruffled her feathers. "Dump *me?* You've got that backward. He's so disgusting I don't know how much more I can tolerate." She dangled the golden charm that refused to be discarded. "And all this bad luck is ruining my plans. What am I supposed to do? My life is in shambles, and my tips are down."

"You could try to be nice," Sheyenne said.

"How is that going to help anything?" Esther shrieked.

Robin gave her legal opinion. "We're in a gray area here. The bad-luck medallion was a tip, freely given and freely accepted, and because the wizard made no guarantees, implied or explicit, it'll be hard to impose damages. We could file a letter of complaint with the Better Business Bureau, which would then be available for Glenn's potential customers to see. As a long shot, we might succeed in getting him censured in magical professional organizations, and there would be a fine, but you'd probably receive very little in monetary damages."

"Damages?" Esther cocked her head. "I don't want damages, I want revenge! I'm stuck with this thing!"

I lied again. "Because he felt so sorry for what he did to you, Glenn told me how you can get rid of the bad-luck charm. It might help your situation."

She perked up. "Who do I need to kill? What sort of sacrifice do I have to make?"

"Glenn gave it to you, and you accepted it. The obvious solution is for you to give it away to someone else, who will also accept it."

"Give it away?" She clutched the medallion in her talons. "But it's mine! *Mine!*"

"It could be the only solution," Robin said.

"That's the stupidest thing I've ever heard." Annoyed, Esther spun about. "You've been no help at all."

When she left, all three of us let out a sigh of relief, even though two of us didn't need to breathe.

CHAPTER 42

By that afternoon, an uneasy anticipation was building in the air around the Unnatural Quarter. In any normal month, part-time werewolves would anticipate the rise of the full moon and revel in their temporary bestial freedom. A few months ago, I remembered how Miranda herself had been far more interested in the full-moon party with her friends than she was in the major crackdown on Jekyll Lifestyle Products and Necroceuticals.

This time, however, the two types of werewolves planned more than frenzied running and howling like hyperactive puppies on their first visit to a dog park.

Miranda and Hirsute stopped by our offices. "Just a few matters to wrap up, sweethearts. Legal specifics, dotting the i's and crossing the t's." She had a shine in her eyes, and she licked her lips more often than usual. Hirsute also had a simmering energy; his fists were clenched, and his arm muscles bulged far more than was appropriate.

"Ms. Jekyll, I finished the paperwork to convert your were-wolf sanctuary into a not-for-profit corporation," Robin said.

"A straightforward matter, and I'll have MLDW list it among the monster-supportive charity organizations." Sheyenne brought out the case folder as well as the notary stamp and record book, ready to formalize the documents so they could be filed with the clerk.

"Good to wrap that up—Hirsute and I plan to be busy this evening. The rumble is going to be quite spectacular. It might appear to be slumming, but those bastards asked for trouble. You saw the cockatrice shit all over me. Who's going to pay for the assault? Who'll pay for my dress? That was a brand-new Vera Wang—and *not* off the rack!"

Hirsute growled deep in his throat. "I'll make them pay, my dear."

Miranda giggled. "I know you will—you're so chivalrous it makes my blood run hot!" Then she snapped her attention back to Robin. "That brings up another subject. Hirsute is going to defend me during the gang violence, but we'll need some sort of disclaimer or hold-harmless document that clears me of legal responsibility if either of us inflicts damage upon those pathetic Hairballs. And I also want to be able to recoup any dental expenses I might sustain if, for instance, I chip a tooth while sinking my fangs into a victim."

"That won't be possible, Ms. Jekyll," Robin said in a warning voice. "My advice is to steer clear of the violence, for your own safety."

Miranda chuckled. "I'm not worried about my *safety*, sweetheart. I have Hirsute to protect me. I just don't want legal headaches afterward, when the mangy Hairballs turn out to be sore losers."

Robin shook her head. "I'd like to help you, Ms. Jekyll, but if you attend the rumble, you do so at your own risk, and you accept responsibility for any damages to your dental work or to the throats of your victims."

Miranda was already on the edge of violence this close to moonrise, and her temper flared.

Robin quickly amended, "We do have some recourse, however. Since Dan witnessed the excrement-balloon assault, we can sue Mister Furguson and seek damages for the cost of cleaning your dress."

"It couldn't be cleaned, sweetheart. That cockatrice acid burned right through the fabric."

"Replacement costs, then."

Hirsute flexed and extended his hands, impatient. "Wait until tomorrow—if any of them survive tonight, we file the suit." He nuzzled Miranda's ear. "That dress wouldn't have lasted long, anyway. I was ready to tear it off you."

"Sorry you didn't get the opportunity." She turned and waved farewell. "Hirsute and I have to change into casual clothes. It's a seedy part of town filled with undesirables. I'd hate to get my good jeans dirty."

After they left, the imminent rumble continued to weigh on me. I phoned McGoo to let him know the rumble was supposed to take place at the ruined Smile Syndicate warehouse on the other side of town. He was grateful for the tip. "How the hell did you learn that, Shamble? The department's been trying to find out where we should send reinforcements."

"Werewolves aren't very good at keeping secrets. Ask around. I wouldn't be surprised if people living nearby were selling tickets for good seats."

"Damn scalpers," McGoo said.

"That might not be the best word choice."

"Seemed appropriate to me."

I hung up. Robin had already gone back to her office and now emerged triumphantly holding a folder. She had that look on her face.

"Since the donation receipts didn't match the pieces for sale on the warehouse shelves, we were already convinced Cralo was illicitly obtaining body parts, but we didn't know where he got them. This racket is even bigger than we guessed. One corporation owned by another corporation, but I connected the dots." She smiled at me. "Guess who owns a majority share of Joe's Crematorium?"

"Would I be right if I said Tony Cralo?"

Sheyenne was listening in. "If Cralo owns the Spare Parts Emporium, why would he be burning bodies?"

I grasped the answer. "Because he's not burning them— that's what happened to Adriana Cruz. The bodies come in for cremation, but instead of putting them in the furnace, Joe Muggins loads them into a truck and sends them off to the Emporium for disassembly. Cralo probably has a chop shop in the back room where he can strip out the parts he needs."

Sheyenne drew in a quick imaginary breath. "And then he gives the bereaved family members an urn full of burned hickory or mesquite ashes. Nobody knows the difference."

"Still doesn't explain the scalped werewolves, or the vampire stripped of his organs," I said. "A vampire wouldn't end up in a crematorium."

"So, somebody had to murder Ben Willard to harvest especially valuable body parts," Robin said. "Maybe he liked to go to rough nightclubs, and he picked up the wrong person."

Then something else about Joe Muggins went *click* inside my head. I'd first seen the crematorium owner in the Voodoo Tattoo parlor, getting a hidden tat of *Bite Me* on his shoulder. What if Joe had gone out hunting for some rough trade of his own, met Ben Willard, brought him back to the Motel Six Feet Under, set him up . . . ?

"You two put the evidence together and tell McGoo to get an arrest warrant. In the meantime, I'm going to make a quick visit to Joe's Crematorium."

CHAPTER 43

For an edgy vampire who prowled rough nightclubs sporting a *Bite Me* temporary tattoo, Joe Muggins struck me as awfully wimpy.

The crematorium receptionist had already gone for the day (since she was a Monthly werewolf, this was a big social night for her). Business hours were almost over, so I walked past the front desk and found the meek-looking vampire in his office.

"Sorry, we're not accepting any more—oh, it's you, Mister Chambeaux." Joe Muggins seemed nervous as he rose from his desk. "My, my, I thought we'd taken care of that . . . that other matter. Has there been more trouble?"

I shambled through the door. "You've been a very naughty boy, Mister Muggins."

He stammered. "Wh-what are you talking about?"

"Does the name Ben Willard mean anything to you?"

He thought hard for a moment, then shook his head. "No. Who is he?"

"Okay, maybe I shouldn't have led with that. *Bite Me?* The club scene? Hard-partying vampire in search of a good time, maybe a little hardball sex? A room by the hour at the Motel Six Feet Under?" I let that hang.

"Ben Willard—so that was his name! He told me to call him 'Frisky.' " Now alarm crossed his face. "But the fact that I have a tattoo—*had* a tattoo, because it's worn off now—doesn't prove anything."

"He was murdered, all his organs removed, and the vampire body parts leave a trail back to Tony Cralo's Spare Parts Emporium. Also, Cralo is a majority owner of Joe's Crematorium, and we have proof that you aren't actually cremating the bodies you receive—you sell them to the Emporium for disassembly and redistribution."

The vampire was on the verge of panic. "What are you, some kind of detective?"

"I thought you knew that already."

I loomed in the doorway of his small office. He looked for a place to run, but I had him cornered. If I'd known it was going to be this easy to get him to confess, I'd have called McGoo ahead of time, but my BHF was too busy preparing for the gang war.

The crematorium's back door burst open, and two burly forms shouldered their way in, guffawing. "Hurry up, scrotum-face!" Scratch shoved his companion aside. "Let's make this delivery so there's time for a beer before the rumble starts."

The two biker werewolves saw me and pulled up short. Sniff demonstrated his extensive powers of observation. "It's that zombie detective guy again."

Scratch let out a giggle and a snort. "Hey, does anybody call you a *stiff dick?*"

"Gee, never heard that one before," I said.

Desperate, Joe Muggins wailed, "Get him! He knows everything!"

The two Monthlies bristled. "What do you mean, he knows everything?"

"That's an exaggeration," I said. "I'm a smart guy, but I can think of dozens of subjects that I know nothing about. Like sports teams, for instance. Couldn't care less." I was thinking fast, trying to figure out what to do next.

I could handle Joe Muggins, but I hadn't counted on these two coming in. Having seen Scratch and Sniff roar away from the loading dock of the crematorium, their choppers piled with wrapped packages—for organ deliveries?—I should have guessed they were involved.

"He figured out about the bodies and the wood ash, and the corpses we deliver to the Emporium—even the vampire we killed and culled!"

"I hadn't figured it *all* out, Mister Muggins, but you're doing a good job of filling in the blanks." I reached for my .38, but Scratch seized me before I could draw my weapon.

"What's he think he's going to *do* about it?" Sniff asked.

"Not very damn much." Scratch lifted me off my feet. Sniff joined in the fun.

"You said you were in collections," I said to the biker were-wolves.

"We collect organs," Scratch said. "Just the high-value pieces, take them right over to the Emporium. The rest of the bodies come over later in the big wagon."

Now that I was safely contained, Joe Muggins was brave and full of himself. "Vampire organs are a niche market—very hard to obtain."

Scratch and Sniff both chuckled. "But *fun* to get."

"So you went out clubbing," I said to Joe, "found a horny young vampire, lured him back to the motel?"

"I told him we were playing a bondage game," Joe said. "He didn't figure out that the handcuffs were silver until too late."

"After that," Scratch said, "we played a long, slow game of doctor."

"I won," Sniff said.

I was pretty sure that Ben Willard had lost.

"And so all the corpses that show up for a nice clean cremation become part of Cralo's organ and body-part scam?"

"Not a scam," Joe said. "It's being environmentally aware, a form of recycling. We can't let all those perfectly good parts go to waste."

I couldn't move in their grip. I looked from Scratch to Sniff. "I hate to dampen your excitement, boys, but I'm pretty sure there's no market for already-used zombie parts."

"Not much. Bottom of the barrel," Joe agreed from his desk. "But we've got to do something with *you*, even if we only get scrap prices."

Scratch looked at his watch. "You two gab like a couple of teenage girls going to the bathroom. Let's get a move on! Sniff and I have big plans tonight."

Joe looked at the two as-yet-untransformed werewolves. "Wrap him up and deliver him to Mister Cralo over at the bathhouse. He'll decide what to do."

"How the hell am I going to get a zombie on the back of my chopper?" Sniff said. "Shouldn't we cut him into portable pieces first?"

"He could wrap his arms around your waist and hold on tight," Scratch suggested with a malicious snicker.

"Don't be girlie. He can snuggle up next to you!"

Joe cut the argument short. "I've got rolls of butcher paper in the side room. Wrap him up like a package. Add enough twine, and he's not going anywhere."

That didn't sound pleasant to me, but neither did snuggling my arms around Sniff's waist.

"We've already got the proof of your activities," I said. "I informed the police."

"Oh, I'm soooo scared," Scratch said in a falsetto voice.

Even Joe did not seem worried. "That's what the last four people said. We'll risk it."

They relieved me of my .38 and my cell phone. Joe placed the gun in his desk drawer while Sniff smashed my phone on the floor, then stomped on it for good measure.

"That was my good phone," I said.

"Time to upgrade," Joe said, then supervised as the two wrapped me in sheets of white coated paper like a mummy (or a fresh-cut roast) until I couldn't see.

The biker werewolves picked me up—one by the shoulders, one by the feet—and carried me out of the crematorium.

CHAPTER 44

Choppers aren't made for passengers, especially not for passengers wrapped up as packages, and it was a long, bumpy, unpleasant ride. Scratch and Sniff had propped me with my paper-shrouded face close to the blatting exhaust pipe. Not exactly "easy riding."

Since the full moon would rise soon, the two biker werewolves were anxious to get rid of me so they could get to the rumble in time for the opening salvo. I could tell, however, that they were intimidated by Tony Cralo and wouldn't cut corners on an important job—such as disposing of me.

The choppers pulled up at their destination, but I couldn't see a thing through the wrapping. Scratch and Sniff manhandled me off the bike, straightened me—a relief to my aching joints—and carried me away. I felt them climb a set of stairs and wrestle open a creaking door. They bumped my head against the door frame (the butcher paper provided very little cushion) and took me down a hall, where I heard voices, dripping water, a splash. After they propped me like a garden rake against a wall, somebody tore the butcher paper off my face so I could see.

We were outside a sauna/steam room at the Zombie Bathhouse, with Cralo's two business-suited guards regarding me. One bodyguard glanced at a clipboard and scolded the two thugs. "This isn't the delivery we were expecting. Look at your paperwork—it says two kidneys and a gallbladder, pronto."

"Joe told us to bring this over." Scratch self-consciously wiped his hair back. "We don't have time to argue."

"Possible problems," Sniff said. "Mister Cralo will want to know about him."

The bodyguards looked at me without interest. "What's so special about this one? He's just dead meat." They sniffed in unison. "Not even fresh."

"He figured out the whole operation—even the part about the vampire organs," Scratch said. "Claims he already told the police."

The bodyguards rolled their eyes. "That's what the last four said." The one on the left sighed. "All right, unwrap him and bring him into the steam room. Mister Cralo needs to have words with him."

The other guard lowered his voice. "I bet the boss will be glad for the distraction from that harpy in there, even if it's about a threat to his operation."

After liberating me from the twine and butcher paper, the bodyguards opened the sauna door, and a waft of noisome steam burbled out—not invigorating steam from water ladled over hot rocks, but foul-smelling fumes like the armpit of a stagnant swamp.

Esther stood in front of the sauna door, a white towel wrapped around her body, her harpy face pinched in a disapproving expression. Her moist plumage drooped. I heard a loud burring sound, like a dragonfly drowning, then an extended belch from

Cralo's other end. Esther called back to a hulking form on one of the benches. "Tony, I love you, but sometimes your out-gassing is disgusting." She gave me her usual look of disapproval. "And you have a visitor."

The bodyguards shoved me into the miasmic room. The obese zombie sat surrounded by the steam, a towel over his shoulders and another one covering his lap; both were the size of bedsheets. "Come to file another complaint, Mister Chambeaux? Just how many dissatisfied customers do you represent?"

"Same one, and he's still dissatisfied," I said. "But I'd like to expand my complaint to include your spare-parts gathering from Joe's Crematorium, and the murder of a vampire for his organs."

Cralo did not look amused. He turned to the two biker werewolves. "What's all this about?"

Scratch and Sniff were eager to take credit. "He was roughing up Joe, but we captured him and brought him here."

Cralo looked to me, and the sunken eyes in his round face blazed brighter. "You think you're smart?"

"Above average," I admitted. "We've already delivered our evidence to the police. The law is closing in on you, Mister Cralo. They'll arrive soon enough."

Scratch and Sniff laughed. "Cops are going to be busy with the werewolf gang war, boss. You don't need to be in any hurry."

The fat zombie shook his head. "You're a pain in the ass, Chambeaux . . . as if I needed any extra bodily aches. Maybe I should leave town after all, lie low for a while—fortunately, the rumble gives me time to pack up and get away without leaving any loose ends."

When he rose to his feet, the towel around his waist fell off. I turned away as quickly as I could, as did Esther, the two bodyguards, and Scratch and Sniff. The guards came forward, eyes screwed shut, carrying what looked like a white terry-cloth camping tent, but it was merely a Tony Cralo–sized spa robe. "I'll go underground, *deep* underground—sewer level. Esther, sweetie-magpie, I want you with me. Don't worry about your clothes or your jewels, I'll get you pretty new things. We'll find a hideout just for you and me, like a little love nest."

Esther tightened her own towel and winced at the stench in the air. I wondered if even sewer dwellers would want someone like Cralo around. She daintily waved her taloned hand. "Oh, my poor thing! That sounds delightful and romantic, but I can't go with you. I have my job, my career." She flounced to the door of the steam room. "I'll wait for you, baby—so long as you bring me expensive things. Call me when you get back."

She hesitated at the sauna door, and I watched her expression brighten. "Wait, I have something for you." From the folds of her feathers, she pulled the gold medallion Glenn the wizard had given her. "Here, take this as a token from me."

Cralo reached out a pudgy hand. "What is it?"

"It's for luck." He accepted the charm, and Esther beat a hasty retreat out of the bathhouse.

Although they loved the possibility of having to dispose of my body, Scratch and Sniff were impatient. "Believe me, boss, the Monthlies and Hairballs will be all the diversion you need to get out of town. You should start packing."

"I'll put a bonus in your next paycheck." Cralo wrapped the thin chain of the charm around his pudgy wrist. I doubted I'd survive long enough to benefit from Cralo's newly acquired bad luck. "In the meantime, what do we do with *you*, Chambeaux?"

"If you're looking for suggestions, I vote for letting me go with a stern warning."

"I'll take that under careful advisement." He paused for a

nanosecond. "No, I'm afraid not. We should bury you under cement. You're already dead, so it won't kill you, but you'll be awfully bored encased in concrete under the foundation of a building." Cralo looked at his two bodyguards. "Do we have any building foundations being poured tonight?"

The two looked at each other, shook their heads. "Not until next week, boss."

Sniff suggested, "Could put him in a pothole in the parking lot of the Emporium and cover him over. That lot really does need repaving."

"We don't have that kind of equipment right now. Besides, I'm still taking bids for the job," Cralo said. "Damned contractors, they're all corrupt. That'll take too long."

"It's a shame," I said. "All I really wanted was a brain. If you had a better customer service department, I wouldn't have had to keep digging."

"I appreciate the feedback. We should improve that part of our business." Cralo smiled at me. "If it's any consolation, I did receive the troll brain you returned, and I already disassembled the customer service rep who gave you so much trouble. I sent a high-priced replacement brain directly to Dr. Victor, and he was very happy to receive it. You can rest in peace."

"Thanks for that, at least," I said. "But is it the brain he wanted?"

"Better—I gave him the vampire brain. Those organs are genuine die-hard quality. It'll perform far beyond your client's expectations. Besides, after that transplant debacle, the rest of the vamp organs were too hot to move through regular channels."

I feared what would happen when Archibald installed the vampire brain into his newly constructed body. If the murderous creature in the heart-transplant ward was any indication, I doubted the coroner's house trailer could contain the violence.

I would have rushed off to save him, but at the moment I had bigger problems.

Cralo clipped on a gold Rolex as he got dressed, glanced at the time. "I've got to start packing. Just wrap him up again, take him to the crematorium, and put him in the furnace." The fat zombie laughed close to my face, and his breath smelled as bad as his farts. "You're about to make an ash of yourself, Chambeaux."

CHAPTER 45

Wrapped up again and unable to move, I endured another noisy and bumpy ride back to Joe's Crematorium. This time, fortunately, I was propped away from the exhaust, though I doubt Scratch and Sniff did it out of consideration for me.

Private investigators are solo types, and we work on our cases without an entourage. It's not that we don't play well with others, but detective work isn't exactly a team sport.

I usually chided McGoo when he went off half-cocked without calling for backup, but here I was, tied up, relieved of my weapon, and heading for a cozy evening in a couple-thousand-degree furnace. It was damned poor planning. This was going to be very unpleasant, and in a very unpleasant way.

But live and learn—or if that didn't work, *die* and learn.

The choppers pulled around the back of Joe's Crematorium with double-barreled muffler blasts. Scratch and Sniff man-handled me off the bike and hauled me inside.

When Joe Muggins saw the burly pair, he scowled. "My, my, why did you bring him back here?"

Scratch ran a hand through his slicked-back hair, which

seemed even more fluffy now in anticipation of the full-moon transformation. "Mister Cralo says it's time for a barbecue. Extra crispy."

The little vampire shuffled his feet. "All right, if that's what he thinks is best."

"Could I put in a dissenting vote?" I said.

"Shut up," Sniff said; his forearms were growing noticeably hairier. He shoved me toward Joe Muggins. "Hurry up and take care of this. We've got places to be."

"No waiting in furnace number four," said Joe. "Take him over there."

I struggled. With my legs and arms still wrapped up, I looked like a drunken caterpillar who couldn't break free of a cocoon. As the two werewolves carried me—Scratch by the shoulders, Sniff by the feet—Joe scuttled into a back room and returned with a cardboard box from toilet paper rolls sold by the gross. "We were about to break down these boxes for recycling. This one will do for a makeshift coffin."

"A toilet-paper box?" I asked. "Really? You can't get me something of higher quality?"

Joe pursed his lips. "Why go to the added expense? Should I send a bill to Chambeaux and Deyer?"

"No, that probably wouldn't work," I said.

Robin had paid for my fine embalming job the first time, as well as a quick-release casket and a nice burial plot in the Greenlawn Cemetery. This time, though, it would be a cardboard box, disposed of after hours in a crematorium with no one else watching.

Scratch and Sniff lifted me up and placed me in the box. With the butcher paper and twine bindings, I couldn't move my arms, couldn't separate my elbows, couldn't free my hands.

Grunting and growling, the two lugged the cardboard box toward one of the crematorium furnaces. Hurrying ahead, Joe swung open a metal hatch like a doorman at a fancy hotel.

Through the open box top I could see a black-encrusted chamber built to accommodate the largest coffins.

The two werewolves tipped the box onto a rattling line of rollers that would feed me into the furnace. At the controls, Joe turned a knob to start the jets, but nothing happened. "Damn pilot light went out again. Sometimes the breezes come in and—"

Scratch snarled. "Hurry up! Moon's rising in half an hour!"

Joe fiddled with the pre-burner, found a box of long wooden fireplace matches, struck one, and leaned into the furnace. Tiny blue gas jets lit, and the vampire straightened, nodding. "There, that should work just fine."

"Good. We're outta here!" The two headed out, annoyed that they wouldn't have time for a beer before the rumble.

As he rattled my cardboard box along the rollers into the soot-caked furnace, Joe leaned close. "I have slow-cooker settings or broiler—do you have a preference?"

Neither option sounded particularly enjoyable. "Bite me," I said. It seemed clever at the time.

Joe seemed antsy. "Broiler it is, then." He gave my box one last shove into the furnace. "I've had to go to the bathroom since before you arrived. Sorry for the rush." He nudged my head down farther into the toilet-paper box, made sure I was situated in the center of the cremation chamber. "Thank you for your patronage." Squirming as if his bladder were about to burst, he swung the vault door closed. I heard the clunk of the latch.

A few seconds later, the flame jets spurted higher, and fire gushed out to lick the sides of the box. I could smell the cardboard crisping, the acrid smoke curling around. Joe Muggins hadn't even bothered to add hickory or mesquite for seasoning. I was going to be plain bland ash . . . not that it made much difference. The fire crackled around me. My hair singed.

There was only so much the Wannovich sisters' restoration

spell could accomplish. I hoped the witches wouldn't be too disappointed at the abrupt end of their potentially successful Shamble & Die series. (Linda Bullwer could probably concoct more adventures on her own, however.)

Smoke filled the chamber. The cardboard box was in flames now, and the butcher paper wrapping my body had turned brown and started to smoke. I wouldn't have minded so much if the cremation had happened before I came back to life, but now I'd had a change of heart. I could understand why Adriana Cruz didn't want to demand completion of the promised services.

The first time around, I hadn't known I was going to die, hadn't heard the killer approach, barely had time to react to the cold gun barrel pressed against the back of my head before the quick *pop*. It was a complete surprise. Now, as flames consumed the box around me and black smoke closed in, the anticipation was downright terrifying.

I still had cases unsolved, and I was especially upset that Archibald Victor would find himself in mortal danger the moment he installed a vampire brain in his do-it-yourself body kit. Nobody would be able to warn him.

Worse, I knew how much I was going to make Robin grieve, *again*. And I would be separated from Sheyenne, too . . . unless I came back as a ghost, but the odds of that happening were lottery-jackpot small. As I had demonstrated by my current situation, I'm not that lucky.

Or maybe I was.

Unexpectedly, the gas jets died down, and the bright flames retreated into their nozzles, leaving only tiny pilot lights. The cardboard box was on fire, collapsing into black ash and embers. The butcher paper still burned, which had damaged my sport jacket, among other things.

I heard the latch slam aside, and the heavy vault door swung open. A blast of fire-extinguisher mist filled the furnace chamber, chasing out the smoke. I couldn't see a thing, but at least I wasn't roasted.

"Beaux! You in there?" Sheyenne's voice sounded wonderful.

"I'm sure glad to see you." The paper wrapping had burned and crumbled, and this time when I strained, I managed to snap the cords binding me. When the smoke and fire-extinguisher fumes cleared away, I saw Sheyenne hovering outside the furnace. Her face looked more translucent than usual, her expression distraught. She blasted the metal rollers, cooling them enough that I could scramble, slip, then scramble again until I reached the oven door.

"I'm glad you didn't wait one minute longer," I said. Ten minutes earlier would have been even better, but I wasn't going to complain. I clambered out and straightened myself, brushing my singed jacket, my singed hair, and my singed grayish skin. "I'm thinking a big hug at you right now."

"You told us you were going to the crematorium, but you took way too long. Glad I was impatient."

I looked around the crematorium. "We've got to arrest Joe Muggins. I want that weasely vamp to spend a few decades in a bright, sunny cell. I hope he didn't get away—"

"Oh, Joe's not going anywhere," she said. I heard a muffled shout and a pounding; a door rattled. Sheyenne had jammed a chair under the doorknob of the small employee bathroom, trapping the little vampire inside.

"One more reason to offer you a raise," I said.

"You know you don't pay me, Beaux."

"Then I'll double your salary—tomorrow. I've got a few more fires to put out tonight."

CHAPTER 46

With Joe Muggins locked in the crematorium's employee bathroom, I had more urgent concerns. The Monthlies and the Hairballs were about to start World War Werewolf. By now, Tony Cralo would be making his escape, if he hadn't already skipped town. And Archibald Victor was about to install a vampire brain into his build-your-own body kit, and he was bound to unleash a wild monster whether or not he intended to reanimate it.

Sheyenne rushed off at her spectral speed to let McGoo know about the zombie crime lord. The UQPD would be preoccupied by the werewolf rumble, but if Cralo escaped into the underworld, they might never find him again.

Meanwhile, I retrieved my .38 from the drawer in Joe's desk and headed off to the mad scientist's trailer, hoping I could get there before he installed the brain and inadvertently unleashed a homicidal monster.

Dark was just falling, and the full moon hadn't risen yet. A brewing violence hung in the twilight, and the Quarter felt deserted, as if everyone were getting ready for High Noon . . . or Full Moon.

I made my best speed toward the trailer park. Because the Parlour (BNF) was right on my way, I burst through the door, hoping that Harriet Victor could get in touch with her husband before it was too late.

Not surprisingly, the beauty shop was devoid of customers. Rova was barefoot and doing a contortionist act in one of the chairs, trying to give herself a pedicure, but not doing a good job. When she glanced up at me, she scowled as if she had just gargled with sour-lemon mouthwash. "You're not allowed to come within fifty yards of me—didn't you read the restraining order?"

"What restraining order?" I asked.

"My attorney drew it up. He was going to serve it on you, for harassment."

I didn't have the patience for this. "First of all, a lawyer can't serve his own papers, and second, I haven't had time to receive any restraining orders. Where's Mrs. Victor? This is an emergency!"

The bearded lady came out from the back room, her arms around an open cardboard box filled with crème rinses, shampoos, and skin lotions to display on the Parlour's shelves. The hair on her head, face, hands, and arms was freshly permed, curled, and adorned with colorful ribbons. She said in a chirpy voice, "Mister Chambeaux! Archibald was delighted to receive the surprise package—he's been waiting for that new brain. He called me from home an hour ago, couldn't wait to get to work. I think he puts in more hours in his home lab than at the morgue."

"We have to get in touch with him, Mrs. Victor! He can't use that brain—it's a vampire brain, very dangerous. If he installs it, he could create a monster."

"Well, of course he's creating a monster. That's the whole point."

"Not like this. A similar thing killed a dozen people at the hospital. We'd better stop him before he gets hurt. Can you call him?"

The hair all over her body began to uncurl. "My poor Archibald! When he's trying to concentrate, he always turns the phone off so it doesn't interrupt him."

No time to lose. I turned around and lurched toward the door. "I'm heading over there."

Harriet grabbed her purse. "Then I'll come with you."

We must have been a strange sight, a singed zombie detective and a bearded lady moving like two bats out of hell. In the trailer park, we rushed to the Victors' double-wide with its pretty flower boxes and wind chimes. Harriet removed the house keys from her purse, fumbled with the lock, and pushed the door open. "Archibald, are you all right? Mister Chambeaux says you're in danger."

I entered, hot on her heels. "Step away from the brain, Dr. Victor! It's not safe."

In the back lab, I could see that Archibald had gone to work with the fervor of a truly mad scientist. His experiments filled the cozy trailer: Bubbling chemicals and strange mixtures covered the dinette table, the kitchen counter, the coffee table, the sofa. The brawny build-it-yourself body lay on the hobby table, with all the main pieces now put together.

I spotted the gift-wrapped box from the Spare Parts Emporium, the lid set aside, the box empty—then I saw with weak-kneed relief that the brain was still in its transparent jar, next to the empty cranial cavity of the mostly assembled monster. Archibald hadn't had a chance to install the brain yet. We were safe!

In the meantime, he had been working on something else.

As the mad scientist emerged from the bedroom laboratory, Harriet and I stared in astonishment. We barely recognized him. His voice was supercharged with excitement. "It works, sweetie! We're going to be rich!"

Archibald Victor had given up his toupee, for good. The little coroner no longer needed it—not by a long shot. Except for his ping-pong-ball-sized eyes, I would not have recognized him. He looked like a Neanderthal hippy.

Hair sprouted from every square inch of his pale skin. His eyebrows had turned into ferns. Hair poured from his scalp, growing visibly as we watched. His jaw and chin sported a full beard that rivaled his wife's. Fur sprang out from his neck. His chest hair was a forest sprouting from the open collar of his lab coat. He swiped at his face with hair-covered hands to push his overgrown eyebrows out of the way so he could see. His mustache ran over his lips and continued all the way down to his chest.

"It works, it works!" he repeated. "No one ever has to be bald again!"

"And *this* is preferable?" I asked.

"It should stop growing soon," Archibald said. "I designed the formula that way."

Harriet grabbed a pair of scissors from the chemistry-strewn counter and raced to her husband. "You need a trim, Archibald. This is alarming!" She began to shear handfuls of hair from his face, clearing his lips so he could speak plainly, cropping in front of his eyes so he could see.

"But look how effective it is, Harriet—I never dreamed of results like this! Maybe it has something to do with the full moon."

"At least we're in time to stop you from using the replacement brain," I said, getting back to the main emergency. "We've got to destroy it."

Archibald looked distracted (at least as far as I could tell, under all that hair). Harriet fussed over him, stroked his wild locks. "We were so worried you might be in danger."

"Oh, a silly body-building competition doesn't matter anymore! Yes, I was about to install the brain, but then I had a breakthrough idea. I had to try the new tonic, and it works! Did I mention we're going to be rich? This is the most important discovery in the history of human civilization, and only I have the formula!"

Harriet nudged her husband into a chair by the kitchen table. "And you've created plenty of business for barbers and stylists everywhere, but you might still need to fine-tune the recipe," she said. "Let me give you a full haircut, make you presentable before we release any announcements." She snipped and clipped, trimming him in all directions. By the time she finished one circuit of his overly enthusiastic follicles, she had to go back and trim again.

While she fussed over the no-longer-hairless coroner, I went to the body-building table to take care of the vampire brain. One disaster averted. Now all I had to worry about was stopping the werewolf gang war. I could leave Harriet and Archibald to their own tangled mess.

Then I spotted something I wanted to see even less than I wanted to see a hair-covered Archibald Victor.

On a separate table, a row of large petri dishes was connected to bottles and flasks that were bubbling over Bunsen burners. Each petri dish was the size of a blue plate special, filled with a greenish liquid. In the petri dishes, like round hunks of sod, sat four burbling werewolf scalps connected to electrodes, twitching and writhing in a chemical bath. They looked as fresh as the day they'd been removed from their original owners.

CHAPTER 47

When Rusty the werewolf had hired me to track down his attacker, I never expected to blunder into this. Archibald Victor was also my client, and I got involved in the conflict only because he received some bad brains. It should have been a simple customer service issue, but I found myself knee-deep in shady organ dealings.

In their jumbo nutrient-filled petri dishes, the gruesome living scalps throbbed. I blurted out, "*You're* the one who's been scalping werewolves?"

Archibald saw where I was standing and tried to squirm out of the chair. Harriet, still trimming the persistent strands streaming down the coroner's face, gave her husband's bangs a last snip. "Archibald, why can't you clean up after yourself?"

"I have to report this, Dr. Victor." After being caught unawares at Joe's Crematorium, this time I drew my .38 without giving them the benefit of the doubt. "Why would you stun and scalp werewolves?"

"To find the secret, of course." The mad scientist grimaced, spitting out hair that had gotten into his mouth. "Have you seen the thick head of hair on a full-time werewolf? I wanted to reproduce that! Werewolf hair growth is nature's best, and I'm not one to think small. I wanted to develop a werewolf-based hair-follicle treatment that could be marketed to normal balding humans. We'd capture the entire market, and Harriet and I would earn millions! I'd quit my job as the coroner and just do autopsies as a hobby."

Harriet said, "And I could keep the Parlour (BNF) afloat for months."

"As diabolical schemes go, that one's way out there." I remembered the bloody gang violence that was about to start. "Do you realize what you've *caused?* You provoked a werewolf war!"

"It's all in the name of science and personal styling," Archibald said. "The donors didn't feel a thing. I knocked them out before I took their scalps, and they'll heal. Werewolves are good at that."

I thought of Professor Zevon recovering in the hospital, poor Ernesto and Arnie in their shantytown, covering their heads with old stocking caps, Rusty with his bandanna wrapped around his scabbed head. I held the gun steady. "You didn't think there was anything *wrong* with assaulting werewolves? Committing grievous injury?"

"Not grievous injury, Mister Chambeaux. It was surgery," Archibald said. "And I needed living scalps to test the hair follicles, to study the growth of each strand, to separate and identify the specific hormones—in particular the chemical changes that promote such persistent hair growth, enhanced by the light of the full moon. They weren't going to give up their scalps just because I asked nicely."

The mad scientist truly was mad. "Sorry to shatter your dreams, Dr. Victor, but you've got to come clean about this—

right now. I'll take you over to where the rumble's due to start. We can still stop the werewolf violence and save a lot of lives. I've got a friend on the police force—maybe he'll cut you a break. But we have to spread the word before the gang war breaks out!"

During our tense conversation, Harriet had stopped cutting her husband's hair, and his face was completely covered again. He pulled the strands away from his mouth and eyes once more, just so he could meet my gaze.

"No, they'll confiscate my formula! No one can have it. I worked and sweated and concocted—this is my life's mission. Besides, I haven't applied for a patent yet. I'm not going to let anyone take away our nest egg."

Harriet moved so quickly that she surprised me. She threw herself upon me—and was damned lucky she didn't get herself killed (and not just because she was running with scissors). I wasn't about to shoot a lady, bearded or otherwise. She knocked my gun hand aside, and as I wrestled with her, Harriet yelled, "Get rid of the stuff, Archie! Destroy the evidence—you can always recreate it!"

She was a sweet hairdresser, former circus attraction, and caring business owner, but when she saw her beloved mad-scientist husband threatened, she turned into a mama grizzly (and looked the part). Harriet was strong, too, as she grappled with me.

The Neanderthal-hairy coroner leaped from the chair and scuttled over to his test tubes and beakers, trying not to trip on his own hair. I thought he would try to dispose of the incriminating scalps, but apparently his top-secret hair formula was more important to him.

Before I could break free from the bearded lady, Archibald grabbed the flask of his hair-growth solution and stumbled to the bathroom. Barely able to see where he was going, he upended the flask and poured the solution down the shower drain.

I wrenched my gun hand free, extricated myself from Harriet's clinging grasp, and lurched away, swinging up my .38 again. "Look, I really don't care about the formula! I just want to stop the werewolf war." I glared at both of them. "Remember, I came here to save *you* from a murderous vampire brain."

I eased myself over to the hobby table where the mostly constructed monster body lay, picked up the transparent jar with the offending brain, and smashed it on the floor. Just to be safe.

"That'll stain my carpeting!" Harriet objected.

"Don't worry, love," Archibald said. "With my formula, I'll be able to buy us a castle."

"*When* you get out of prison," I said. "Right now, we need to stop the werewolf war. You're coming with me, Dr. Victor—so you can do the right thing."

"I can't let poor Archibald go to jail," Harriet wailed.

"I only did it for you, sweetie," the coroner said, "so I could have hair just like yours."

"Oh, Archibald, I didn't care about your hair. And I wish you'd never worn that silly toupee. Can't you just look like yourself, the man I fell in love with?"

My urgency increased now that the full moon had risen and was shining through the trailer's windows. "Very heartwarming, but can we put a pin in that? We've got to get to the Warehouse District before the fur starts flying!" I hoped we could get there in time.

It's always something, though.

I can't remember the last case where I solved a mystery and closed a file without any complications. Even in Penny Dreadful's fictionalized versions of my cases, nothing was ever so simple.

Before I could march the Victors out of their trailer, the shower drain began to groan and burble, like a dragon with severe intestinal distress. Archibald lifted his long eyebrows away from his face so he could see. Harriet covered her mouth with a hand.

Hair sprouted from the shower drain. Maybe *sprouted* isn't the right word; *exploded* is more accurate. Tangled auburn strands writhed out of the drain, growing at an astonishing rate and lashing like tentacles.

I realized that Archibald's amazing hair-growth tonic had been derived from werewolf hormones, and with the added impetus of the full moon, the chemical became supercharged. Within seconds, the shower stall was filled with a writhing, angry sargasso of hair that burst out of the shower, streamed across the bathroom—then went on the attack.

"Do something!" Harriet cried. "Stop it!"

The hair tsunami kept rolling forward, some strands curled in a perm, others stringy and straight. I fired three rounds into the maniacal hairy outburst ... which, not unexpectedly, did nothing.

Harriet tried to stop it. She grabbed her haircutting scissors and dodged past me to dive into the ever-growing mass.

I tried to stop her. "Stay away from there!"

But the hair kept growing, and the tentacles wrapped around the bearded lady and pulled her into the thicket. Harriet lashed with the scissors, snipping and trimming as quickly as she could, but not fast enough.

"Harriet!" Archibald cried. Unable to see because of his hair problems, he stumbled forward to rescue his wife. The eerily sentient hair reached out, as if knowing the mad scientist was to blame for scalping the werewolves, or maybe it was instinctive affection since the detached hairs came from his adoring wife. Whatever the reason, the python-like clumps of hair wrapped around Archibald and lifted him up, twisting him in a tight, murderous snarl. He flailed, but couldn't escape the constrictive grasp; the living hair was lustrous and full of body.

One of the hairy tentacles knocked me sprawling into the sofa. I couldn't possibly reach them.

Harriet's hand worked its way free, questing for the bottles of hair product on the countertop. She snagged a squeeze-tube of detangler, but it was much too little and too late.

"Harriet!" Archibald wailed, and he struggled, trying to break free and get to her. The hair surrounded them in an impenetrable clump, squeezing them tight. It drew them into the dense heart of the thicket, squeezing, crushing. The couple fell silent.

Deadly tresses continued to boil out of the shower drain, pushing into the main room, where they engulfed the brainless but otherwise complete monster body. The mad scientist had said he designed the formula to expire after a certain point, but I had no idea when that might be. As the awful strands quested toward me, I jumped out the front door. There was no telling how much more the demonic tangle would grow.

Trailer-park neighbors emerged to stand on their porches and watch the spectacle. "What's Dr. Victor doing now?" asked an old toothless gargoyle who sat on a folding lawn chair.

"Just more of the same," said a witch from two trailers over.

Backing away, I saw the sides of the trailer bulge. The windows shattered, and hairy strands burst outward, curling around the roof of the double-wide. I worried we might have to call in an air strike to stop the tangled monstrosity, bombers dumping barrels of high-end conditioner designed for controlling unruly hair.

But then, with a sigh, the twitching strands quested outward one last time, until, exhausted, the hair became limp and lifeless. The mad scientist's trailer sagged and fell silent.

I stared for a long moment, thinking about the Victors. Then it was time for action. I had to get over to the rumble and stop the massacre.

In the last hour, I had survived a crematorium furnace, stopped the activation of a murderous vampire brain, and barely escaped a wild tangle of killer hair.

But the night was still young.

CHAPTER 48

As I ran from the trailer park, the bright moon was just above the skyline, which meant that the Monthlies would be fully transformed by now. I hoped I wasn't too late. Police reinforcements had already converged out at the ruined Smile Syndicate warehouse, but I doubted an entire riot squad would be enough to stop the violence if all the werewolves in the city were howling mad. If I could let the two hairy gangs know that it was actually a well-intentioned mad scientist who had done the scalpings, not a rival werewolf, maybe they would shake paws and go home as friends.

Yeah, I know how that sounds.

The Warehouse District was on the other side of town, but I headed off at my best possible speed, hoping to find an open business where I could make a call. I had to pass by the Spare Parts Emporium, and I realized the zombie crime lord might be making his escape even now . . . but Tony Cralo was not highest on my most-loathed-persons list right now. Funny how things can change in only an hour.

As I neared the skeletal bridge under which the homeless

unnaturals huddled, to my surprise, I heard a chorus of howls, and a rival set of growls, yips, and barks echoed out into the night. It sounded like someone training the inhabitants of an animal shelter for barbershop quartets. Barbershop? Not a good image at the moment. I suppressed a shudder and started to shamble faster.

I hesitated. Something wasn't right. Larry had made a point of telling me exactly where the rumble would take place. Why would so many werewolves be *here,* if the big clash was supposed to be taking place across town at the Smile Syndicate warehouse? Maybe the ruined Smile Syndicate warehouse was already booked for another event?

Taking a chance—although my gambles hadn't paid off lately—I entered the persistent fog bank that hung around the Emporium. The full moon looked like a blurry yellow streetlight filtered through the mist. Shadowy figures moved among the battered transportainers and the large delivery trucks parked on the lot. The cardboard-box houses and tar-paper shacks under the bridge were abandoned—no trolls or vampires or even the forlorn ogre.

Just an entire furry army.

Two armies, in fact—werewolves of one form or the other. They faced off like football teams across a scrimmage line. The Hairballs and Monthlies snarled curses at one another.

Larry was the first figure I blundered into: hunched over, flexing his muscles, ready to fight. He whirled when he heard me, claws extended for a mauling, then he relaxed. "Hey, it's Dan Shamble! How'd you find the party? We weren't supposed to invite non-werewolves—better check with Rusty."

"You lied to me, Larry. You said the rumble was happening in the Warehouse District."

He showed his fangs, but it might have been a grin. "Not *exactly.* I said the Warehouse District would be a good place for it. You filled in the rest. A little bait-and-switch. Rusty knew you'd blab to your cop friend, so we used you to get them out of our fur, send them to the other side of town."

I felt exasperated. "That's not fair—I'm trying to do the right thing here! I have proof that the Monthlies aren't responsible for the scalpings. It was a mad scientist collecting specimens . . . and he was killed when his own experiment backfired. You don't need to go to war!"

Larry sniffed. "It's a free country. We werewolves can tear each other apart if we want to. It's our right."

"It might be your right, but all the reasons are wrong," I said. "I've got information that affects the entire basis for the rumble. Can I borrow your phone?" I needed to let McGoo know where the real clash was taking place.

"Shamble, I live in a cardboard box. You think I have a monthly cell plan?"

"I suppose not. Sorry."

Rusty saw me and lurched forward. In the light of the full moon, some of his scalped fur had grown back, though it looked like a different color and poked up in all directions. "Out of the way, Mister Shamble! You had your chance to solve the case—now we're taking matters into our own paws."

Furguson came up, all gangly arms and legs, bouncing from side to side like a kid on too much caffeine. "Ready to go, Uncle Rusty!"

"But the attacks had nothing to do with either gang," I insisted. "The Monthlies didn't scalp you!"

The nearby werewolves grumbled at this, but ultimately they didn't care. Rusty shrugged. "We've got enough reasons to fight, even without that. Don't rock the boat now, Shamble."

"*Chambeaux,*" I said, knowing it wouldn't do any good.

I also saw Professor Zevon, who had recovered enough to join the fray. Patches of fur sprouted from his scalped crown, but the appearance was like the aftermath of a clumsy back-room hair transplant, rather than his original lavish head of silver fur. As I continued to shout about Archibald Victor and his hair-tonic experiments, the professor said, "An interesting hypothesis, sir, but irrelevant at the moment." He fumbled with his necktie, tossed it aside, then unbuttoned the top button of his white shirt. He did not, however, remove the nice tweed jacket he had worn for the occasion. A group of his students stood beside him, growling, ready to fight for their teacher's honor—strictly in theory, of course; as academics, they were there only to chronicle the event and preferred to stay back from the fight.

On the other side of the parking lot, the Monthlies were gathering, shoulder to shoulder, baring fangs. The howls grew louder.

Hoping I'd have better luck with the other team, I raced across the open area. Monthlies did spend more time *acting* human on the nights when the moon wasn't full. Maybe I could get through to them.

Now transformed, the gathered Monthly combatants looked the same as the Hairballs, and I wondered how the two sides would tell each other apart in the middle of the fray. Different colognes? Then I recalled that the gang members had specific tats, courtesy of Antoine Stickler and Voodoo Tattoo.

At the forefront of the Monthlies, Scratch and Sniff were now snarling man-beasts, holding their rusty meat cleavers in clawed hands and ready to do damage. Even covered by all that fresh fur, their myriad tattoos were visible. Sniff's beard had grown much longer.

When the two biker werewolves saw me, they growled in unison. "You're supposed to be dead!" Scratch said.

"Still am—and I'll deal with you two later."

On the edge of the angry lupine crowd, I saw the transformed Miranda Jekyll next to an enormous brute who could only have been Hirsute. While Scratch and Sniff roared challenges and brandished their little choppers, Miranda and Hirsute were content to be spectators.

Hoping Miranda would be more reasonable, I approached her first. She waved at me. "Oh, look, we have a zombie cheering section! Thank you for coming, sweetheart, but stay clear so you don't get hurt."

Hirsute drew in a huge breath to swell his chest. "Can you smell it in the air? Mayhem and bloodletting . . . quite an aphrodisiac." He stroked Miranda's muzzle, and she licked his paw, growling low in her throat.

"I'm tempted to drag you into a dark alley and have my way with you, Hirsute," she said. "Or do you really want to stay for the rumble?"

I interrupted her cooing. "Miranda, can I borrow your phone? I have to make an urgent call."

"Of course, sweetheart. My purse is right over there, with my dress."

Miranda's phone was in a sparkly diamond case, and I had to close out a game of Curses with Friends before I found the dialing pad and called the office. Robin answered right away; I could tell she was worried about me. "Dan! Sheyenne told me—"

"I'm not done yet," I said. "Dr. Victor and his wife are dead, and I'm at the werewolf rumble now, but they won't listen. Tell McGoo the werewolf gangs have gathered by Cralo's Emporium, *not* at the warehouse. Get the riot squad down here right away. I need some muscle."

Robin sounded concerned. "I'll call—but by the time the cops get there, it'll be too late. Sheyenne's the only one who's fast enough."

I heard her voice in the background. "Already on my way, Beaux!"

"She's a ghost! Sheyenne can't touch anybody—how can she help during a brawl?" Regardless, I knew I'd do better with Sheyenne's support.

Robin was on edge. "I'm not going to be the one to keep her away. And I'm coming, too. Be there as fast as the Pro Bono Mobile can carry me. Calling Officer McGoohan first." She hung up. Robin's old Ford Maverick couldn't go very fast, though, so I had time.

I would try to defuse tensions meanwhile, although nobody seemed interested in hearing the real story about the scalpings. The two sides began howling and roaring even louder challenges, only seconds away from declaring open war.

I pulled my .38, as if that would threaten anyone, and bolted into the parking lot, waving my hands. "Stop—the rumble has been canceled."

As the two sides snarled, I suddenly felt like a meat-flavored rag doll about to be fought over by two very hungry rat terriers. I swept my gun from side to side. "You all need to calm down. The first person who comes forward gets shot."

Rusty stood there in his overalls, burly and angry. "You got silver bullets in that thing, Mister Shamble?"

The question took me by surprise; I couldn't remember, so I bluffed. "Usually."

"He doesn't," Scratch called from the other gang of werewolves.

"Didn't think so." Rusty stepped forward and plucked the gun out of my hand. He threw it to one side, where it bounced on the gravel, skittered, and vanished forever into one of the crater-sized pothole puddles. "Furguson, make yourself useful. Help me out here."

Rusty and his nephew seized me and carried me over to the bridge and the shantytown. Despite my struggles, they lifted me up and shoved me feet-first into one of the rusty barrels half-full of moist ash from old fires. They wedged me down with my hands trapped at my sides, and I was stuck like a cork in a bottle (only much less dignified).

"Stay there, Shamble. This fight is for members only," Rusty growled, and they bounded off. Like a wrestling announcer, Furguson yelled to all the werewolves, "Are you ready to *rumble?*"

The Monthlies surged forward. The Hairballs roared and pounded their chests, ready to meet them.

Just then Antoine Stickler appeared.

The Jamaican vampire sauntered into the midst of the two groups, yin-yang tattoos and peace signs visible on his arms—freshly re-inked. The dreadlocks looked like the tentacles of a baby kraken that was suckling on his scalp.

"Now, you all done heard Mister Chambeaux," he said, in a calm tone, but his accent was more pronounced, probably due to the tension. "There won't be no peace and happiness in the world unless we listen to each other. I've been impartial—I put gang ink on both sides. I tried to help you be mellow and show you that violence is never an answer. I made voodoo dolls of every one of you, put balm of Gilead all around you and on you, spelled you all to make you think peaceful thoughts—but *damn,* you are stubborn!" He shook his head and made a disgusted sound. "Now you're making me haul out the *Big Ink.*"

The rival werewolves stared at him. Antoine's lecture was getting an even worse reception than mine had. I struggled in the barrel, rocking back and forth, trying to dump myself over.

From a clip at his waist, Antoine removed a small battery-powered tattoo gun, made a fist of his right hand, and held out his forearm. A new tattoo stood out on his vampire flesh, an intricate mandala pattern. "You all have gang tats, but I loaded every one with special magic—a variation on an old impotence spell."

Rusty growled from across the parking lot.

"Sorry about that, Rusty." Antoine nodded toward him. "The first one was a mistake. *This* one's on purpose. It's a non-violence spell."

Werewolves on both sides were snarling now. "Don't ruin our fun!"

"We had *plans* for tonight!"

"You got no right!"

"Oh, I got no right? You think so?" Using the gun, Antoine completed a pattern, connecting dots on his mandala. "There! Now don't worry, be happy."

Suddenly, all the Hairballs and Monthlies who had been snarling looked disoriented and confused, but very relaxed about it.

"Whoa," said Furguson, swaying, looking around at the crowd. "With all these wolves, let's have a block party!" He called across to the Monthlies. "Hey! You guys could bring a keg."

Some of the Monthlies scratched themselves, perplexed. "We'll need some chips, too."

Antoine Stickler let out a sigh. "Now you see the light." He inhaled deeply, as if imagining a long toke, then he sauntered away, his work done. He called over his shoulder, "Now, resolve your difficulties like cool people."

I finally managed to tip over the rusty barrel, which crashed to the ground. My shoulders hurt, but I wriggled and began to work my way out of my embarrassing confinement. Not exactly the most dignified way to solve a case.

The groups of combatants began to break up, unsure. Though the voodoo spell hadn't affected Miranda and Hirsute, who had not sullied their bodies with tattoos, the pair simply lost interest and ran off to the nearest dark alley together. Which was probably what they wanted anyway. The professor and the students also backed away, relieved not to have to fight, although Professor Zevon had been hoping to derive an academic paper from the material.

Other rumble participants did not have voodoo gang ink, however, and their anger remained unslaked. Scratch and Sniff were having none of the curious détente—and neither was Rusty.

As the first Hairball to get a voodoo tattoo, Rusty had been afflicted with the impotence spell—but that was before Antoine had added his fail-safe trick on the other gang tats. As Rusty looked around at his sickeningly mellow companions, he let out a roar with even more bestial fury than usual—and I knew we were in trouble.

He stalked over to two large tarpaulin-covered cages like the ones I had seen at the cockatrice fights. He wrestled away the fabric covering . . . and I suddenly recalled the mysterious blacked-out coop in his backyard.

Rusty threw open the cage doors and turned away, covering his eyes with a furry forearm. He shouted in a loud guttural voice, "Loyal Hairballs—remember the drill! Squint!"

I heard a shrieking, hissing caterwaul and knew what it was. Not domesticated cockatrices this time. *Real* ones.

CHAPTER 49

Three angry, snapping, writhing shapes exploded out of their containers. Since I was flat on the ground trying to squirm out of a rusty barrel, I didn't get a good look—fortunately.

Rusty kept his eyes pressed into the crook of his elbow and staggered out of the way. Though the Hairballs were stunned and lethargic from the peace tattoos, they were well trained and reacted by closing their eyes, averting their heads, and slinking away.

At the forefront of the Monthlies, Scratch and Sniff were spoiling for a fight. Their tattoos were healing spells, and not of the peace-inducing variety. Since Rusty was vulnerable with his eyes covered, the two troublemakers bounded in for the kill, their pelt jackets flying behind them. They raised their meat cleavers, bared their long fangs, and let their tongues loll out.

Scratch and Sniff sprang in front of the purebred cockatrices—and froze. Their muscles petrified, their eyes widened and then whitened. I heard a cracking sound, like a sheet of ice shattering on a frozen pond. The two troublemakers turned into perfect ferocious-looking statues, as if some sculptor had captured the essence of lycanthropy.

Hearing the warning, Professor Zevon dutifully covered his eyes and stumbled about, calling to his students, "Can someone gather data? It would make a most interesting paper!"

One student said, "I'll do it, Professor! I've got my lab notebook." He raced forward—and also turned to stone.

Even though the werewolf gangs had been mellowed by Antoine's peace tattoos and no longer wanted to claw out clumps of their rivals' fur or sink fangs into their throats, they could still panic. They began to scatter.

The last thing in the world I wanted was to catch an eyeful of *ugly*. I finally managed to squirm myself free of the barrel and climbed back to my feet, turning my face away.

The beautiful blond, blue-eyed Sheyenne appeared before me, hands on her spectral hips. "You are really having a bad night, Beaux."

"Tell me about it, but it's better now that you're here with me." I was covered in ash. "Don't go near the cockatrices. One glimpse—"

Sheyenne chuckled. "I've already had a look, Beaux. Yes, they are hideous, but what's a cockatrice going to do to a ghost, turn me into ectoplasmic stone? I'm safe—it's you I'm worried about. I don't dare let you sneak a peek."

Rusty stumbled over to us, still pressing the flat of his paw against his eyes. He was chuffing with laughter. "Did you see those two morons? Scratch and Sniff—serves them right!"

"Yeah, great job, Rusty," I said, keeping a hand over my eyes as well. It was an odd way to have a conversation. I cocked my head in the direction where I thought he was standing. "You've caused the deaths of three people, and your deadly cockatrices are on the loose. How do you plan on catching them?"

"I've got burlap bags right by the cages. We just snag 'em and bag 'em."

"And how exactly are you going to do that?" I asked. "One glimpse, and we turn to stone."

"Oh." Rusty paused. "Maybe I'd better have Furguson do it."

Sheyenne retrieved the necktie that Professor Zevon had discarded prior to the fight. "Use this as a blindfold, Beaux."

I lined it up over my eyes and cinched it tight, putting the knot up against the bullet hole in the back of my head, to hold it in place.

"No peeking," she said.

"I feel safer, but how does that help us? I can't see a thing."

I should have known Sheyenne already had a plan. "But you and I are a team. We're going to take the burlap sacks and catch the cockatrices. I'll guide you to them—like in a game of Marco Polo."

"Never was much good at that game," I said.

She guided me to the cages, where she picked up a burlap sack and pushed it into my hands. I fumbled with the rough sack and pulled it open. After the cockatrice fights, Rusty and Furguson had snagged two of the domesticated creatures and stuffed them into sacks without too much trouble. But Rusty and Furguson hadn't been blindfolded at the time, and these purebred cockatrices seemed larger, meaner, and—judging from the stony effect they had on their victims—even uglier.

Amid the panicked turmoil of fleeing werewolves, I heard someone let out a grunt of surprised disgust, then that crackly ice sound again as he turned to stone.

"This way, Beaux," Sheyenne called. I followed her voice, stumbling across the gravel parking lot. "Hurry! They've split up, but this one's close." I heard hissing, a clacking beak, a slither of scales, and the clatter of talons on gravel. I remembered how vicious even their kinder, gentler cousins had been in the fighting ring.

"It's right in front of you, Beaux. Three steps, now hold the sack open!"

I lurched forward, flailing with the open sack. The cockatrice let out a squawk and scuttled in the opposite direction.

"To your left, your left!"

I swooped with the bag and dove forward—only to land in one of the big muddy potholes. At least it washed some of the ash from my slacks. I stumbled back to my feet.

Sheyenne was close. "I'll drive it to you. There—at one o'clock, Beaux! *Lunge!*"

I dove forward with the burlap sack and, to my astonishment, snagged the creature. It flapped and flailed inside the sack, but I yanked the mouth shut, twisted the burlap around, and made a quick, solid knot.

"One down, Beaux! Good work!"

She whisked away for just a moment, then returned and thrust another burlap bag into my hands. "Come on, two more to go—no time to rest. I've got a spare sack."

"Which way now?" I asked.

"Turn right a little. Then straight ahead. One of them is perched on the new Sniff statue."

"Proud of its work, no doubt," I muttered. I could hear it cawing and hissing like a rooster guarding its territory.

Sheyenne was so intent on chasing the creature herself that she forgot to warn me about obstacles. I barked my shin against a parked truck's bumper. She was ahead of me, calling back. "Come on, follow my voice!"

The cockatrice hissed and squawked, and Sheyenne yelled, "Hey, ugly!" The creature sounded offended at being unable to turn a ghost to stone.

I smelled a foul stench and guessed the cockatrice had opened its bowels to leave a hefty, smoking decoration on the statue's shoulder. I lurched forward and distracted the thing, and Sheyenne managed to throw the sack over it, catching the thrashing, angry creature by surprise. The flailing cockatrice nearly tore free of the burlap, but I helped Sheyenne wrestle it off the statue and down to the ground.

"My poltergeist powers are wearing thin," she said. "I don't usually exert myself for so long."

I fumbled blindly until I tied off the sack and tossed the annoyed cockatrice to the side. It accidentally landed in one of the crater mud puddles. (I would have done it on purpose if I'd been able to see.)

"The third one's getting away, Beaux! Quick—it's almost to Cralo's warehouse!"

I stood up again, holding the sack. "Just guide me to it, Spooky. I'll take care of this one."

I hoped the Emporium delivery doors were closed; I didn't want to imagine a madcap blindfolded chase through the aisles of the spare parts showroom.

"We've got to head it off! Hurry—it's going around back!" Sheyenne shouted.

It's not easy to hurry when you can't see where you're going; nevertheless, I shambled forward, stumbling across the uneven parking lot, tripping in a deep tire rut. I heard a car engine start somewhere behind the Emporium.

The cockatrice squawked and hissed like a turkey being chased by a poodle. I followed, picking up speed; at this point I didn't care whether or not I damaged myself. I was going to have to ask Mavis and Alma Wannovich for an early refresher spell this month. I certainly had some good stories to share with them by way of payment.

Sheyenne floated beside me, telling me to dodge left or right, offering loving encouragement while also urging me to greater speed. Then her voice changed as I heard the engine roar, the tires squeal. "It's Tony Cralo's limo—that fat zombie's getting away!"

I staggered blindly ahead, flailing my hands. Considering

the singes from the crematorium, the ashes from the barrel, and the mud from the parking lot puddles, I must have looked like a frightful decomposing shambler.

Hearing the cockatrice, I ran recklessly ahead and sensed the large shape of a limousine coming toward me. I stopped. So did the limo driver—right after the front bumper thumped into me and knocked me flat on my back. The limo windows were down, as if Cralo wanted one last breath of fresh air from the Quarter before he fled underground forever.

Tony Cralo's voice yelled, "What are you stopping for, Rudy? Just run him over, whoever it is!"

"Can't see, boss," said the hunchbacked chauffeur. "We were in such a rush I forgot my seat cushion, and I'm sitting too low. I'd better step out and take a look."

"I'll do it—you move too slow, and we're in a hurry!"

The limo's back door opened, and I heard Cralo emerge, cursing, grumbling, and outgassing. Gravel crunched, and he stood over me. "Wait, that's Chambeaux! How the hell did he get away from the crematorium?"

The last cockatrice was close by. I heard Sheyenne's voice whisper, "Shoo! Shoo!"

Cralo paused, and I heard the cockatrice prowling outside the limo. It came around the car and let out a challenging hiss. "What is that ugly—?"

The crackling-ice petrification sound came louder than I'd heard before as the fat zombie turned to stone with a final disgusted groan and a last toot. Next, it sounded like a felled tree tottering and a loud crash—accompanied by a surprised squawk and a wet squelch.

Then silence.

"Spooky! What just happened?"

"The good news is you can take off the blindfold now, Beaux."

I touched the necktie blindfold, then paused. "We didn't catch the third cockatrice yet."

"Tony Cralo did."

I yanked the necktie from my eyes and blinked.

Near me, the enormous form of Tony Cralo had turned a chalky grayish-white, and the stone zombie had fallen flat on his face. A few feathers and a lumpy claw of the last cockatrice protruded from beneath the toppled statue.

Rudy, the small hunchbacked driver, was slung low in the driver's seat of the limo. His hands clutched the steering wheel, but he could barely peer over the dash, much less see the ground. "So, is it taken care of, Mister Cralo? Should I be driving now?" Rudy strained to raise his head above the steering wheel.

"Your boss isn't going anywhere," I said. In fact, I had no idea how we'd even move him.

Chapter 50

By the time McGoo and Robin arrived at the scene—followed by truckloads of armored police loaded for werewolf—the mayhem was all over. The riot squad had been ready to crack down on a rumble, and they were disappointed to find the crisis wrapped up before they found the right address.

McGoo shook his head. "We wasted hours over by the Smile Syndicate warehouse. Nothing was happening. An old security guard tried to shoo us away, but he hadn't heard anything about a rumble."

Seeing how battered I looked, Sheyenne intangibly fussed over my stained jacket and singed hair while Robin checked me over. "You need a good cleaning, Dan, but there's no severe damage that I can see. Nothing that can't be fixed."

Sheyenne hovered next to me. "Every once in a while, Beaux just needs to be reminded that he can't do without me."

"I'd rather not be reminded again soon," I said. "But I'm glad to have your company anytime." I flexed my arms, winced. "Maybe I should try one of those new zombie energy drinks."

McGoo finished pacing around the parking lot crime scene,

taking notes for his report. I asked, "Have you been to the crematorium yet? Sheyenne locked Joe Muggins in the bathroom over there. He's another one of the bad guys—stuck me in a furnace."

"I rescued Dan," Sheyenne said. "As usual."

"Attempting to cremate a zombie against his wishes is a serious crime," Robin said. "I can find several relevant statutes."

McGoo nodded. "Sheyenne tipped me off, and I had a team arrest him at the crematorium. I think he's confessed to anyone who'll listen by now. He was just relieved somebody let him out of that bathroom—it has a big, barred east-facing window that's not blacked out. He would've fried in the sunlight if nobody came before dawn."

I snorted. "That might have been the only *real* ash the crematorium ever produced." I found it hard to feel sympathy for the guy who had shoved me in a cremation furnace and adjusted the settings to Extra Crispy.

I told them the full story about how Archibald Victor was the one scalping werewolves to gather specimens for his experiments, and also how I'd tracked down and destroyed the vampire brain before it could be transplanted. I still felt saddened by the deaths of the mad scientist and his wife, but they had tangled their own fates and there were no more split ends.

We stood together outside the limo, where the enormous stone Cralo lay facedown in the parking lot. A uniformed cop drove a forklift out of the Emporium loading bay and rumbled over to the obese statue.

Lowering the tines and easing forward, the forklift driver raised the heavy stone figure off the ground. The diesel engine groaned, and exhaust fumes curled into the air; the forklift teetered, unbalanced, as the operator drove away with its heavy burden.

"Better not look down at the smashed cockatrice," I said. "Just in case."

"It's fine. The thing is pulped beyond recognition," Sheyenne said. So we all stared anyway. The tangle of feathers, claws, scales, and blood would have been ugly in any configuration, but now at least it wasn't fatally hideous.

McGoo shuddered. "Compared to that *thing*, the Tony Cralo statue is practically a work of art." He followed the departing forklift as it rolled into the warehouse loading dock.

Robin stared at the big showroom building. "I don't know if the Spare Parts Emporium can be made into a legitimate business, but I'll bring the full force of MLDW to bear. The new management will have to keep very careful records from now on."

"Same with Joe's Crematorium," I said.

Robin was already running possibilities through her mind. "Pending investigation, all the Emporium's inventory will have to be returned to the original owners or their estates. Lacking any legal claimant, maybe we can get the pieces donated to the Fresh Corpses Zombie Rehab Clinic."

"It would be nice to have some good come of this," Sheyenne said.

Near the limo's open door, I caught a glimpse of gold chain on the ground, a flash of yellow metal that Tony Cralo must have dropped when he stepped out of the vehicle.

Before I could bend to see what it was, a voice interrupted me. "Hey, um, Mister Chambeaux?"

I turned to find Larry the werewolf. "It's all over, Larry. You can go back home to your box now."

"I've got something for you—and for Ms. Deyer." The werewolf handed both of us folded packets of paper bound in blue. "You've been served." He backed away quickly. "Sorry, I needed the money." He vanished before Robin could tear open her envelope.

Sheyenne hovered close to see for herself, and Robin looked at me as if she had bitten into a spoiled pickle. "It's a temporary restraining order—we're both required to stay away from Rova Halsted."

"That is correct," came a man's voice, brittle and professional sounding. Don Tuthery stepped out of a nearby shadow, his wire-rimmed glasses glinting, not a gray hair out of place, his conservative business suit painfully immaculate in a setting of so much mayhem. He looked as if he meant to smile in triumph, but couldn't figure out how to make his lips curve in that direction. "There shall be no direct contact. Neither of you is allowed to approach within fifty feet of the Parlour (BNF), and you're forbidden from getting your hair cut there."

I chuckled. "I can live with that. I've taken enough risks already for one week."

Robin recovered her cool and aloof manner. "When you get to your office tomorrow, Mister Tuthery, you'll find a little surprise of your own—I've already received a preliminary ruling."

From the expression on his face, Tuthery was not aware of any ruling, so Robin was happy to explain it to him. "Since our client, Mister Halsted, has expressly clarified his wishes, the judge ruled that fifty thousand dollars in insurance monies—or the equivalent amount in liquid, tangible, and/or capital assets of the Parlour (BNF)—are to be immediately placed into trust in the name of Jordan Halsted until the proceedings are complete. The Court has appointed a Guardian Ad Litem to represent Jordan's best interests and elect potential trustees. And Rova Halsted cannot be a trustee."

Tuthery stared at her. "I'll contest that."

"Go right ahead," Robin said. "The judge has already looked at the Better Business Bureau complaints about the Parlour (BNF) and is not convinced that the beauty salon is a good investment for the child's future."

"Complaints against a business cannot be used in custody issues," Tuthery sputtered. "You know that."

"The haircut snapshots were offered for character reference only," Robin countered.

"Ms. Halsted is a fully qualified stylist!"

Robin smiled. "I invite you to have your client retake the Boards for her license, just to prove her competence in the field."

"Or you could just have her cut *your* hair," I suggested.

The attorney flushed red. "Your client is not getting visitation rights, and we'll fight him for child support."

"Already arranged, Mister Tuthery—you really should spend more time at your desk," Robin said. "Mister Halsted has agreed to pay *reasonable* child support, now that he is gainfully employed. And so long as his payments continue as promised, the judge grants him access to the boy."

"But he's a . . . zombie!" Tuthery looked at me as if I'd actually help his cause.

"Not sufficient grounds for discrimination," Robin replied. "Especially not to deny a father the right to see his son."

Though I had been through several ordeals in a row, I felt good as I turned to walk away; Robin slipped her arm through one of mine, and Sheyenne pretended to hold my other one. The three of us strolled across the parking lot, heads held high, leaving a livid Don Tuthery standing by the limo.

I glanced back at him and saw that something had caught his eye. The lawyer bent down beside the limo and picked up a gold chain with a small gleaming medallion that had fallen to the ground—Esther's bad-luck charm. He furtively glanced around to see if anyone had noticed, and slipped the charm "for luck" into his pocket.

I thought about warning him, but decided that wasn't my place. Instead, we walked away, letting Don Tuthery accept the luck that he deserved.

CHAPTER 51

Two days later, Robin had wrapped up and filed the paperwork to establish a charitable werewolves-only wilderness preserve in Montana. When she came into our offices, Miranda Jekyll was pleased, impatient, and aloof—typical Miranda. Robin handed her the documents, already stamped and notarized by Sheyenne, in a nice black binder. "I am proud to announce the Miranda Jekyll Memorial Werewolf Preserve, as you requested."

Perplexed, I pointed out, "You don't usually name a place 'Memorial' something-or-other until after the person is dead."

Miranda laughed and raised her hand, which the ever-present Hirsute seized, kissed, then nibbled, much to her delight. She struggled to continue, "Sweetheart, what good does it do me if people don't remember me *now*?"

And so the name stayed.

Miranda walked over to the fly-specked window that looked out upon the dingy streets and ramshackle buildings. She sounded wistful. "While I was in the middle of nowhere, I longed to come back to the Quarter. A person can take only so much fresh air, sunshine, and scenery." She turned around and looked at us. "But I forgot what a pain in the ass monsters can be. Good thing Hirsute and I left that unpleasant rumble when we did." She shook her head. "I hear cockatrices are attracted by perfume."

"They would have been drawn to your sparkling personality, as well, my dear," Hirsute said.

"I'm still a city girl at heart, but I may get used to my role as a country bumpkin." Miranda toyed with her pearls. "Scratch and Sniff are going to make adorable statues out at the gateway to the preserve. A matched set! We're having them crated up and delivered in a few days. In fact, Mister Chambeaux, I understand your friend, Steve Halsted, is a reliable truck driver?"

I smiled. "I believe he is."

Miranda said, "I have to think Scratch and Sniff would like to be up at the preserve. And now at least we can control those boys. Sometimes they were too unruly even for werewolves. They deserved what happened to them."

One of Professor Zevon's students and two other werewolf bystanders had also been turned to stone, however, and they hadn't deserved such a fate. Glenn the wizard was now working to develop an anti-petrification spell; someday, maybe they would all be cured.

Anxious to bring the criminals to justice, McGoo was particularly hoping to restore Tony Cralo so the zombie crime lord could face charges, alongside Joe Muggins. Personally, I figured it was best to let the statues stand for themselves.

And Rusty had to make restitution as well for his part in the tragedy.

Miranda said her farewells, took Hirsute's arm, and left our offices with a last invitation. "If you ever want to take a long walk through the deep, dark woods, we've got what you need in Montana. We're even opening the sanctuary to Girl Scout troops for campouts. It gets chilly out there in the forest, so we're providing all of them with nice, warm red riding hoods. It'll be marvelous."

We said we'd consider visiting, but made no promises.

Back at my desk at last, I reviewed pending cases and enjoyed the quiet for about five minutes before I felt the need to go out again. That "restless zombie" thing again. I was not made for a desk job. Real private investigation involves meeting people, keeping ears and eyes open, being aware of when something just doesn't smell right. Like cockatrice poop.

Sheyenne had closed out the case file for Archibald Victor and was now boxing up the mountain of documents from Cralo's Spare Parts Emporium for delivery to the district attorney. She had taken the time to highlight the most incriminating entries with colorful tape flags.

As I walked the streets, I bumped into McGoo out on his beat. He was writing a citation for an illegally parked hearse outside of Bruno and Heinrich's Embalming Parlor. "See you at the Tavern tonight, Shamble?"

"You know I'll be there."

He finished writing the ticket and placed it on the windshield of the hearse. "Do you know what kind of monster is machine washable?"

"You got me, McGoo."

"A wash-and-werewolf."

"Right. See you tonight." We parted company.

I stopped by Voodoo Tattoo to thank Antoine Stickler for his attempt at stopping the werewolf gang violence. When I entered the tattoo parlor, I saw that he had a customer—a hairy-backed red-furred werewolf who was sprawled facedown on the padded table. Rusty turned his muzzle, glanced at me, and let out a long contented sigh.

"Mister Shamble, so nice to see you! I need to pay my bill,

don't I?" His voice was languid, drifting, not at all like the gruff and growling werewolf I knew.

"Did you give him valium, Antoine?" I asked.

The Jamaican vampire was humming as he worked with his needle gun. "Even better." The needle whirred as he continued drawing his pattern. "Permanent peace-and-mellowness tattoo—better than antidepressants. Rusty's not gonna let the stress get to him anymore. He'll be mellow all the time."

After taking a deep, slow inhale, Rusty let out the breath. His tongue lolled as he seemed to melt into the padded bench. "I can even tolerate my nephew now. . . ."

Antoine tossed his dreadlocks and grinned. "I can do one for you, too, Mister Chambeaux. Special discount rate for friends."

Permanent peace and mellowness? "There are times I'd like that, but I need to keep my edge. You don't see many mellow private detectives."

"Don't see many *zombie* detectives either," Antoine said. "Takes all kinds in the Quarter."

"How did you convince Rusty to submit to that?" I asked. "After your peace tattoos ruined his rumble, I thought he'd be angry with you."

"Court order for anger management and restitution," Antoine said. "And I made him a deal. I figured out how to modify the impotence tat. No way to get rid of it—one hell of a persistent spell—but I inked on an extra design . . . makes the impotence impotent, but only for a couple days each month." Antoine winked. "At full moon, he'll be as virile and hairy as ever."

"But won't he be too mellow to go on the prowl?"

"Don't need to go on the prowl." Rusty closed his eyes and relaxed. "They come to me. I've always been a bitch magnet."

"I don't suppose there's an anti-clumsiness tattoo you can use on Furguson?" I asked.

"I've got some ideas cookin'." Antoine smiled and finished connecting a line on the shaved patch on Rusty's shoulder. As I watched, the fur began growing back into place, covering up the lines.

"Glad you stopped by, Mister Chambeaux. You and I, we're men of the same mind-set. I've got something for you, something special—and I don't do this for just anybody." Antoine stood up, patted Rusty on the back. "You relax there awhile."

Rusty nodded slowly. "Relax . . ."

With great pride, the Jamaican vampire walked to the effigy dolls on his shelves. He displayed the lifelike werewolf figures he had so painstakingly made before the rumble. Scratch and Sniff, Rusty, Furguson, a dozen more, both Monthlies and Hairballs. From the top shelf, he took down a gaunt pale-skinned doll with a fedora, a sport jacket complete with tiny stitched-up bullet holes, even a mark in the middle of the forehead.

"Had to work from memory, but this is sure to be effective. Special keepsake with a thousand uses. Made it with angelica root to ward off evil, bring good luck. I even got the skin color right."

I didn't know what to say. I wasn't even sure I wanted the thing. "That's . . . very kind of you, Antoine. Would it be too much trouble to unmake it? I'm not comfortable having that around. What if it fell into the wrong hands?"

Antoine chuckled. "Aww, who would want to do harm to you, Mister Chambeaux?"

"I've already been murdered once, remember?"

He looked disturbed. "I thought that was a one-time thing. Well, I can keep this doll for you here, put it in my portfolio—it's some of my best work."

Though I wasn't sure what use I'd have for my own personal voodoo doll, I didn't like Antoine's solution, either. "I'll take it with me after all, since you did all that work. We'll keep it in our offices." *Locked up in the safe where no one else can get at it.*

I put the doll in my pocket—gently—and headed out.

CHAPTER 52

When my dirt buddy Steve Halsted came back to the offices, he was all smiles. Accompanying him, his ex-wife Rova was not smiling, but she looked less bitter than before. In fact, she seemed shaken and resigned. Even after all the unpleasantness she had shown toward so many people, we could at least share grief over the death of Harriet Victor.

"Rova and I have business to wrap up before I start my drive," Steve said. "Got a new rig and a long-haul delivery to Montana."

Robin looked uncertainly at Rova Halsted. "Where is your attorney? The restraining orders are still in effect, and we're not allowed to talk with you."

"I had the orders withdrawn this morning. Mister Tuthery wasn't very happy about it. Can I see your copies?" Sheyenne brought them to her, and Rova tore them in half. "We don't need these anymore. Time to settle this, just me and Steve."

"You shouldn't be here without counsel," Robin warned. "I can't vouch for—"

"Don Tuthery tried to grab my ass, then he tripped on a

desk mat and fell face-first into a stapler. Broke his nose." Rova snorted.

"Bad luck," I said innocently.

"He always seemed so suave, but now I see him for what he really is. Needless to say, I terminated my relationship with the Addams Family Practice. I'm representing myself as of now. Steve and I have decided to be adults about this."

"That's always the best course of action," Robin said, "though we rarely see it in this business." She led us into the conference room, while Sheyenne brought in the case files. Even for a zombie, Steve had more of a jaunty step.

Robin said, "Ms. Halsted, I need to remind you that a trust must be set up in the name of your son. The liquid and capital assets of the Parlour (BNF) are, per court order, under the control of a trustee until such time as the full amount of fifty thousand dollars is reached."

"We have the money now," Rova said. "Harriet Victor named me the beneficiary of *her* insurance. It's more than enough to fund Jordan's trust and also keep the business running. I think I'm going to install two more tanning beds."

I doubted that was a wise business decision, since the original tanning beds were never used, but what did I know about running beauty salons?

Steve said, "We both want to make sure Jordan's taken care of. I understand how hard this is for him, but I still want to see my son once a month or so."

"I've decided to accept the situation and make the best of it," Rova said. "A boy needs his father, even if he's a zombie. And Steve has agreed to make himself as presentable as possible before each visit, so it isn't so . . . jarring."

Robin looked back and forth, surprised and relieved. "I'm so happy for all of you."

Steve's eyes were bright. "I saw Jordan yesterday, and we played catch, threw a ball back and forth a few times." He shook his head in wonderment. "I'm not as nimble as a dad should be anymore, but it's still our time together. Jordan even wants to take me to school, for show-and-tell. There's a day where the students get to describe what's special about their dads. Apparently they're all anxious to see me."

Sheyenne said, "I bet they don't usually have a zombie show up in class."

Steve made an embarrassed gesture. "Not because I'm a *zombie*—Jordan wants to show me off because I'm a truck driver."

These days, Mrs. Saldana spent much of her time at the zombie rehab clinic—and she had extra work to do, with so many body parts from Cralo's Emporium being donated for charity work. But the old woman's first love was her mission.

When I stopped in at Hope & Salvation, I was surprised to see the patchwork but energetic Adriana Cruz working as a volunteer. Despite her scars and awkward movements, her mood was upbeat. She helped Jerry, the mission's undead assistant, fold and stack metal chairs against the wall.

When I entered, Jerry looked up and smiled, showing his rotten teeth. He had been much more lively company since Chambeaux & Deyer tracked down his lost heart and soul.

Mrs. Saldana had just finished her sermon, having given the monsters their breakfast, and everyone left satisfied for another day of existence. Cheerful as usual, the old woman gathered the hymnals to put them away on a library book cart.

"Good to see you back at the mission, Mrs. Saldana," I said.

She brightened. "That'll happen more often now, since I have Adriana to assist over at the rehab clinic. She's a born administrator."

"I've decided to do something with myself," Adriana said. "I can still make a difference. I'm glad I wasn't cremated after all."

"Good to hear. I wanted to let you know that the crematorium is shut down. Joe Muggins is in prison. All of their crimes unraveled."

"You're an inspiration to all of us, Mister Chambeaux," Mrs. Saldana said.

"I am? What did I do?"

Jerry slid out a wooden piano bench and eased himself down upon it. He cracked his knuckles loudly and prepared to play.

Adriana said, "You made me see that I can keep being useful. Just because I'm dead doesn't mean I can't live my life the way I want to."

I was embarrassed, but no longer capable of blushing, thanks to the embalming fluid. "Glad to hear it," I said.

Mavis and Alma Wannovich also called me an inspiration, and they arranged for Linda Bullwer to join us when I stopped by their apartment for the much-needed refresher on the restoration spell.

Mavis bustled about, pleased to have company. "Happy to do it, Mister Chambeaux. We owe you a great deal."

"In royalties?"

"In favors," Mavis corrected.

The plump vampire ghostwriter sat on the sofa with a notebook propped on her lap. "I need to get to work on the next Shamble and Die novel," Linda Bullwer said. "I've decided to frame it around Senator Balfour and his Unnatural Acts Act, tie it together with the Smile Syndicate, even the troubles at the Full Moon Brothel. Readers love titillating storylines. Throw in a little sex, and you increase your sales."

"Sales are quite fine," Mavis said, "from the initial release."

Alma circled the apartment, snuffling along the baseboard. She made a series of loud grunts to remind her sister of something. Mavis said, "Oh, yes, I almost forgot! The reception at the Worldwide Horror Convention was quite positive. The fans loved the book. There's even been talk of awards."

"Awards?" I asked. "Really?"

Linda Bullwer tapped her pen on the notepad. "I'm campaigning behind the scenes, so we'll see. Penny Dreadful may have a long literary career ahead of her." She took off her cat's-eye glasses and wiped them on her fuzzy sweater. "So long as you have a long and interesting career, Mister Chambeaux."

"I'll do my best," I said.

Back in the office, Robin had mounted a certificate of appreciation in a standard black document frame. The award acknowledged her charitable work for the Monster Legal Defense Workers. "It's good to be appreciated," she said.

"I certainly appreciate you," I said. "And Sheyenne. We make a great team."

Sheyenne drifted in with a stack of papers, which she placed on Robin's much-cleaner-than-usual desk. "Now that the Cralo paperwork is gone, this office seems almost clean for a change. Time to start a new pile. Here's the sewer documentation you asked for."

"What sewer documentation?" I asked. "Did we get a new case?"

"MLDW has called a meeting. Zoning troubles with the sewers. The underdwellers are complaining about the amount of effluent."

"Too much or too little?" I asked. In the underworld, it could have been either.

"That's the heart of the dispute," Robin said.

"I'll leave you to it."

I went into my own office, and Sheyenne followed, wearing her flirtatious smile. "I've been resting up my poltergeist energies since the werewolf rumble, Beaux. I think I've got my strength back. I could try on the body suit again tonight . . . if you're interested."

"If it's you, Spooky, how could I not be interested?" I leaned back in my chair as she drifted out of the office toward her desk, where the phone was ringing.

Even with all the murder and mayhem in the Quarter, all the treachery and corruption I exposed, all the slime (or effluent) I had to deal with, this wasn't so bad. You take whatever life—or afterlife—hands you, and you make the best of it.

The office door crashed open, and another monster staggered in, looking distraught—as they always do.

Time to get back to work.

ACKNOWLEDGMENTS

Going over rough draft manuscripts is a grisly job and not for the faint of heart. Rebecca Moesta, Louis Moesta, Deb Ray, Nancy Greene, and Melinda Brown dug down to the bones of this story and offered invaluable commentary and support. My Kensington editor, Michaela Hamilton, sinks her teeth into every Dan Shamble novel, and everyone at Kensington has shown great enthusiasm for the series. Shamble on!

Want to enjoy more zany adventures
with Dan Shamble, Zombie P.I.?

Don't miss the previous entries in the series . . .

DEATH WARMED OVER

UNNATURAL ACTS

STAKEOUT AT THE VAMPIRE CIRCUS

Available from Kensington Publishing Corp.

Keep reading for sample excerpts. . . .

CHAPTER 1

I'm dead, for starters—it happens. But I'm still ambulatory, and I can still think, still be a contributing member of society (such as it is, these days). And still solve crimes.

As the detective half of Chambeaux & Deyer Investigations, I'm responsible for our caseload, despite being shot in the head a month ago. My unexpected murder caused a lot of inconvenience to me and to others, but I'm not the sort of guy to leave his partner in the lurch. The cases don't solve themselves.

My partner, Robin Deyer, and I had built a decent business for ourselves, sharing office space, with several file cabinets full of pending cases, both legal matters and private investigations. Although catching my own killer is always on my mind, paying clients have to take priority.

Which is why I found myself sneaking into a cemetery at night while trying to elude a werewolf hit man who'd been following me since sunset—in order to retrieve a lost painting for a ghost.

Just another day at work for me.

The wrought-iron cemetery gate stood ajar with a Welcome

mat on either side. These days, visiting hours are round-the-clock, and the gate needs to stay open so that newly risen undead can wander out. When the gates were locked, neighbors complained about moaning and banging sounds throughout the night, which made it difficult for them to sleep.

When I pulled, the gate glided open on well-oiled hinges. A small sign on the bars read, MAINTAINED BY FRIENDS OF THE GREENLAWN CEMETERY. There were more than a hundred ostentatious crypts to choose from, interspersed with less prominent tombstones. I wished I had purchased a guide pamphlet ahead of time, but the gift shop was open only on weekends. I had to find the Ricketts crypt on my own—before the werewolf hit man caught up with me.

The world's a crazy place since the Big Uneasy, the event that changed all the rules and allowed a flood of baffled unnaturals to return—zombies, vampires, werewolves, ghouls, succubi, and the usual associated creatures. In the subsequent ten years, the Unnatural Quarter had settled into a community of sorts—one that offered more work than I could handle.

Now the quarter moon rode high in the sky, giving me enough light to see the rest of the cemetery. The unnatural thug, hired by the heirs of Alvin Ricketts, wasn't one of the monthly full-moon-only lycanthropes: He was a full-time hairy, surly beast, regardless of the time of month. Those are usually the meanest ones.

I moved from one crypt to the next, scrutinizing the blocky stone letters. The place was quiet, spooky . . . part of the ambience. You might think a zombie—even a well-preserved one like myself—would feel perfectly at ease in a graveyard. After all, what do *I* have to be afraid of? Well, I can still get mangled, for one thing. My body doesn't heal the way it used to, and we've all seen those smelly decomposing shamblers who refuse to take care of themselves, giving zombies everywhere a bad name. And werewolves are experts at mangling.

I wanted to avoid that, if possible.

Even undead, I remain as handsome as ever, with the exception of the holes left by the bullet—the largish exit wound on my forehead and the neat round one at the back of my head, where some bastard came up from behind, pressed the barrel of a .32 caliber pistol against my skull, and popped me before I got a good look at him. Fortunately, a low-slouched fedora covers the big hole. For the most part . . .

In the broader sense, the world hasn't changed much since the Big Uneasy. Most people go about their daily lives, having families, working jobs. But though a decade has passed, the law—not to mention law *enforcement*—still hasn't caught up with the new reality. According to the latest statistics by the DUS, the Department of Unnatural Services, about one out of every seventy-five corpses wakes up as a zombie, with the odds weighted heavily in favor of suicides or murder victims.

Lucky me to be on the interesting side of statistics.

After returning to life, I had shambled back into the office, picked up my caseload, and got to work again. Same as before . . . sort of. Fortunately, my zombie status isn't a handicap to being a private detective in the Unnatural Quarter. As I said, the cases don't solve themselves.

Days of investigation had led me to the graveyard. I dug through files, interviewed witnesses and suspects, met with the ghost artist Alvin Ricketts and separately with his indignant still-living family. (Despite Robin's best mediation efforts in the offices, the ghost and the living family refused to speak to each other.)

Alvin Ricketts was a successful pop-culture painter before his untimely demise, attributable to a month's worth of sleeping pills washed down with a full bottle of twenty-one-year-old single malt. (No sense letting it go to waste.) The ghost told me he would have taken more pills, but his insurance only authorized a thirty-day supply, and even in the deep gloom of his creative depression, Alvin had (on principle) refused to pay the additional pharmacy charge.

Now, whereas one in seventy-five dead people returns as a zombie, like myself, one in *thirty* comes back as a ghost (statistics again heavily weighted toward murder victims and suicides). Alvin Ricketts, a pop-art genius, had suffered a long and debilitating creative block, "artistic constipation" he called it. Feeling that he had nothing left to live for, he took his own life.

And then came back.

His ghost, however, found the death experience so inspirational that he found a reawakened and vibrant artistic fervor. Alvin set about painting again, announcing he would soon release his first new work with great fanfare.

His grieving (sic) family was less than enthusiastic about his return to painting, as well as his return from the dead. The artist's tragic suicide, and the fact that there would never be more Alvin Ricketts paintings, had caused his existing work to skyrocket in value—until the ghost's announcement of renewed productivity made the bottom fall out of the market. Collectors waited to see what new material Alvin would release, already speculating about how his artistic technique might have changed in his "post-death period."

The Ricketts family sued him, claiming that since Alvin was dead and they were his heirs, they now owned everything in his estate, including any new or undiscovered works and the profits from subsequent sales.

Alvin contested the claim. He hired Robin Deyer to fight for his rights, and she promptly filed challenges while the ghost happily worked on his new painting. No one had yet seen it, but he claimed the work was his masterpiece.

The Ricketts heirs took the dispute to the next level. "Someone" broke into Alvin's studio and stole the painting. With the supposed masterpiece gone, the pop artist's much-anticipated return to the spotlight was put on hold. The family vehemently denied any involvement, of course.

That's when the ghost hired *me,* at Robin's suggestion, to track down and retrieve the painting—by any means necessary. The Ricketts heirs had hired a thug to keep me from succeeding in my investigation.

I heard a faint clang, which I recognized as the wrought-iron cemetery gate banging shut against the frame. The werewolf hit man wasn't far behind me. On the bright side, the fact that he was breathing down my neck probably meant I was getting close.

The cemetery had plenty of shadows to choose from, and I stayed hidden as I approached another crypt. BENSON. Not the right one. I had to find RICKETTS.

Werewolves are usually good trackers, but the cemetery abounds with odors of dead things, and he must have kept losing my scent. Since I change clothes frequently and maintain high standards of personal hygiene for a zombie, I don't have much of a smell about me. Unlike most unnaturals, I don't choose to wear colognes, fancy specialized unnatural deodorants, or perfumes.

I turned the corner in front of another low stone building fronted by stubby Corinthian columns. Much to my delight, I saw the inhabitant's name: RICKETTS. The flat stone door had been pried open, the caulking seal split apart.

New rules required quick-release latches on the insides of tombs now, so the undead can conveniently get back out. Some people were even buried with their cell phones, though I doubted they'd get good service from inside. *Can you hear me now?*

Now, if Alvin Ricketts were a zombie, he would have broken the seal when he came back out of the crypt. But since ghosts can pass through solid walls, Alvin would not have needed to break any door seals for his reemergence. So why was the crypt door ajar?

I spotted the silhouette of a large hairy form loping among the graves, sniffing the ground, coming closer. He still hadn't seen me. I pulled open the stone door just enough to slip through the narrow gap into the crypt, hoping my detective work was right.

During the investigation into the missing masterpiece, the police had obtained search warrants and combed through the homes, properties, and businesses of the Ricketts heirs. Nothing. With my own digging, I discovered a small storage unit that had been rented in the name of Gomez Ricketts, the black sheep of the family—and I was sure they had hidden the painting there.

But when the detectives served their warrant and opened the unit, they found only cases and cases of contraband vampire porn packaged as sick kiddie porn. Because the starlets were actually old-school vampires who had been turned while they were children, they claimed to be well over the legal age—in real years if not in physical maturity. Gomez Ricketts had been arrested for pedophilia/necrophilia, but he was out on bail. Even Robin, in her best legal opinion, couldn't say which way the verdict might go.

More to the point, we didn't find the stolen painting in the storage unit.

So I kept working on the case. Not only did I consult with Alvin's ghost, I also went over the interviews he'd given after his suicide. The ghost had gone into a manic phase, deliriously happy to put death behind him. He talked about awakening to find himself sealed in a crypt, his astral form rising from the cold physical body, his epiphany of throwing those morbid chains behind him. He had vowed never to go back there.

That's when I figured it out: The last place Alvin would ever think to look for his painting was inside his own crypt, which was property owned by the Ricketts family (though a recent court ruling deemed that a person owned his own grave in perpetuity—a landmark decision that benefitted several vampires who were caught in property-rights disputes).

Tonight, I planned to retrieve the painting from its hiding place.

From *Unnatural Acts*

CHAPTER 1

I never thought a golem could make me cry, but hearing the big clay guy's sad story brought a tear to my normally blood-shot eyes. My business partner Robin, a lawyer (but don't hold it against her), was weeping openly.

"It's so tragic!" she sniffled.

"Well, I certainly thought so," the golem said, lowering his sculpted head, "but I'm biased."

He had lurched into the offices of Chambeaux & Deyer Investigations with the ponderous and inexorable gait that all golems have. "Please," he said, "you've got to help me!"

In my business, most clients introduce themselves like that. It's not that they don't have any manners, but a person doesn't engage the services of a private investigator, or a lawyer, as an ordinary social activity. Our visitors generally come pre-loaded with problems. Robin and I were used to it.

Then, swaying on his thick feet, the golem added, "And you've got to help my people."

Now, that was something new.

Golems are man-sized creatures fashioned out of clay and

brought to life by an animation spell. Tailor-made for menial labor, they serve their masters and don't complain about minimum wage (or less, no tips). Traditionally, the creatures are statuesque and bulky, their appearance ranging from store-mannequin smooth to early Claymation, depending on the skill of the sculptor-magician who created them. I've seen do-it-yourself kits on the market, complete with facial molds and step-by-step instructions.

This golem was in bad shape: dried and flaking, his gray skin fissured with cracks. His features were rounded, generic, and less distinctive than a bargain-store dummy's. His brow was furrowed, his chapped gray lips pressed down in a frown. He tottered, and I feared he would crumble right there in the lobby area.

Robin hurried out of her office. "Please, come in, sir. We can see you right away."

Robin Deyer is a young African American woman with anime-worthy brown eyes, a big heart, and a feisty disposition. She and I had formed a loose partnership in the Unnatural Quarter, sharing office space and cooperating on cases. We have plenty of clients, plenty of job security, plenty of headaches. Unnaturals have problems just like anyone else, but zombies, vampires, werewolves, witches, ghouls, and the gamut of monsters are underrepresented in the legal system. That's more than enough cases, if you can handle the odd clientele and the unusual problems.

Since I'm a zombie myself, I fit right in.

I stepped toward the golem and shook his hand. His grip was firm but powdery. "My partner and I would be happy to listen to your case, Mr. . . . ?"

"I don't actually know my name. Sorry." His frown deepened like a character in a cartoon special. "Could you read it for me?" He slowly turned around. In standard magical manufacturing, a golem's name is etched in the soft clay on the back of his neck, where he can never see it for himself. "None of my fellow golems could read. We're budget models."

There it was, in block letters. "It says your name is Bill."

"Oh. I like that name." His frown softened, although the clay face was too stiff to be overly expressive. He stepped forward, disoriented. "Could I have some water, please?"

Sheyenne, the beautiful blond ghost who served as our receptionist, office manager, paralegal, business advisor, and whatever other titles she wanted to come up with, flitted to the kitchenette and returned with some sparkling water that Robin kept in the office refrigerator. The golem took the bottle from Sheyenne's translucent hands and unceremoniously poured it over his skin. "Oh, bubbly! That tingles."

It wasn't what I'd expected him to do, but we were used to unusual clients.

When I'd first hung out my shingle as a PI, I'd still been human, albeit jaded—not quite down-and-out, but willing to consider a nontraditional client base. Robin and I worked together for years in the Quarter, garnering a decent reputation with our work . . . and then I got shot in the back of the head during a case gone wrong. Fortunately, being killed didn't end my career. Ever since the Big Uneasy, staying dead isn't as common as it used to be. I returned from the grave, cleaned myself up, changed clothes, and got back to work. The cases don't solve themselves.

Thanks to high-quality embalming and meticulous personal care, I'm well preserved, not one of those rotting shamblers that give the undead such a bad name. Even with my pallid skin, the shadows under my eyes aren't too bad, and mortician's putty covers up the bullet's entry and exit holes in my skull, for the most part.

Bill massaged the moistened clay, smoothed the cracks and fissures of his skin, and let out a contented sigh. He splashed more water on his face, and his expression brightened. "That's better! Little things can improve life in large ways." After wiping his cheeks and eyes with the last drops of sparkling water, he became more animated. "Is that so much to ask? Civil treatment? Human decency? It wouldn't even cost much. But my people have to endure the most appalling conditions! It's a crime, plain and simple."

He swiveled around to include Robin, Sheyenne, and me. "That's why I came to you. Although *I* escaped, my people remain enslaved, working under miserable conditions. Please help us!" He deepened his voice, growing more serious. "I know I can count on Chambeaux and Deyer."

Now that the bottle of sparkling water was empty, Sheyenne returned with a glass of tap water, which the golem accepted. She wasn't going to give him the expensive stuff anymore if he was just going to pour it all over his body. "Was there anyone in particular who referred you to us?" she asked.

"I saw your name on a tourist map. Everyone in town knows Chambeaux and Deyer gives unnaturals a fair shake when there's trouble." He held out a rumpled, folded giveaway map carried by many businesses in the Quarter, more remarkable for its cartoon pictures and cheerful drawings than its cartographic detail.

Sheyenne flashed me a dazzling smile. "See, Beaux? I told you our ad on the chamber-of-commerce map would be worth the investment." Beaux is Sheyenne's pet name for me; no one else gets to call me that. (Come to think of it, no one had ever tried.)

"I thought you couldn't read, Bill," I said.

"I can look at the pictures, and the shop had an old vampire proofreader who mumbled aloud as he read the words," Bill said. "As a golem, you hear things."

"The important thing is that Mr., uh, Bill found us," Robin said. She had been sold on the case as soon as the golem told us his plight. If it weren't for Sheyenne looking out for us, Robin would be inclined to embrace any client in trouble, whether or not he, she, or it could pay.

Since joining us, postmortem, Sheyenne had worked tirelessly—not that ghosts got tired—to manage our business and keep Chambeaux & Deyer in the black. I didn't know what I'd do without her, professionally or personally.

Before her death, Sheyenne had been a med student, working her way through school as a cocktail waitress and occasional nightclub singer at one of the Unnatural Quarter high-end establishments. She and I had a thing in life, a relationship with real potential, but that had been snuffed out when Sheyenne was murdered, and then me, too.

Thus, our romance was an uphill struggle.

While it's corny to talk about "undying love," Fate gave us a second chance . . . then blew us a big loud raspberry. Sheyenne and I each came back from the dead in our respective way—me as a zombie, and Sheyenne as a ghost—but ghosts can never touch any living, or formerly living, person. So much for the physical side of our relationship . . . but I still like having her around.

Now that he was moisturized, Bill the golem seemed a new person, and he no longer flaked off mud as he followed Robin into our conference room. She carried a yellow legal pad, ready to take notes. Since it wasn't yet clear whether the golem needed a detective, an attorney, or both, I joined them. Sheyenne brought more water, a whole pitcher this time. We let Bill have it all.

Golems aren't the smartest action figures in the toy box—they don't need to be—but even though Bill was uneducated, he wasn't unintelligent, and he had a very strong sense of right and wrong. When he started talking, his passion for Justice was apparent. I realized he would make a powerful witness. Robin fell for him right away; he was just her type of client.

"There are a hundred other disenfranchised golems just like me," Bill said. "Living in miserable conditions, slaves in a sweatshop, brought to life and put to work."

"Who created you?" I asked. "Where is this sweatshop located? And what work did you do?"

Bill's clay brain could not hold three questions at a time, so he answered only two of them. "We manufacture Unnatural Quarter souvenirs—vampire ashtrays made with real vampire ash, T-shirts, place mats, paperweights, holders for toothpicks marketed as 'stakes for itsy-bitsy vampires.' "

Several new gift shops had recently opened up in the Quarter, a chain called Kreepsakes. All those inane souvenirs had to come from somewhere.

More than a decade after the Big Uneasy brought back all the legendary monsters, normal humans had recovered from their shock and horror enough that a few tourists ventured into the Quarter. This had never been the best part of town, even without the monsters, but businesses welcomed the increased tourism as an unexpected form of urban renewal.

"Our master is a necromancer who calls himself Maximus Max," Bill continued. "The golems are mass produced, slapped together from uneven clay, then awakened with a bootleg animation spell that he runs off on an old smelly mimeograph. Shoddy work, but he doesn't care. He's a slave driver!"

Robin grew more incensed. "This is outrageous! How can he get away with this right out in the open?"

"Not exactly out in the open. We labor in an underground chamber, badly lit, no ventilation . . . not even an employee break room. Through lack of routine maintenance, we dry out and crumble." He bent his big blunt fingers, straightened them, then dipped his hand into the pitcher of water, where he left a murky residue. "We suffer constant aches and pains. As the mimeographed animation spell fades, we can't move very well. Eventually, we fall apart. I've seen many coworkers and friends just crumble on the job. Then other golems have to sweep up the mess and dump it into a bin, while Maximus Max whips up a new batch of clay so he can create more golems. No one lasts very long."

"That's monstrous." Robin took detailed notes. She looked up and said in a soft, compassionate voice, "And how did you escape, Bill?"

The golem shuddered. "There was an accident on the bottling line. When a batch of our Fires of Hell hot sauce melted the glass bottles and corroded the labeling machine, three of my golem friends had to clean up the mess. But the hot sauce ruined them, too, and they fell apart.

"I was in the second-wave cleanup crew, shoveling the mess into a wheelbarrow. Max commanded me to empty it into a Dumpster in the alley above, but he forgot to command me to come back. So when I was done, I just walked away." Bill hung his head. "But my people are still there, still enslaved. Can you free them? Stop the suffering?"

I addressed the golem. "Why didn't you go to the police when you escaped?"

Bill blinked his big artificial eyes, now that he was more moisturized. "Would they have listened to me? I don't have any papers. Legally speaking, I'm the necromancer's property."

Robin dabbed her eyes with a tissue and pushed her legal pad aside. "It sounds like a civil rights lawsuit in the making, Bill. We can investigate Maximus Max's sweatshop for conformance to workplace safety codes. Armed with that information, I'll find a sympathetic judge and file an injunction to stop the work line temporarily."

Bill was disappointed. "But how long will that take? They need help now!"

"I think he was hoping for something more immediate, Robin," I suggested. "I'll talk to Officer McGoohan, see if he'll raid the place . . . but even that might be a day or two."

The golem's face showed increasing alarm. "I can't stay here—I'm not safe! Maximus Max will be looking for me. He'll know where to find me."

"How?" Sheyenne asked, sounding skeptical.

"I'm an escaped golem looking for action and legal representation—where else would I go but Chambeaux and Deyer? That's what the tourist map says."

"I've got an idea," I said. "Spooky, call Tiffany and tell her I'll come to her comedy improv show if she does me a quick favor."

Sheyenne responded with an impish grin. "Good idea, Beaux."

Tiffany was the buffest—and butchest—vampire I'd ever met. She had a gruff demeanor and treated her life with the utmost seriousness the second time around. But she had more of a sense of humor than I originally thought. Earlier that afternoon, Tiffany had dropped in, wearing a grin that showed her white fangs; she waved a pack of tickets and asked if we'd come see her for open-mic night at the Laughing Skull, a comedy club down in Little Transylvania. Maybe we could trade favors....

I knew Tiffany from the All-Day/All-Nite Fitness Center, where I tried to keep myself in shape. Zombies don't have to worry about cholesterol levels or love handles, but it's important to maintain muscle tone and flexibility. The aftereffects of death can substantially impact one's quality of life. I worked out regularly, but Tiffany was downright obsessive about it. She said she could bench-press a coffin filled with lead bricks (though why she would want to, I couldn't say).

Like many vampires, Tiffany had invested well and didn't need a regular job, but due to her intimidating physique, I kept her in mind in case I ever needed extra muscle. I'd never tried to call in a favor before, but Sheyenne was very persuasive.

Tiffany the vampire walked through the door wearing a denim work shirt and jeans. She had narrow hips, square shoulders, no waist, all muscle. She looked as if she'd been assembled from solid concrete blocks; if any foolish vampire slayer had tried to pound a stake through her heart, it would have splintered into tooth-picks.

Tiffany said gruffly, "Tell me what you got, Chambeaux." When Bill emerged from the conference room, she eyed him up and down. "You're a big boy."

"I was made that way. Mr. Chambeaux said you can keep me safe."

After I explained the situation, she said, "Sure, I'll give you a place to stay. Hang out at my house for a few days until this blows over." Tiffany glanced at me, raised her eyebrows. "A *few days*—right, Chambeaux?"

Robin answered for me. "That should be all we need to start the legal proceedings."

Bill's clay lips rolled upward in a genuine smile now. "My people and I are indebted to you, Miss Tiffany."

"No debt involved. Actually, I could use a hand if you don't mind pitching in. I'm doing some remodeling at home, in-stalling shelves, flooring, and a workbench in the garage, plus dark paneling and a wet bar in the basement den. I also need help setting up some heavy tools I ordered—circular saw and drill press, that kind of thing."

"I would be happy to help," Bill agreed.

"Thanks for the favor, Tiffany," I said.

The vampire gave me a brusque nod. "Don't worry, he'll be putty in my hands."

From *Stakeout at the Vampire Circus*

CHAPTER 1

The circus is supposed to be fun, even a monster circus, but the experience turned sour when somebody tried to murder the vampire trapeze artist.

As a private detective, albeit a zombie, I investigate cases of all sorts in the Unnatural Quarter, applying my deductive skills and persistent determination (yes, the undead can be very persistent indeed). Some of my cases are admittedly strange; most are even stranger than that.

I'd been hired by a transvestite fortune-teller to find a stolen deck of magic cards, and he had sent me two free tickets to the circus. Gotta love the perks of the job. Not one to let an opportunity go to waste, I invited my girlfriend to accompany me; in many ways her detective skills are as good as my own.

Sheyenne is beautiful, blond, and intangible. I had started to fall in love with her when both of us were alive, and I still like having her around, despite the difficulties of an unnatural relationship—as a ghost, she can't physically touch me, and as a zombie I have my own limitations.

We showed our passes at the circus entrance gate and entered a whirlwind of colors, sounds, smells. Big tents, wild rides, popcorn and cotton candy for the humans, more exotic treats for the unnaturals. One booth sold deep-fried artichoke hearts, while another sold deep-fried human hearts. Seeing me shamble by, a persistent vendor offered me a free sample of brains on a stick, but I politely declined.

I'm a well-preserved zombie and have never acquired a taste for brains. I've got my standards of behavior, not to mention personal hygiene. Given a little bit of care and effort, a zombie doesn't have to rot and fall apart, and I take pride in looking mostly human. Some people have even called me handsome—Sheyenne certainly does, but she's biased.

As Sheyenne flitted past the line of food stalls, her eyes were bright, her smile dazzling; I could imagine what she must have looked like as a little girl. I hadn't seen her this happy since she'd been poisoned to death.

Nearby, a muscular clay golem lifted a wooden mallet at the Test Your Strength game and slammed it down with such force that he not only rang the bell at the top of the pole, he split the mallet in half. A troll barker at the game muttered and handed the golem a pink plush bunny as a prize. The golem set the stuffed animal next to a pile of fuzzy prizes, paid another few coins, and took a fresh mallet to play the game again.

Many of the attendees were humans, attracted by the low prices of the human matinee; the nocturnal monsters would come out for the evening show. More than a decade had passed since the Big Uneasy, when all the legendary monsters came back to the world, and human society was finally realizing that unnaturals were people just like everyone else. Yes, some were ferocious and bloodthirsty—but so were some humans. Most monsters just wanted to live and let live (even though the definition of "living" had blurred).

Sheyenne saw crowds streaming toward the Big Top. "The lion tamer should be finishing, but the vampire trapeze artist is due to start. Do you think we could . . ."

I gave her my best smile. With stiff facial muscles, my "best smile" was only average, but even so, I saved it for Sheyenne. "Sure, Spooky. We've got an hour before we're supposed to meet Zelda. Let's call it 'gathering background information.'"

"Or we could just call it part of the date," Sheyenne teased.

"That, too."

We followed other humans through the tent flaps. A pudgy twelve-year-old boy was harassing his sister, poking her arm incessantly, until he glanced at me and Sheyenne. I had pulled the fedora low, but it didn't entirely conceal the bullet hole in my forehead. When the pudgy kid gawked at the sight, his sister took advantage of the distraction and began poking him until their mother hurried them into the Big Top.

Inside, Sheyenne pointed to empty bleachers not far from the entrance. The thick canvas kept out direct sunlight, protecting the vampire performers and shrouding the interior in a pleasant nighttime gloom. My eyes adjusted quickly, because gloom is a natural state for me. Always on the case, I remained alert. If I'd been more alert while I was still alive, I would be . . . well, still alive.

When I was a human private detective in the Quarter, Sheyenne's ghost had asked me to investigate her murder, which got me in trouble; I didn't even see the creep come up behind me in a dark alley, put a gun to the back of my head, and pull the trigger.

Under most circumstances, that would have put an end to my career, but you can't keep a good detective down. Thanks to the changed world, I came back from the dead, back on the case. Soon enough, I fell into my old routine, investigating mysteries wherever they might take me . . . even to the circus.

Sheyenne drifted to the nearest bleacher, and I climbed

stiffly beside her. The spotlight shone down on a side ring, where a brown-furred werewolf in a scarlet vest—Calvin—cracked his bullwhip, snarling right back at a pair of snarling lions who failed to follow his commands. The thick-maned male cat growled, while the big female opened her mouth wide to show a yawn full of fangs. The lion tamer roared a response, cracked the whip again, and urged the big cats to do tricks, but they absolutely refused.

The lions flexed their claws, and the werewolf flexed his own in a show of dominance, but the lions weren't buying it. Just when it looked as if the fur was about to fly, a loud drum-roll came from the center ring.

The spotlight swiveled away from the lion tamer to fall upon the ringmaster, a tall vampire with steel-gray hair. "Ladies and gentlemen, naturals and unnaturals of all ages—in the center ring, our main event!" He pointed upward, and the spotlight swung to the cavernous tent's rigging strung with high wires and a trapeze platform. A Baryshnikov look-alike stood on the platform, a gymnastic vampire in a silver lamé full-body leotard. He wore a medallion around his neck, a bright red ribbon with some kind of amulet, and a professional sneer.

"Bela, our vampire trapeze artist, master of the ropes—graceful, talented . . . a real swinger!" The ringmaster paused until the audience realized they were supposed to respond with polite laughter. Up on the platform, Bela lifted his chin, as if their applause was beneath him (and, technically speaking, it was, since the bleachers were far below).

"For his death-defying feat, Bela will perform without a safety net above *one hundred sharpened wooden stakes!*" The spotlight swung down to the floor of the ring, which was covered with a forest of pointy sticks, just waiting to perform impalement duties.

The suitably impressed audience gasped.

On the trapeze platform, Bela's haughty sneer was wide

enough to show his fangs; I could see them even from my seat in the bleachers. The gold medallion at his neck glinted in the spotlight. Rolling his shoulders to loosen up, the vampire grasped the trapeze handle and lunged out into the open air. He seemed not to care a whit about the sharp wooden stakes as he swung across to the other side. At the apex of his arc, he swung back again, gaining speed. On the backswing, Bela spun around the trapeze bar, doing a loop. As he reached the apex once again, he released, did a quick somersault high in the air, and caught the bar as he dropped down.

The audience applauded. Werewolves in the bleachers howled their appreciation; some ghouls and less-well-preserved zombies let out long, low moans that sounded upbeat, considering. I shot a glance at Sheyenne, and judging by her delighted expression, she seemed to be enjoying herself.

Bela swung back, hanging on with one hand as he gave a dismissive wave to the audience. Vampires usually have fluid movements. I remembered that one vamp had tried out for the Olympic gymnastics team four years ago—and was promptly disqualified, though the Olympic judges could not articulate a valid reason. The vampire sued, and the matter was tied up in the courts until long past the conclusion of the Olympics. The vampire gymnast took the long view, however, as she would be just as spry and healthy in the next four-year cycle, and the next, and the next.

A big drumroll signaled Bela's finale. He swung back and forth one more time, pumping with his legs, increasing speed, and the bar soared up to the highest point yet. The vampire released his hold, flung himself into the air for another somersault, then a second, then a third as the empty trapeze swung in its clockwork arc, gliding back toward him, all perfectly choreographed.

As he dropped, Bela reached out. His fingertips brushed the bar—and missed. He flailed his hands in the air, trying to grab the trapeze, but the bar swung past out of reach, and gravity did its work. Bela tumbled toward the hundred sharp wooden stakes below.

Someone screamed. Even with my rigor-mortis-stiff knees, I lurched to my feet.

But at the last possible moment, the vampire's plummeting form transformed in the air. Mere inches above the deadly points, Bela turned into a bat, stretching and flapping his leathery wings. He flew away, the medallion still dangling from his little furry rodent neck. He alighted on the opposite trapeze platform, then transformed back into a vampire just in time to catch the returning trapeze. He held on, showing his pointed fangs in a superior grin, and took a deep bow. On cue, the band played a loud "Ta-da!"

After a stunned moment, the audience erupted in wild applause. Sheyenne was beaming enough to make her ectoplasm glow. Even I was smiling. "That was worth the price of admission," I said.

Sheyenne looked at me. "We didn't pay anything—we got free tickets."

"Then it's worth twice as much."

With the show over, the audience rose from the bleachers and filed toward the exit. "The cases don't solve themselves," I said to Sheyenne. "Let's go find that fortune-teller."